an inheritance

an inheritance

a novel

mark albert

atmosphere press

for Sara

1

When I stepped into the hospital room, my father was alone. And silent. A thin white blanket lay loosely over his boney body. His eyes were tightly closed. His eyebrows knitted as if he were somehow conscious of his pain. Several days had already passed since the accident and there were still no signs of improvement. An array of vigilant machinery surrounded him. A long, clear line transporting vital fluids from a bag hanging above his head traced into the man's yellowing thin flesh and another line, this one clouded, emerging from under the sheets led out to a bag tied to the underside of the bed. His body had been reduced to an intermediary step entangled within a web of mechanical processes. The red and green lights, blinking in their slow, steady synchronous rhythms, were the only indications that any life whatsoever remained.

I studied my father, while sitting on the deep ledge of the hospital room's window. Others had described Dad as handsome, with a broad squarish face and a thick, now graying mustache. He had been robust, his dominant characteristic. He maintained throughout his life a muscular physique, and until the day he died was as fit as any worker he ever employed. Vibrant even at age eighty-one, he had worked steadily until that last minute on the back porch of the Nichols' house.

He would get out of bed every day with some idea in his mind, wrong or right; he didn't care and set off for work. His face was rough from its many years in the sun. From a touch of the man's hands, dry and iron-like, one knew right off that manual labor had been a consistent thread throughout his life.

People who knew my father as a younger man consistently mentioned his charisma. And I often heard from those same people declarations of our physical resemblance. But when I compared old photos of us, even trying to match our ages, the connection to me seemed less than obvious. Our builds were similar; he was two inches taller and, in his prime, narrower around the waist. Also, I saw myself with softer eyes, indicating a more reflective personality.

But on that last day I saw him, his face was swollen and not yet peaceful. Even though the accident and his time in the hospital had transformed his appearance into a different person than the one implanted in my memory, and even with his eyes shut, I had no problem recalling the stern set of his eyes. That seldom distracted gaze. His dark, near-black eyes were for me, his most memorable aspect, always unwaveringly directed at whomever he was speaking to. For most folk, it was accompanied by a broad, friendly smile. For me, his eyes telegraphed a different story, one usually accompanied by judgment or anger.

The hospital room's lighting had been set for night mode. A dim fluorescent fixture above his bed provided just enough illumination for the steady sequence of nurses to execute their defined missions. In and out, each entered the room, each courteously saying hello, each seemingly happy with their job. We exchanged pleasantries. It seemed like there were dozens, and it was hard, but I tried to keep track of their names. They moved efficiently about the room, checked the device that related to their specialty, made notes on their laptops, and sanitized their hands. And as each one exited the room, I said, "Thank you."

With one of the nurses, Doris, I developed a bit of a rapport. She visited several times in my few hours there. She would linger but never long enough to sit down. She would ask questions about my dad, my family, and most particularly about my younger brother, Andy. She had been on duty when my dad was admitted and was concerned about how Andy was reacting to our dad's accident. She didn't say anything explicitly, but she clearly sensed his lack of composure. I tried to alleviate her concern, first affirming that my brother was perhaps more emotionally sensitive than most men, and then telling her that after missing the better part of two nights' sleep, he had finally gone home for some badly needed rest.

Beyond her affable character, a small odd detail about Doris stuck with me. I noticed that when she lifted her arm to check the time, she wore two watches on the same wrist. When I questioned her about the strange habit, she answered, pointing with her finger, "This black plastic digital one, I wear for its accuracy. This other one," shifting her gaze from me and almost as if addressing the watch, she said, lightly touching the gold-banded watch with its small white face, "it doesn't really keep good time. Actually, I have to reset it every few days. I wear it every day because it belonged to my mother and before that, her mother, a gift from my grandfather." She ended softly, almost as if I weren't intended to hear her, "I have a boy — but soon I hope to have a girl, and one day I'll pass it on to her." I wordlessly acknowledged her story, nodding my head, jealous of her deep sentiment. And then, obedient to her other obligations, Doris typed a few stats into the computer and quickly said goodbye.

Left alone again with my father, I settled back in my seat, my back to the impenetrably black window. I watched the slow, subtle heave of his ailing chest as the muscles strained to keep their host alive. His finely wrinkled skin tenuously gripped the waning muscles. His always-shaven cheeks were bristly from a lack of attention. With his advanced age acting as a co-conspirator, this once solid man was devolving with surprising speed into a gaunt sack of sticks. And as each successive hour passed, the large hospital bed sucked him further down, as if it were slowly consuming him. The outcome was certain, and no earthly power was capable of reversing it. Dad was wilting like a plant without water.

It had only been three days earlier when Andy had called, leaving me message after message, one at the house, one at work, and another on my cell phone, with no telling of his purpose. Each message repeating the same exact words, "Call me. It's important." It was my brother's habit to quickly default to panic. And that's what I heard behind his simple words, panic.

Andy's problem threshold was lower than for most of us. From a non-clinician's perspective, after first meeting Andy, one might jump to the errant conclusion that he was some-where "on the spectrum," meaning he possessed some degree of autism. Not only would that be wrong, but it would also require the arrogance of confidently professing who is normal and who is not. Although I witness those sorts of judgments all the time, aren't we all somewhere on one spectrum or another? Who should judge another like that? And for what reason?

Andy and I often went for months at a stretch without talking, but when he did call, especially in rapid successive beats like this, I was certain he was struggling with a supposed new tragedy.

Yes, Andy was reserved, a bit awkward in many social situations, but he moved easily about in society — and had prospered. For years, he had been a well-regarded high-school teacher. The classroom, with its memorized structure, provid-ed a comforting pattern. But back to my point here, he had limited bandwidth for problems in situations for which he hadn't been conditioned, and when the standard rhythm broke, he was slow to adapt. To attend to Andy's occasional anxiety attacks, I would have to summon my maximum patience. Learned over the many years of dealing with my brother, my equally instinctual and, I suppose, cynical reaction led me to slow down and default to complacency — *What, another crisis?*

Most often, he was worried about how he had been perceived by others. Being less than adept at casual conversation with new people, he could badly stumble on his words, ruminate on how he had embarrassed himself, and self-flagellate until his self-esteem was near zero. Sometimes, the complexity of the situation, its import, or its newness would confound him. He loathed confrontation and was often prone to passivity. He had to be certain that he wasn't making a mistake in how he reacted. As a worshiper at the church of intellect, as Andy was, it is easy to realize how much you don't know about the world, and you can feel, most benevolently, humble, but in Andy's case, he would feel stupid or worse a fraud. The result, with the pressure of trying to be right, he over-thought almost every decision.

These character traits led to a proclivity for internal suffering. But even so primed, either by a strange set of correlations or reverse causation, catastrophes did tend to follow my brother more closely than most. Maybe it was an unlucky star that followed Andy on his path. By a prejudiced fate, he entered the world as a victim of unfair circumstances. One could easily understand this self-view as the legitimate reaction to losing our mother to cancer when we were both quite young, Andy being three at the time and me a bit older, six. Although brothers, our dispositions were natively different, and our reactions dramatically opposed. Maybe there was a slight variant in our DNA that predisposed Andy towards passivity. Maybe it was the difference in our ages that primed us for our disparate adaptations to such a tragedy. Maybe it was his own doing and a matter of consistently poor choices. Wherever the genesis, he often and easily fell into the role of the victim. His was a life accepted, rather than one wrested free from the constraints the world offers us.

Dad's accident was clearly an event he was not prepared for. No one anticipates these tragedies. Although worry was native to his personality, in this case, it was appropriate.

I was busy at work and waited to respond to my brother's messages until it was convenient for me. His insistent neediness made Andy oblivious to where I was or what I might be doing. He couldn't muster the patience to appreciate my schedule.

I had assumed his rapid sequence of calls had to do with another exaggerated sense of injury, odds heavy on it having something to do with his ex-wife. She had expected before and during their marriage a lifestyle that Andy was incapable of delivering — and I don't know with what evidence — he was a high school teacher. Even now, post-marriage and without her own means, she nonsensically still held the same expectations. I thought she probably needed money again.

On the morning of his calls, I had made the boys breakfast, drove Kevin to school for an early workout with the basketball team, and was sitting in my office by 7:45, preparing for a meeting to iron out the details of a big property purchase we were working on. So, it wasn't until two hours later, after I had responded to a dozen emails and finally had a chance to breathe, that I picked up the phone to call Andy.

Andy answered my call without even a hello. "Dad's in the hospital."

My brother's typical lack of pretense or pleasantries was strangely right. Of all the reasons for Andy to call, Dad in the hospital was unthinkable. Even at this age, Dad was busy seven days a week. He quit for nothing. He had been that way his whole life. The Marines, framing houses, starting his own construction business. The man was unconquerable, sturdy as a rock, immune to tragedy. I had never known him to suffer anything worse than a cold. The line stayed quiet.

"Andy, I'm sure he'll be fine."

"No ... no, I don't think so. This is bad ... really, really bad. He's not responsive ... nothing." Andy's voice stammered. "They're still trying to figure out what's wrong..."

I waited for Andy to regain his composure and tell the story in his time.

"Sorry. It's already been a long day ..."

"It's okay. Take a deep breath and tell me what you know."

"Anyway, with all this time waiting, I've been trying to pull the story together." Andy paused again. I could hear his deep breathing. "The best I can figure is that Dad, yesterday afternoon, drove to the Nichols' house. You know the Nichols couple?"

"No, Andy, I really don't know much about his tenants."

"Well, they're an older couple. They live in one of Dad's rent houses in the south part of town." As Andy began recounting the details, his voice became stronger and its tenor more solid. "They've been tenants forever. Really sweet people. But they can't do a thing for themselves. Too old and too fragile. Can't even manage to change a light bulb. And literally, it was just that, a light bulb. Can you believe, a freaking light bulb?"

"Andy, I don't get it. How does this connect?"

"That's why Dad was at the Nichols' house. When he got there, nobody was home, and he, from what I can tell, parked his truck back behind the house, next to their garage. He pulled out his ladder and set it up on the back porch where the light was out."

"So, are you telling me he fell?"

"Yeah, he fell..." Andy's voice started wavering again. "I'm sorry. I just have this horrible vision in my head of him lying there on this porch with nobody there to help him..." Again, I patiently waited for Andy to recover. "So sorry, this is hard... and it gets worse. The Nichols didn't get home until after dark. Knowing the light was out, they parked out front along the street, not wanting to park in back like they would normally do. From the front yard, there was no way they could have seen Dad's truck. It wasn't until later, much later, like nearly midnight, when Mr. Nichols was taking out the trash, that he found Dad lying on the porch. He must have been like that for hours. Can you imagine? Laying on that cold hard porch. I'm sure Mr. Nichols' first thought was that he was dead. Awful. Just plain awful. By the time they called me, and I made it over to the hospital, it was already three in the morning, and I didn't get to see the doctor for another hour or so. That's when I tried to call you."

"And what'd he say?"

"It was a she, by the way. She couldn't tell me anything for sure. But, I can tell you this, to my eyes, it doesn't look good — not good at all. I'm thinking this could be the end."

That evening, I jumped on a plane to Denver, crossing the two time zones as quickly as I could.

Sitting in the hospital, I stared at the motionless man laying in front of me, contemplating his life. He was a man who prioritized his obligations before all else. Having a family, running my own business, and knowing all the associated challenges, I could look back at his long list of accomplishments with unqualified respect and judge him a noble man.

But, for the first time in my life, I felt my father inert, powerless, incapable of rising, of control. His presence had been an overwhelming one, an overseer in every aspect of my life. As a teenager coming home late at night, even when he seemed to be asleep in his favorite chair, the TV loudly chattering, he sensed my return. He knew to the minute what time I had snuck back into the house. For a single male parent, as hard as that was, he checked all the right boxes. He had provided well for his two sons. We were never aware of any scarcity. We were well-educated. He taught us to differentiate right from wrong and, above all else, how to respect others. Dad was a role model for duty to a higher cause and conscientiously directed us to follow him along the same clear path that he knew so well, a relic of his Marine training.

In no clear order, forty-five years of memories tumbled out. But my charitable perceptions were soon taken over by an emotional storm. My thoughts spiraled downward. His overbearing assertiveness. His uncompromising nature. His long list of rules, limits, and boundaries. Discipline, quick and firm. Belittlement. Unfair comparisons. A poverty of empathy. He could be downright mean. He could be ignorant. At the recollections, my shoulders tensed as if I were again preparing for battle. Mentally, I braced for a nonexistent counter-reaction. Even now, with his body motionless and silent, I had to protect my esteem from being crushed. Resilience or resistance were my choices. The needless tension grew. I closed my eyes and took a deep breath. I had to remind myself that the man who lay before me was now inert and would be forever more.

The last time I was this close to death was decades ago with my mother. But I didn't know it at the time. We were alone together in her bed, nestled under the covers. It was early morning, and a cool breeze was coming in from the nearby screened window. Mom and I were looking at family pictures. But at that moment, I had been told nothing yet about her cancer. She nor Dad offered not a clue about the gravity of her situation. I was six, Andy three, when our mother, only thirty-eight, died. I was certainly being protected by their good intentions.

She held in her lap a small plastic box that looked very much like a tiny TV, and to her side was a shoebox full of small yellow boxes. She would pop in a slide and examine it through the backlit magnifying screen, then share the photo with me. The Kodachromes were brilliant. The water an iridescent aqua. My mother's dress safflower. The striped umbrellas cherry red. And a bright pale-blue sky background. The images were of Mom, Andy and my five-year-old self, taken during the previous summer. We were swimming at the public pool five minutes from our house. There was a broad concrete terrace scattered with umbrellas, tables and chairs. A parade of other kids danced in and out of the background, each with their own inflatable toy. Invisible but close by, Dad was taking pictures of an obviously very happy mother. Lit by the bright midday sun, Andy leaned next to Mom, who was leaning back in a lounge chair. I was captured in various poses, standing next to both of them, angling my head in with that say-cheese smile. I saw a simple, comprehensible world, completely unaware of, as a child should be, and completely untethered to the complex assemblages of my future responsibilities. It was impossible for me to know that that intimate moment would be the last time the two of us would talk together. I wished somebody had warned me.

For one brief moment, during the flipping of slides, I saw a tear in Mom's eye. She turned to me, eyes directly into mine, and said in a quiet declarative voice, "You are a wonderful, loving big brother. I know you'll always take care of him." Dropping in the next slide, she wiped the tear away. And just like that, my life's mission had been established. How did she know? How did she know my character so well? And Andy's? Or was she at that moment shaping them, the both of them?

At that time, my mother was the only person I had been close to that had died. This reality remained true until now, facing my father's death. Both sets of grandparents were gone long before I was born. I knew none of them. Mom and Dad were each an only child, so no aunts or uncles. There weren't any really old people around in my life. Death was a foreigner. I didn't recall feeling grief when Mom died, but it must have been present. Without doubt, I must have run through the entire gamut of emotions. I remember that at school, I met several times with a psychologist, meeting before lunch on Wednesdays for the rest of the year. Her small office was near the school's entrance, with her office window looking out onto the front sidewalk and the tall, resolute flagpole next to it. I do not know what we talked about, but from this distant perspective, almost forty years later, I still remember feeling comfortable and safe sitting on that soft gray couch in that very nice woman's office. It was a pleasant refuge where I felt attended to, felt understood. I hadn't felt that same focused kind of compassion since.

After my mom's passing, there was a tangible absence around the house, something almost physical. I can't articulate or describe precisely the suite of emotions racing around my head, but I felt a large hazy void floating about, knocking me off balance according to its own arbitrary will. While I felt disoriented, Dad remained his solid, stoic self, marching back and forth with his military-like urgency. I never saw him cry over his wife's passing, never abandoning his confident resolve. Without missing a beat, his job description easily expanded to include all the domestic chores. He got up early like he always did, but instead of rushing off to work, he stayed home, promptly made his bed, something I had never seen him do before, and by the time Andy and I crawled into the kitchen, bleary-eyed from sleep, breakfast would be on the table. I don't remember talking about Mom, but how could we not have had those conversations? One doesn't jump from before death to after death like flipping to a new chapter in a book. But that's my memory of it, Dad, Andy and myself, three boys, sitting at the kitchen table struggling to talk about school, uncertain about how to navigate our feelings, whatever they might have been. There was mostly silence.

How accurate were my memories? Were those images and sounds immutably seared into my neurons since the time of their creation? Or had I subconsciously edited and manipulated the memories to suit the narrative I needed? Where were the gaps? What was missing? Had time been compressed or perhaps lost? I doubted what had previously felt like truth. This history, real or not, this retrospection, was tiring on my brain, and while gazing at my dying father, I decided there was no further utility to any of it. Why question the past? None of it affected tomorrow.

And now, anticipating my father's imminent death, I felt emotionless, as if I had already been here before. The denial, the anger, the bargaining, the depression, and the acceptance were all stages that I had traveled through and swiftly moved beyond. While not the man, the relationship had died years ago, and I found little difference between the two. I had no words to share, and worse, no motivation to share. And even if I did, it wasn't like he would hear me. He never listened to anything I had to say. We hadn't had a meaningful conversation in ages — if ever. I gave up on that goal a million years ago. Our visits had become routine, absent of affection and not much different than I might have had with a check-out clerk at the grocery store. As I aged, a sadness about the relationship had set in. Worse was the fact that it was nothing personal. It was a generic sadness, one where a father and son had failed to connect, like I was watching somebody else's movie. I had long ago purged myself of hope, then later anger. The only thing still remaining was a dry emptiness. That is what I had learned to accept. I stared at him, saying nothing.

There was nothing I could do to help the man. Same as

when I was a boy, I had no influence over him. He never wanted my help. Too firm in his ways, there was no allowance for anybody else's opinion. He had Andy. And I had to get back to my work. Andy would soon return, take my place and continue the vigil. No telling how long this dying was going to take, but I had no stomach for it. I put my hand on Dad's shoulder, "Dad, I gotta go. I know you'll understand, but work is calling me, and right now, it needs me one hundred percent. Andy will be here soon."

I headed back to the airport. I didn't expect to be sad, and I wasn't.

2

I sat on a kitchen barstool after making a quick breakfast of coffee and scrambled eggs; the newspaper spread out to the side. While the TV mutely displayed the national news, I studied Liz's photo wall near the breakfast table on the other side of the room. There was an arrangement of framed family pictures, like a genealogy chart stirred up, her parents, her sisters, nieces and nephews in every possible combination. The display was carefully curated to include a small measure from my side of the family. There wasn't a lot to choose from. Her side of the family was large and met frequently for holidays and birthdays. My side was just my brother, my dad and me, and we rarely got together. The one decent photo of me, my dad, and Andy together was from twenty-plus years ago at Andy's college graduation. A rare artifact showing us each with a self-satisfied smile. When the photo was taken, Andy had reached the triumphal apogee of his education, finishing school in a dense three years. Meanwhile, I was prospering at work, and Dad was spotlight-proud of his two accomplished sons. Although she had often requested for us to take a new one, Liz didn't have a more recent photo to replace the old one. I couldn't fathom how fast the time had flown and, within that twenty-year-plus period, how few times the three of us had assembled to celebrate anything.

That was my entire side of the family, just us three guys. Mom and Dad were both orphans. I had to believe that commonality was their crucial bond. We grew up isolated from any idea of a broader family. As good as Dad was at making friends, none of those people entered his sons' lives. None of them were ever invited over to the house for dinner, something I later discovered typical parents might do. None of those quote-unquote close friends of dad would we ever call uncle or aunt, all distant strangers, names muttered in passing.

As I was putting my dishes in the sink, Liz appeared in the doorway. She was wearing her workout clothes, her default morning attire. She squinted in my direction as if the kitchen's glare was a bit too bright.

Liz and I had met in college. We were both taking a life drawing class. I was looking for an easy A and an elective with no homework. Plus, I couldn't resist the cheap thrill of drawing naked women. The thrill part quickly dissipated, replaced by unsolvable frustration. I could never master the difficult hand control required to mimic what was before my eyes. I was tempted to drop the class except for the delicate girl to my right, who shared the same set of problems, and who was politely sympathetic to my efforts. She wasn't a natural artist either. She was there because she needed the studio hours to supplement her art history degree. Contrary to my experiences in high school, I was bonding with someone over a common weakness.

One day during the following semester, I knew she was mine after we had given up on the folly of being artists. I was waiting for her to finish a class, standing in front of the main dining hall at one end of a long quad, when I saw an indistinct figure running towards me. Liz was in a full gallop; her face lit up like a floodlight. Beaming, she flew into my arms, wrapping her whole body around mine. I had never felt love like that before. Her commitment to me was instantaneous, surprising and unshakable. Prior to Liz, I had never felt such unconditional acceptance, and I'm still not sure why.

"What time did you get in?" Liz asked.

"Late. Came in around two-thirty. I slept in my study so I wouldn't wake you."

"But it's not even six. You've got to be exhausted?"

"I am. I can't tell you how drained I feel, but I've got to be in the office soon. Our deal closes this week, and there are a million moving parts left that we need to nail down."

"Cole, sweetheart, I'm worried about you. I don't know... how can you focus on any of that with your dad so sick?"

Like the rest of the world, except for my brother and father, Liz called me by my last name. The change came during my sophomore year in high school, roll call during the baseball team's first meeting in late winter. I was one of two from my class to make the varsity team that year. I can immodestly say I had a laser-accurate right arm and was already at my full height of six foot even. In short, I was the perfect candidate for the open position at third base. As the coach read through the roster for the first time, he yelled out, "Cole," and looked up, scanning the group of guys. I hesitated for a second, not sure he was talking to me. I would much later understand his tactic. The coach, like so many of his kind, enjoyed using our last names. He was essentially disconnecting these proto-men from their previous softer home-worlds and moving them into the depersonalized performance-based world where all that matters is your stats. We were no longer sensitive young boys. We were seen as implements to be used for his purposes. He was hardening us. It was only the first step in his reconfiguring of our personalities. I raised my hand and responded, "I'm here." The time was right. I was ready. Tommy no longer seemed appropriate. Like a snake shedding its skin, I enjoyed the transformative properties of the new name. That simple,

clear syllable quickly became my teammates' and then everyone's habit. From then forward, I was known as Cole to the
wider world, only hearing my boyhood name at home.

Liz gave me a tight hug before pulling out her usual box of
granola.

"Hear anything new about your dad this morning?" she
asked.

"Not yet. But Liz, could you please do me a favor? I don't
have the time today to make the boys' breakfast or, much less
drive them to school. Could you do that for me?"

With her mouth full of granola, Liz nodded.

"Got to run. Love you."

3

I sat down at my usual place, at the end of our long white gray-veined marble conference table. Me, along with the table and its two rows of carefully aligned black leather chairs, waited passively for our weekly meeting to begin. The conference room's broad spread of floor-to-ceiling windows looked over a gridded mosaic of building rooftops. Large cubical engines expelled short-lived vaporish gray clouds, quickly vanishing in the dry fall air.

After business school, knowing that it was the nucleus from which all the world's money flowed in to and out of, I couldn't find my way to New York fast enough. Eager for almost any job in the investment world, I oddly stumbled on a job with a real estate investment company. I say 'oddly' because the company that hired me, in a very abstract sense, worked much like my dad's small business, but on a scale a million times larger and with all the protocols and hierarchies of the corporate world. Instead of buying and renovating modest rent houses, the company was buying multi-story office buildings and apartment complexes containing hundreds of units. The principles are basically the same, and the industry's jargon sounded very much like what I heard at home around the dinner table.

I began as one of a dozen analysts building spreadsheets, going way beyond my father's back-of-the-envelope calculations, figuring out internal rates of return, a financial concept my father had never heard of and would never be able to understand by its textbook definition, but it was one he felt intuitively. In those first few years, I learned how large investors measured risk and by which metrics they measured success. I had to project growth rates into the distant future. It didn't take long to figure out that my crystal ball, like everyone else's, was very cloudy. I couched my predictions in terms of probabilities with pages of disclaimers.

Soon I was dealing directly with the industry's biggest investors, who were not people per se but corporations, but corporations populated by people just like me situated somewhere in the middle of another corporate structure, who so happened to sit on the other side of the table. Within three years I had graduated from cubicle life and moved into a large corner office.

We worked in mind-numbingly large numbers, tens of millions to hundreds of millions of dollars. So large, the numbers were unrelatable abstractions, totally disconnected from a twenty-seven-year-old's annual budget for rent and food. We relied on the miracle of compound interest over decades of probable income estimates to build wealth for insurance companies and pension funds. From the perspective of those institutions, good profits versus disappointing losses were measured in the tenths of a percentage point.

Unlike many of my cohorts, I didn't mind the continuous stress, the eighty-hour weeks, the excruciating focus on microscopic details, or the unforgiving judgments. I enjoyed the challenges and the dependability by which one's performance could be calculated. There was no room for subjectivity.

The salaries were strong, but the serious financial rewards went to the heads of the company, those at the top, whose compensation was measured in, essentially, parts per million, but because of the huge numbers we were working with, added up to some very large take-home pay. Being impatient to wait for my turn at the top, I left the firm and started my own firm. I was determined to siphon off my share sooner than later.

Although being a few minutes early for the meeting, I was unable, as was my typical habit, to review our weekly meeting's upcoming agenda. Instead, I was distracted by what lay far out beyond the city, beyond the horizon. My mind was back at home. The quiet moment gave me a chance to call Andy.

Since I had left the hospital, Andy had begun the habit of regularly texting me descriptions of Dad's schedule, much like entries in a detailed diary. Which doctor came in. At what time. What medicines were given. When he was cleaned, although I looked between the stats, I could discern no hints of hope. On the other hand, it was evident that even while unconscious, the old man remained relentless, refusing to give in. All completely consistent with Dad's character. Death was going to have to wring every last iota of life out of the man. The texts Andy sent conveyed facts but nothing of his state of mind. My less frequent phone calls with Andy weren't any more informative than the texts. His monotone voice rarely revealed much of his inner life, but still, I wanted to hear his voice to see if I could pick up on any emotional nuance. True to form, his oral accounts were dry and weightless; he spoke of our father's lingering on the edge of death. When I pressed and asked directly how he, Andy, was doing, he shrugged it off and said, "Fine. I'm doing just fine." I'd come to believe that *fine* was the least informative word ever invented, a surrogate for not wanting to talk — at least about anything serious. That morning, I kept my conversation with Andy brief, promising to check back a little later.

I opened up the projects binder and began flipping through its tabs, reviewing the calculations. At the opposite end of the room, above the whiteboard, a digital clock stared at me. It read 08:23:24, twenty-plus minutes until the meeting's scheduled start.

The clock idea came to me a couple of years ago when my son Kevin's junior league basketball team was playing in the league finals. A firm believer in the benefits of team sports, the camaraderie, the shared responsibilities, and the common goal, I insisted that the boys pick a sport and stick with it. Baseball, which was my sport, is a game without a clock and without any sense of urgency. It is semi-pastoral in that way. But basketball is nothing if not urgent, non-stop and relentlessly tiring. I learned a lot from going to Kevin's practices and watching him perfect his skills. On that evening, watching his team play, I could appreciate the lesson of a time-limited game. It reflects the true nature of our modern world better.

From my seat high in the bleachers, I watched as both coaches mismanaged the remaining time. The game was coming down to the final couple of minutes, and neither team had any timeouts left. With the game about to end, the coaches had lost their ability to pace their players and the game. They were frantically yelling commands from the sidelines with the crowd yelling their own suggestions. Chaos abounded, and the boys looked for the moment, frozen by the disorder. They couldn't disentangle the message from the noise. The boys had no choice but to ignore their superiors. A mutiny of sorts, but I saw it as a demonstration of self-reliance. They trusted their intuition and months of training. They became who they needed to be by ignoring the non-essentials. On their own, in those few remaining moments, they were empowered, untethered from the coaches. With no way to stop the game, their focus and energy peaked during those precious last few minutes. Keeping one eye on the clock as the seconds ticked away, I was spellbound watching the boys' increased intensity.

During the drive home, that energy stayed with me, and I wondered how the idea of a ticking time clock would work in the office. The meetings lasted much longer than necessary. Too many people enjoyed the sound of their own voices, adding nothing but irritation.

To test my theory, I installed in the conference room a large digital clock. I limited the meetings to forty-five minutes; no matter what, hard stop. A typical round clock with its gently sweeping second hand is almost soothing; it lacks the necessary visceral stress. A digital clock, on the other hand, with its large pulsating orange seconds flashing in a steady sequence, overtly exposes the unrelenting erosion of everyone's precious time.

Distilling a problem down to its essential ingredients and expressing it in a few carefully crafted sentences is a skill that I admire. Those that don't possess such skillset should learn it in a hurry. After its installation and observing its effect on the others, I began to very much like the clock.

The seconds ticked away as I waited for the others to arrive. I opened my laptop and answered a few emails. Steve, my newest hire, was the first to walk in at 08:38:04, seven minutes early, taking a seat at mid-table.

"Morning. How was your weekend?" Steve said.

"Fine." A social lie. I wasn't ready to talk about my father. I had decided to keep the news of his fall to myself. It would be a disturbing distraction from the office's much-needed focus. Too much personal information distorts efficiency. Plus, in the back of my mind, I worried that somehow the information could be misused. It intuitively seemed better that nobody knew.

I continued typing, pausing only momentarily to briefly

glance at Steve, who was engrossed in his computer. He had been working for me for less than three months. I had met his wife and two little girls at an office-wide weekend get-together soon after I had made the hire. My boys behaved as excellent big brothers to his toddlers. At the time, I remember the girls' names striking me as so odd, Esther and Miriam, so old-fashioned, like echoes from the Bible. Why would parents want to burden their kids that way?

Michael walked in a minute later and set his laptop down to my immediate right. Michael and I had met in business school and ever since have worked together. In school, we became quick friends but freighted the relationship with a steady diet of friendly competition. We made small bets — whoever scored best, the other would buy drinks for the other. If I had to guess, by the time we arrived at graduation, the net result was a push. Our similar ambitions and personal drives were well matched for each other. After leaving school, we both had the good fortune of joining the same real estate firm.

But I got fed up first. I had reached a point where I couldn't stand working another minute for somebody else. My dad, with his fierce independence, had drilled a basic philosophy into my head, *Don't allow someone else to profit off of your time; work for yourself.* When I was a teenager, I found my father's bumper sticker quotes boring and trite, another overly simplistic truism. But as I moved through the corporate world, the principle slowly resonated with me. The firm was exploiting my time for the sake of the higher-ups' profits, and I didn't see that situation changing anytime soon. So, to maximize my income, I went off on my own. I left on good terms. It was not an unusual path. I was following a long line of previous hires who sought the brass ring. My bosses wished me good luck, and I set out to control my own destiny. With two clients willing to follow, I had all that I needed. A year later, Michael saw what I had accomplished and joined me as a partner.

In those early days, there were brief periods when I wondered if my departure had been too rash. Although I was seeking autonomy, I hadn't anticipated the larger picture. I was still young and naive. I hadn't thought through the complexities of running one's own company and how interwoven and dependent my needs would be with those of my clients and, worse, my employees. Building a business environment was a completely different skill set than negotiating a property purchase. I had to quickly master a sobering reality, one completely contradictory to my initial intent: no matter what your job, or your title, there was always somebody to whom you are beholden. To close deals, I needed investors, I needed bankers, I needed partners. They all exuded their own particular form of pressure and expectations. Eventually, I came to peace with the fact that this business, like every other one, is a service business. Once I finally learned how to appease everyone's various needs, growth appeared unlimited.

Although Michael, by outward appearances, was handsome but slightly round. He was unathletic and hated physical activities. He was shorter than me by several inches and wore small round glasses, unintentionally creating a studious and non-threatening look. When we were together at meetings, he was often assumed to be my associate rather than my partner. Funny how people innately react to the alpha-male body image stereotype, and it's one that's difficult to dislodge from our primal brains. But Michael was a gregarious soul and made friends easily. He wasn't married and had none of the obligations of the home life. For that reason, he readily volunteered to meet our visiting clients for dinners or drinks. But contrary to his easy-going disposition, he was a fierce competitor and didn't back down easily. He took on the role of protector, the anchor to my speedboat. His first instinct was always caution. He'd claim that things couldn't be done, outlining a litany of problems as evidence. He was an effective challenger. While at first a contrarian, if and when he became convinced of his adversary's position, he quickly became an acolyte. He had no pride in any particular opinion; his only metric veered toward winning, but, and this was crucial for him, following the path of least risk. He didn't mind playing the long slow game. He was a good chess player.

Michael approached me and started to say something, but I motioned for him to join me out in the hall. He was the one person in the office I had told about my trip out west to see my father and Andy, but I couldn't remember if I had emphasized to him my intention to keep the trip secret from the rest of the firm.

"How's your father doing?" Michael asked, his face displaying an unusually concerned look. Much like me, he wasn't one for overt expressions of emotion, especially in the business environment. Doing so might signal weakness to one's opponent. I knew Michael cared. We had been friends forever.

"Not good. It doesn't look like it will be long." I held his gaze, not sure how much to add at this moment.

"That's terrible." He continued to stare at me, his eyebrows squished together in confusion. "So then ... why are you here?"

"There? Here? What difference does it make? There's nothing I can do? I can't sit passively in that sterile hospital room and watch the man slowly die."

"But you should ... I mean, you should at least be there for your brother," Michael said, slowly shaking his head. "Andy needs you with him, and I can take care of the office, or whatever ... but that said ...."

I patted him on the shoulder, "Don't worry. I'll handle the meeting. Thanks for offering."

"Understood. But really ..." Michael shook his head again. "So sorry about your dad."

Behind us, the younger associates were entering the room,

each offering a quick hello before walking in.

I was about to head back into the conference room when Michael grabbed my arm, pulling me back. He looked around to make sure he wasn't being overheard.

"So, I guess you haven't heard yet?" He spoke in a hushed voice. "The London call was canceled. An email came in about an hour ago. I looked for you, but you weren't in your office. They're done with the deal in Atlantic City. They're pulling out."

The trade was not particularly complicated, a large apartment complex, a deal like we've done dozens of times before, but we were just days away from closing. It was of no relevance to the deal, but visiting the site and working on this specific purchase reminded me of my good luck. It was in Atlantic City one spring break that I had won a decent amount of money at a casino. At the time, I was exercising my odds-making muscles, applying principles I had gathered from my several classes in statistics. I hadn't discovered some previously unknown gambling theory nor found some magical money-making technique. My success was a good string of luck, and I simply recognized that fact. Something told me it was time to quit. I felt if I had continued to play, that irrefutable law, regression towards the mean, would have led to me ultimately losing money. But I recognized my brief moment of good luck. I took my winnings and went home happy. The strange city had since held a fondness in my heart.

I've always tried to keep luck in perspective. When I was a junior analyst at my first job, by dint of the sheer number of hours I spent building spreadsheets, I learned how much study went into each trade. The expectation was for me to produce only three to four deals a year that might lead to an outsized return. But no matter how much work you did, you couldn't entirely eliminate the element of luck. It was impossible. And no matter how hard you tried, you would lose a fair number of bets. But if the dice happened to fall in your favor, you might find that special sweet spot that led to permanent financial independence. That was why we played the game. But absent the dreams, at the end of the day, after dozens of trades, the reality check was measured by the couple of percentage points separating the wins from the losses, and I attributed that narrow margin to the triumph of hard work over luck.

But here I was, outside the second standard deviation, hit by a circumstance, a disingenuous partner, a problem I hadn't anticipated. I was pissed.

"You're kidding. What do you mean 'done'? Not now ... They can't do that. The deposit is in the title company. They can't back out now." I was caught expecting a slow pitch down the middle of the plate, not that curveball. Actually, I thought the ball was already heading out over the centerfield fence. "Didn't we solve all of their questions and concerns? I didn't realize we had any problems left. We've invested months in planning this purchase. I don't get it ... They're idiots. This is a solid bet."

"I can't tell you for certain. But in the email, all they said was that their decision was based on the quote-unquote, current risk environment. They say they can no longer tolerate the risk inside the currency trade position. Their pound has moved in a negative way against the dollar. They want their money back."

"I've got a bunch of my own money already locked inside this deal." Michael didn't notice or choose not to react to my admitted vulnerability. Business had been great recently. In fact, we had been on a long winning streak, and as my confidence increased, I committed to a larger and larger cut of each deal, doubling down frequently. Plenty of money was flowing my way, enough to support Liz's lifestyle, the house, and the boys' private schools, but I steadily plowed my profits back into the business. That's where the best returns were. I was so confident in the Atlantic City deal I had increased my line of credit.

Michael, on the other hand, being the cautious type, only put enough of his own money in the deals to symbolically prove to our investors that he had a stake. And not being the titular head of the company, there wasn't the same expectation on him to commit. He had more of the Warren Buffett mentality: slow, steady growth and don't spend a nickel if you don't have to. And in the expense category, he had next to none, with the benefit of not being married, with no children. He lived in a gracious well-appointed condo. An elegant bachelor lifestyle, but with zero overheads.

"I need this deal to work," I said.

"I know that ... and I know we ..." Michael emphasized the pronoun, "have a lot of money tied up here, and if we," again with emphasis, "want to hold our position, we either need to quickly find a replacement partner or be willing to commit the extra cash ourselves."

"This is such bullshit."

"This has nothing to do with us. Don't be so defensive. You're right; the deal is solid. But these London guys clearly have developed ... how should I say it? ... a contrasting philosophical perspective. You know everyone calculates risk differently. Whether you think it rational or not, they want out."

"Fuck that," I said. "A deal is a deal. Are they incapable of keeping their word? After all this time, all these meetings, and you're telling me now that they're experiencing a sort of, as you say, philosophical epiphany? It's clearly some negotiating ploy. They think they have their hands around my balls and can outplay me. No fucking way. They wait for the last minute to screw with me. They're not thinking clearly. This is a great deal. At this point, we can't untie the deal without taking a big hit." Suddenly, I was struck by another possibility. "Do you think they found a better deal somewhere else without telling us?"

Michael said, "Now, you're really getting paranoid."

"We need to fly out there, sit down with them, and walk them through the trade one more time. Maybe I'll take a couple of lawyers with me."

"I don't think even you can fix this. And you can't sue them. Doesn't make sense, would take too long, and in the end, hurt our reputation more than help."

Michael's emphasis on the pronoun, this time, 'you', was again deliberate, but I couldn't tell if this was an objective assessment or if Michael had embedded a bit of sarcasm. I couldn't tell if he, too, was becoming a skeptic ... although it was his default nature. Could it be that he did not want this deal to happen and had lost his stomach for the risk? Did he have doubts about my judgment? Could this be disloyalty?

"I think it's a much bigger picture," Michael continued. "The other night, when we were out for a drink, one of the London guys started talking politics. He thinks the Middle East is once again on the verge of exploding. The alliances out there keep shifting like wind on a sand dune. Our saber-rattling president has created a fucking mess. A lot of unnecessary tension ... and for what? It's honestly hard to find clarity in this chaos, and some people are starting to talk about war."

"And so what in the hell does that have to do with our deal?"

"If they actually spoke those words out loud in public, some people might take those comments as some sort of international political insult. Plus, they're way too polite to be that honest. They don't want to do our deal — or probably anybody's deal. No secret conspiracy. Just risk-averse. End of story. I don't think there's any way to convince them. They're looking for a way out without admitting that they're truly a bunch of weak-kneed little girls."

It wasn't my language, but it re-bolstered my view that Michael was an aggressive advocate for our position.

"Who knows about this so far?" I asked.

"You and me. That's it. I want to keep it tight for the moment. I'd like to think this through before reacting rashly."

"Agreed. No need to put everyone into an unnecessary panic." I set my hand on Michael's shoulder and nodded. He nodded back in agreement. We walked back in and took our seats next to each other. I looked up at the clock. It read 8:44:35.

"Great, we're right on time. Since everyone's here, let's get started. Steve, you have three minutes. Tell us about your Woodland trade."

Steve started his presentation. Though halfway into the second minute, I couldn't follow his train of thought. "Stop right there." I was about to rise out of my chair. "All this talking, and you haven't yet mentioned the most important detail, ... what's our internal rate of return? Is this an efficient use of our capital?"

Steve looked up at me from the papers he had been reading from. He stammered, "Well ... it depends on the time frame."

"Of course it does — do you think I'm an idiot? We all learned that in school."

I heard myself getting overheated. And sarcasm wasn't going to help. Steve glanced around the table for help, but he was on his own, which was the way it should be. All eyes focused on him, and I could see him sweating. I had rattled him. I backed off a little, and in a more measured voice and trying carefully not to sound like a kindergarten teacher, I ventured, "So, what time horizon are you suggesting?"

A pause, five seconds longer than it needed to be. "Well ... I'm not sure," Steve finally admitted. He started shuffling through his binder, looking for some hint at the answer.

"Seriously, Steve!" His hesitation irritated me. He choked on the simplest softball question. My anger rose again. "Okay, listen up. This is how it works here; there's one metric — money. How much goes out, how much comes back, ... and when! When is a crucial factor. Steve, I'm trying to help you out here, but first you have to know your target date. You have to know your material, and you have to have enough conviction to make a stand. Nobody is ever absolutely certain about anything, right? The future will always be murky. Chaos and the laws of nature are intertwined. But you, Steve, are here to make a reasonable guess. If it's not reasonable, these dozen partners around the table will straighten you out. ... Understand?" I was almost climbing out of my seat. Maybe hiring Steve was a terrible mistake.

"Go back. We have time on this. Do some more thinking and be ready next week ... and I mean ready to defend all challenges. You might be wrong. Be prepared for that. That's okay. There's no shame in striking out, but you have to be swinging. If you don't start out with conviction, you're cooked. If you're always in doubt, you'll never make a decision. You've done a lot of great work to get to this point. You're now a part of this firm, but that doesn't mean you now have an eight-to-five entitlement. Are you willing to reach for a position of power, or are you going to waste your talents? For this to be your career, you've got to earn it every day. And if that's not your attitude ... we have a line of people standing outside that door ready to take your spot. Got it?"

The table's attention was rapt. All eyes were on me.

"Hold on," Steve said. I saw a sudden straightening of his back. He opened his binder and flipped a few pages back and forth. The room stayed quiet, everybody watching. Steve typed rapidly into his computer and, after thirty long seconds, said, "We can hit our target rate of return before six years, but it's acceptable through nine, which should be enough time to accommodate a possible interim negative swing in the market."

"Thank you." I gave Steve a nod, grateful to be finished

with the unneeded anxiety. I decided to give the poor boy a pass and skip the rebuttals. I shifted my focus to the other side of the table. "Now, Bob, tell us where you are with your project."

I heard the words come out of Bob's mouth, but I couldn't focus on their meaning. His lips were moving, but my ears had turned off. I was back focusing on the London group. These dueling agendas plagued my mind for the rest of the meeting, with neither benefiting. I watched the seconds on the clock tick away, my chest tightening. My weapon of choice had turned on me. At 09:31:27, only a minute and a half late, I closed the meeting.

"Nice recovery," I said to Steve as he walked towards the door. Steve nodded, but clearly he had been spooked.

"And by the way," I asked. "How are those girls of yours doing, Esther and Miriam?"

"Very well. Thank you for remembering." Steve said as he left Michael and me by ourselves in the room.

I leaned back in my chair and let go of a long, strained sigh.

We both stood to leave.

"We'll be fine," Michael said. Then he hugged me. I couldn't remember him ever doing that before.

4

Returning home after seeing Dad in the hospital, I decided to return as quickly as possible to my routine. It was for the sake of my sanity. I felt isolated in that world of sickness and an urgency to be back in another. I had no understanding of how to toggle between the two. I thought that the best way to seize control was to dive straight back into work. I spent even more time than usual at the office. Michael correctly tried to evict me from all future office meetings, but I stubbornly refused. I continued going through the motions, day after day. Attempting to inhabit normality was my goal. But despite the effort, I discovered myself lost. There were frequent moments when I'd be at my desk, staring at the computer screen, trying to decide which button I should press next. I'd tab between one email to the next, not remembering what I'd read five minutes earlier. I would gaze out the window looking, without thought, towards the distant horizon, numbly watching the clouds float by — as if the answer to my unasked question could be found out there.

My mind unburied events I hadn't thought about in years. Boyhood recollections, playing ball in the front yard with my neighborhood friends. Remembering the time when Andy first arrived home as a baby. Or little vignettes, like Dad sitting at the kitchen table, my bedroom with the long shelf of baseball trophies, Andy's room with the glow-in-the-dark constellations dotted onto the ceiling. These were pieces of time that I had held at a distance and hadn't accessed in years, yet they were as real as yesterday.

One morning, from my desk, I picked up the phone and called Andy. We were now talking several times a day. I was concerned with my brother's well-being, worried about how the loss would affect him. Dad was by far the most meaningful relationship in his life. That distinction, once, a long time ago, had belonged with me, but that special place ended when I left for college.

Andy had few male friends, and those that he had were only superficially related via their common time together at school. The only real hobby he had — and even this was not something he was particularly dedicated to — was photography. But that was a solitary affair for him. No friend ever broke through that thinly shared space and had become a best friend. I knew of nobody with whom he could share his personal problems. And to make matters worse, Andy resisted those sorts of conversations entirely. He was even reluctant to share his interior thoughts with his only sibling.

Andy's marriage to Sally didn't last long. I knew it was doomed before it started. Sally was an unrepentant narcissist, and she saw Andy as someone who would conform to her every need. If she ever possessed any satisfaction in their relationship, it quickly dissipated. Soon after marrying him, she began blaming Andy for her, and it was well-known to everybody but Andy, constitutional dissatisfaction with life. I never did understand the how or why of Andy's attraction to her, nor how their relationship had turned into a marriage. Andy had been duped by her. For some brief moment, he must have received from Sally the kind of attention he lacked elsewhere. The marriage was a mistake, but at the time, of course, I couldn't say anything for fear of being accused of being negative and not supportive.

After his divorce from Sally, Andy sought solace with Dad. But I don't think they shared intimate details with each other. That would have been counter to each of their natures. Somehow mere proximity was satisfactory enough.

Although following his divorce Andy and Dad grew closer, and they were together often. I'm not sure they spoke about anything other than the day-to-day mechanics of life. What to cook for dinner. When they would next go out to the mountains. It wasn't Dad's way to be a comforting therapist. To put it bluntly, in a way he might have appreciated he wasn't good with his words. His mastery was in action, doing. It was his answer to every problem. "I'm going to do something, even if it's wrong." And if Dad was wrong at the beginning, sheer persistence would eventually make whatever it was right. Doing was solving. Talking was seldom the solution. Andy depended on Dad's stolidness, but Andy's increased isolation from everyone else reflected an unhealthy malaise. I suspected he had clinical depression. He had seen therapists over the years and had tried various drugs, but nothing had ever seemed to truly restore the young Andy's joie de vivre. The person I had once known was now absent, distant. Perhaps gone for good. And I hadn't yet figured out how to relate to this new version. In my heart, though, I owed Andy a debt. There were reparations due for the way I had abandoned him. I wasn't sure how to frame the payment.

Over the years, there were occasional moments when I felt like we were like young brothers again. A happy birthday call, where we laughed about silly jokes. But in those conversations, we always reminisced about the past. Our present lives never came into play. Although enjoyable in the moment, the calls reflected a dormancy in our relationship, not fertile ground for the future.

Between losing his job, his marriage, and now losing his father and closest confidant, the well he was stuck in was dark and deep. Our own relationship had long ago been tarnished, perhaps for no good reason. I had to question my own culpability in that. I knew it was my fault. The leaving and the resulting fracture had nothing to do with Andy. It had to do with me needing the distance from home. The torn relationship with Andy was unintended collateral damage, not something I had consciously wished for. Realizing my guilt took me many years, and owning it took me a few longer. While Andy was innocent and still young, I had severed the relationship. The break had been made during that brief period of life when the three-year difference between a seventeen-year-old and a fourteen-year-old feels like a vast chasm, a space where mutual interests naturally diverge and where the need to individuate requires leaving others behind.

My former idea of home no longer mattered. I had left it. Without the thought of any other possibility, I took classes in business. Business was rational. That choice at least had the side benefit of Dad's strong approval, being that it was practical and would probably lead to a job. My views rapidly evolved. The universe expanded at warp speed. The old world became irrelevant, and my focus was one hundred percent forward. I felt authentic to myself without feeling judged or monitored. I was excited for my future. That was when I felt the most free in my life. My growing self-confidence reinforced my decisive emotional break with home that went along with the physical one. I felt like I was becoming my own man.

Andy's moves fell into an expected linearity, science in high school, science in college, and then teaching science as a career. His youthful enthusiastic curiosity devolved into a non-reflective pattern of pre-ordained expectations. Or, at least that's the impression I had from back then. It could also just be that we didn't know how to talk to each other about our areas of interest. Or that we didn't build the opportunity or space in which those conversations could grow roots. Years later, after so much time apart, my little brother and I shared precious little beyond the memories of being boys together.

But our frequent calls about Dad's status and the recent dislodging of ancient memories made me long for the closeness of our early relationship. The calls were a stark shift from our prior habit of the rare and perfunctory birthday wishes. At the start of Dad's illness, I looked to Andy for the medical updates. Soon though, with the doctors eliminating hope and with Dad's death all but certain, the constant monitoring of his condition became unnecessary. I knew — everybody knew — that Dad was about to die. When was the only mystery. There was nothing I could do about that. When I attempted to ask Andy directly how he felt, he shared nothing with me. "Fine, doing just fine." But I knew otherwise.

5

A couple of days later, I was threading my way to work through the typically hurried Third Avenue proletariat. The early October air was unseasonably warm. The still low sun scattered long slivers of yellowish light off the buildings. When stepping into the broad crowded plaza just in front of my building, my phone rang. The nurse on the other end of the line caught me mid-stride. I stopped to listen.

"Your father has died."

She spoke frankly, only adding that his passing was peaceful.

I should have predicted this call, should have been prepared — but I wasn't. Why now? Of all the times? I was initially irritated by the interruption. Without even realizing it, I had fallen back into my everyday rhythm. My morning alarm, my workout, my quick breakfast of oatmeal, kissing goodbye to Liz, driving the boys to school, then in my office by seven-thirty. My brain had again become fully consumed by my daily routines, although clouded, clouded about the London deal going bad. Although I had ceded control to Michael and had been banished from the calls, the deal loomed larger in my head than it should have. I was persistently ruminating on the deal's demise. I had slipped into a parallel world.

The nurse's call pulled me back to that other world. Its impact surprised me like a sucker punch to the side of my head. A loud atonal noise roared through my head like a vacuum cleaner sucking at my brain's every synapse. I couldn't unring the bell. I put both hands over my ears as if that might help. My head felt light and foggy. I was surrounded by people, but I felt disoriented and alone. The passersby, annoyed by the sudden obstruction, weaved around me, but one kind person paused, putting a hand on my shoulder. Faceless, I heard him ask if I was all right. I waved him off quickly, saying, "I'm fine. I'm fine. It's okay." That brief human connection straightened me up. I gasped for a sip of oxygen. The kind person walked on back into his own world.

Finding a seat on a nearby planter, I closed my eyes and tried to isolate my senses and recollect my bearings. It worked. The pause allowed clarity to slowly reemerge. My father was dead. I stiffened my back and raised my face, seeking the sun's burn. I opened my eyes, looked up and above me, a million windows glistened like so many stars in the daylight, reflecting shards of broken light haphazardly across the plaza's stone floor. I rested for the moment in my own sanctuary. The buzz of the street became as indistinct as ocean waves.

My dad appeared to me in a stirring succession of images. I was not standing in a hospital room looking down at the old man lying motionless in bed as I saw him last week; I was in the front yard standing below the bottom step, looking up at him while he postured on the porch, at his knitted brow, him waiting impatiently for me to return from playing in the street; I was at the dinner table, knife in hand, with him concentrating on his food, and me concentrating on him, worried if he was going to glance my way; I saw him in a plaid shirt, throwing a judging glance over his shoulder as he walked away. The images were from when I was young, when he was most frightening. It was as if I were reopening the first few pages of a long-forgotten photo album. The effect was nauseating.

I closed my eyes again, seeking isolation within the chaos, but less successfully. The noise about me rose in volume. I was angry with myself, or perhaps disappointed. My thoughts had jumped directly to the negative. And of all the possible emotions, my first instinct was to reject regret. It wasn't my fault. I had heard on the news so many stories about children who regretted not asking their recently past parent some burning question, about some missing essential component of their relationship, some version of "Why didn't you love me more?" With me, it's not that I had the answer so much as I knew there was no answer to be had. I had done my part to try. I had tried to bridge the gap, but the man was impenetrably unselfconscious and incapable of empathy. He never acknowledged a problem between us. I knew what made him tick, the cause and effect of my actions and his reactions, but I never knew him intimately. What was his pain, his longings, his inner motivations. I had known him too long and, strangely, not long enough. I understood all that was inaccessible. He remained a mystery that I wrote down as being unsolvable. What you saw was what you got, and all that was available was available on the surface. There never existed any possibility of reconciliation or cathartic embrace.

My father had, when I was young, filled a large, robust space in my life — or more precisely, he had dominated my early life. Doubly so, after my mom passed away. And with the enormous effort required to get along with a man who was not easy to get along with, meant there was never much remaining energy for me to generate my voice. I felt like I was planted in a small pot packed with dense soil. My role in this play was to react and comply; his, and only his, agenda drove the action. I was reactive to his proactive.

Waking up on any given day, I never knew exactly which

Dad might walk into the room. That uncertainty kept me confused but also on my toes. There was the man who was well organized, reflecting his military background, and starting the day with a clear schedule. There was the provider, a man who took care of all our needs, making sure we lacked for nothing. There was Dad, the rule setter, who specified how one was to behave and who made clear what his expectations were. Connected to that Dad was the authoritarian. This man who could, without warning, pass judgment and mete out punishment with a swift swing of his formidable right arm, a frightening symbol of violence. When unshielded by a shirt, it revealed a long, jagged red scar along the length of his forearm, a result of Dad having been pushed through a glass door when he was a young teenager. Each version of Dad came uncorrelated to any perceivable pattern. His unpredictability nourished a permanent unsettledness. The only way I knew to preserve order was by distance.

With my eyes still closed, an image of my mother floated into my head. Another vague memory seeking anchor. Most of my recollections of her could only be accessed by the occasional visits to the box of old photos set on the top shelf of the hall closet. Although one silver-framed wedding picture was not hidden. It sat prominently on top of Dad's dresser. The two of them, Mom and Dad, frozen in the middle of a dance. My dad's arm was around my mother's waist, hers around his shoulder. They were wrapped close, and my mother wore a broad joyful smile. There was certainly something she once found in Dad to love. I felt a surge of empathy and sadness for her loss, an odd feeling, finding empathy with someone who was long ago dead, who, moreover, I never really knew and certainly couldn't feel this particular pain.

I drew a deep breath, lingered on it, and exhaled it out slowly. Another breath and then another in an unhurried cadence. My eyes opened, and I finally felt I had rejoined the real world. The fall air was cleansing and fresh. A breeze of relief blew through me, a reprieve from a long-endured battle with my memories. It was sobering to think that my father's passing was the only possible resolution to our strain, but he was never going to change, and I was never going to win. I had thought that my anger had dissipated. I had set it aside. But now, I was surprised at how that anger had instantly leapt free across all those years.

I couldn't imagine why I hadn't heard this news from Andy. Why did the nurse call me and not him? Was he so distraught he couldn't call? That didn't seem plausible. Where was he? He depended on me.

I had lost track of time, and with reality seeping back in, the London deal came back to the forefront of my consciousness. Suddenly the competing urgencies of the moment asserted themselves and battled my work versus my obligations to my father. But a funeral? A memorial? A wake? Some public acknowledgment of the man's death seemed necessary. When would all this happen? Could I leave work now? The logistics of death. I had no training for this. And how was I going to handle the estate? I anticipated a mess there. Too much was closing in on me at once. Above all, I still didn't understand why the nurse had called me instead of Andy. I imagined that Andy would have been at Dad's side when he died. Was Andy okay?

I dialed Andy's number. No answer.

I called Liz. Always dependable and never without her phone, she picked up quickly.

"What's wrong?" she asked with extrasensory intuition.

I can't imagine what her clue might have been, how she knew instantly that there was a problem. Liz's worldview was inaccessible to me, like she was watching a different network on a different frequency. I had long understood that my view was mechanical, limited to action-reaction, cause-effect. Liz sensed forces that were invisible to me but no less influential. It was like our marriage manifested the wave-particle duality. We were in the same reality but with two opposing schemas, two world views that overlapped only because they were both attempting to explain the same phenomena. But at the same time, those views were completely divergent because their foundational principles were irreconcilable and couldn't co-exist with the other – yet somehow they did. When there was no evidence apparent to me, she sensed when the tide was coming in or going out. My attempt at a rational explanation to this phenomenon was that she subconsciously read people's micro-expressions or perceived the tiniest variations in their speech. As far as I was concerned, it was like a magic trick. Perhaps today the tell was the timing of my call, so soon after having left the house. If I had called earlier, she might have thought I had merely forgotten something. A half-hour later, she would have thought I was calling about a calendar change. But none of that analysis mattered, nor was it verifiable. We were cut from different fabrics, but in the combination there was certain strength. Years ago, I had learned to trust her intuition and even embrace it.

I told her about the nurse's call.

"I'm so sorry. I can hear the distress in your voice," she said.

Liz's tone was soothing and perfect, her words practiced as if she had spoken the same script a thousand times before. I further heard her projecting on to me how she expected I should feel as if I needed to be told. Slightly bristling, I chose to follow her lead, not share with her my true ambivalence about Dad. I did feel sorrow – or perhaps some emotion close to it – but it was countered by a large measure of relief. Perhaps, more authentically, I felt confusion, an agitating confluence of emotions simultaneously pulling me in opposite directions. I took a deep breath and listened to my wife.

My anxiety intensified as I self-analyzed. How could a son be relieved by his father's passing? It felt wrong to feel as I did. I was certain though that I wouldn't miss those dark, judging eyes, always seeking fault. I needed to look forward.

Liz went on, "... these events, you can never predict how they'll affect you."

Her words started to sound like pablum, and I needed to move on. "I'm not sure what I'm supposed to do next," I responded. "Of course, it falls on me to figure out the funeral plans. Andy isn't capable ... but I'll figure it out."

"You underestimate your brother, Cole."

I knew Liz could and certainly would help make the appropriate plans. She was accomplished at event planning, any event, even from a great distance. It nevertheless felt odd to ask her to plan the funeral for a man she had met only a handful of times. It was my responsibility.

After a few more supportive words from Liz, we hung up, and I started to walk away from my office. I wasn't ready to face those people. I headed north, trying to take to heart what Liz had just said and give myself a little time to amble and think.

I arrived at the crosswalk, and a turning delivery van clipped the curb, barely missing me. I jerked back out of the way. The driver hit his brakes hard and, in the same instant, leaned on his horn. With the barest of his remaining momentum, he struck a bike messenger who had been weaving out of the maze of vehicles and pedestrians. The blow wasn't severe, but enough to knock the bike and the boy to the ground.

I jumped in front of the van, banged on its hood, yelling at the driver, "You fucking asshole! You could've killed somebody!" The driver glared at me and vigorously gestured his righteousness. He stayed put behind the windshield without even bothering to check on his victim. I felt the urge to further confront the driver but was relieved by the boy rising up. He couldn't have been more than nineteen. He straddled his bike slowly, sneering at the driver all the while. Continuing to take his time, he grabbed the tail of his shirt, dabbing the spot of blood dripping from his elbow, before finally riding off.

The crosswalk remained momentarily chaotic, and the disentangling crowd thwarted my progress. I stepped back onto the curb, letting the commotion dissipate before I followed in the same direction as the boy. I had no particular destination in mind, only wanting to move on.

Was Dad ever aware of what had happened to him? In one moment he was standing on a ladder, and in the next random beat, he lay helpless on the Nichol's porch. Did he call for help? Was he instantly unconscious?

What if he had been found sooner? The fall from the ladder could have been an inconsequential event — not unlike the boy on the bike. A dozen alternative scenarios could have prevented the tragedy. What if Mr. Nichols had asked his neighbor or one of his children to help with the bulb? Dad was never bothered by driving across town for the smallest chore. He liked his houses to be kept in a near-perfect state, and most of all, he enjoyed his tenants. Those small conversations and interactions sustained his days as he grew old.

I walked another block.

What if the Nichols had driven to the back of their house as they typically would have done? What if Dad had waited until he knew the Nichols would be home? But Dad had his own schedule. He did what he wanted when he wanted. The what-ifs could go on forever if I let them. I took another deep breath. And another.

One theory held that he had a stroke and that the fall was subsequent to that. But with so much trauma, a test couldn't be conclusive. In any case, it didn't make a difference. At this point, none of that mattered, and I couldn't find any moral to the story. My father was dead. Case Closed. Past tense. Present tense conjecturing wasn't going to change a thing, not the result nor its predicate. It was one of those random and unpredictable life events.

The reality was that by the time the paramedics came, it was too late.

Andy, and his absence, re-dominated my thoughts. It was troubling, and I still had no idea what to think. It was a couple of hours earlier in the morning for him. The sun wouldn't even be up yet — where was he? I tried him again. No answer.

At the next intersection, the green light granted me permission to cross. The choreography now was more fluid. I began to relax. The impact of the news dissipated, and in its space the London deal reclaimed the moment. Instantly, I was worried again.

"*Shit! ... What time is it?*" I checked my watch. Only seven minutes until my meeting. I made a U-turn and hurried back to my office.

6

I froze at the threshold of the conference room. The clock read 9:05:46; I was five minutes late for my own meeting. Michael looked over at me as I paused, then rose from the table and walked over to me.

"You okay?" he asked with an obvious look of concern.

I chose not to self-assess and refused to answer. I scanned the room. Thankfully, the hunched-over group of guys and one girl sitting around the table were consumed by their work. None noticed my presence.

Michael put his hand on my shoulder and urged me into the hall. "you look pissed," he said. "Tell me, something bothering you? What is it? ... Is it your father? How is he?"

"Dead," I said. Michael's eyes widened. "I heard the news a few minutes ago while I was walking into the office. Haven't even talked to Andy. ... I don't get it; he won't answer his phone."

"Man, what the hell is wrong with you?"

"This deal is important. I'm nervous about it and couldn't see canceling the call. Besides, we weren't that close. In fact, worse than that ..." I stopped myself, turned from Michael's eyes and started for my seat.

"Com'on Cole." Michael yanked me back out into the hall.

With his nose nearly touching mine, and in a barely hushed voice, exclaimed, "You've got no business here. None. I've never seen anything like this. Man, this is your father we're talking about! You ought to have more important things on your mind than this." Michael let his arm sweep across our view of the now full conference room, "... like Andy ... like yourself. Go. Get out of here. Leave all the worrying about these assholes to me."

We stood in silence. Through the open door, I stared past the occasional curious face and out through the huge windows. The mountains of steel and glass glared back at me harshly. Feeling judged, I was tense and angry. I looked back at Michael. He also looked to be on the verge of anger, even ready for a fight. Anyway, he was right. I had to go. I had to find Andy. There was nothing to argue about or defend. I needed out of there.

"It's time. Go to your family. I'll send you updates. ... and please, take care of yourself."

Leaving Michael on his own, I walked the short hallway down to my office, shut the door and sat at my desk. It felt good to lean back in my chair and lock the door. Opposite my desk and above the sofa was my collection of photos, all the prominent people I had met over the years through business deals, charity functions, golf tournaments or symposiums. Amongst all those pictures, I was shaking hands with two of the past three New York City mayors and our senior senator in Washington with his arm hanging over my shoulder. I had all their cell phone numbers and could fully expect they would answer my call. But now, gazing beyond all those proofs of resume, across the horizon, to the place of my youth, I remembered the wilderness of my dad's property, where he would regularly take Andy and me. It was a fanciful daydream that I occasionally elicited to seek relief from work's tensions. I couldn't pin it down, but the wild was beckoning me. I had an intense need to go somewhere, anywhere. Just to go. To escape. Mostly just so that I was moving, feeling my body's physicality, its place in the world.

I called Andy and felt an instantaneous wash of relief when he picked up after the second ring.

"How are you holding up?" I asked, confident we both knew the same basic facts about Dad's death.

"It's been rough. This sucks. No two ways about it. It sucks. ... and I can't believe how exhausted I feel. I can hardly tell you what time it is or the day of the week. ... and you? How are you?"

"Worse than I imagined. I was caught off-guard. With all that was going on at work, things falling apart, my mind was elsewhere" I could hear Andy's footsteps echoing in a hallway, voices coming in and out of the background. "... where are you?" I asked.

"I'm back at the hospital, picking up Dad's stuff. And now they're quizzing me about where to send the body. ... and I'm just not ready for that." Andy's voice was cracking, and he was doing what he could to stifle his emotions.

"Just tell them to wait. That's so rude. Don't worry about any of that; I can negotiate those details."

"But, I wanted to be with Dad at the end ..."

The rising background noise of voices was becoming unbearable. "Andy, you've got to find a quieter place. I can barely hear you."

I heard his footsteps and then quiet.

"I'm in his room now," he said. "I've shut the door. Is that better?"

"He's not still there, is he?"

"No. No. He's gone, in some room down in the basement."

"Where were you this morning? How come I didn't hear from you?"

"Tommy, I wasn't with Dad at the end, and it really, really bothers me."

"But where were you? Why didn't you pick up my calls?"

"I'd been spending most nights right here in Dad's room, in this recliner. Terrible place to sleep; hard to get more than an hour of quiet between the IV machine alarm going off, the nurses coming in and out at all hours, and that strange machine that cleans the hallways ... it's like a tiny Zamboni with a whine that could wake the dead. Maybe that's why they use it."

I chuckled.

"I wanted to be here when the doctors came by. But you know, you can't predict their schedules. When they might drop in, it seems completely absent of any understandable order. I never found the right rhythm. I was exhausted and stayed exhausted. So, last night, I just couldn't do it any more. I just had to go home to get some ..." Andy paused. It sounded as if he had put his hand over the phone. A second later, he continued, his voice not as secure, "... you know, to shower and catch a few good hours in my own bed, a couple of hours of good sleep. That's all I wanted."

Although understandable, Andy's despair was in sharp contrast to the Andy I knew since childhood. His emotions had always been flat or near flat, like a sine wave with a very low amplitude and a long wavelength. If a psychologist had told me back then that Andy was somewhere on the spectrum, I wouldn't have argued differently. He was rarely rattled, but he seemed to miss the highs, too.

"Andy, there's no reason to blame yourself for anything. You couldn't have done any more than you did. Don't worry. Dad would've been proud. You've been a loyal son, as good as any."

"I wanted to be there with him. I owed it to him. He had always been there for me when I needed him ... but I crashed.

I let him down. I ended up sleeping for like fourteen hours ... and even when the hospital called, I didn't hear the phone ring. I was so tired."

"Dad would understand."

"It's not how I wanted it. I didn't want him to die alone. I tried. I tried so hard, but I was just so worn out, all that time at the hospital, such a tiring place to be. And in the end, he was alone."

I heard Andy sobbing through the muffled phone. I didn't know what else I could say, and for some moments we hung in an awful asymmetry. Andy cried. I listened. It was the wrong time to remember this, but I couldn't help thinking about how Dad reacted to crying, at least to my own crying. When I was young, I must've been about eight, and something stupid went wrong at school, like not getting picked to play for the soccer team. I came home in tears. After a two-question quiz to determine the reason, Dad said, "Okay, you're done now. Quit. Men don't cry. Let's get over this and move on to the next thing. You'll show them." I wasn't sure of his intentions, but my takeaway was that I was never again to show Dad any sign of weakness. I don't know if Andy received the same lesson or not. Or if it didn't take, or if he didn't care. Or if it was simply the wrong advice altogether.

"Sorry, I'm better now," Andy said. I heard a long exhale and a moment's pause.

"It's okay. I'm here. I get it." I said.

"I've got no one else I can talk to."

"Nobody?" I asked out loud, but internally I tried to think of who Andy was close to and quickly realized that I didn't know any of those people.

"No one I can share this with, not this."

"I know you saw a therapist not too long ago; don't you still see him occasionally?"

"I called, but I can't get in for a few days. ... But, tell me,

I've been talking too much, what about you? How are you coping?"

"Like I said, mostly numb. It's hard for me to process it all right now."

I felt that Andy needed me. I wasn't sure in what capacity, but my instincts suddenly were to be close to him.

"Don't worry," I said. "As soon as I can get on a plane, I'll be back home."

Home? I caught myself thinking of that strange word. How odd using that word so effortlessly after all this time away. Home? I said it to myself several times. That word in any other conversation with any other person would have meant the place I lived with Liz, Kevin, and Alex. I suppose for most people, where one spent their childhood will always be, in some sense, home. But, I hadn't thought of that place where Andy and I grew up as home in a very long time. For years, decades really, I had framed it as the place where I was raised, not home.

I felt an urgency to go back right away. The impulse came from some place deep inside, and it felt genuine. I didn't question it. I called Liz again and told her my plan was to fly out that evening. She expressed no surprise at the announcement and was, in fact, supportive. There were a bunch of emails I'd have to rush to finish, and I'd have to figure out how to delegate whatever work remained. Liz, being Liz, offered to book my flight and messenger a packed suitcase to the office. We decided it would be better if she came later with the boys, after I knew what was going on in terms of a funeral.

That evening, in the cab to the airport, slowly moving down the FDR, the cumulative turmoil of the day finally caught up with me. Exhausted, I sank low in the seat, giving in to the mesmerizing stream of lights sliding past the window.

7

Despite having trekked miles through two crowded airports and spending four hours crammed in the plane's back row, next to the bathroom, and despite the long day, and despite my flight's late-night arrival, Andy insisted on meeting me as soon as I landed. He suggested an all-night diner a few blocks from his house.

I arrived at the diner five minutes after eleven. I spotted my brother at the back of the room, firmly settled in a booth. Hunched over, he was scribbling into a small notebook. His hair was longer, grayer, and thinner than I had remembered. His shoulders were gently rocking back and forth, and stuck in his ears were a pair of white earphones. Immune to the outside world and my approach, his body shifted in a subtle rhythm known only to him. Nestled in his open sandals, disregarding the cold weather, were his sock-less feet tapping up and down at a different, slightly uneven pace.

When I broke into his peripheral vision, he jumped up and moved towards me, his long, thick, green sweater swinging open like a loose robe. Splattered with globs of gray paint, it looked unclean, causing me to hesitate briefly before accepting his embrace. This instantaneous pulling back, due to his unruly appearance, induced within me a spark of doubt regarding who I was in relation to this man, this man who I call my brother. But his hug was tight, and it lingered. It felt genuine.

We sat down in the booth opposite each other. His eyes looked tired and sad, but in contrast, he put on a pleasant smile. I appreciated the effort and sensed he was grateful for my arrival. We stared at one another for a moment without saying a word, each of us assessing the other. The table's faux walnut wood pattern had long ago been worn to a dullish gray. I pulled a paper napkin from the black shoebox-like dispenser and wiped at the bit of grime in front of me, but unfortunately, the grunge was a now permanent feature of the table. Recentering himself in the booth, Andy folded his notebook and pushed it to the side. He cradled the large cup of steaming coffee in front of him, absorbing its warmth.

"What is that you're writing?" I asked. "A novel?" I added, my attempt at a small joke. I could never imagine Andy to be the novel-writing type.

"Actually, it's my journal. I find it therapeutic and best done with a little Thelonious Monk in the background."

"So, that's new. When did you start doing that?"

"My therapist suggested it — like right after the divorce. So actually, it's been a habit for a few years. I thought you knew."

"If you told me, I forgot. ... Sorry."

"At first, it was a daily habit, but I've gotten to the point I only write when I'm feeling anxious. It is ..."

"Andy, you interested in ordering any food?" Dressed in crumpled black pants and a white shirt with the diner's logo over the pocket, the waiter interrupted Andy, asking his blunt question with no warmth but with an obvious familiarity.

"Paul, coffee only for me, but my brother might want something."

"Nice to meet you," the waiter said, continuing with his lack of sincerity.

I was hungry, having avoided the airplane food. I ran my

finger quickly across the menu as Paul refilled Andy's coffee. I settled on the club sandwich with extra crispy fries to go along with my own much-needed coffee. Paul picked up the menus, leaned across the table and set them back in their proper slot next to the ketchup, mustard and honey.

Andy's eyes glanced briefly into the dark coffee, then back up at me. They were more bloodshot and swollen than I had first noticed. Whatever he was getting ready to tell me a minute ago had evaporated. "Tell me about the boys — what are they up to? I haven't seen them in well over a year. Feels though like a lot longer." The question was delivered dryly, almost as if it were an obligation, but I grabbed onto it as a good way to start the conversation with something positive.

"Kevin has just started seventh grade." I felt awkward at first, not quite at ease outlining the basic facts. "Surprisingly, he's turning into a pretty good student, which is not what I expected after his lower school struggles. Twelve, it's just a terrible age ... the worst, highly unpredictable. The beginning of that weird, uneven transition from being a soft-faced little boy to a man. It tears at you. Who is it you're trying to please, your parents or your friends? And it seems like those forces are always in opposition. You're always off-balance and having to make hard choices. His body is beginning to look manly, and he's almost as tall as me, hairy in places he wasn't a year before. But on the inside, he's still sweet — hugs his mom every morning before he leaves for school."

"I seem to remember he enjoys history, no? Is that right?"

Barely breaking stride, Paul dropped off a cup of still boiling coffee and a handful of synthetic creamer pods.

"Good memory. I find it odd how he's always looking backward, always asking about the backstory, curious about how things came to be the way they are. He's a strange kid. Reminds me of you in that way."

"But I bet he's like his dad when it comes to sports?"

"Sort of, but it's not baseball he's interested in. For Kevin, it's basketball. He's always out in the driveway dropping free throws, like a thousand a day."

"And Alex?" Andy asked, skipping any follow-up questions about Kevin. It was as if he was simply moving on to the next box on his to-do list. Andy had some other topic dominating his mind. These questions were his attempt at following the proper social convention — which it was, but as was Andy's way, he was doing so without much grace. Even so, I knew his interest in the boys was authentic, and I wished for him to better know his nephews.

"He's still a work in progress. I have no idea where he's headed yet. He's in the fourth grade and, for the time being, following after his big brother, trying to be cool. Just a smaller version."

"And Liz? How's she?" He was asking me questions but wasn't listening to any of my answers or caring. His mind wasn't focused on this conversation. His eyes surveyed the room, and his leg was nervously bouncing up and down.

"She's good," I answered with a self-edited brevity. "Either on the tennis court or volunteering on one of her million charity committees. I don't ask any more; it's too confusing."

Andy nodded, acknowledging he heard me, but his expression was passive. He was hearing but not processing. His interest in family talk had reached his limit.

"And you, Andy ... what's going on with you?" I was ready to coax out of him whatever it was he had on his mind.

I had no idea how he filled his days and almost regretted asking for fear of putting him on the defensive or forcing him to invent for me a list of activities that made him appear busy. He had lost his teaching job almost ten years ago. It was an unfair firing, having been unjustifiably accused of improper conduct with a young student. He spent years with lawyers defending his name. He not only was exonerated, but he also collected as damages a nice sum of money from the school, so much so that he was in such a good financial position he didn't have to work. Although he wanted to work, actually needed to work to prove his own self-worth. Over the last several years Andy floundered, bouncing around between one odd thing and another, applying for positions below his capabilities, and taking the occasional class. I felt sorry for him, and I didn't know how to define him any more. He had loved that school and teaching science perfectly suited his personality.

"Perhaps some good news," he said, although his expression didn't mirror the expected happiness. "I'm not sure what it'll lead to, but I've been offered a part-time job at the junior college. It's only a couple of classes per week, but it's teaching again ... an introduction to astronomy. Starts right away."

"That's great to hear. I'm happy for you." I was relieved to hear such positive news.

Paul plopped the hard plastic plate holding my sandwich onto the table, refilled my cup with the inky coffee and silently moved to the next table.

Andy shrugged. "Maybe. We'll see." He looked back into his coffee, then around the room, and then back to me. Apparently we were done with the catching-up part of the conversation, and the job opportunity was not what was dominating his mind. Andy now looked at me expectantly, like he wanted me to talk next.

Not in any sense a multi-tasker, my little brother could only focus on the single issue that was occupying his mind at that particular moment. In math class, if there were a decidedly difficult problem, he would stick with it for days if that's what it took to figure out the solution. Admirable, certainly, but this tenacity came at the expense of his other assignments, the ones that were less interesting to him. He always did solve the problem. He was stubborn in that sense. That selected myopia, though, resulted in a deficiency in areas that were not subject to a logical formulation. He was disinterested in literature or poetry, completely unable to untie those murkier knots. There was room in his mind for only one thought at a time. This didn't make him simple-minded, but it did make his approach to life appear more simple than for most other people, who were constantly reacting to the mind-numbing rush of modern life's multiple stimuli. He knew how to cut out that noise.

With Andy still staring at me, I started to ask about our schedule for the next day. It was close to midnight now. I was tired, ready for bed, and I knew that Andy had scheduled a meeting at the funeral home — and that we needed to get in contact with Dad's attorney. But before I could start my question, Andy spoke up. "Tell me the truth. What does Dad's mountain property mean to you?" I was dumbfounded that this was the subject that had been troubling him and then confused by the ambiguous phrasing of his question. I didn't quite understand what he meant by "mean." Was he asking about my memories of the place — good or bad? Was he ready to reminisce about the good old days? Was he asking about the property's possible financial value? I stared back at Andy, wordless. I didn't know what was going on inside his head.

Miles from the city, the property, a large primal tract of land deep in the mountains, contained a small rustic cabin. It was Dad's constant refuge. For a good part of our childhood, we spent many weekends there, good weather or bad, leaving Friday evening and returning Sunday afternoon. After I had left for college, Andy and Dad maintained the habit, at least until it was Andy's turn to leave for college. Dad's motivation lessened after that. "Lonely" is what he called the feeling. Without either of us, Dad's trips to the mountain cabin became less frequent, and the place slowly started slipping into disrepair. But when Andy returned from school years later, he sensed Dad's heartache and arranged his summer breaks from teaching so that he could accompany Dad on the occasional visits. Within a few years, the pattern transformed. Perhaps at first, Andy was motivated by some obligation, or maybe it was simply force of habit, but he used almost all of his time off from work to hang with Dad. They enjoyed working together on the repairs. I don't know who was more loyal to whom, Andy to Dad or Dad to Andy. After his divorce, Andy suffered. His limited social world had revolved around his wife's friends. When that dried up, he even more depended on the anchor of familiarity, and Dad relished in his son's uncritical attention. Whether they were consciously aware of it or not, their internal attraction to one another was unimportant. Their external interests were clear, mutual, and frequently expressed, and they all centered on Dad's mountain property.

As the years caught up with Dad, the pattern twisted yet again, with Andy becoming the motivator. Dad's energy had declined. He no longer enjoyed the physical labor integral to the experience, but his vicarious connection through his son's involvement compensated. Andy's spirit galvanized, and he continued making the trip even with Dad's frequent regrets. He had no problem being out there by himself. Dad more and more stayed in town, although he continued to support the property financially. It remained an important symbol for Dad, a sanctuary of sorts, unencumbered by outsiders. Their shared passion for the property persisted as the unambiguous binder for their interdependence. Eventually, I knew it formed the basis for almost every conversation between them.

"The property, to me?" I answered. " … Well, not a whole lot."

"Don't you remember? We had so many years of great fun up there," Andy said; a new animation came into his voice. He almost sounded like a used car salesman intent on making his first sale. His enthusiasm was awkward, even naive, but it was authentic. "Exploring the woods and shooting cans off the fence posts. Didn't you enjoy all that?"

"Sure. I did."

Dad had bought the property soon after our mother died. So, perhaps at the outset, the purchase was a reaction to the loss, a distraction from his sadness, an activity to focus his attention when otherwise it would focus on emptiness. Or maybe it was a longing he couldn't express while our mom was around. Maybe she had squelched the idea. But after her death, Dad felt our suburban three-bedroom house confining. He persistently mentioned the fresh air and the freedom that could only be felt in the woods, outside the negative energies of the city. The wilderness had a beckoning call. He sought escape from the pressures of the city and work. He trusted the land.

The mountains were also where Dad, least distracted by the urgencies of his work, felt free to elaborate on his longer-term expectations for his sons. We endured constant mini-speeches about hard work, grit, setting goals, and getting ahead. The mountain land became the hearth from which he attempted to forge his boys into men.

The rules at the cabin were the reverse of the rules at home. At home, the standards were about order, obsessively so. His strictures revolved around the mechanics of getting through the day and the week, keeping the house clean, clothes picked up, and doing our homework. In the mountains, the attention to our bodily hygiene and the mental acuity required for schoolwork took a back seat to our physical endeavors, meaning manual labor, maintenance, and the never-ending list of repairs. We learned to cut and split wood, laying out cords and cords of wood, stacking them in an area down the hill near to the cabin. We accumulated a reserve of wood that could've lasted for years, leaving me with the impression that the exercise was not about the wood but instead work for the sake of work. Lots and lots of unnecessary busywork. But to Andy's point, although our pedagogical chores were many, they were offset by hours upon hours of unsupervised adventure and absolute freedom.

"I was wondering," Andy continued. "Since you're going to be in town for a few days, and, I know, it's been a long time since you were last there, maybe you'd like to go with me out to the mountains ... an overnight visit? For old-times' sake? What do you think?"

The lumpy booth was uneven and uncomfortable. I felt like I was tilting to the side. I shifted over in my seat, moving closer to the wall.

"Thanks for the offer, but I don't think we'll have time."

Andy's face dropped. He didn't like my answer.

"The place doesn't hold the same warm and fuzzy place in my heart as it does yours," I tried to explain.

Andy scratched at the side of his scruffy beard, parroting my words, "Warm and fuzzy?"

"It's been a long, long time since I've set foot on that place. Perhaps there's some nostalgia there, but what's the point? Especially now, with everything that we have in front of us."

"Well, what about how I feel? Can you get warm and fuzzy about that?"

Paul approached us once again with a coffee pot in hand. I made eye contact. He wisely picked up on the clue and turned the other direction, having for once the good sense to leave us be.

Andy was still looking at me, waiting for my response.

I chose not to.

Andy rarely challenged me, but he felt emboldened. I could see it in his expression, "How is it possible that my own brother doesn't know me? I mean ... where's your compassion?"

His attack wasn't leading us towards common ground, and it did nothing to engender my sympathy. It worked in reverse, actually. I heard neediness. I heard weakness and his inability to stand independently on his own two feet. But I chose not to say any of this to him. Being that I had dropped everything to be with him, at this point, I was not going to engage in a refutation of my supposed lack of empathy. Especially now, with my exhaustion so deep, I could have just leaned over in the booth and taken a little snooze. I shifted in my seat and let my gaze drift out the window, a deep, black square hole framing one glaring parking lot light. The light blinded my ability to see anything else, but I continued to stare into the undifferentiated darkness. I wasn't sure what else my brother and I had left in common ... after Dad, probably nothing. Surprisingly, we had arrived through the same bloodline.

I turned back and leaned toward my brother, "Andy ... it's not my memories that matter here. I'm not here to force my feelings onto you. You're certainly entitled to feel however you want, but, as far as I'm concerned, I have no interest in visiting that old decrepit cabin in the mountains."

"I was just hoping to spend a little quality time with my brother ... and I think the last time that really happened ...was out there."

I settled back into my seat, drew in a deep breath and let it out slowly.

"What's that sigh about?"

I felt defensive. I couldn't pinpoint what nerve he had struck, but what Andy had said was true. It had been a long time since we had talked as brothers should. In recent memory, when we did talk, it was about superficial things, mostly general issues easily found in the national news. Andy didn't follow sports much, didn't play golf. That domain didn't go very deep. We did occasionally find common ground about travel. While he didn't venture out much, he was curious about all the trips Liz and I would take. But we never talked about us, our relationship, how over the years it had slipped into this artificial formality. Nor did we revisit much about our past — the good of it, the bad, anything.

"I'm not asking for much here," Andy, his eyes narrowed as if on the verge of anger, continued to press his point. "Just a couple of hours drive. I'm certain if you were to go back and see the property again with your own eyes, you'd fall back in love."

I leaned across the booth. "But Andy, how can I be more clear? I haven't been there in, ... thirty-what years. I'm not interested in reliving some silly romantic notion from child-hood. There are more important things to worry about now. We have a lot of work here in town with Dad's estate. And I know this doesn't mean anything to you, but I have some really serious problems back at my office. It's a fucking mess."

"Sorry, didn't mean to upset you," Andy said, "but I actu-ally thought a trip away might be an antidote to all that stress. The place is calming. It has a way of dissolving time — I, with all my heart, believe that. Being there has allowed me to connect with something bigger. I'm going. You can come or not. But, instead of being out there alone, I thought ... was thinking how great it would be, at this time that's so painful to both of us, to be on Dad's land with my brother. ... Back in the day, out in the mountains, no distractions, the two of us together, exploring the world." He looked down briefly into his barely touched and now lukewarm coffee and then back into my eyes. "Now, I feel like I'm not worthy enough to fit in your busy schedule."

"I'm sorry you feel so let down." I was resolved to stand my ground.

"Are you really that ... that callous? I know you're busy and have a lot on your mind. But you know, I could ... could have used some help these last few weeks. You fly in for one evening ... grace us with your presence, and ... then you're back to work like everything's just fucking normal. Meanwhile, I'm days and days sitting next to our comatose father. You owe me."

"Come on, Andy. That's not fair and you know it. Let's hit pause on this conversation. It's well past midnight, I just flew halfway across the country, and I'm beyond tired. Please stop pushing me."

"Why did you come out here?"

"That's a stupid question. To be with you, of course … and to bury our dad. How quickly did I come?"

"I bet you'd rather be working on your big deal than be here with me. Right?"

That barb stung. We were sitting across the table from one another, but the distance between us had grown to miles.

We sat in an awkward silence for a while until, finally, Andy waved at Paul, making the universal "bring me the check" scribbling gesture in the air.

Before Paul could even lay down the bill, Andy, having already calculated the exact total, including tip, handed Paul an assortment of bills. "Thank you," he said.

Andy looked my way and briefly waited like he was expecting me to say something.

"It's late. I'm going to bed," he said, leaving me alone at the table. He moved quickly through the empty restaurant. As he walked out, I looked out the window but could see nothing of him. He was lost in the dark blind of that single parking lot light.

I was too tired to move, too exhausted to think about what had just happened. The conversation would need to be unpacked, but I couldn't do that at the moment. I rubbed my face and thought about a good night's sleep. I ate two more bites of my long-ignored sandwich, then pushed it aside. Looking like a steady, invariable fixture of the old diner, Paul sat on his stool near the cash register, concentrating on a spread-out newspaper. He even seemed to be done with me.

Summoning my last bits of energy, I started to slide out of the booth. To my left I noticed Andy's journal lying next to the menus. I picked it up and returned to my hotel room.

8

When I arrived at the hotel, I set the journal down on the table. I opened my suitcase, shed my shoes, and sat on the edge of the bed. But the journal radiated an increasingly strong mystery. I kept glancing back at it while I was unpacking. The journal was bound in soft black leather, heavily worn along its edges. The cover was blank, but its coded message was obvious. It might as well have had the word "PRIVATE" printed boldly across the cover, like a teenager who pins a "do not enter" sign on his bedroom door, a bit naive in his belief that such a message might be an effective deterrent. In reality, such a sign is a proclamation, a desire to individuate, to define and protect one's own space. Against those who respect other people's privacy, it's a sufficient deterrent.

Having finally undressed, still coasting on the coffee high, and overwhelmed by curiosity. I grabbed the journal off the table and put myself on the edge of the bed. Thumbing through the pages, I saw the density of Andy's words, but was not yet willing to examine their meaning. In the upper corner of each page there were preprinted, stenciled numbers. The pages were unruled, but the script was small, dense, straight and even. And he consistently used the same fine-point blue pen. The book was nearly full, with just a few empty pages remaining. Clearly, it had been a long-standing project. I closed the cover and set it on the nightstand.

The part of me that said to ignore its call, to hand it back to Andy unread, was rapidly losing the battle to my blasphemous side. While I washed my face and brushed my teeth, I couldn't stop thinking about the book's contents. I moreover wondered — really wondered — how I was being portrayed in his story.

Five minutes later, ignoring my urge to close my eyes and give in to sleep, I propped the pillow against the headboard and opened the notebook to a page in the middle.

The writing was rambled, with incomplete phrases interspersed with thoughtful sentences. It was a transcript of Andy's stream of consciousness, a reflection of his inner self, unedited. I turned to another page and then another. Within its meanderings and lilting, half-dazed wanderings, some of the passages captured small essences of Andy.

> ... *nobody asked me for my version of the events. I was judged and punished in one quick motion. ... My life disintegrated from good to disaster in a heartbeat. ... the default position was not to believe me. What had I done to deserve this distrust? My whole life, I'd always done the right thing and followed the rules. All I had done was ask a young girl to stay behind. I wanted to help her understand the material, and I thought some extra tutoring might help. What did I do wrong? I failed to open the classroom door. I left it closed for all of five minutes ...*
>
> ... *down the hallway, the parade of students, teachers and staff left the building. My suspicions increased by the minute. Once the building was empty, Ms. Pearson came back to the office. ... She told me to gather my things, leave the building and have absolutely no*

contact with any student or teacher from that point forward. While she wasn't judgmental, she didn't either offer a single word of support. No compassion. No allowance for all the years we were friends, ... and then suddenly ice-cold. ...

... A couple of days later, a letter from an attorney arrived, terminating my employment. What about the principle of innocent until proven guilty? ...

... even after the exoneration, the school decided not to bring me back. They claimed that the accusation couldn't be expunged; they couldn't tolerate any cloud on any teacher's record. I had to clear my reputation so that I could work again. I had bills to pay. ... handicapping their odds, the school calculated how costly a negative verdict could be. ... The settlement was substantial ... but I had been robbed of my purpose. ...

... I lost Sally's trust. I'm not sure if she believed the accusations or not. We had other issues, but during that time, I was so consumed with my self-accusations of basic negligence ... I don't think I could have been good friends with anybody, much less be a good husband.

His telling of the firing was described in microscopic increments. In an attempt to heal his psychic scar, he was probing, breaking down just the beginning of what obviously felt like a long series of injustices. He had been unfairly victimized. Andy didn't enjoy fighting; it was counter to his character, but when it came to defending his character, he had no other choice. Thankfully, he won and was vindicated. He was ethically right and, as it turned out, legally right, something that over my career I've discovered aren't always in alignment. But this reliving of the events, writing it down in detail, seemed to keep the wound open rather than helping him heal. I didn't see any softening of his anger over the long passage of time. The handwriting felt urgent; the letters stark, engraved into the paper.

On another page, I found a softer Andy while nevertheless still feeling his angst. Waxing poetic, he reminisced about his first date with Sally, how she coerced him to go to the symphony.

... I was engrossed by the arrival choreography, the red-jacketed ushers, the cool austerity of the voluminous hall, and the serious demeanor of the jewel-laden women as they processed toward their seats ... looking at the carefully articulated curving marble stairs, the bold gestures, and the fastidious attention to all the details made me wonder why I had never seriously thought about architecture as a career path. ... I felt like the odd man out, the one guy who didn't understand what was going on. ... I lied when asked how I enjoyed the evening. Pleased that I had, she said we'd have to do it again. I didn't know what else to say.

I flipped ahead several pages. I couldn't discern any order to the entries. He bounced from one subject to the next with no apparent connection between them. I stopped on an entry regarding his brief foray into photography.

For a brief time, I tried my hand at capturing those moments of beauty... I liked the old-fashion darkroom, the chemicals, the magic of watching an image emerge from the developing liquids... I liked its adjacency to science. The process was engaging. It felt logical and comprehensible. ...although my results were less than satisfying... Why preserve the ethereal? By doing so, you destroy its essential charm. ...the images felt average, trite, boring. ... I have drawers of pictures that nobody but me will ever see. ... Who cares? ... Photography felt like cheating, too easy to make, point your camera in any direction and who is to say that picture is any better or worse than any other? ... we're inundated with pictures, like so many leaves falling from a tree; one more won't change anybody's life one iota? ...

I enjoyed reading Andy's occasional poetical sentiments. I knew Andy had a softer artistic tendency but hadn't paid attention to how deep those roots ran. They were a pleasant discovery, capturing an aspect of Andy I wished he had paid more attention to — the latent artist pushing out from inside the rigid scientist. Although his attempts at strict logic and rationality dominated the scribblings, every once in a while, shining out from a crack, I saw alluring glimmers of the illogical.

He was correct in saying that creative work needs an audience. Fostering a dialogue is the whole point of art. Otherwise, it's like shouting into an empty field. Art must be seen or heard, or read. If it's only for oneself, it's self-gratification, perhaps therapeutic, at worse narcissistic.

But buried not very deep underneath those few words lay Andy's strange self-destructive logic. He couldn't unlink his intrinsic joy of creating art from how others might perceive his work. Andy was competent in the craft, but his self-judgment and self-confidence about his artistic capabilities were impaired, if not entirely absent. He had no internal gauge. He couldn't trust his own opinions. He couldn't discern good from bad without external validation, a metric he desperately needed but was unwilling to seek out.

I hadn't paid attention to how thoroughly my younger brother had squelched his own passions. While I sat there reading his words, I wished Andy could have given in more to that subjective realm. It was so close to the surface. But he had chronically found excuses to suppress his urges. By nature, he looked for quantification, an objective measure. That's why he thrived in school. The answers could be measured. They had to either be right or wrong, or someplace on the scale from zero to one hundred. I wished he could have liberated himself from that necessity of being measured, but then again, I had known the feeling as well.

His rejection of photography reflected his frustration with not being heard. I had had that feeling growing up as well. If your father won't listen to your feelings, how can you expect somebody else to care? Dad was so focused on his certain agenda for us boys he had no reason to call upon his empathy. He didn't bother with understanding either of his boys' interests. It hurts not to be seen, as you believe you should be seen, and worse to be seen only as some preordained outline of your father's expectations. For me, the problem manifested most acutely with baseball. He worried that I spent too much time on the sport. He could have cared less about the details, asked no questions, and took no interest, assuming it was a small distraction from his larger plan. He never attended a single one of my games and never once asked if I was enjoying my time.

I knew for sure that this artistic side of Andy was one that our dad had no capacity to relate to. Dad understood grades, what they meant for one's future success — but that's all. Desperate to please him, Andy gravitated to the classes where he was confident he could make an A. Andy didn't want to challenge Dad's worldview; he let his innate trust in his father override his own perceptions. Dad's approval was doled out in a narrow range, and Andy's self-worth was thus limited to that range. From an early age, he surrendered to the path that Dad had defined for him.

Andy easily aced the higher levels of math and science,

achieving the top scores with little effort. But our school wasn't designed for such excellence and couldn't provide Andy with any further challenges beyond their limited curriculum. He, therefore, never had to put in the long hours that others had to. Ironically, these easily conquered challenges promoted a learned laziness. He readily quit or simply avoided the challenges outside his competencies before giving himself a sufficient chance to profit from the benefits of long hours of hard work, staying focused on that narrow range.

Like Andy, I wanted Dad to pay attention to my passions. But eventually I had come to accept that Dad was congenitally incapable of that sort of un-judgemental support. I eventually forgave our father for that failure. I had moved beyond the inflicted damage; no other choice. I had to be my own man, not some predefined version. Andy, on the other hand, desperately chose to please Dad. Andy had forfeited way too much power in that regard. But truthfully, the problem was that Andy lacked any self-induced ambition. He wasn't internally motivated to stretch himself. He could never grow into his authentic self — whatever that might have been.

A few pages later, I discovered a passage where my name jumped out.

> *... Tommy and I were inseparable when we were in grade school, and I had no reason but to expect the same going forward. As it turned out, the reverse became true ... Tommy lost interest in me. ... I suffered through the comparisons to my older brother. I hated that. ... even Dad would say, "Tommy aced history. So why shouldn't you." ... even my friends would say, "Your brother pitched a great game." His baseball buddies became his all-consuming society of friends. ... I was dropped. I became the irritating little brother. ... The world treated Tommy like a star... Tommy was*

praised for his athletics by his wide group of friends ... and for some strange reason, he felt like Dad was constantly criticizing him, preferring me over him. I really can't see where that attitude came from. ... it was the complete opposite. ... after my relationship with Maggie, my first attempt at having a girlfriend fell apart ... I felt awkward ... I was hurt and had nobody to talk to. ... I couldn't talk to Tommy any more. He would have laughed ceaselessly about my naivety. I was too embarrassed to tell him ... he was so involved in his world he wouldn't have noticed one way or another what was going on with me. ... Dad, too. ... neither could take the time ...

I had finally found a reference to me and it was a hurtful one. I didn't know what I had expected, but I decided not to put too much importance on Andy's words. I was a teenager back then, as was he. Emotions at that age are not fully formed. Everyone super sensitive to the slightest perception of slight. Although my interest continued to be piqued by my brother's innermost feelings, I could no longer resist my weariness. The clock was rolling past two a.m. I awoke the next morning as the sun shone through the crack in the shades. Andy's journal lay butterflied on the other side of the double bed.

9

I was set to meet Andy at the funeral home just after lunch. Having no agenda for the morning was welcome. I enjoyed an extra hour of sleep, ordered room service, coffee, a couple of fried eggs and sausage, no carbs, and worked out in the hotel gym, using a few minutes towards the end of the morning to catch up with Michael. He had no news yet on an alternative plan to deal with the London group, and further he had to remind me that it had barely been twenty-four hours since our meeting. It was as if I had been transported to a new planet, not simply two time zones, and it felt like several days had passed since I had last been in the office; I had lost an objective perspective on time.

Sitting on a long yellow stiff sofa, some designer's idea of lightening the mood of a naturally and overwhelming dour environment, Andy and I waited for our sales associate to finish his prior appointment. Andy broke the quiet and asked me, "Do you have my journal?"

"No." My response was instantaneous, carelessly obeying an abhorrent impulse. I lied, and I wasn't sure why.

"That's weird. Paul said the diner doesn't have it. It's not in my car. Can't imagine where it went."

I hadn't given any prior thought to such an obvious

question. I could have easily admitted taking it with the intention of returning it to him. But to reverse myself after saying 'no' would be an admission to a lie. That now seemed to be worse and more confusing than just continuing to claim no knowledge of the journal's whereabouts. My tongue felt large, fat and dry. I hated myself. I couldn't decipher why I made the decision to lie. It was as if I had no choice, no free will.

Relief arrived quickly as a strong-backed young man presented himself to Andy and me. He looked much like a better-dressed version of one of my newer associates, with a well-tailored suit, a crisp white shirt and a blue and gold striped tie. Introducing himself, we learned his name was Brad, and I immediately felt a certain sympathy with his situation. Brad's words were correct, evoking sympathy in their strict definition. But he lacked the proper tonality. Unintentionally mechanical, his words sounded like a practiced presentation, and his face likewise revealed no emotion. Not being family or even a friend, though, how could he behave otherwise? Death was a daily commodity for him, and he had acquired an immunity to grief. He had been charged with an impossible task and one he had chosen to do on a daily basis.

Brad invited us back to a well-organized office where, opposite his desk, we found another sofa, a pair of side chairs and a coffee table. The room was set up like a cozy family den. Ominously a shiny catalog with a picture of a casket sat on the table between us. Neither Andy nor I had any idea of what we should do for Dad. We weren't sure what he would have wanted, only presuming he would have liked to be buried next to our mother. Dad himself had never said a single word to either of us about the topic. We struggled with the idea of even having a church service or not, whether it was appropriate, and if it was, where to do it. With no religious tradition to go by, we were strangely looking at this twenty-something-year-old for guidance.

Listening to our uncertainty, Brad nodded, an obviously self-conscious gesture designed to encourage us to talk more, as if he were a practiced therapist. When he did finally speak, he offered a solution to our mysterious state, one he clearly had in mind before we walked in. He suggested we contact the preacher from a nearby church before making any decisions, assuring us the man had a good reputation. The preacher, apparently a friend of our father, had already called the funeral home, not knowing how to contact us directly.

10

The preacher, Preacher Dan, as I quickly learned, was the name our father used and the one he preferred. As it turned out, he was a player in Dad's occasional poker group, a group of guys I had never met. They apparently met and came together several years after I left home. Only occasionally had I heard Dad even allude to their existence. Preacher Dan shared with me more details than I had even known through Dad. They played a penny, nickel, dime game, meeting in another member's back house, a sort of man cave, as I heard the preacher describe it, with a refrigerator full of beer and multiple TVs on the wall. I was pleased to learn Dad had found such good fellowship at this later stage of his life, a good way for him to fill a portion of his ever-increasing free time. Not knowing how to reach either Andy or me, Preacher Dan had started his search with the hospital and then followed the link to the funeral home and then on to us. He was just as Brad described, and we were expertly advised over the next couple of days about an appropriate service. He contrived a feeling of rightness, and I couldn't explain how. I just accepted it. This, at least, was a pleasant relief from my mounting anxieties.

I had met Preacher Dan in his small whitewashed office while Andy was off interviewing a bookkeeper to help sort out

Dad's business affairs. The office felt appropriately monastic, containing no bookshelves, no cabinets, and no art other than a polychromed cross on one wall, looking like some artifact from Mexico. Below the single large window, he had positioned his block-like desk, outfitted with a large Bible carefully aligned to one corner and a brass lamp stationed on the other corner. Although not derived from the strict definition of his words but clear from his tone, the preacher conveyed certainty, comfort and sympathy, a temperament that Brad from the funeral home was incapable of delivering.

He spoke briefly about Dad, describing my father as never boring, always working on a new project, and always with a story to tell. I passively let Preacher Dan talk without offering an alternative point of view or anything other than a nod in agreement.

Preacher Dan reassured me that taking care of the service arrangements would be an honor he'd happily perform. He then shifted into talking of all the church's current financial constraints and all the good it performed for the community, a not-so-subtle message implying a commensurate reciprocity. I wasn't surprised by the ask and was all too happy to comply, having even brought a blank check with me. Knowing that Preacher Dan couldn't explicitly state his price, I had a hard time determining what the proper price should be. As he talked, I thought of a number that might be fair and acceptable, then doubled it. Once he examined the check, he was visibly satisfied. Extending the fiction, he said, "Thank you. This is not at all necessary but much appreciated. You are a very generous man, much like your father."

Two days after my meeting with Preacher Dan, and a mere four days since Dad's death, I was sitting in a church waiting for the funeral service to begin. It was the first time since — I can't remember when, an uncomfortable hypocrisy weighed on me. Religion of this particular rendition, or for that matter, any sort, was never part of our lives growing up. In our childhood household, there wasn't even a theology for me to reject. We simply hadn't been raised that way. Dad steadfastly refused the idea of a supernatural deity. He didn't understand the function of religion in our modern world. It was an antiquated form of social control, designed for people who were incapable of thinking or acting for themselves. For Dad, the world was a series of mechanical processes whereby people operated solely out of their own self-interests, with frequent clashes along the way. Accounts of the pious and pure altruism rang inauthentic to him. He always detected some hidden motivation behind the posturing. The worst possible trait in his book was the advertising of one's personal virtues. Nevertheless, Dad wasn't radical in asserting his opinion on others. He figured everybody made the decision that worked best for them. More than being an atheist, or even an agnostic, he claimed ambivalence. And I had followed his path.

For Liz, yes, religion had always been a part of her lifelong weekly routine. She grew up with her family's social life centered on the Methodist church. Its annual rhythm of holidays provided an incorruptible structure upon which everything else in life seemed to depend. Dad, Andy and I, of course, claimed no such pattern. As far as my boys were concerned, by default of not expressing any opinion, I deferred to Liz. Kevin and Alex were now used to Liz's family's weekly rhythm.

Liz and the boys had arrived in town the previous night. They sat quietly to my right while we were waiting for Preacher Dan to appear at the pulpit. Frayed from the long day of traveling, the boys appeared tired, having been transported into a new and unusual world with a brand new set of expectations. They sat sullenly with their hands folded in their laps and heads bent over, mirror images of each other. A half-hour earlier, the family had met with Preacher Dan in his small office while he outlined the protocols for the ceremony. Andy had not yet arrived when Preacher Dan walked us down the long red-tiled hallway into the sanctuary. He pointed to the first row of seats, then disappeared through a side door, abandoning us without a word. I glanced over my shoulder at the back of the room, only to be met by a sea of inquisitive eyes. Rows of people I had never met were there, along with supposed friends who had arrived for the spectacle. Not wanting to engage with any of them and knowing my cloak of grief would protect me, I maintained my focus forward.

When Andy and I discussed how to bury our father, the idea of setting him into the ground without any ceremony, without some marking of the event, struck us as cold and dishonorable. The fortuitous hookup with the preacher provided us an easy out. We deferred to his practiced guidance, and in return, he lifted some of our worries.

Painted the soft light filtering through the stained-glass windows, an ethereal mosaic laid across the stone floor in front of me, painting for me a concise moment of aesthetic enjoyment. The pew was hard, but I was as psychically uncomfortable as I was physically. For a person who avoided attention as much as he did, I viscerally sensed my deceased dad's unease, and by proxy, it was mine as well.

The plain wooden coffin, though, hopefully pleased the man who had enjoyed a sparse life. It was the last on his list and the least expensive choice in Brad's brightly colored twelve-page catalog. Luxuries of any kind didn't impress Dad, with him thinking of them as compensatory pronouncements for those short on self-esteem. As far as he was concerned, living was all about efficiency, pulling the maximum value out of the least expense. He fully depreciated every asset. But the cost of even a simple coffin had startled me. I'm certain that if Dad had anticipated the need sooner, he would have taken the time to build his own. Brad, who had patiently outlined for us the fifty options and half-dozen species of wood, refused to utter the word 'casket,' insisting on the term 'final resting place.' I resisted the sarcastic impulse to parrot him. It would have upset Andy. We declined all the funeral home's many options. Both my brother and I only had one criteria, cost.

Behind the set-piece where the casket, with my father inside, was displayed, a couple of short steps led to a shallow apse that was void of the expected iconography. Devoid except for one disproportionately small wooden cross hanging on the back wall. The freestanding pulpit to the right was equally austere, decorated with a subtle floral pattern carved into the top panel. It looked like a donation from a woodworking hobbyist. Situated at center stage, the casket rested on a silver trimmed white cloth, one that hung almost to the floor but remained high enough to reveal the large rubber wheels that eased the transport of the dead from room to room. This glimpse of clinical mechanics broke the carefully cultivated church atmosphere and briefly threw me back to the sterility of the funeral home.

I checked my watch. It was two minutes before the hour. We had been sitting in the pews for seven minutes, but it had felt like an hour.

Michael had called the day before, sending his regrets. He was working on a lead to replace the London group and felt that making that call was more urgent than the funeral, I concurred, although wordlessly. Liz, having known Michael for all these many years, had never truly enjoyed his company. Liz felt that he talked way too much about himself and work and seldom inquired into her well-being or that of the boys. She regarded this failure to show up as an infraction, a grave malfeasance. The two of them had never bonded. At first, I tried to force congeniality by organizing dinners with the three of us, but it didn't take long before I gave up, seeing that there was no chemistry between them. Michael was abrupt and always focused on business. After I relayed the news to her last night about Michael's absence, she felt liberated to speak at length and disparagingly of his choice and, more astoundingly, of him as a person. She exclaimed her disappointment for me, how selfish and callous the man was, and how this latest instance was another example of a long string of slights against the family, firmly demonstrating that his priorities were misplaced. She denounced his behavior as rude and outright disloyal to me. I withheld my defense of Michael's behavior and especially my consent for his steadfast commitment to the company. Michael didn't know my father, and I certainly didn't need any symbolic fidelity.

Preacher Dan reappeared through the side door and slowly ambled across the room to the organist. They talked in hushed voices and turned through the pages of music, sharing a few chuckles that felt entirely inappropriate for the circumstances, adding to my unease.

A couple of long minutes later, through that same side door a few steps to the right of the pulpit, I saw Andy cautiously peering into the chapel. His unkempt hair, still looking wet from the shower, hung over the collar of his outdated brown suit. He scanned the room from side to side until he made eye contact with me. He made his way over to the empty seat at my left. And as he sat down, he wrapped an arm around my shoulder, pulling me close. It was bizarre. I wasn't used to receiving hugs from Andy. His behavior felt like playacting and only served to amplify my unease. My brother's eyes seemed dark and clouded. After the hug, he shifted his attention to the preacher and didn't otherwise attempt to engage. He lifted his glasses and held them out at a distance as if examining their function. He wiped his eyes with a crisp white handkerchief. And then stared out into the empty space above the coffin.

Having finished fidgeting, Andy sat quietly, waiting for the ritual to begin. Neither one of us said a word. Maybe it was simply that my perspective of time had been thrown off, but whatever the case, my impatience was growing. The urge to stand, move, walk about, do something physical, anything, was tearing at me. I was bored with the waiting. Down the row, the boys were quiet, their hands folded in their laps. I wasn't quite sure if that was how they were instructed to behave by their mother or whether they knew this intuitively. I was the one who was shifting about, anxious, trying to find comfort on the thin pew cushion. I couldn't tell if my restlessness distorted time or if Preacher Dan was, for some reason, purposefully making us all suffer just a little extra, part of his setup for the ceremony. The agreed-on protocol was for the family to come in at the last minute and the preacher to start right away. Now that Andy was seated, I couldn't for the life of me figure out what was taking the man so long to move into his position.

Liz reached over and took hold of my hand, an overt attempt to calm me. Even and unblemished, several shades lighter than mine, her hand was a pleasant reassurance. I slid my hand out from her light grip, placing my hand on top of hers. It disappeared entirely underneath my palm. Lightly squeezing it, her hand felt narrow and delicate. My squeeze was firm while cautious of her fragility. The result of much lotion, little housework and frequent manicures, Liz took a particular pride in her hands. The evidence found in her weekly salon charges. Stroking her soft skin with my thumb, I thought about the long distance I had traveled – from a motherless and entirely masculine childhood to a wife who adored all things feminine. I couldn't recall any aspect of my mother's hands, not their appearance nor their feel. Until this moment, I had never even considered what they might have felt like.

With a subtle underhand swing of his arm, Preacher Dan at last directed his young helpers to their places. At a painfully slow pace, he walked across the room to the pulpit and shuffled his papers into a new order. I wondered why he hadn't put them into their proper order before walking in. I leaned back in my seat and took a deep breath, continuing to wait.

I looked over at Andy. He was still staring blankly at a spot some place far beyond the casket. His eyes were swollen, and he kept wiping the end of his nose with the bright new white handkerchief. Long ago, we shared secrets, traveled as a team, imagining conquering the world together. We strapped on backpacks and went exploring up and down old mountain trails, naming the peaks as if we were the first explorers to have seen them. There was 'The Hump' and 'The Double Hump' and 'Flat Top.' There was a pond out along one of the trails we called 'Ugly Lake' due to its marshy nature and being inundated with reeds. And the pond right next to the cabin we simply called 'The Pond.' We learned that a hand's breadth between the sun and horizon gave us about an hour to get home. Orienting ourselves in the wild became second nature. We went everywhere together, and I used to know what he was thinking. Now, I had no idea. I hadn't in years.

"You doing okay?" I asked.

"Fine, but I just wish they'd get on with it."

"Me too. It's well past ten, and people are still coming in. Do you know who they all are?"

"Not a clue."

"I didn't think Dad had this many friends."

The organist softly began her measured melody, and like a period at the end of a sentence, the chatter from the back of the room abruptly stopped. For several minutes she played a soothing melody to the hushed room. The music calmly began its work on me. Closing my eyes, I gave myself over to it. I felt my tension lessen. The last note faded to quiet, framing Preacher Dan's measured voice.

He read several passages from Scripture before beginning his eulogy. He spoke about the old man as if they had been the closest of friends. There were platitudes explaining that while the man, my father, didn't spend one iota of time in the church nor subscribe to any religious tenets, he lived his life as if he knew the holy path well. His absence from the church was not a liability but a teachable parable. Preacher Dan described Dad's "life as a text," a person to be emulated. His voice gently rose and fell into a practiced rhythm, but after a while, the sounds faded into white noise. I gradually retreated into a numbing fog of quietness. Every third sentence or so, I came out of my cloud and realized this so-called friend of my father's didn't really know the man, or perhaps, he knew little of the father I knew. Understanding that he was telling the outsider's perspective, I tried to reconcile his telling with my own memories. The talk about my father being kind, loving and generous didn't strike me as false so much as not fully accurate. I knew intellectually that the balanced and nuanced view of a man's life is not appropriately given at his funeral, but the image being painted of my dad was from a different universe than the one I had grown up living in. By abdicating my expected role, I suppose I had contributed to this problem. During one of my sleepless nights, I had, in fact, drafted a eulogy, one that leaned positive. But as the moment approached, I realized that I lacked the courage to lie in public. Instead, when Andy and I had met with the preacher for the second time a couple of days earlier, I had given the preacher all the glorious facts, the conquests, the impossible challenges and consequent successes. I'd uttered none of the negatives, the harsh judgments, the abuses. But now, hearing the sanitized version out loud from a stranger's lips, the dissonance irritated me. This was not the man I knew.

After Mom's death, Dad's initial attempt at normalcy was to hire a sequence of housekeepers to do the cleaning, shopping and cooking. But his impatience with each of them was on constant display. It might have been their particular work habits or their personalities, or that they stole, or that he just didn't like people he didn't know in his house. Whatever the case, after a couple of years and a long series of women, they were gone, all of them. Dad dropped the idea altogether. We could do all the work ourselves. The change increased the burden on all of us. He shifted the bulk of the housework onto Andy and me commanding us in minute detail what our responsibilities were. Unaware that there was any other option, we, without dissent, complied.

As the years went on, our responsibilities grew. We learned how to do our laundry, clean the bathroom, and cook. When we came home from school, we let ourselves into the empty house and from there were left pretty much on our own. While our school work was only perfunctorily supervised, our housework was subject to our father's sporadic but thorough inspections. When the mood arose, occurring according to some astrological rhythm, Dad did the military thing, checking the bed's corner folds and wiping his fingers across shelves. He expected everything to be in its place and aligned. Lack of adherence to the rules might elicit a polite, "you could do better," or, more harshly, a spanking. When we were older, judgment was rendered with a belt across the ass. My father's power derived from the fear that we never knew which version of him, mean or just strict, might be walking through the door on any given day. We never knew what was going on at his work or what even forces were working in the interior of his mind. I looked for tells, the set of his narrow eyes or a worried brow, but to no avail. His was an undecipherable book closed to my eyes. Andy and I, therefore, depended on each other for protection. When one of us was criticized for failing to clean the kitchen properly, we'd both do the work. If Dad came home unexpectedly early, one might distract him for a moment while the other would run back and pick up the dirty clothes from the floor. The tension kept us on our toes and in a constant, low-level state of fear. Dad called it respect, and it took me to adulthood to understand the difference.

His motivations, I believe with all my heart, were pure. He wanted nothing more than for his sons to be respectful and to have a strong work ethic. But he was controlled by a set of internal forces that I don't believe he was aware of. He was certain of his standards, that they had to be imposed, that they weren't native to our being. He simply couldn't trust us; behaving as if left to our native instincts Andy and I would devolve into some combination of hedonism and sloth. For him, we needed to be constantly prodded, to be directed down a particular path in accord with some set of secrets that he had discovered through his own personal tribulations. A successful life was achieved but by one path — his way and only his way.

Early on, I figured out he was wrong. The world was full of possible paths, plainly evident from a simple glance around. I could easily see this through his faulty vision simply by watching my friends' parents correlating their individual parenting styles to the character of the child. There wasn't much correlation. From a young age, I understood the debate between nature and nurture and how incalcitrant nature can be.

I also learned that what he couldn't see right in front of his own eyes, he didn't care about — it didn't exist. Therefore, as long as I was in his presence and behaving according to his expectations, I was in good standing. When I snuck out of sight, he was blind to me and what I did. He rarely inquired about where I was or who my friends were. More hurtful from my now distant adult perspective, he never asked how I was feeling — about anything, never. He had little interest in my life except how he might best be able to mold it. Dad focused on what was important to him and never on what was important to me

Once I left for college and tasted independence, with the paternal constraints distant, I reshaped my life, pushing Dad's influence off to the side. I set my own standards. His opinions became inert. I took zero advice from the imaginary man standing over my shoulder. I didn't have to, not any more. As the years of separation increased, I hardened myself, achieving a careful non-confrontational indifference to him. I found a place where I could patiently listen to his rants about greed, politics, hypocrisy, and life, knowing that he was reliably naive about the world, at least the world I had come to know.

I suppressed my instinct to argue, to defend my own perspective. There would have been no point. He couldn't or wouldn't have heard me. So what else was I to do? I couldn't make him listen, make him understand, or make him care about my life. My transformation was hard-won and vital — and it was entirely internal to me. But on some level, he as well must have felt the distancing. Dad never talked about his feelings and I never asked. In a sad symmetry, I felt his emotions toward me had turned equally bland, further cementing our distance. Rote would have been the best word to describe our relationship. And after all that work, cultivating my emancipation, I never imagined that his death could possibly be a liberating event. Before he died, I had already fully separated from him.

Staring at his casket, though, on the threshold of this new reality, Dad's absolute physical absence, the ether felt surprisingly very thin. As opposed to liberating, there was an undefinable thread now tethering, thick or thin, I couldn't tell. But there was some energy binding me to whatever aspect of him that was left hovering inside that wooden "resting place." Suddenly, I felt an uncomfortable tension emerging in my shoulders. An anger growing. There was nothing to fight against, nothing for my arms to wrestle from, but still I was mad. My pushing had no resistance; the friction had been removed. It was like trying to punch air, like arriving to play ball and the opponent not showing. Like swinging and missing a slow pitch. My antagonist was gone, but something sticky still remained — and I wanted to shed it.

Living far away, with an insanely busy life, I didn't visit Dad often, and he rarely came to see us. I only saw him as much as civil protocol demanded, a determination that was entirely in Liz's domain. In her view of the world order, family was paramount, and a fundamental part of that order was for the boys to know their grandfather. I didn't protest and put on a welcoming attitude when we were all together. Liz conceived of the year as stringing time between hooks, the traditional holidays, the family milestones, the birthdays, graduations, and anniversaries, with the time in-between ordered by the preparations for the next family event. In this way, she always had something to look forward to.

The last time Dad flew out to visit us was several months before his death, on Memorial Day. Andy had also joined him on that trip. Liz, the boys and I were inaugurating our new pool and launching into the summer with a celebration. Just like she does for every other event, Liz had seemingly invited the whole world over to our place. Throughout that day, Dad sat comfortably under the cabana's overhang in a large lounger. Sipping his beer, there was a huge smile on his face. He kept calling the boys over for a rub on the head, then patted them on the behind, sending them off again to fly into the water. Even though they seemed too old for either the rub or the pat, the boys seemed to enjoy the attention. I had spared the boys from my psychological baggage; it would have been mean of me to poison that well. They were entitled to their own relationships on their own terms. In an odd bit of irony, I enjoyed feeling the jealousy. Dad was relishing the relationship with his grandchildren in a way that he never had with his own sons. As I stared out from the kitchen window, watching his smile, I wondered what about my father had changed over all that time. Or what was there that I had never been able to see.

The preacher's gestures were studied and precise. Andy's composure had improved. He appeared calmer. With his voice rising and falling ever so slightly, Preacher Dan's rhetorical flourishes pulled me back to attention.

"There is a resistance to this new reality ... It may be that the hardest job of living is separating from the dead and continuing life without them. ... Their comfort and strength gone ... and you may feel abandoned and lost ... but we shouldn't have to negotiate for temperance and kindness; it should be the common coin of our relationships with one another. ... We stare into the abyss, a dark nothingness, finding no refuge, nowhere to cling. ... a loneliness that will remain with us forever. ... embrace your vulnerabilities ... acknowledge the pain you have felt and the pain you have inflicted ... You must accept ... The balm is to hang together. ... The work we do now is for ourselves and those that remain."

But as the speech devolved into so many platitudes, I again quit trying to make sense of them.

Instead, I envisioned what lay inside of the coffin. Already beginning to desiccate, my dead father, drained of color, his body stiff and motionless. The stern, gray-headed, calloused old man had finally been subdued. It was hard to grasp that a man who stayed in constant action would now be forever still, powerless. When alive and even simply sitting in his favorite chair, his reading glasses at the end of his nose, a directed gaze could bristle with energy, instantly fused with judgment. Now with his eyes eternally shut, I felt relief that I would never see his narrow pupils again.

The last visual of my father, my dead father, will stay forever etched in my memory. The old man's body was laid on a long stainless steel table. Exiting my previously known reality, I had entered the mortuary's viewing room by myself. The mortuary's dimly lit holding room. Absolute silence. My distorted senses were unreliable. They played tricks on me. In my memory, the room appears as a dark stage set, the walls' edges lost in blackness, a single spotlight illuminating a crisp white shroud pulled up just shy of the old man's shoulders. The collar of his dark, freshly pressed suit and only the knot of the tie were visible. The pale bluish face. I cautiously approached his face, examining it in a way I was never able to do while he was alive. There was no guessing as to what his reaction might be. I gently touched his cheek. Was taken back by its coldness. Freshly shaved, his face felt smooth again. His mustache was trimmed straight. His bushy eyebrows tamed. What I saw before me was at once reminiscent of my father and, at the same time, entirely alien. It was not at all flattering — in fact, it was horrifying. I wished then — and wished now — that there was some way to erase that final image.

That was my last memory of him. And I hated it.

"I'm not sure I'm going to miss him," I whispered to Andy.

"Maybe later. You need to give it time."

11

The family and I left the sanctuary first. We walked down the wide passage, followed by the soft clicking sound of our heels reverberating off the stone floors. The reception was in the rectory, and much like the chapel, it was a plain and carefully ordered room. A wall of windows along one side opened to a small garden with a delicate fountain at one end. Centered in the room was a large round table graced by three dozen white flowers. Along the table's outside edge were evenly spread several silver trays of slender white finger sandwiches. Interspersed throughout were smaller trays containing carefully aligned rows of white cake, each piece centered on top of a lace-like paper doily.

Liz, Andy, the boys, and I positioned ourselves after the preacher, forming a receiving line in front of the windows. I stood silently with my hands clasped as we waited for the other mourners to make their way down the long hall.

The situation's formality brought to mind Dad's constant admonitions to address each and every one of his friends as "Mister so-and-so," to answer each question with a "yes, sir" or "no, sir." By itself, these admonitions were tolerable, not an odious job. But when grouped with all the dozens of other good-manner rules — "say thank you," "don't interrupt older people," "don't talk with food in your mouth" — it became difficult for a twelve-year-old to keep on top of. I remembered one particular evening when all three of us, Dad, Andy and me, were out at a restaurant, some fried chicken place with red checked table cloths, when a friend of Dad's stopped by the table. As trained, Andy and I jumped up to shake the man's hand, no matter that our hands were irretrievably greasy from the chicken. He was friendly, asking the standard questions about school and sports. In one of my responses, though, I failed to add the required "sir." Instantly, and I mean in a nanosecond, I received a head-jolting slap on the back of my head. Then in a voice loud enough to humiliate me in front of the entire restaurant, "Son, why don't you try that again?"

I brought my attention back to reality and the first mourner in line, Dave. A tall thin man with perfectly groomed gray hair and a well-tailored solid black suit. Dave was another one of Dad's poker-playing buddies and also a friend of Preacher Dan. He carried himself with the formal confidence of a bank president. He firmly clasped my hand with both of his.

"Even after witnessing his work all of these years, I still don't know how he does it. Isn't it masterful? I love watching him do his work up there." It took me a second to realize Dave was talking about Preacher Dan. "From behind the pulpit, like he's channeling a greater power, pulling it out of some hidden place."

Dave went on. "He did his job well. Don't you think? I don't suppose you know him at all ... the preacher, I mean."

"I met Preacher Dan for the first time just a couple of days ago. I only spent a few minutes with him, at that. But I can say for sure; he is a very sympathetic man."

"I'd say. I believe he found your father's spirituality, exposing sparks of divinity that your father would never in a million years acknowledge possessing. Your father most assuredly avoided that kind of language. You and I know that. But even though he never talked about it, I know your dad saw himself as part of some larger order. It was clear in the way he carried himself and how he treated others."

I was relieved by his shift in emphasis to my dad but wondered if Dave were speaking in some sort of code. I didn't understand him. Just like Preacher Dan, Dave seemed to be talking about a different man than the one I knew.

"Your dad was one of the most forthright people I've ever met."

"Yes, sir, never any doubt about where he stood," I answered.

"He never said an unkind word about anybody. And he was always willing to go out of his way to help someone who he saw was in need." Dave smiled broadly at me with a directness in his eyes, immediately dismissing my sense of some secret code. "I hope you aren't upset with our insistence. Maybe you see it as an intrusion. But Preacher Dan and I knowing your dad's lack of religious direction, ... well, we thought that organizing these arrangements might be helpful to you and your brother."

"My brother and I were surprised and at the same time very appreciative, pleased with the suggestion. We were at a loss as to — how can I say it — appropriately frame the loss. This ceremony, with all of his friends present, in such a dignified venue, was perfect. Just perfect. A beautiful way to honor the man. Thank you for taking the initiative."

I had let Dave monopolize my time, and the line of mourners was crowding in behind him. Needing to move on, I said goodbye and offered my hand again. He grasped it firmly with his right hand and then laid his left hand on top, lingering a little too long with the hold.

After my new best friend moved on, I shook hands, smiled and repeated my thank yous and appreciations a thousand more times. Going through the many motions of kindness was tiring and didn't allow room for any of my emotions to seep in. Perhaps though, there weren't any to be found. By the end of the reception, I had shaken dozens of solid hands, the many men who had worked alongside Dad building his homes. I had heard mention of these men over the years, but only by the rare accidental encounter had I ever met them before today. They were all slight variations of the same animal, with leathered skin and stern expressions. A quiet group for the most part. Those that did say more than a word or two of condolence spoke of Dad's drive, his unbreakable determination, or his steadfast integrity. Mixed into the group were also some of Dad's tenants from his various rent houses. This seemed to be a more diverse and gregarious group, one that nevertheless consistently spoke of the man's frequent forbearance, which to a person had spawned an intense loyalty.

Out of the group of renters, one stood out. He was a man about my age or maybe a few years younger. Short, with an easy smile even here at a funeral. When he approached, he didn't just settle for a handshake. Instead, he slung his arms around me, giving me a bear hug. It was as if I were reuniting with an old cousin, someone I had known my whole life. "Thomas," he exclaimed, using the name of my dad's language, "so glad I finally get to meet you. Your dad loved to talk about his sons. Every time he came by, it was something new. I heard all about your baseball days in high school and your brilliant business successes. He was so proud of you and your brother."

"Remind me again, what's your name?"

"Billy. Billy Swenson. Your father was a great man. Back when I was having some money troubles, he allowed me to work off the rent. I did a few repairs on the house and, after that, on his other houses. I'm in a really good place now, and it's thanks to him. I know you're busy now, and I don't want to take up too much of your time, but call me should you ever need anything. Anything at all. Please, I'd love to help. Anything you need. I owe it to your father." He put a business card in my hand before moving over to talk with Andy, "What an amazing role model," he said as he left.

Billy's description of Dad exacerbated my growing dissonance. No one had ever told me that my dad was capable of a profusion of pride about his son. Dad had never shared anything resembling pride with me, at least not directly to my face. My experience had been the exact opposite of the one Billy presented.

I didn't know what to make of Billy's story, whether to be pissed off that Dad never took the time to share with me the compliments he shared with others or to be happy that he was at least with some people proud enough of me to brag about my accomplishments. A strict, humorless man, Dad spent all of his time trying to fill the coffers. When he wasn't in the field building houses, he was caring for his rent houses: doing repairs, making them ready to lease, collecting rent. My wants, my needs and especially my feelings fell to the bottom of Dad's priorities. In the basic parental sense and by all objective measures, he had performed the duties of a father with all the grace of a carpenter driving in nails with a twenty-four-ounce hammer. No bullshit. No distractions. Straight to the point. Precise. Systematic. But was that the best way to bring up a child, especially one who had already lost his mother.

I'm sure Preacher Dan's, Dave's, and Billy's heartfelt renditions of a kind-hearted man were honest. And there's no reason to think they were acting on any agenda to influence me. Still, reading their nuances, I felt as if they were trying to convince me that my perception of my father was limited by my hardened bias. Being a single father in a time when such things weren't talked about on afternoon talk shows, there's no question Dad had faced a higher hurdle than most. There was good reason to be respectful of those accomplishments. I knew that. I could muster respect. Who he was to those men, though, wasn't who he was to me or Andy.

Sunday through Sunday, he worked every single day. Except, this being a crucial distinction, for when we left town for the mountains. But even at that, the trips to the mountains were never a holiday; it was simply a new venue with a different kind of work. In town or out of town, he was always clean-shaven with his mustache closely trimmed. He was a lean 180 pounds and as solid as a 4x6 beam. His clothes were always the same: jeans, work boots, and a plaid shirt. He had no hobbies, not unless his refuge in the mountains could be labeled as one. He had no interest in pets. He would cringe when someone pulled out a photo of a dog or horse or, worse, a baby. He cooked as if it were another job. Food brought him no particular pleasure. He methodically made his lunch every morning the same way, putting a salami sandwich and a piece of fruit in a brown paper bag. In the evenings, after all the chores were done, he would sit down and watch whatever it was that first popped up on the screen, never changing the channel. He would sip his Crown Royal neat, always having only one.

He created a small construction business that paid the bills. Money was always in the bank. He competently performed his fatherly duties, adequately providing for his sons' sustenance and education.

The outer world could see all that clearly. Andy and I lacked for none of the basics, but luxuries were non-existent. Growing up, the middle-class neighborhood we lived in was immersed in a virtuous prosperity dynamic. It was the nature of the local economy. The time and place were ripe for unrestrained growth. It seemed with each passing year; our neighbors were buying newer and bigger cars. Our friends wore the coolest clothes, and their vacations were becoming more and more exotic. But only twice did Andy and I leave town for a vacation, and even at that, the trips were connected to Dad's work, a convention in Las Vegas and another in Houston. Because he never worked on more than a couple of houses at a time, Dad's business was limited, and he never grew the company in any substantive way. In comparison to our neighbors, we stayed the same while simultaneously falling behind.

Andy and I worked every summer in Dad's construction business, sweeping and picking up trash, only occasionally doing a chore as sophisticated as staining a fence. It was no accident my father ended up building houses. Innovation was glacially slow, and the best tried-and-trusted methods were decades old, if not centuries old.

Dad had set aside money for our college and never complained about writing the check. Although there was plenty of money, we were expected to not only study hard but also to take on-campus jobs to pay for our personal weekend follies. By then, the work ethic had adhered to my temperament. I knew no different. My favorite side job was at the media center. There I was the projectionist for the history of film classes and was exposed for the first time to the craft of moviemaking and storytelling. I must have seen *Citizen Kane* and *Touch of Evil* ten times each.

Yet absent from Dad's mix of positive qualities was an essential element of fatherhood, one that I wasn't able to understand or label when I was young. But later, when I did identify the lack, I put it aside, refusing to use it as an excuse. Correcting for what he had seen as his own personal failings, Dad raised Andy and me the only way he knew how. We did push-ups and sit-ups at night before bed because when Dad joined the Army, he found himself weak and vulnerable — and he refused to stay that way. So that we wouldn't struggle in math class like he did, he bought math workbooks home from the drugstore. What I learned in my childhood was to satiate Dad's needs. His agenda ended up taking so much room that I never discovered my own needs. My desires were overlooked by both my dad and me. All under the assumption that he knew what was best for me. For the years that we spent together, he never understood me. At one point, I tried yelling in an attempt to be heard. Not only were these disruptions ineffective, they just made him mad. For fear of the belt, I gave up. Nothing cemented Dad's opinion more than confrontation. I was treated as a malformed version of him. Hot metal needing to be hammered and cut to a preordained pattern. He was oblivious to my difficult to define urges, my possibilities, and the dreams I didn't yet know how to articulate.

12

The morning after the funeral, Andy and I drove to Dad's house. When I got out of the car, I paused at the curb and watched Andy walk down the straight sidewalk towards the front door. Forty years after being poured, the sidewalk still laid level with hardly a crack in it. A testament to its builder. The gray roof, too, was in perfect shape. The lawn was neatly manicured, and the trees were ten times taller than my ancient memories. It was the same house we were in when Mom died, the same house Andy and I had grown up in, the same house I abandoned when I was eighteen. The same tainted house I had avoided in those many years since. But overnight, the house had lost a bit of its meaning. It felt less alive as if it had been instantly transformed into an artifact from a past era. It felt as if I were about to step into one of those faded photographs kept in a large, never opened box sitting along the back wall of the basement.

I followed Andy through the open front door, and the illusion of walking into the past became somewhat believable. When Andy turned right into Dad's office, the former dining room, I continued straight ahead, walking into the den. I briefly glanced into the back yard and then turned into the bedroom hallway. Andy's was the middle room and to the right, at the end of the hall, was Dad's room. To the left was my room. It had a window to the front yard, one that, on occasion, in the middle of the night, I would escape out of. Nothing in the room had changed since the day I left some thirty years earlier. The bed, and chest of drawers, were all still in their same places. The Jimi Hendrix poster still on the wall. All I could think about was absence, inert lifeless things, no animation. Even an absence of sound, having been absorbed by the dated plush yellow carpet, the noises of years past no longer echoed. Mom was gone, and the earlier versions of Andy and I were gone. Each room was frozen in its own particular moment, the moment it had been abandoned. Now Dad was gone, too, his bedroom now frozen into the exact moment he left it to fix the Nichols' light bulb. Room by room, the house had quit growing as its inhabitants abandoned it. The house was dead. Those hazy ghosts were in the final stages of evaporating. I turned back towards the dining room, instantly knowing I'd never visit these rooms again.

I found Andy sitting in Dad's chair at the center of the dining table, thumbing through a spiral notebook. The room had taken on the aura of an office. Behind Andy were a row of beige filing cabinets lined up in front of the mirrored wall. The dining table's surface was covered by multiple stacks of colored spiral notebooks, each with large black numbers written on their covers. The dining table's other matching chairs were gone; I assumed they were stacked in the garage.

Dad's accounting system was, as expected, idiosyncratic but easy to follow. He had a separate spiral notebook for each house, each page aligned in carefully crafted columns, with everything handwritten in pencil. Organized by its house number, we determined there was a notebook for each rented house. The street name labeled in a much smaller text provided a secondary subtitle. Dad had a computer, but for some reason it was set on the kitchen counter, clearly serving no useful function.

By the osmosis of years of proximity, Andy and I had obtained a basic familiarity with our father's work habits. At night, as we'd watch our TV shows, Dad would sort through a stack of invoices. First, he'd run his pencil down the column of numbers, double-checking the quantities and the addition. Then he'd make a notation in one of his notebooks, after which he'd write the check. It was an easy imaginative leap from seeing him at work behind the dining room table those so many years ago to the aged bookkeeping artifacts before our eyes. We were always surrounded by his business. There was no separation between the man and his work. He desperately wanted to bring us inside his tent. When we reached the age of ten or so and could competently follow instructions, and perform basic physical labor, we followed Dad out onto his construction sites. At first, we labored during the summers performing menial jobs, picking up trash and sweeping up after the workmen, or painting primer on the porch columns. When we were a little older, we were allowed to use the spraying machine to stain fences. Although the work was tiring and the hours long, we were never paid a nickel. "It's a privilege to work for your father," Dad repeatedly said, permanently forestalling any discussion of wages. Although it wasn't about the money, neither Andy nor I needed more cash. We had allowances that were disconnected from our labors, and these were sufficient to cover everything we needed. I didn't feel like my work was important enough, contributed enough to the overall project to justify being paid. I didn't feel valued. Work was a family ethos. It's what we did to help each other out, no matter the circumstances, paid or not. It was part of some unmentioned but well-understood familial contract.

To Dad's never-stated but obvious disappointment, neither Andy nor I ever considered joining him in business. The requisite manual labor was beneath my ambitions. Maybe and just maybe, if he had found the right window of opportunity, and if he had properly explained to me the concept of income — how one accounted for expenses to arrive at profit — I might have found some path towards an understanding and appreciation of his business. Dreams like that popped in and out of my head quickly. The reality was I couldn't see a world beyond the openly implicit obligation to work for my dad as a serf. The relationship could never have evolved into one of strictly business or anything resembling peer-to-peer respect. Dad was incapable, in a dozen or a hundred years, of delegating his authority to anyone, even his sons. It would never have been working with him; it always would have been working for him. I couldn't envision anything other than a power struggle, father versus son.

Marcus Miller was Dad's longtime friend and attorney. After Dad's passing, we called him right away and scheduled a meeting for the following morning at eleven a.m. Seeing no reason why the probate process shouldn't follow a simple series of inconsequential rituals, I anticipated a perfunctory meeting. The work, I thought, could be easily handled by Marcus or, more economically, one of his assistants.

After introducing myself to the receptionist, I sat down in the faux-living-room-like waiting area. With heavy, thickly padded chairs embraced by large rolled arms in a distressed dark brown leather, the room evoked a ranch setting. Hanging on the wall behind the sofa was a full-size reproduction of a Frederic Remington painting, one depicting a posse of cowboys cresting the ridge, rifles raised high, creating mayhem. There could be no doubt that ranches and farms were Marcus's field of expertise and that he was not averse to confrontation. I couldn't help intuiting sympathy for those on the receiving end of so much real or imagined violence. The room reinforced the idea that the client was amongst his own kind.

For me, though, the atmosphere induced a contrary effect. It wasn't so much that I felt out of my realm. I had spent plenty of time in Marcus's world, complete with its antiquated tropes and artifacts. Despite all my childhood visits to Dad's mountain property and the intimate association with his world that I had, I still felt like an anthropologist analyzing a foreign culture. I could understand the appeal of the country. And I enjoyed it as a contrast to the hustle of city life, but it worked only briefly.

Furthermore, the culture that went along with the country life irritated me. That world steadfastly remained in a deliberate anachronism, one that romanticized the lone cowboy struggling to find a place in the vast western plains. It was an overdone metaphor that long ago had worn thin for me, all the playacting, with the boots and horse and hat. If I weren't so immune, it would have made me laugh.

Waiting for Marcus on that dark brown leather sofa, a tension within me began building. The tedium associated with becoming his executor was now coming into focus — the court filings, redirecting bills, changing names on accounts. After the few glances I had spent studying Dad's affairs, I realized how complicated the process would be. I wanted to instantly put Dad's affairs into an order that didn't require my constant attention, and I was distressed thinking about how long that transition might actually take.

The clear imperative was to sell off Dad's properties as quickly as possible. Dad's rent houses, scattered across creation, would be difficult to sell as a group, at least at anything approaching a market price. They would have to be sold one by one. That process could take months or even years. Although I was confident that each of the properties would eventually find its appropriate buyer, the search would take time, time that I wished could be better spent on more productive work. I felt burdened by the hundreds of decisions that still lay ahead of me.

Familial obligations on one side, on the other, I felt the urgent pull to race back to New York. My conversations with Michael about the London group had been too infrequent, and his reassurances were no longer satisfying. I was isolated from the action, from where I needed to be, a physical distance that couldn't be adequately bridged with emails. With the London group so adamant about exiting the deal and retrieving their escrow money, my imagination ran wild with the possible counterattacks they might be conjuring. The deal that I had spent so much time creating had fallen into a strange, remote parallel universe. I sensed it was also irretrievably dying. Death was everywhere. I squelched my instinct to jump into the fray, being self-aware enough to know that my capacities were currently compromised. Until I could hand off my executor's responsibilities to Marcus, I had to, for the moment, defer to Michael's judgment. This wasn't my life here in Colorado, and I felt out of place.

Most importantly, my focus had to remain with Andy. As rocky as Andy's life had been up to this point, this had to be his deepest valley. Now, with our new shared agenda, the settling of Dad's worldly affairs, Andy and I were in closer communication than we had been in years. That it had taken our father's death to bring us back together was a sad reflection on our relationship. Despite that taint, the frequency of the dialogue had the effect of warming the atmosphere between us. I could see the potential for a new brotherly rapport.

The first priority was the management of Dad's rental properties. The ordinary tasks of a landlord had given Dad's life structure and a purpose. But without him able to do the daily work, Andy and I had to learn quickly how to step in. Dad had enjoyed those banal routines, but in the aggregate, and for someone else for whom the routines were new, the job was menial.

Fortunately, with Andy's free time and close proximity to Dad's dining room office, it would be easy for him to check the mail frequently and make the proper deposits. Dad had all his rental affairs well-organized inside his head, to be sure, but that order existed nowhere on paper. Being an astute science teacher, comfortable with classification and order, I was confident that Andy could decipher Dad's books and filing system. Andy, though, knew next to nothing about business. Over dinner the previous evening, he had bombarded me with a barrage of questions about the funeral costs and legal fees. How and who was going to pay for them? Now that he was dead, how would we cash checks made out in Dad's name? All these questions highlighted my brother's entrepreneurial naivety. He did not expressly say, "I need your help," but he implicitly expressed all his worries. As such, I was going to do my part. I thought about what I could manage from back in the city. It would be easy to go online every few days and pay the water, gas and electric bills. I could monitor the bank accounts and deal with the paperwork. Thinking about implementing these routines made my tension rise even higher. My schedule was already too full, and trying to help Andy out would take energy I didn't have.

The choice of lawyer for Dad's estate was not a choice at all. Marcus had been Dad's lawyer for as long as I was aware that such a profession existed. As close as he was to my dad, he was nevertheless off my radar. I knew of him, but I didn't know him. Growing up I had met him dozens of times, sure, but I had no concrete memory of him other than a large smile, his tannish cowboy hat and a vise-like handshake. Twenty years or more must have passed since the last time I'd seen him. My deep-rooted sense of the man was that he was gregarious and attentive. I looked forward to reconnecting with him after so many years.

After a few minutes of waiting, Marcus emerged stage right from the adjoining hallway, looking true to my memory of him. He was tall, solidly built, with a full head of longish gray hair swept straight back, sharply creased jeans and shiny boots. His age was probably somewhere halfway between Dad's and mine. We exchanged pleasantries. He apologized for making me wait, saying he didn't want to hang up on a very talkative client. He offered coffee, which the receptionist obediently retrieved, then he escorted me to a small conference room with a favorable view of the street below.

Marcus asked, "Are we expecting your brother?"

"He should be here shortly. I wouldn't have expected him to be exactly on time."

Unlike the many uptight lawyers I was used to dealing with, Marcus was relaxed. He tilted back in his chair. I even half-expected him to put his boots up on the wooden table, but he didn't. Although he seemed to already know quite a bit, he began inquiring about my life. I didn't let the conversation go on long before turning the tables, becoming the questioner. Since the funeral, I had become curious about my father's life outside the family. I was still having difficulty resolving the father I knew with the portrayals that the outer world kept feeding me. I wanted to better understand the outsider's perspective.

Marcus started, "When your dad first came to town, he joined the Masons."

I shook my head, acknowledging receipt of the information and at the same time displaying my total ignorance of that fact.

"He didn't last long, maybe a couple of meetings, max. I guess he was trying someplace new to find friends. While he certainly could get along with people just fine, as you certainly know, he wasn't much for belonging to any group. In any case, that is where we first met. I had just left a big firm and was going out on my own, and joining the Masons seemed like a great way to network."

As he spoke, I began to notice the persistent presence of the large 'G' squeezed between the mason's square and compass inconspicuously visible inside each of the photos on the wall.

"Your dad was just starting his business, and he reached out to me for a little help. It was a nice gesture and — how should I say it — we matured together. He hasn't been, by any stretch, my biggest client — actually not even a good one, financially speaking, but we developed a solid friendship."

"No offense intended here, but I always thought that Dad didn't really much trust lawyers."

"Trust wasn't the issue. He just thought they got in the way more often than they helped."

The smile lingered, and with a chuckle, he continued, "I tried hard to get him to stop writing his own agreements. But, man, was he stubborn. He really didn't want to hear an answer other than what he had decided on when he walked in. Every once in a while, he'd call me to untangle a mess. I'd see him after work for a beer, and mixed in with politics and sports talk, he'd ask for a legal opinion. But you know, it was his ability to get along with people that allowed him to do what he did. He was a man of his word. People trusted him. The legal stuff was an afterthought."

Marcus paused for a second, "I know it's cliché to say, but it was me that got the better end of the deal. Your dad was great company and always had a joke to tell or an interesting story. Never was he at a loss for words. Plus, it was your father who convinced me to get involved in the rural property business."

With the flood of new information to process, I was shaking my head once again.

"When he bought his first mountain property, I had to drive way out to the county courthouse a few different times. I ended up meeting the nicest people."

"You said, 'first.' How many were there?"

"I'd have to check, but somewhere around seven or eight. Where the cabin is, came first. After discovering how much he liked it out there, he'd keep adding adjacent tracts as they became available. He assembled quite a bit of land out there."

Marcus' anecdotes about my Dad were inducing within me an entirely new line of questions. But before I could start in, at exactly twenty minutes past nine, Andy was led through the door by the receptionist. The first words out of his mouth were, "Sorry, I hope I didn't miss anything?"

Andy explained that on his way over, he had detoured to meet with Dad's banker and retrieve his will from the safe deposit box. He cautiously placed on the table a narrow black binder, then opened it up, exposing a well-organized set of tabs and labels.

Obviously his handiwork, Marcus briefly glanced at the binder, then abruptly closed it, sliding it off to the side of the table and directing his gaze directly at Andy, "We were just reminiscing about your father. I loved that man, almost like a brother."

Reluctantly shifting his gaze from the binder, Andy accepted the compliment, "Lately, we have been hearing a lot of people saying nice things like that. Thank you."

"I was telling your brother about how I started doing ranch and farm work." Marcus paused for a second to recompose his thoughts, "To cut to the chase, not long after I met your dad, I bought a small building in Wilbur not far from your dad's place, opened up a satellite office there. As far as I'm concerned, it is a more authentic and fulfilling version of the law.

I get to know people and their families. I see them in the diners and at the grocery store. They drop by my ranch. I get to practice a broad spectrum of law, everything from wills, domestic disputes, and bankruptcy to large real estate deals. No two days are the same. And now, I'm trying to figure out how to spend more time out there and less time here in town, in this office. Maybe work a few less hours."

"I feel the same way," Andy said. "I would love that, more time out in the woods."

Marcus scooted his chair closer to the table, opened a manila folder and began running his finger down a to-do list. To nobody's surprise, Marcus pointed out that Dad's accounting methods were chaotic. He carefully explained the protocols and listed due dates. Being similar to the work I saw every day; it was clear Marcus' process was thorough and orderly. Relief enveloped me. I could see that in the near future, all of the upheaval involved in unwinding Dad's affairs would eventually end. We were in good hands.

Dad spent his whole life moving like time was about to run out. But it wasn't the pace that was the problem. The priority was all about the doing, and doing for doing's sake, as opposed to setting a specific goal and conforming to a thought-out agenda. Forethought was not in Dad's makeup. He bounced from one job to the next, one subject to the next, without any clear direction. In his hands, life was like a complex braid with too many strands to count. Many of them were abandoned somewhere along and left frayed — but he didn't care; he just moved to the next project — never a regret.

The only time Dad ever wrote anything down was after dinner. During the day, it all stayed in his head. As a kid, after Andy and I cleared the table, I would see Dad spend the entire evening at the dining room table, tracking his checks and deposits in his fifty-cent notebooks. He'd write down columns of figures, adding in his cryptic notes, then later file his cheap books in a growing array of cabinets.

Despite his relative success, Dad never allowed himself luxuries, and he truly desired none. He was proud to find a shirt on sale at JC Penny's and had the habit of buying his shoes out of a catalog. His parsimonious life was natural to him; learned early on and engrained deeply within him.

The narrative from my father's deep past, the years before I was even conscious of the idea of a past, those years before I was born and through the time of Mom's death, only emerged through our rare conversations about his family's history. Dad's early life remained vague to me. He didn't enjoy talking about anything beyond yesterday; he avoided the past as if it were toxic. I surmised that he was embarrassed by his childhood poverty; at least, that was my sense. Both his parents were only children, and they themselves had lost their parents as youngsters. When Dad was a teenager, they died in a car accident. Andy and I, therefore, had no known relatives. I couldn't tell if it was borne out of any tension with his parents, but all his life Dad had a native disregard for authority. I could easily see him being a rebellious, untamable child. By his own admission, he couldn't tolerate the regularity of school. He hated reading, leading me to speculate that in today's world, he would have been characterized as having some degree of ADD. Consequently, school didn't suit him, and he had poor grades. After losing his parents in the car accident and having no family and no money, not yet a senior in high school, Dad's only option was to sign up with the Marine Corps. Fortunately, he missed the Korean War and never actually went overseas. But it was in the Marines that he discovered an aptitude for engine repair, working on the Corps' many trucks and jeeps.

After his military service, Dad moved west, finding a job as an apprentice carpenter at a Ford assembly plant. Quickly learning the trade, he shifted his skill to houses and soon began his own contracting business. He was doing his small part to transform old family farms into hundred lot developments for the working class. As demand shifted, he moved further west. He found his place in the world of construction and stayed in it for over forty years.

His wife, my mother, died when Andy and I were just six and three. After that, Dad's life was centered around work and his two boys, in constantly varying proportions but usually biased towards work. There was no third thing, just work and his sons. There was no other family. I never considered it while growing up, but as far as I knew, there was never another woman, at least not one that he ever introduced to his sons.

By its nature, his work was unpredictable. The construction business constantly oscillated like a pendulum, and invariably there were two polar opposite constants, not nearly enough work to pay the bills to being overwhelmed with the dizzying number of projects going on at the same time. As became obvious to me later on in life, his anxiety was inversely proportional to the amount of work he had. This put Andy and me at a disadvantage. In those years when he had the most time to give us, he was simultaneously apprehensive about finding new work. Conversely, when work was good and plentiful, his bank account flush, he was too absorbed with his projects to have any time for us. I never knew which it was going to be, nor for how long it would stay that way. As a child and teenager, my life seemed to fit in only when work for Dad was absent, his anxiety at its highest.

Along the way, Dad developed a side business, one designed to try and soothe his business and his own internal volatility. He started buying older, broken-down homes in forgotten neighborhoods. He would fix them up, mostly by his own efforts, then rent them out. Paying off one and then buying another. And then doing the same thing again. And again. Although Dad worked for the big developers six days a week, on the seventh he worked for himself, on his own account. Over time, as the rental income became steady, he found that he could live comfortably inside his narrow set of needs. Eventually, he sold off the construction business to one of his long-time employees. And that was that — a self-made man.

Dad sacrificed spending time with Andy and me to build a business that would pay for his retirement. He rolled every dollar he made back into paying off the latest rental house loan so that he would be able to move on to the next purchase. There was a compounding effect, gradual but incessant. Over time he accumulated a dozen or so properties. The plan was ad hoc, or maybe you could say he got lucky.

But everything was in land. He felt it was solid, tangible, secure, an investment that one could touch and feel. Stocks and bonds were indecipherable to him. Cash was transitory, an abstraction that he couldn't trust. So, Dad's bank account mostly held just enough money to pay his monthly bills, plus a little in reserve.

Always moving to the next project, never pausing, my father was the personification of persistence and proof positive of its potency. Still, the man's homilies about hard work never ended. They ended up having the opposite effect; they simply ended up boring me. Through my own experiences, I had found that hard work was only one part of the long equation. It also had to be incorporated with intelligence and strategic thinking.

Leaning forward in the midst of our reminiscing about Dad, Marcus pulled out a new page from his file and said, "I actually have here an inventory of your dad's properties." With a pair of raised eyebrows, as if to impart a special meaning to what he was about to say, he continued, "To the best of my know-ledge." He paused here to let that idea settle in. "I believe this list is complete, but as you know, your dad's records weren't always the best."

Andy and I both nodded, fully recognizing his meaning.

"And as I understand you, it is your intention to sell the entire lot."

Now, from my new position having to oversee Dad's "mini-empire," I felt like Andy and I had just become slum-lords. Dad's properties appeared to me as liabilities. Their age and condition, coupled with the amount of time it took to manage all the details, hardly seemed worth the little bit of money they brought in. I knew of more efficient ways to make money. Neither Andy nor I had any interest in sustaining the rental house business. It was an unwanted inheritance, a nuisance more than a legacy. They were scattered across all parts of the city. Dad spent half of his days driving from one house to another, fixing the plumbing or collecting the rent.

I suppose he found moments of joy intermixed with all the work. I heard Dad talk about his frequent sits on his tenants' front porches, drinking tea or beer, depending on the time of day. That was his life, not one I wanted.

That all the properties were to be sold in the most efficient manner possible and that the proceeds be simply split fifty-fifty between Andy and me was an easy decision, at least in theory. There were complications, for sure. First, tracking down what Dad actually owned. Record-keeping was poor. The half-dozen filing cabinets back at the house were packed with papers, and the order of the files was not easily discern-able. He was prone to making deals with a one-paragraph scribble and slapping the paper on top of his desk with the last four years of correspondence underneath, or worse yet, just a handshake.

In our discussion with Marcus, we came to discover that our father had given generous arrangements to many of the families who rented his houses. Marcus wasn't even sure whether all the arrangements were technically legal. It was going to be challenging to put things in proper order, and it was going to take some time. Only with death would order finally be brought to my dad's life.

Marcus glanced back and forth between Andy and me before adding, "You boys are going to inherit a nice estate here. All of these small houses will add up to something substantial."

Marcus began to read off the inventory of properties to be put up for sale, address by address, as well their latest appraised values. In total, the list was several pages long, with a couple of dozen houses. Then he arrived at the property description for the mountain property. At that, Andy, who had been intently listening to the details, taking notes on a legal pad, raised his head. With a confused expression, he asked, "What? Why's the cabin on this list?"

It was only now, through our discussions with Marcus, did I understand how much money he had actually diverted out to his mountain property.

"Andy," I said. "Yesterday on the phone, when we were planning this meeting. Remember. You and I talked about all this. We decided to sell all of all Dad's real estate and split the proceeds. It's the obvious thing to do. Neither one of us wants to manage that mess. You know that."

"I never considered the mountain property to be a part of that list." Andy's annoyance sounded as if he were explaining to his students a difficult concept. He punctuated his words emphatically. "The mountain property with the cabin is different from the rent houses. Yes, I agree with you. All the rent houses, let's sell them. But," Andy's irritation emerged, his voice fractured and stressed, "I mean ... really? How could you possibly, even for a moment, think ... that we would ever sell Dad's cabin?" Andy was not comfortable confronting me, but he was trying hard to be assertive.

"I don't care one bit about the mountain property. But do you realize how much that property has grown in value?"

"I can't believe you're talking like that. There isn't any money equivalent to what that property means to me."

"You certainly could use the money to upgrade your life a little. Get out of that old beaten down house. It would even give you a decent retirement account."

"I'm quite happy with my life. Thank you. ... Besides, why do you care how I live?... And you? You couldn't possibly need any more money. All your big deals and that huge new house. You're just fine. Don't act like you need anything more."

Not wanting to explain my current financial stresses or engage any further, I stood up, effectively cutting the meeting short, "Excuse us, Marcus, but we clearly need to work out a couple of these details between us. We'll talk again next week."

"Typical," Andy scoffed.

13

When I made it back to the hotel room that evening, it was after ten. I had a flight early the next morning and felt comfortable leaving the work in Marcus's adept hands. Our meeting was productive, with a satisfying sense of order emerging. The rhythm of packing my bags and its limited nature was now a satisfying distraction. Packing is a mindless protocol. The mind focuses on a simple problem and forgets about everything else. Over the years, I had developed a particular system with an array of specialized accessories, one for shirts, another for socks, and so forth. The one disappointment is that I am now so familiar with the process it takes very little of my time. It's like an already solved crossword puzzle.

Marcus's command of the situation and the consequent feeling of relief that command gave me made my heading home feel right. It was only a matter of time before the chaos of Dad's passing would be put behind us, and I could return to my problems, the problems of my own life. For the time being, I had parked the London deal in an empty spot in my brain, placing my faith in Michael and his team. I knew that they were doing everything that I would have done had I stayed behind.

The caller ID flashed Andy's name. Picking up the phone, I could feel my chest tighten and my anxiety level escalate. I felt totally self-aware. I summoned my patience and took a deep breath. I knew what he was calling about. He and his feelings about Dad's mountain property were the one remaining unresolved problem regarding the estate. And there was no way he was going to let it rest until he saw a solution.

"Andy, what's up?"

"I've asked for some time off from the school."

"That's good. No sense putting that pressure on yourself yet."

"The reason is, ..." Andy paused, as though he were either reluctant or uncomfortable with the next half of the sentence, "... I want to talk to you about Dad's cabin."

His logic, not untypically, leaped. So, I was for a moment confused. It was unlike Andy to be this assertive with me. I didn't immediately grasp the connection between his time off from work and his midnight obsession with the mountain property. In the same way that he'd stay engrossed in a math problem until he solved them, Andy remained fixated on our earlier disagreement. He wanted a resolution — as did I. But I was irritated that he wanted to press me now. It was late. I was exhausted, not ready for any more discussions about Dad's affairs. I didn't share Andy's urgency. The conversation certainly could have waited till morning. Over the next week or two, in the due course of our continued conversations with Marcus, there was no question we'd figure out some formula balancing Andy's desire for the property with an equalizing distribution to me from some other asset. It was simple math.

Andy went on, "With Dad gone, it's only you. You're my family."

"Yeah, I understand." His preamble was setting me up to be even more apprehensive.

"Without you, I'm alone, and I'm not ready for that. I was

hoping you could stay a few more days. And I thought, kind of like in the old days, we could spend a couple of days at the cabin."

"Andy, c'mon, there's no way." I was aggravated by his explicit attempt to guilt me. "We've already talked about this. I have major problems at work and I've got to get back."

"I know your reasons," Andy said. "But ..."

"There's no 'but.' You're not understanding. I can't. Just can't."

Not sure from where it came, but I felt rising inside of me an almost instinctual sense of futility. Andy and I hardly ever fought. This conversation suddenly reminded me of my arguments with Dad. Maybe because we were talking about the mountain property. With time, I could usually convince Andy of my point of view. With Dad, though, it was another story. No matter how hard or long I tried, it was always impossible to win. For years and years and years, it never happened. Not once. Even after our arguments were over, never resolved in my favor, my blood would continue to a boil. There was always a residual anger. You can't win an argument with a crazy person; under no circumstance would the man ever admit defeat.

Andy continued, his voice remaining disarmingly calm, "Listen to yourself. You're not being reasonable. It's easy. Two days over the weekend. You're already here in town. It couldn't disrupt that much of anything. You've got smart people helping you out back in New York — isn't that why you hired them?"

While I listened to Andy talk, I wondered how his relationship with the mountain property would change now that Dad had died. Would it still have the same meaning for him — without Dad?

Growing up, Dad had pushed two irreconcilable principles on his sons. One was self-reliance, to be independent, to depend on nobody but oneself. At the same time, he rejected any challenge to his rules. Independence for him meant being free of any societal norm but not independent from his sense of order. What he had discovered about life was incontestably true — at least to him. His revelations, I came to see later in life, were actually the correctives to his own self-perceived deficiencies, but he thought what he had found was universal. He was doing us a favor, for Andy and me, by insisting on the veracity of his findings onto us. Dad sincerely believed he was molding the next generation as an improvement over his own. Admiring their rugged individualism, their ability to make something from nothing, my father incessantly praised the 19th-century pioneers and cowboys. He viewed himself as a direct descendant of that lineage. And his sons were next in line.

Andy said, "And if I'm right, you might find the property really does mean something to you as well. I really don't want to sell the property — actually, I can't sell it. Not under any circumstance."

I pulled the phone away from my ear and briefly thought about hanging up. I was tired. Annoyed. Andy was repeating himself, and I didn't want to respond by me repeating myself — saying, "No. No. No." At this point, we were on a merry-go-round, one that I couldn't jump off of. Andy was in a seriously bad spot. Not sure which way to go, I remained silent. I took a deep breath and waited for Andy to continue.

I checked myself and listened. Andy was not Dad. I paused and let my pulse die down. I know I could have imposed my decision on Andy, but in this context, it felt arbitrarily mean, even pointless — maybe heartless.

He started again, "We're just talking a couple of days. We could leave on Friday and be back by Sunday evening."

"I hear you, Andy. But I have other pulls on my time. Liz wants me to spend more time with the boys, and she has plans for us this next weekend." At this point, I was just making up shit.

"It's important to me."

I hung up the phone without saying "No" again. But I hadn't committed myself to anything either.

I fell back onto the hotel pillows. The TV was black. The glare projecting from the bathroom fluorescence overwhelmed the inadequate bed lamp. When Andy and I were young and shared a room at the old house, Dad would come in to check on us, say goodnight, then shut the door, extinguishing all the light in the room. After Dad walked out, Andy would get up, being the one closer to the bathroom, turn on the light, and crack the door ever so slightly. He knew I needed the bathroom light on so that the room wouldn't be quite so dark.

Having hung up the phone, frustrated, I was now sick to my stomach. There wasn't anything Andy said that was false. There were many excellent memories from when we were young of hanging together, exploring, and learning to shoot.

I was worn down. Even to my own ears, my resistance to Andy's weekend mountain excursion sounded weak and self-serving. But I had no rational retort. In any case, I owed Andy at the very least the courtesy of my attention. He was emotionally spent, as was I. Looking back, our conversation at the diner, his making this late-night call, his forthright petition for this silly trip, had all taken their toll on Andy. These assertions of self had been difficult for him.

The property, for me, had always been entangled with the essence of my father. Now that Dad was gone, I wasn't quite sure whether or not the property would feel as contaminated as it had before. If I were to go, it would be just Andy and me. That had never happened before. Sure, it would take some extra effort to stay in touch with the office. But taking a few extra days off for a long weekend was a logistical problem with an easy solution. I had Michael to depend on. I could manage, and so could he. In an earlier life, the opportunity to go to the mountains was cause for excitement and anticipation. To be free, running feral through the forest. Perhaps I had been too childish with Andy, unfairly projecting my conflicts with Dad onto him. He depended on me. There was no one else who could take my place. If I didn't go, I was afraid my connection with Andy would be forever frayed. He'd never understand, seeing my refusal as a serious slight, an insult, and never forgive me. I picked the phone back up, called my brother, and told him, "Okay, I've thought about it again. Let's go."

I put the phone down and fell instantly to sleep.

14

The phone woke me. The time zone difference was immaterial to Michael. He spoke quickly and systematically, laying out the sequence of calls that he recently had between him and the London fold. Listening to his measured outline, I slowly adjusted to a waking state. But I was fully conscious by the time he reached his last point, "The deal is officially dead." He enunciated each letter to make his point redundantly crystal clear, "D-E-A-D, dead!"

He let that bullet sink in, then added, "Worse than that, London wants to sue if they don't get their money back in twenty-four hours. They claim we've committed some sort of egregious fraud on them, and every day is costing them money."

"They do understand the original deal, don't they?"

"Sure they do. It's simple and nefarious at the same time. They're screaming extortion, knowing it's a false claim. The facts don't matter any more. Just like our politicians, it's part and parcel of the era we live in now. A deal is not a deal, never a deal, until ... actually, never. Any failure has to be somebody else's fault. They are the poor helpless victim when, in fact, they are the ones with the power. Power rests with those who have the most gold and, right now, they've got it. They'll fight like hell for no reason other than to preserve that power. Nothing else matters. They have no remorse for stealing money from the ignorant, the weak or those who have stumbled ... like us." Michael's shrill, aggrieved tenor of his voice was its own form of coffee. I was certainly up now.

I wasn't surprised by their strategy. I didn't need Michael's cynical little "it's all about power" speech to understand. I've lived in that world long enough, both sides of it.

Identifying an opponent's vulnerabilities has to be one of the most useful. But, confident that the deal was a good one for both sides, I hadn't identified the London group's weak spot, never bothering to look. I naively believed we all had our mutual interests at heart. I foolishly didn't anticipate this deal falling apart. *Never trust your partners* was one of my long-trusted maxims, a truism that says at the end of the day, everyone will revert to their self-interest and what's best for them, no matter how long the relationship or how much damage it might inflict. These guys were behaving true to form. I should have known better.

Thinking about the many everythings swirling around me — Dad, Andy, London, all of it — I felt myself fighting for breath. I was clutching the phone in my hand as if it were a weapon, as if it were the thing that was going to save me.

Fight or flight? I never ran from a confrontation. I enjoyed the challenge of a good fight, but at this moment, flight felt like a distinct possibility. Dad's death had drained me. I didn't have the energy to fight. Not right now.

On the end of the phone, Michael provided me with no comfort. "What do you want to do next?" he asked.

There was, however, a third choice, feint. We weren't going to fight, at least not just yet. Nor were we going to run. All of a sudden, the timing of a mountain escape with Andy felt perfectly right, an apropos alignment of the stars. I liked the idea of some time alone, away from these worldly worries. A retreat felt enticing, a place where I could breathe freely and clear my mind.

I said to Michael, "Right now, I don't care. If the assholes want to sue, let 'em. It's a meaningless threat. Don't respond. Let's go dark on them. No communication by anyone, not a word, radio silence. Let them stew for a bit. In the meantime, schedule a conference call between the partners and the attorneys for Monday afternoon. I should be back in the office and settled by then. Nothing will happen over the weekend."

15

Andy had left for the cabin earlier in the day. He wanted to be there ahead of me so that he could clear out some boxes from my room and make the cabin ready for both of us. The Cadillac sedan I had rented a couple of days ago, although sporty, was unsuitable for the rough roads I was about to encounter, so I needed to go to the rental company and trade for an SUV. The trade, though, turned out to be not quite what I had hoped for. The agent didn't have anything close to a Jeep or a Volvo. He could only offer me another Cadillac, a large black Escalade trimmed in bright chrome bands. Although functionally suitable and certainly luxurious, the gestalt was at odds with my purpose, but I had no other option. Showroom ready, the car sparkled, making me a bit anxious about how it would look on my return. I hadn't been outright dishonest with the manager about my trip to the mountains. Nevertheless, I worried, albeit slightly, that any hint of my off-road adventure would force him to nix the deal; it almost certainly being a violation of company policy. But he didn't ask and I didn't tell. The trip would clearly be the vehicle's first venture off the pavement. Overreacting to my concern about the car's pristine black finish, I paid for the unreasonably expensive extra-protection plan. When I finally climbed into the driver's seat, I felt more like a premium Uber driver than the outdoorsman I was striving to be.

I used the touch screen navigation system to find the nearest sporting goods store and spent a quick half-hour buying a small wardrobe of outdoor wear, the sort of clothes I hadn't worn in years. Plus, a new pair of trail shoes. I threw my few purchases into the voluminous back storage space and, by mid-afternoon, had set out for the cabin. I touched the destination on the screen. The car instantly calculated the distance, including the travel time down the narrow county roads, estimating my arrival time to be in one hour and thirty-eight minutes. I was on track, and if all went according to plan, I would be there an hour before sunset, in time to help Andy situate things around the cabin.

I headed south out of Denver, and as I merged onto the interstate for the first time, I felt a sincere enthusiasm for the adventure. The immersion in the leaving process induced a bit of a rush. I felt reconnected to what was once very familiar and comfortable. I suddenly had access to my deeply etched memories of the route and could anticipate each step along the journey: the long highway drive, the turn-off by the diner, the steep dirt roads, the routines for opening the cabin, and finally settling into the quiet peace of the mountains.

After only a couple of miles the traffic slowed to a crawl. I hugged the car bumper in front of me. With my massive chrome grille looming in his rearview mirror, I'm sure it irritated the hell out of the guy driving his compact commuter car, but whenever I had let the gap with the car in front of me stretch to anything over a car length, some anxious driver from the next lane would immediately squeeze in trying to shave five nanoseconds off their drive home. I had to fight for every foot of concrete. There were thousands of agendas navigating the road, and each thought their needs more important than everybody else's. Ayn Rand's philosophy of selfishness is made plain in the evening commute. She got one thing right, human nature.

I felt the adrenaline building within me. Maybe it was left over from work. Maybe it was part of the anxiety about getting away on time. Maybe it was simply traffic irritation. In any case, it fueled me in my battle for every inch of asphalt. And then, thirty minutes into the drive, the traffic came to a complete stop. I had traveled less than ten miles from the hotel and had well over a hundred left to go. All that built-up energy was frustrated by my stalled progress and, worse, my total lack of control. There wasn't any strategy I could follow to make the situation better. And to top it off, my call with Michael about our errant partners started cycling through my head... In an attempt to self-soothe, I took a series of deep breaths.

In theory, I might have left the city by way of the side streets and then weaved through the countryside on the various county roads. A path like that is what Dad would do when the weather was good, when he had the time — or when he was in the right mood, or when he simply thought that Andy and I might enjoy seeing a cow or two. But I hadn't traveled that route in many years. I had no memory of those old twists and turns. And with the subsequent growth in the suburbs, the alternate route was certainly less efficient than it had been those many years ago. That travel time, though, would be closer to days than hours. It was another nostalgic memory that had no use.

I suspected there was something more going on than just the typical Friday afternoon traffic. I pulled out my phone — something I had just cussed another driver for doing seconds earlier — and checked the map. Not surprisingly, the app indicated there was an accident about four miles down the road; the two left lanes were closed. Along with the rest of the world, I settled in for the wait.

Feeling the opportunity, I called Michael to check-in, only to remember once I heard his voicemail greeting that he was on a plane to Houston. An email that morning had told me he was pitching an investor there, and now he was on his way to see them in person. I felt grateful now for his insistence that he lead the parade. My mental state would have prevented me from having the necessary calm to start a new negotiation.

What with it being the end of the day on Friday, my other calls back to the office also went to voicemail. I particularly wanted to hear from Steve and get his perspective. I wanted to give the guy a chance.

I called Liz and actually felt a moment of relief that someone had answered the phone, but we talked for just a second. She was gearing up the boys to see some friends for an evening at the mall and a movie.

I explored the menus on the Caddy's dashboard, experimenting with the satellite radio, but the intricacies of the multiple screens diverted my attention from the road. The Caddy annoyingly beeped at me, telling me I had apparently crossed the dashed white line. Eventually, I settled for a sports station on the satellite radio and quit playing with the car's too-many features. After twenty minutes of eighth-grade school-yard blabber, I tuned into some meditative music and tried to find my Zen mind. With a deep breath, I resolved to calmly wait through the traffic jam. These forces were beyond my control. After a few minutes, the sounds of the radio faded from my consciousness. My mind began to drift.

About a month ago, on an early Sunday morning, while watching the morning sky brighten through the bedroom's sheer curtains, my life felt better than normal. I lingered in bed a bit longer than usual, content with my place in the world.

"How do you know?" I asked Liz.

"Know what, dear?"

"Know that if I had hit the water, I would have died."

"I'm sorry, but what are you talking about?"

It took me a moment to realize that Liz had drifted back to sleep and had already lost track of our conversation. I had to forgive her; I had been pondering the logic of her comment for some time.

"My dream."

A few minutes earlier, I had awoken suddenly. Quickly sitting up, I looked over and saw Liz's eyes open. I wasn't sure how long she had been resting like that. Maybe it was my startle that woke her, or maybe she had been like that for a while. It had sadly long been a habit of hers to lie awake for hours on end, and she may have been lying there for a while trying to again fall sleep. The poor women had for years had terrible problems with sleep. She attributed it to an incessant focus on planning, thinking about the future, most pointedly the boys, their studies, their friends, their next event. I had no theory of my own and took her explanations at face value. She refused to even think about sleeping pills, worried about the addiction stories she heard from her friends. In any case, I needed to share with her what had just happened with me; perhaps I could rely on her normally reliable insight into my anxieties.

As dreams go, this one was quite bizarre — even compared to the standard confusing nature of dreams. I couldn't recall precisely how I found myself in this position, but I could clearly recount how the final sequence unfolded. I saw myself on the very top of a sailing ship's mast. A tremendously large ship with several masts. The ship was naked, all the sails down. It floated silently in calm water. Meanwhile, I was hundreds of feet up in the air on the ship's tallest mast. I felt secure in my position and was not at all worried. Thinking back, the scene was certainly a dislodged remnant memory from our recent vacation. Liz and I had taken an anniversary trip to San Diego and toured one of the historic tall sailing ships. It was a ship like that. My brain, for some reason, was hanging on to the image, conflating life with dreaming.

Some sudden inner compulsion pulled me to jump. I didn't know the reason. This is where I needed Liz's intuition. There was no one chasing me, nor was there fire on the deck. I felt no fear. Did I jump just to experience the thrill? Never before had I had the desire to leap from a high perch. Even as a kid at the community center pool, the high board was always too intimidating for me. Senseless adventurous thrills had never been a part of my life. I was much too nervous as a kid, worried about the long list of negative consequences. But here, in the middle of a vast ocean with no land in sight, I was acting as if this were but the one last item on my bucket list. In the dream, I jumped with no hesitation. I was drawn into the emptiness. As soon as I leapt, though, the ship was no longer close at hand. Instead, it was set off in the middle distance, still and adrift in the open waters. There were people on the ship's deck, but no one was paying attention, at least to me. Except that is for a young boy standing on the back of the boat. He was looking in my direction, albeit without any discernible emotion whatsoever. The fall was long and steady. Throughout my descent, I was strangely aware of the sensation of falling. As I continued down towards the water, still in freefall, the ship appeared even farther away, almost to the horizon. It no longer felt like my beginning point. I was falling out of an open sky. I started to contemplate my splash into the water. It occurred to me that once I hit, I would be floating alone. I would merely be a tiny dot in a vast ocean. I wondered if that emotionless boy was still watching, and I worried how long it would take for the ship to make its way back to me. Worse, if they could even find me. My anxiety increased as the texture of the waves became visible, the impact inevitable. I worried not about the force of my impact upon the water but about the seeming endlessness of the blue-green waves, my isolation, bobbing in an endless heartless sea. I was not afraid but alone.

The moment I touched the water, I awoke. Heart beating hard. I opened my eyes, taking a quick moment to restore my bearings. It was just a dream. I was drenched with sweat but pleased to discover the stability of my bedroom.

After patiently listening to the telling, Liz said, "Nothing surprising here. That's how you see yourself, as an unattached individual swimming by yourself in a vast ill-defined world." Adding, "It was a good thing you woke up when you did. You know, it's a well-known fact that if you die in your dream, you will be truly dead."

Lying there, I actually tried to unravel the Gordian Knot she had presented me. My mind was puzzled by Liz's bizarre logic. With it being early in the morning, however, I was foggy and disoriented, not thinking clearly. But in the moment, the answer felt important. How could such a fact be known? We can't question the dead, nor can we forensically determine what they might have been dreaming in the moments prior to their death. That's when I asked her, "How do you know?"

The question was admittedly foolish on my part. I shouldn't have bothered. Knowing my wife, I could anticipate her answer. According to Liz's view of the world, old wives' tales, superstitions, and urban legends assuredly contain some element of truth to them. Otherwise, why would they persist?

A few seconds later, Liz added, "You know all dreams are, in the end, positive. The challenge is to find within that irrational mess, where's the constructive prediction."

Hearing that, I instantly discarded the spinning conundrum and turned towards getting on with my day. Liz was of no help here as an interpreter. Dreams were dreams, scrambled nonsense. Let them be. I decided not to let some murky nonsense ruin the rest of my day.

Ever since we moved into our new house, my Sunday morning routine began with working in the garden. To beat the anticipated heat, I headed outside early, gathering my tools from the shed on my way.

I knelt at the edge of my small garden and welcomed the moment of peace. Gardening had recently become a welcome ritual of solace and serenity. It was new to me. Moments as it were separate from ordinary time. The habit of gardening had begun when the architect — with surprising psychic precision — suggested that a small garden outside my study window would be a beneficial antidote to the hours at work spent buried under the harsh fluorescent lights. Having never gardened in my life, at first, I was skeptical, reluctant to commit. Nothing, no activity or distraction up to this point, had successfully interfered with the consistently coercive obligations I had towards work. But the pleasures of physical labor were immediate. I didn't realize it was something that I had been missing. The simple act of moving real objects about in the physical world was a welcome and gratifying contrast to the moving of abstract symbols, words and numbers on an electronic screen. I enjoyed this renewed contact with the earth.

For years I had submitted willingly and succumbed to all of the professional demands set upon me, success being directly related to the number of hours applied to the task. Some derisively call it workaholism, but like it or not, the formula is fundamental; the more hours spent on a job, the better chance at success. But, as my net worth grew, somewhere along the way, I found myself with little else in my life other than work and family obligations. Nothing resembling a hobby had ever surfaced. Coinciding with the decision to build a new house with gardening, I felt as if I had finally crossed a long-sought threshold that almost magically permitted me to enjoy the benefits of my hard work. Being part psychologist, the architect properly intuited my need for a dramatic counterpoint.

I gave it a try. I put my hands in the dirt. The sensation was immediate. The connection with the ground felt primal. Over time, my habit evolved. I loved it. Before heading outside, I parked my phone on the kitchen counter as a conscious act of self-protection.

With a small spade, I dug one small hole after another in aligned rows before laying in my crocuses. I then pushed back the earth, and patted it firmly with my hands. I focused purely on the soil and the pregnant bulbs, extinguishing all outside thoughts from my mind. The process induced a calm as if it were emanating from the earth. While gardening, the office and its worries felt remote and easily ignored. The habit quickly took hold, and I fell easily into a weekly routine. Gardening was probably as close as I'd ever get to what other people call meditation. I imagined next spring, witnessing the first inkling of bloom, the crocuses peering up through the last remnants of the snow.

Absorbed in the garden, time took on a new pace, one that was difficult to measure. So, I'm not sure how much later it was when Liz appeared at the edge of the broad driveway. She called out, "Cole." The air was humid. I grabbed a towel and wiped the sweat from my face. Before I had a chance to respond, she called out again in the same measured but firm tone, "Cole."

"Yes?" I answered Liz, rising and clearing the dark soil from my arms.

Remaining at a distance, in a black knit suit and tall thin heels, hesitant to walk on the soft lawn, Liz announced, "I'm taking the boys to Sunday school. We'll pick up my mother on the way, and then after church, we're off to lunch. Should be back by two."

Church followed by lunch was an important weekly ritual

for Liz — one that we agreed to disagree on. She insisted that the children have a religious upbringing, and also that's where all her friends would be on Sunday. With no religious education, I had no patience for such foolishness. Zero. Those rare times I found myself in the pews, I felt out of place, never quite sure how to behave or what to expect. Although the entirety of the religious spectacle seemed like an elaborate anachronism. I sensed, but was not sure, that somehow if managed properly, the exercise could yield a bit of good, perhaps as a source for moral teachings or simply as a place for people to meet. Yet it remained foreign and undecipherable. The minutiae of the rituals, the contorted explanations, the supplicating to an imaginary power — they struck me as patently irrational. What logic is there in rushing off to a pompous glorifying edifice, standing and sitting, sitting and standing, while a high and mighty anointed clairvoyant in a long robe pretends to have all the answers?

As much as the religious spectacle irritated me, I nevertheless refrained from making such politically incorrect statements in public for fear of societal disdain. Even in private, I was not bothered by Liz's religiosity; it never crossed my mind to challenge her on the issue. She comfortably excused my absence to her friends and the pastor by detailing my near 24/7 obsession with work. This, everyone knew, had been undeniably true since the Thursday evening sixteen years earlier when we went on our first date, sharing a pizza and a bottle of wine.

Liz and I had an agreement that I would not share my opinions with the boys. It was clear, however, that church was mom's thing, not dad's. I voiced no objection to Liz taking the boys to church. It was fine with me if she wanted to make the effort. I wasn't going to argue about it, nor was I going to stand in her way. I knew that Liz's Sunday routine was an emotional necessity, integral, like breathing, a natural part of life.

Hearing the call from Liz, my boys bounded out the front door, racing past their mother into the yard. Kevin, almost twelve, and his younger brother, Alex, age nine, were in their boyhood prime. Entranced by their youthful energy, I watched from the garden. Completely unconcerned that their Sunday suits needed any special care, they ran a couple of quick loops through and around the elm trees and ended up standing attentively before me like little soldiers standing for review.

Alex had his mother's disposition, was gregarious and opinionated. Alex's gaze was suddenly distracted, following something behind me. He pointed and said, "Look, Dad."

Digging in my newly turned dirt was a squirrel either burying a nut or uncovering one. In either case, he was disturbing my work. I turned in his direction, raised my arm, and aimed my finger at the varmint, and saying loudly, "Pow! Pow!" as if I were firing a gun.

"Dad, don't kill him."

"Son, I was just pretending. Don't worry. He's fine. I just wanted to scare him away."

"He wasn't doing anything wrong."

"You're right; that's not a funny joke. He was just doing what squirrels do." Young Alex briefly made me feel ashamed. How was it that my first instinct was to shoot? I could have simply waved my arms and yelled, "shoo!" Instead, I taught my son that violence was the first solution — or at least it was mine.

I studied the boys with a pretend air of scrutiny, "Looking good. Looking real good. A sharp-looking pair." A coat and tie were an integral part of the boys' Sunday morning ritual, a style of dress that a hundred percent was imposed by their mom. I had long ago abandoned those archaic customs in favor of open collars. But, admittedly, I did find a special paternal pride in seeing my sons dressed as handsome men-in-the-making.

Looking at Kevin was like peering through a time-delaying mirror. Quiet mostly and affable, he looked and acted like a younger version of his dad. But, unlike his dad, he was a great student with a natural aptitude for math and science, more like his uncle. With his hand pinching the knot of his tie, Kevin asked, "So, Dad, how do you think I did?" Before I had a chance to answer, Alex jumped on the back end of his brother's question with a self-consciously louder voice, yelping, "Dad, did you see mine? What d'ya think? Good, huh?" I shifted my attention to the younger boy. Seeing the multiple windings and twists, which bore no resemblance to anything from the House of Windsor, I couldn't help but offer a broad grin. "Well done, son." Getting me to smile was often Alex's goal. Satisfied with the attention, he darted back in his mother's direction. I watched as Alex grabbed his mother's hand, wondering how much longer that childlike affection would persist.

Liz, her black suit accented with a single large pearl button near the neck, smiled broadly, clearly enjoying the interplay between her men. She had straight black shoulder-length hair and penetratingly dark open eyes, so intense that quite often, she had been mistakenly characterized as being confrontational; in fact, she was anything but. She was a peacemaker. Of average height, she nonetheless thought of herself as short, especially when standing next to her much taller husband. She almost always wore extremely high heels to compensate. It did not escape her self-appraisal that they helped show off her spin class-toned calves. Her fitness and her clothes were all part of her appearance's careful composition. It was Liz's form of artistic expression. Assured in her style, she could quickly assemble the appropriate outfit for every occasion. Even venturing out into the garden without the appropriate shoes was anathema to my wife's being. So, there she stood at a distance away on the sidewalk.

I crossed the lawn towards Liz with Kevin on my heel.

I turned back to Kevin, his eyes tracking my every move. He had patiently waited for his accolades, but his face had fallen. Kevin needed more of me. "You did well, too," I said, pressing a finger into the silk just below the knot, then pushing it snug to his collar, "A proper knot will have a dimple just below it. Like this." As I patted him on the back, "Soon enough, you will be your own man, and you won't need your old dad any more." Kevin displayed a deferential smile, but I saw an easily read the 'Dad, is-that-all-you've-got' look on his face.

Liz waved her arms, propelling the boys forward, "Come on, we'll be late." Kevin raced to beat his brother the short distance to the car but lost by half a step.

As the boys climbed in, Liz asked, "Are you sure you don't want to go with us?" This was a question I had heard almost every week since the kids were old enough to walk. Ostensibly about the church and lunch ritual, at its heart, the question was really about Liz bargaining for more of my time. Answer to the question wasn't required. But in the gap of where an answer might have been, Liz responded with a resigned sigh.

The sigh was something new. Hearing it, I knew a response was required. I tucked my gloves in my back pocket but caught myself just before putting my certainly still perceived dirty hands on Liz's shoulder. I deliberately ignored the deeper question, answering only the more superficial one, "You know I'll never interfere with you, your mom and the boys. You and the boys go and do your thing. I'll finish my work. This is where I need to be now."

"Cole, please. I don't think you understand. The boys see how you dismiss what's important to me. Family is important – more than anything else. My mom included. I'm afraid they're going to follow your lead and one day turn away from me. I don't want to lose them — ever. I want us all to stay together. Please, do me a favor. I need you to support me every once in a while. I want you to be more involved, especially with the boys."

Paralyzed between the desire to accommodate and knowing what I truly needed, I decided that this was neither the time nor the place to continue this discussion, "I know. Let me think about it. We'll talk later and find a solution."

Knowing my words didn't supply much comfort, I leaned towards her cheek, careful to keep my soiled clothes away from hers, and kissed her. "Don't worry; it'll work out fine."

But I knew what she knew. We both knew. Nothing was going to change any time soon.

We separated, each to our own mission. Liz paused mid-step on her way to the car. "And don't forget Kevin's birthday party is coming up Thursday, after school. It's important that you be there for him. Put it on your calendar."

I watched as she and the boys drove down the drive. I returned to my work in the garden. I needed to divide the tulips and move them slightly up the hill towards the house, thereby making more room for the crocuses. The idea of a sweeping mat of delicate bluish-purple flowers arising towards the spring sun seemed like a pleasing prospect. I got back to work.

Tired of the radio, I turned it off and called Michael again.

This time he picked up. "In Houston, just got off the plane."

"I hear you have a good prospect lined up. With whom?"

There were probably a hundred companies in the city with both the interest and capacity to do a deal like this. But within that large group, I couldn't imagine who Michael had a relationship with. He was a smart guy, but not in the networking sort of way. There had to be some intermediary involved.

"Cole, don't get too excited. It's a long shot."

"You don't want to share?"

"Not really. Relax this weekend. Enjoy your brother."

That answer irritated me. But neither was I in the mood to argue. I said, "Hey, I'm just trying to keep up with the progress ... or lack thereof."

"I can handle this. Cole, let go a little. I'll work it out. Trust me."

Trust me. I hated those two words. They made me suspicious and often had the opposite effect of what was intended. My conversation with Michael ended with no new information. Moreover, now I was worried about all the negative permutations. Who was Michael hooked into? Did I know them? Were they going to want a bigger cut? Who would be interested in a deal already going south, and wouldn't they instinctively want to take advantage of our desperate position? A winning scenario was hard to imagine. I was worried about losing our escrow. It would take several years to earn it back. I gripped the steering wheel tight until my hands were tired. On a highway, motionless in the middle of nowhere, I had no power.

Seeking some reliable comfort, I called Liz again, hoping she now had time for me. I asked, "How are things?"

"Fine now. The boys are out with some friends. I won't see them until tomorrow morning. Alex has a friend's birthday, and Kevin wants some new clothes. I think he wants to impress his new girlfriend."

"Really? He's got a girlfriend?"

"Cole, come on. Really? You saw them together at his party, sitting by the pool."

"Me, 'come on.' Seriously, Liz, I can't be expected to remember all their comings and goings, who his friends are this week, who his teachers are. I'm busy. Too busy. Work is crushing me lately."

"You know, for the longest time, I believed that 'I'm busy'

line. Now I'm beginning to think you just don't care enough to focus on the kids or me."

"Do we have to do this now?"

"It's a Friday evening, Cole. I'm home alone. No place to go. My friends are out with their families. I've got nothing else to do. We can talk now."

Navigating the traffic while on the phone suddenly became more challenging. "That's not fair. I'm upset about work and you know that. I'm on the freeway, have been trapped in traffic for hours, and now am about to spend more time than I can imagine with my helpless brother. Something you've been preaching I should've been doing all along, and also something that I've had very little interest in pursuing ... especially now. You know all that too. You think right now is a good time to whine about being lonely?"

"I can't play this game any more. You're right. You win."

The phone went dead.

I called back. Voicemail.

I tuned into the news station and heard more about the world's latest disasters. This, in turn, brought me back to thoughts about how all of that ultimately affects international business, then, in turn, reinforcing my problems with the London guys. This was the first time I had done any business with an overseas group. I could easily see this being my last. I went back to the satellite radio, scrolling through the endless choices until finally arriving at the 90s station. There was an instantaneous sense of comfort, reminding me of high school. I settled there. It was the best way to engender an alternate state of mind, a more optimistic one.

A half-hour later, I approached the accident scene, with the scattering of emergency vehicles and their dozens of flashing red and blue lights. I hoped that nobody was hurt. By the time I got there, one of the damaged cars was being hauled onto a wrecker. The damage looked insignificant and disproportionate to the disruption it had caused to the rest of the world. It irritated me that some careless driver not paying attention, probably on their phone, caused a fender bender, ruining an entire afternoon for a thousand people. Soon, the momentum increased, thankfully back at the posted speed limit. I still had eighty or so miles left, at least an hour and a half's drive. I was way behind schedule.

The traffic remained dense for a while longer. I drove by yet another accident, this one off on the shoulder, but slowing down my pace yet again. I hadn't seen this section of highway in years and was unaccustomed to the breadth of the freeway and the density of traffic this far out of town. There were long lines of cars backed up on exit ramps where there were no visible signs of civilization, not even a gas station. Just a turnoff onto a lonely county road. I couldn't fathom where everyone was going and how far people were willing to commute. I was surprised to discover the number of people living so far out. The thought crossed my mind that it was a Friday afternoon; maybe these folks were headed to their weekend place. Then again, there were way too many cars for that. Instead of imagining the peace and quiet of the countryside, it was probably more realistic to envision rows and rows of new boring homes on a freshly planned grid of streets.

An hour later, there were fewer regular cars on the road, more eighteen-wheelers. I was now driving alongside dusty ten-year-old Ford pickups. My new, shiny, black SUV with its huge chrome wheels and grille felt embarrassingly out of place.

16

The curves of the road and the rising mountains became familiar again and soothing. This was a path I had traveled many times as a boy. My dad driving, my nose to the glass, I observed the gradual evolving horizon, the hills growing into mountains. And as the mountains steepened, the slopes thickened with green conifers. The recognizable sequence of peaks and passes welcomed me back as though I were re-entering a tattered old photograph and watching it reanimate.

Large and impossible-to-miss changes disrupted my dream. Signs and pylons, painted in their well-known graphics and primary colors, screamed for attention. Cubes of brick and aluminum trim crawled against the natural backdrop advancing the unstoppable edge of urbanization. But the further I drove through this battleground, the miles unspooling, the more the commercial activity thinned. The roadside clutter increasingly gave way to large gaps, through which I was permitted views of the unspoiled, primal world.

The commercial activity never entirely ceased, however. Its tentacles were still evident at my exit off the freeway. Where I remembered a pasture had once laid like a broad welcome mat, a truck stop now sided the road. Out front were a dozen rows of gas pumps, framed by columns of parked trucks. The station's bluish lights were bright even under the late afternoon sun.

I rolled past the truck stop and approached the familiar intersection. I eased my black monster onto the shoulder just short of the stop sign. Removing my sunglasses, I listened to the final notes of Pearl Jam's Breathe, a fortunate coincidence placing me in a calmer, more reflective mood.

Past the truck stop, the view was much the same as it was all those years ago. This intersection marked for me a distinct transitional point, from leaving one world and entering another. That contrast between conflicting worlds remained clear now, decades later, as I sat in my car observing the landscape through my windshield. Behind was the fast-paced world of multi-laned highways, the never-ending din of traffic, and civilization's incessant, grinding energy. Straddling the unsettled allure of the primal world, its raw timelessness, was the relentless ignorance of humanity, the false security of the known, structured world. Ahead was nature, pristine as it was formed at creation, untamed, quiet. Begging to be explored but resistant.

On the corner nearest to where I stopped, suffering from years of neglect, rested the old diner at which we ate frequently. Seeing the pale blue front door, with its small ocular window, invoked memories of fried catfish and checkered tablecloths. The plywood-covered windows and the weeds emerging throughout the parking lot lent a dystopian contrast to the nearby gleaming truck stop.

A row of small real estate signs at the property's edge directed the curious to the temptation of small enclaves in the foothills ahead.

Leaning slightly to the left, the stop sign in front of me had faded to a dull pink. It appeared to me as being more a symbol than a traffic sign. It demanded attention — like a divine forewarning signal, one intended to make me think again about my plans. Despite all the distance and effort, the aggravations conquered, the arguments, traffic, my resignation — an intuitive voice gently whispered to me: *Abort this trip to the past. Stop. Turn around. Go back home.*

Recognizing the silliness of such hollow symbolism, I found myself grinning. A counterbalancing aphorism, one that Michael frequently quoted, had come to mind, "Sometimes, in order to get a deal done, you have to run a stop sign." The quote had been stated in the course of dealmaking, sometimes one has to commit a minor but necessary infraction on the way to achieving some larger goal, like a speed bump. But the metaphor rang true here as a life lesson. This weekend was a small sacrifice. Anyway, I couldn't break my promise to Andy. The only option was onward.

Situated on the other side of the stop sign on the far corner, across the intersection, was the oblong-shaped sign framing the little green dinosaur — a prehistoric relic surviving to remind us of an earlier era. The building that the sign stood in front of was also long past its heyday. But it was clearly being maintained. The paint was fresh. The parking lot was clean. The once orderly service station slash corner grocery, once bright and shiny, had lost its pumps but still looked to be in the same business of selling essentials. Next to where a pump once stood was parked a single newish pickup. In sharp contrast to it and barely visible behind the building were an assortment of decaying broken vehicles. On the far side where the service bays once had been, bright lights glistened behind plate glass windows, and above the door, a hand-painted sign read "tacos y bebidas." A half-dozen or so cars were parked nearby.

I crossed the intersection, parking my car next to the pickup. I went into the store, planning to buy a few groceries for the weekend.

A bell rang as I swung the door open. Straight ahead

through an interior door past the register, I saw a young man seated at a gray metal desk, his back turned to me, dressed in khakis and a pressed white shirt. On hearing the bell, he stood up and approached.

"Good evening."

No response. He looked me up and down. "You must be Andy's brother," he said.

"Wow! How did you know?"

"You guys really resemble each other — same eyes and nose; plus, he was just here about two hours ago. ... I'm Pete's grandson, Pete Peterman."

"Named after your granddad. That's a nice honor. I remember him as such a respectful man. How's he doing?"

"Passed about fifteen years ago."

"So sorry ... I should have figured. And your dad?" After the first answer, I was a little apprehensive about asking this one, but my mouth worked faster than my brain.

"Passed not long after that — lung cancer. Smoked a lot, you know?"

Pete gestured towards an empty chair next to his desk, inviting me into the back office, "Suppose I get you something to drink – beer? Soda?"

Before I could consider my options, Pete continued, "We've managed all right. Mom moved in with my wife and me. She helps with the kids. ... and I've been operating the store ever since."

Taken aback by this unusual hospitality, instant familiarity, and curious about the goings-on of the area, I answered, "A Dr. Pepper seems appropriate — like the old days. Thanks."

I was a little nervous about the chair; it looked to have belonged to the grandfather. I sat down, but was careful not to lean back.

Pete disappeared, quickly re-emerging from the front room with a can of soda in each hand. When he sat down, I asked, "How's business? I mean, things are so different from the last time I was here, with the new truck stop just down the road. I imagine they stole most of your customers."

"Different is an understatement, especially with all the rich folk moving out here. The car repair business is long gone. Gas business, like you guessed, went down the street. No real harm, though — it was never much of a moneymaker. Couldn't compete with the national chains. But I'll say keeping the old Sinclair sign creates a bit of nostalgia. The locals have stayed loyal. And likewise, we kept the grocery store going for our old friends like your dad and Andy. Maybe our sentiments confused our business sense."

Gesturing to his left, Pete went on, "A couple of years back, we leased the old service bays to a Salvadoran couple, the Garcias. They've been doing a bang-up job ever since. The place is packed on the weekends. You really need to try it while you're here. Best enchiladas for thirty miles. That all said, I make ends meet. I bought a dozer and hired a guy to drive it for me — thinking about buying a second, bigger machine. This place works as a convenient office. All these real estate folks who are out here need somebody to cut their roads and level their lots. I'm easy to find here. And since I know everybody around, I started brokering a little real estate. That's where the real money is at."

He paused a second. "It was sad hearing about your dad. A really nice man. Great storyteller. I wanted to go to the funeral, but running this business by myself, I couldn't leave. I hope you understand."

"It's hard to leave in the middle of a deal."

"What about you? I see Andy every once in a while. From what he tells me, it sounds like you've done pretty good for yourself."

I was a little put off that Andy was talking about my private affairs. "Yeah, I've been lucky," is all I said about that.

I leaned back on my chair, testing its strength, then surveyed the room, "If I remember correctly, back in the day, the store had four or five tables over there by that front window. Dad would drink coffee and eat your grandmother's pie. And there'd almost always be two or three other guys discussing either the weather or politics — but it seemed like mostly talking about fishing. They'd sit there for hours as if there was absolutely nothing else to do. With all that time to kill, Andy and I would grab a couple of Eskimo Pies out of the back freezer and sit out front watching the traffic."

Pete looked at me but didn't look like he was in any hurry to say anything.

"A lot has changed since then," I said

"I heard from another broker that you guys are going to sell."

"We've talked somewhat about it. I can't say for sure. I suppose you keep up with the real estate around here? I heard that acreage like ours is a hot commodity now. Is that bullshit or just half-true?"

"No. True. Definitely true. Developers are all over the place. They're taking acreage like yours and carving it up into tiny ranchettes. That sort of thing has gotten real popular — you know, appeals to the Sunday-only outdoorsman, anywhere from five acres to fifty acres. I'm surprised that they haven't tried to buy your property yet. I'm getting calls all the time for this old falling down rathole memory of a gas station. Be terrible though to throw out the Garcias and see a Taco Bueno come in behind them."

I looked down at my watch and saw that I had totally blown my original schedule, "Hey Pete, I really need to get going. Thanks for the drink. Hopefully, I'll see you around. But before I leave, I wanted to pick up a few things."

"You needn't bother. From what your brother bought, you won't need anything else for a long while. You're set. He's like your dad in that way, likes to buy in bulk." Pete reached into his shirt pocket, "Let me give you my card. If that road up to the cabin needs any work, let me know. I'll work you a deal."

I found Dad standing at the kitchen counter scribbling on a pad of paper, making his lists for our Saturday shopping trip. As always, mesmerized by the morning cartoons, Andy was sitting in the middle of the living room floor.

The ritual was born out of necessity, and I enjoyed it perhaps because of its regularity. It was the one time of the week that it was guaranteed that the three guys were together. During the week, Dad was thoroughly busy with the details of his work. Even in the evenings when we were all home, he only superficially paid attention to our needs. He took calls during dinner, staying on the phone calling subs and workers about what they had done that day, then discussing with them what was planned for the next. These calls would go on well past our bedtime.

On Saturdays, we'd usually wait until after lunch. Before Andy and I got up, Dad would be already gone, making his job site visits. The shopping trips were planned with the idea of buying for the entire week ahead. Dozens of multipacks, everything we bought came in large quantities. We had a large pantry, and for items like twenty-four pack toilet paper, there was the back of the garage. On some days, it looked like a small warehouse. Dad also loved sales, often buying things that he thought would be needed at some later point. Like a four-pack of insect spray in January or a 24-case of WD-40, one that I don't think he ever broke into. One of the odd things he loved was canned fruit cocktails. He would buy the gallon size, peeling the top off and leaving it in the refrigerator for days while he ate out of it.

But on this particular Saturday, the workers either were

off, or they didn't need Dad's supervision. Leaving early usually meant burgers and milkshakes. I stood in the kitchen next to my dad, watching him write, knowing not to disturb the man while he was in the middle of a project, any project. The scribbling finally stopped, and Dad looked over at me, "What's going on with you?" he needled.

"Nothing."

"You've got your new glove, so how come you're not outside playing catch with your buddies?"

"Mr. Blankenship's dog chased after our ball and chewed the leather off." I pulled the ragged mess out from the glove's pocket. Even if the dog hadn't accelerated its decline, it probably would have lasted only another week or two.

Dad looked at the ball and gave me a concerned, "Hmmph."

Tearing the sheet off the pad, he suddenly said, "Grab your brother; it's time we run our errands."

Our first stop was the grocery store, specifically Aisle 2. Dad loved his vitamins. He respected the *Readers Digest* as the source of the most reliable information about health. In turn, this dictated his daily routine, meaning an ever-shifting array of colored pills, the whole alphabet soup: A, B2 through B12, D, E, potassium, calcium, and all the other minerals. Like everything else he bought, he bought the largest container available so that he could have the lowest cost per unit. The large, white plastic bottles filled the shopping cart, and they eventually filled an entire cabinet in the kitchen, a short reach from the breakfast table.

Apparently in good humor on that Saturday, Dad expanded our route, and he drove us to the sporting goods store. We could pick out something with our allowance money, he said. In those days, baseball was all I ever had on my mind. I was working with a coach, learning the basics of pitching. With a baseball in hand, I came back to Dad.

He frowned at me, saying, "You can't learn to pitch with

just one ball. Let's go back and get some more."

"But Dad, I have only enough money for one ball ... and a Snickers," I said, smiling.

Ignoring my lame attempt at humor, Dad insisted, "To get good at pitching, you need to throw a lot of balls. Can't do it with just one."

And so we went back to the baseball aisle. Not seeing what he wanted, he called over a stock boy, then asked him to call the sports department manager. I didn't understand the exact details, but the next thing I knew, the stock boy pulled down three cases of balls off the top shelf, thirty-six balls. I was dumbstruck, not knowing how to act.

"Now, you can throw some pitches," Dad said proudly.

"But Dad, I don't have the money for any of this."

"I tell you what. You give me the money you brought for the one ball, and I'll buy the rest. Sound like a good deal? And you can still have your Snickers."

"Well, yeah!" I was thrilled.

"Grab the balls and let's go."

"I can't wait to start throwing."

"Let's wait until we get out to the cabin. I've got a plan."

A couple of weekends later, at the cabin, Dad's plan became another one of his fabled projects. First, he scoped out a level location, one that coincided with where we sometimes shot cans. He then ordered Andy and me to get his toolbox. Next, he hung an old tire from a tree limb, setting up the strike zone. Next on the list was measuring out where the pitching rubber should be, but instead of rubber, he set into the ground a flat white stone, immovable. Finally, for a backstop, Dad hauled out a long section of an old chain-link fence. It vaguely resembled what I might see in an actual game at the park. Dad had thought out the details thoroughly.

Andy and I quickly took to playing games, making up our own rules about points, through the tire for more and fewer points for merely hitting the tire. Over time, my accuracy increased as well as my confidence.

One day, Dad found me on the ground doing my stretches.

Dad walked up. "Don't bother with that."

"But Dad, my coaches told me ..."

"That's not necessary. You'll loosen up by throwing catch. Ready?"

"But Dad, this isn't how my coaches want me doing it."

"I really don't care what your coaches say. When you're with me, we do it my way. Got that?"

"Yes, sir."

Beginning about fifteen feet apart, we tossed the ball back and forth. Gradually growing the distance between us until eventually we were about pitching mound distance away from one another. All the while, Dad insisted on keeping the throwing pace even – not hard.

"All right now, let me watch you throw."

He watched me throw about five pitches, then walked over. Taking hold of my hand, he spread my fingers around the ball, then flexed my wrist back and forth. Raising my arm to about eleven o'clock, he said, "This is what you're doing wrong. You shouldn't snap your wrist until this point right here. You need to have a bit more patience."

"But Dad, my coach said ..."

"And how's your pitching?"

"Okay."

"Well. ... Hmmph ... Okay, isn't good enough. Okay doesn't get you very far in life. Maybe you need to work on raising your standards."

"But ..."

"Will you quit interrupting me?"

I saw the jagged scar on Dad's forearm come my way. He grabbed my wrist and yanked my arm straight up, almost lifting me off the ground. "Thomas, this is where I want your arm. Here. Right here. And this here is where you snap your wrist. Understand?"

My arm hurt. My confusion acute. And I started to cry.

"Oh, don't start acting like a little baby. Be a man."

Dad knew nothing about baseball, but that didn't deter him from certainty. He had no regard for the coaches, zero respect for them or my point of view. When I was with him, I had no choice but to comply with what Dad wanted. Although, in the back of my mind, I knew that it was a temporary gesture. Tomorrow, I would go back to my coaches' plan. I trusted them more than my father.

"If you're not interested in my help. Good luck. I've got work to do." At that, Dad walked away from me.

That was the first and only time Dad took any interest in baseball — or even played catch with me. I had longed for the moment without the ability to articulate the nature of the emotion. When he stepped on that hope, the pain was acute. Looking back, I realized that I was lusting for some small connection with Dad, some common interest. But it was never to be.

Two minutes after heading north from Peterman's place, I spotted a young six-point buck in the middle of the road. I stopped the car, watching as he took his time to cross the road. No hurry and no concerns.

The first several miles I drove was a newly paved road, no longer the gravel I remembered. The old county road had been transformed into something modern, with a bright yellow sinuous line pointing the way up into the mountains. A violation of the buck's territory.

The highway planners, though, knew something about the future of this area. The roadbed was wide enough to be instantly upgraded into a four-lane road.

Around the first bend, about a half-mile past the store, a newly constructed turnoff to the right caught my attention. The earth's surface had been recently ripped raw. I stopped for a second to study the work. Intrigued, I drove through a gap between the red and white barricades onto the newly bladed road base. As I crawled farther in, I saw the beginnings of a meandering ribbon of newly stripped earth cleaving the acres into abstract, unnatural patches of level ground.

The money spent on the road surely had added value to the adjacent properties. The reach of development surprised me. I hadn't seriously thought before now about the true value of Dad's mountain property — or rather, Andy's and mine mountain property. I still held the vision that the place was nothing more than a personal, rustic refuge. But wilderness was losing the battle. Clearly, more and more people wanted to possess what we had possessed for years, thereby innocently and ironically robbing the land of its natural pristine essence.

I did the basic math in my head: counted how many acres were there; divided by the average lot size; added in the cost for road and utilities; subtract all that from the selling price. The result was a pretty good profit. Or would we be better off selling the whole thing to a developer, letting him take on the risk?

It didn't take me a second to remember Andy's reluctance. I knew that was there. But such a deal could remove his financial worries forever while also providing me with the possible means to make this current Atlantic City deal work in my favor. I had something to think about.

On the way back out to the main road, just off to the side, stood a sales trailer with a sign out front inviting potential purchasers to come in and view their future utopia. A large D5 dozer was parked next to the trailer. Painted on the cab in large black letters was the now-familiar name, *Peterman*.

I pulled back onto the main road, rounded the corner, and began driving the last three-mile stretch to our property.

The sun had now settled behind the mountains, but there was still plenty of light for the rest of the drive.

"Thomas, your turn."

"Dad! It's not legal."

"It's time you learn to drive. Here's as good a place as any. This is a quiet road, a good spot for your first go at it. There's a couple of miles of easy driving ahead. Then we'll switch back."

...

"Son, pay attention! Stay left! Left! You're about to drive us off the edge here. ... All right, you're doing fine. ... Son, I said, pay attention to your driving. Now! Back to the left."

"Oh no! A truck's coming. What do I do?"

"Stay calm. ... Dammit, son, watch what the hell you're doing. You nearly drove us off into the ditch. ... Let's stop here for a minute."

"You didn't have to hit me."

"You need to pay attention. Focus. Focus on the job at hand."

"But it was a big truck. And it was right in the middle of the road. I was scared. ... Now what?"

"Okay, catch your breath. Relax for a second. ... Easy now, let's get back on the road and keep going. Be careful. Focus. ... You have to face your fears. You can't let them paralyze you. ... Let's go now."

After a mile, the paved road ceased to exist; familiar to my memory, the narrowed gravel road wound tightly up the steep slope on its way up to the property. With the civilized world fully dissipated, I now felt completely enveloped by nature.

The diminishing light and the absence of landmarks confused my sense of location. However, knowing the entry gate would be easy to pass, I slowed my pace. Back in the day, our marker had been our neighbor's mailbox, the one that looked like a family of bears — each one of the four with a raised hand and a friendly smile. And soon enough, to my grateful surprise, there were the bears again waving hello, just a few dozen yards before our gate, as always.

A minute later, I instantly realized that there was no way I could have missed our property's entry. Right there at the entrance was a large sign: 'For Sale - approx. 613 acres, Prime Development Opportunity.' Confusion quickly devolved into irritation. I suspected that in all my eagerness to get the estate settled; I had said something that wasn't interpreted properly. It was true that I had mentioned to a real estate agent who had been bold enough to cold call me that even though we weren't ready to sign any listing agreement, he could try to solicit offers. But I had no idea the guy would put up a sign. On the one hand, I found his aggression a little too bold, but on the other hand, I honored his assertiveness. I might have done the same thing myself.

The conversation with Peterman and the drive in had reinforced the agent's hype. I was newly confident that the agent's expectations might actually be achievable. A sale could generate a lot of money.

Looking at the sign dominating the entrance gate, I knew instantly Andy would be angry with me.

I parked in front of the gate and walked to the padlock. The headlights illuminated the lock, which, it turned out, had been left hanging open. Out of curiosity, I twisted the lock's small wheels, straining to see the faint numbers against the glare of the headlights. With the remembered combination in place, I pulled the shackle and was satisfied to see the well-oiled mechanism smoothly latch and unlatch. The combination was the month and day of Dad's birthday.

The first quarter-mile in the Caddy bumped down the untended drive. I was pleased to have traded cars. At the low water crossing, I bounced across the worn stones. The road rose steeply from there. I was quickly gaining elevation. After a few switchbacks and the final long straight section, I arrived in front of the cabin.

The cabin I had remembered to be rustic but well taken care of; now it looked like a weathered Depression-era shack. Of the three windows that looked out onto the front porch, all the screens were torn, and their ragged edges loosely hung to the side. Paint was a distant memory. What was left of the cabin's color was dull and, in this dim light, looked to be a darker greenish hue than I remembered.

But the cool air felt refreshing. I had forgotten how quickly fall came to these elevations.

The cabin was dark, with no light inside or out. And there was no sign of Andy.

Then, a voice erupted from around the side of the cabin, "Hey Tommy, while I get the generator started, why don't you get the broom and sweep off the front porch."

"I can't see shit. Get me some light. And where would I find a broom anyway?"

I didn't hear a response and stayed right where I was next to the car.

In the old days, when we arrived, we immediately hit the ground working. Everyone knew their job, making the cabin ready, sweeping away the cobwebs, pulling the protective sheets off the furniture, unpacking supplies — all sorts of little chores.

Though with no light or electricity, there was nothing for me to do. Not in any hurry, I waited for Andy to finish whatever it was he was doing. In the meantime, I re-discovered the huge flat rock a few yards out from the front porch, a place that Andy and I used to sit and plan our days. Several yards beyond that, past the open area where Andy and I used to throw the baseball, was a half-acre pond. It was always glass smooth, the perfect spot for skipping rocks. It was also a perfect mirror for inverting the view of the mountains. The rock was large and flat enough that even as an adult, I could comfortably stretch out on it. The best I could, I took my hand and brushed the dirt off the top of the rock. I laid down on it. Relieved to be out of the car, I watched the sky turning to a deep purple and scanned the heavens, looking for the first stars.

Andy's four-cylinder pick-up rattled up next to me, startling me out of my accidental nap. The sky had finished its fade to a deep black. Above me spread a million-plus stars.

Andy yelled out from the back of his yellow truck, "Hey, give me a hand." This was the same truck he had driven for the past dozen years. To see it was still running surprised me.

"Where have you been?"

"I was disconnecting the generator cable from the back of the house."

The truck was positioned so that its lights were shining on the shed to the north of the cabin. Constructed from sheets of unpainted corrugated metal, the shed, covered in deep red rust, somewhat protected the cabin's generator. To the machine's side dangled a clutch of unruly disconnected wires.

Shielding my eyes from the bright lights, I looked up at Andy, "What are you doing?"

Without glancing my way, Andy stayed focused on the job at hand. "I've got to get this new generator hooked up. The old one crapped out a long time ago."

"Where did you get this one?"

"A friend down the road let me borrow it."

With only the tiniest edge of sarcasm, I asked, "Have you

ever thought about buying one for yourself?"

"Why spend the money if I don't have to. I hardly ever use electricity. Doesn't seem worth the investment. Grab that handle."

We found our handholds and lifted the machine off the tailgate. Andy led me and the generator to a spot next to the leaning hulk of the old shed. He then dug into his jean pocket, fishing out a handful of nuts and bolts. Next, he attached the black cable on the generator to another black cable coming from the direction of the house. Methodically, in a way that reminded me of Dad, Andy grabbed the red cable and said, "I came up earlier today and tried to clean out the cabin a little for you. I didn't think you'd want to camp out."

"Don't worry about it. I can handle almost anything for one night."

Andy pulled a wrench from his back pocket and tightened the nuts, "After lunch, I had to run back to the hardware store for some tar paper and roofing nails. The roof's in terrible shape, and there's a small chance of rain for tomorrow. By the time I drove out to the hardware store and then over to the grocery, it ended up taking the whole afternoon."

After double-checking his connections, Andy started the generator.

The noise from the machine forced me to talk louder, "It's almost eight now. You're telling me it took you six hours to shop?"

"Tommy, I don't know. Things just take longer out here. Why don't you go inside and see if the lights work?"

With only the glare of Andy's Toyota's headlights to work with, plus worried about rotten wood, I cautiously tested each step. The top board squeaked loudly underfoot as I raised myself onto the porch. Grabbing the handle of the screen door, I pulled it open, cautious that in its current condition it might fall off in my hand. I pushed the front door open and slid my hand along the wall until I discovered the switch. The fluorescent bulbs in the kitchen flickered to life.

While I absorbed the view of the old cabin, Andy walked in, dropped a cooler on the floor, and stood next to me.

"Sure has deteriorated," I said.

"It's not so bad. Works for me. No major problems to speak of." He glanced around as if he hadn't paid good attention to his surroundings in some time. "But, you know, it wouldn't take much work to bring it back to the way it was. We could —"

"Hey, don't worry about it on my account. Like I said, I can handle almost anything."

Andy reached inside the cooler and pulled out two beers, then led me back out onto the porch. He abruptly sat down in one of the several old wooden chairs grouped at the end of the porch. They were all of the same vintage but a variety of styles. Now, as back then, none with a drop of paint remaining.

I grabbed the back of one of the other chairs, repositioning it so that my brother and I were sharing the same view, and sat down. As soon as my butt touched the seat, it was like an electric jolt hit my spine. Instantly I sprang back up.

Andy said, "Man, what's the matter? Something bite you?"

"I don't know, something about this chair. Are these the same chairs as before?"

"The same. Exactly the same." Andy laughed while I reinspected the chair, passing my hand across its seat, before settling down again.

Now comfortable in the chair, I took a long pull on my beer and peered out across the lake into the dark forest.

"Andy, this property truly is beautiful."

Andy nodded in agreement. "I was thinking," he said, "that if ever you wanted to bring the boys up, a few nails and a little paint could go a long way toward cleaning this place up. It could be a fun project."

I confidently shook my head side to side, seeing it clearly for what it was, a thirty-year-old shack that needed only one thing, that being Peterman's bulldozer.

"Perhaps, that could be possible in some alternate reality. But I can't envision bringing the boys all the way here. It would be way too long a trip. And B, really, when you get down to it, staying here was something that was fun when I was a kid. I don't see the me of today being so interested any more ... it just doesn't have the same appeal."

"We learned a lot out here and not the sort of things you can learn about in a school."

The beer was having its effect, and my heart rate slowed. For a few moments, my brother and I both sat silently, enjoying the quiet, the view, and the cool air.

"I've a got a few things to do," Andy said. "You sit here for a bit and relax."

Letting myself indulge in his permission, I studied my view.

A single star, probably Venus, sparkled brightly just above the western horizon, and in the east, the moon hung low, a couple of days shy of full. In the now dim light, I could barely discern the outlines of the nearby and once very familiar pond, appearing smaller than when Andy and I called it "The Lake." Not far from where I sat, off to the left, Dad had constructed a small dock on the pond's edge. But all that remained, almost completely submerged in the dark water, were a handful of planks, which weren't quite bridging the gap between the pair of sunken beams. It was a barely visible remnant that only a past inhabitant with a vivid memory could decipher. In the calm silence, I worked to rebuild the dock, and next to it, I imagined a small rowboat with two fishing poles, ones that had rarely encountered a fish. I also summoned the memory of two pairs of feet dangling off the dock, tickling the cool water.

Between where I sat and the old dock, there spread a large flat grassy area. Depending on the season, it was the ideal place to pass a football or throw a baseball. The vast expanse was one I had to regularly mow. A half-day job, but at least it was one for which I could understand its utility.

Andy took his work seriously. He was in and out of the door several times, with an assertiveness to his mission. I got up from my seat and wandered back into the house to see if I could offer any help. With a toolbox in hand, he walked past me back outside through the screen door. Like a puppy with nothing better to do, I followed him back out. But I was late — Andy and the truck had already disappeared down the hill.

As the rattle of the truck drifted out of earshot, the generator rattled and then fell silent. The kitchen light went out, and I found myself on the porch, alone in the dark.

Out of instinct, I checked my phone. But nothing there. Zero bars. No signal. I hadn't talked to Michael in hours and was worried about how I was going to stay in touch with him. At first, this disconnect felt like a welcome reprieve, but then I realized I would be out of contact with my other world for the weekend. I shoved the phone back into my pocket and glanced outward.

Not sure what to do with myself, I sat back on the flat rock to better absorb the world I had returned to. I was immersed in the dark. At first impenetrable, my eyes, briefly blinded by the phone's bright screen, slowly adjusted. The jagged outlines of the ill-defined trees encircled me like a tall wall — fortress-like.

17

We had been living in a small apartment when Andy came along. Dad and Mom had been there since they were married. A tiny two-bedroom apartment. My only trustworthy memory from that period involves playing in the common hallway at the foot of stairs. The stairs led to the units above us, and our neighbors would politely step around and over my toy cars, offering a smile and "hello" as they passed. The only hazard was the across-the-hall neighbor's dog, a graying dachshund that would tug at its leash and snap at me. I don't remember being scared, though. Only annoyed.

The day Mom and Dad came home with Andy, I was in the hallway, my toys scattered around the bottom of the stairs. With Andy wrapped tight in her arms, I could see an unsteadiness in Mom's short steps. I hurriedly removed my toy cars from her path. Looking up at Dad, he beamed, perhaps the happiest I had ever seen him. Dad accompanied Mom inside, leaving the door wide open. But he soon reappeared in the hallway with a special collection of Hot Wheels cars. It was a good day for me as well.

I was six and Andy just three when we moved out. Our new place was a Levittown-like house; each house barely differentiated from its neighbor except by the color of its trim.

We weren't the first owners but the second. The house was only three years old, and it still felt brand new. Dad had negotiated a favorable deal from the developer, a guy he was doing most of his work for at the time. I later found out that it was a foreclosure, and Dad simply had to pick up the previous owner's payments. Andy and I each had our own bedroom but shared one bathroom. I had space to play ball, and more importantly, there were a lot of other similarly aged kids around. The parallel streets, cloned houses and stringy saplings became the geometry that undergirded my life for the next decade.

The kitchen was painted a vibrant sunshine yellow. Dad and I spent a lot of time at the counter crafting our meals. It was a nice way of reabsorbing Mom's presence in the wake of her absence. The few isolated memories I have of my mother are of her in that kitchen, her long skirts swinging as she moved from the counter to the table, giving off the scent of cleanness. With its evocative smells of cakes and briskets, the room, unlike any other place in the house, conjured up her spirit and brought back little nodes of memories.

It's embarrassing that I don't remember more about that time with my mother. Nothing about walks with her, or going to the park, or school meetings, or other moms. And when I was older, asking Dad to tell me stories about her, his brief descriptions did little to make her real. Something of that time seems like it should have resonated and stayed with me. But it didn't, none of it.

But Dad did proudly report that Mom never complained about doing whatever chores were necessary. It was in accord with the work ethic he was imparting on his sons. Imagining the woman from the pictures I'd seen, she didn't appear exactly as a pioneer woman, but nonetheless, Dad emphasized that she was wholly unafraid of physical labor. Reinforcing Dad's view, the few photos pasted in the family album could have been exhibits in a museum about the struggles of the working class. In them, she wears pale floral prints that were almost certainly bought from Sears. Neither in the photos nor my memories was she ever wearing makeup. Like a caricature lifted out of a Norman Rockwell illustration, she exists for me, laboring incessantly in a small, clean, sparsely-appointed kitchen, leaving the heavy lifting and outside work to her protective husband. Whether or not that version of her has any relationship to reality is beside the point — it's the one that is embedded in me.

Mom was an only child, and that is the single detail that Andy and I knew about her before-marriage past. Dad's story about her began with how they first met. Shopping for underwear at Macy's, Dad met a saleslady with a broad smile, big teeth, bright red lips and long flowing hair. In his telling, she spent half the afternoon with him, selling him far more clothes than he could afford. It was a one-time extravagance that I'm certain he never repeated. After their business was consummated, he mustered the courage to ask her to go out for dinner after work. Two months later, they were married. I was born within a year, and Andy three years later.

Not too long after we had moved into our house, Mom was diagnosed with breast cancer. I remembered clearly the day when the three of us visited her in the hospital. Her appearance had radically deteriorated. She had become extremely pale and thin, to such an extent that I barely recognized her. She must have been on heavy medication because the one question I asked her — "Mom, how are you feeling?" — she never answered. She never came home. So, when I add it all up, Dad only knew Mom for about seven years, a tiny part of his life.

No aspect of her funeral stayed with me. I have no recollection of that moment, perhaps having successfully blocked it. And from what I could tell, Dad moved on quickly, which

167

was completely in character. I never saw him cry or slow down. Life went on, just with some adjustments. Dad never remarried. I'm not even sure he ever went to dinner with another woman.

Looking back at Mom's death from this distant perspective, I recall no real emotional upheaval, only practical hurdles. After Mom's passing, women were simply not around the house much. There were no aunts or cousins. We didn't have any. Not even any female friends came around. My connection with women was limited to teachers and my schoolmates' moms. When I was young, there were the occasional housekeepers. In fact, a whole series of them. But none of them stayed longer than a few months, and there were long breaks when there was no help at all in the house. By the time I started fourth grade, the housecleaners had stopped coming altogether, and it was just the three of us doing all the upkeep and cooking. It was work that had to be done. If there were any difficulties in the transition, I've forgotten them. We had no other choice.

I don't remember any jealousy towards the other kids or their own interactions with their mothers. It never crossed my mind at the time that anything was missing from my own life. We did well enough on our own. Dad worked hard and was gone long hours. That said, he provided for all of our material needs. We lacked for nothing in that regard. Even as small children, he trusted and empowered us to manage our day-to-day lives in almost every aspect. Expectations were high. No slacking. And we obediently fell in line. Homework was done before playing outside began. Strip the bed and laundry once a week. No reminders. Andy and I did our jobs.

Dad, in his attempt to bridge the loss, would bring us together in the kitchen to recreate one of her recipes. There were a few dishes we made, meatloaf and mashed potatoes in particular, that were close to recapturing the remembered tastes.

Even when Mom was alive, Dad was always a stickler for maintaining the house in perfect condition, and he enforced that same attitude onto Andy and me. We could never leave the house without making our beds. And if by chance we were ever to, by whatever circumstance, put a nick into the wall, small or large, we quickly learned how to spackle that hole and repaint the wall.

One of the striking features of our childhood home, and a prime reason Dad liked the house, was the spacious den that looked out onto the backyard by way of a pair of large sliding glass doors. When the doors were opened, the back patio and the den felt like one continuous inside/outside extensive space. But what by day brought in much-desired light and warmth had the reverse power at night. The window then became a black portal that revealed to a timid young boy nothing but terrible possibilities.

By the age of ten, I was beginning to stay up well past dark and frequently had to traverse the den to go back and forth from my bedroom to the refrigerator. Crossing in front of that big black window, though, was not easy. When the den was well lit, it wasn't so bad, but when there was only a single lamp burning, those large sliding glass doors seemed to grow in their immensity. Looming behind them was a black void loaded with endless evils. I don't know what I expected to jump out of that blackness – but all I knew was it was nothing good. Therefore, my habit was to run as fast as possible across the room from one side of the house to the other, focusing on the safety of the bedroom or kitchen, depending on the direction.

One night, when in the middle of one of my nightly sprints, I stopped. Frozen. I straightened my back and stoically faced the window. After I moment or two, I slowly walked up to the black void. I stared out through the glass as if I were searching for the face of God. After a minute or two, my eyes adjusted to the dim light. I began to see what was so clear during the daylight hours: the elm tree that gave its welcome shade during the hot summers, the table and four chairs sitting peacefully next to Dad's grill, the swing set off in the back corner, and behind all of it the pointy wood fence that will forever remind me of an old western movie. All exactly as they had been hours ago in the bright light of day. Where I had previously thought there was nothing but evil, there was actually some bare luminance, enough to render the unknown as familiar.

The mystery was suddenly gone. From that night forward, the void lost its potency for distrust. Instead, I became intrigued by the dark, its subtle shadings and hidden dimensions. As opposed to being frightening, its mystery pulled me in. Eyes wide, I began the habit of peering out of dark windows, watching as details became increasingly apparent as I became more intimate with the dim light. I discovered that the dark was not, in fact, a total absence of light. There was always a pale glow coming from a streetlamp or a neighbor's garage. And never solidly black, the night sky. Those million distant points have for eons been sending their radiance across the endless ether, only to arrive at this place, at this exact moment. There is always light. The less light, the more effort and, therefore, the more pleasure in resolving the puzzle. With a few clues, I enjoyed finding patterns within the dark forms. It required concentration. I began to fall in love with the dark, or rather the dimly lit. Eventually, I came not to fear the dark but to be enchanted by it. It revealed to me the pleasures that come from intensely examining something that most people found difficult to see and would rather not consider at all.

Not long after my spectral discovery, I began dragging Andy out late at night. Lying in the grass, we would consider the stars. And in that way, I felt at least a little responsible for Andy's career in science.

18

The bright lights of Andy's truck rising over the hill removed me from my reveries. He stopped the truck several feet in front of me, headlights blazing, forcing me to shield my eyes. He switched the machine off and, thankfully, the lights as well. Jumping out, he immediately headed inside.

"Anything I can do to help?" I asked.

"I've got it."

"I want to check in with Liz, you know, just to let her know I made it. And ..."

"You discovered there's no cell reception here. If you walk or drive about a quarter-mile back along the road to the crest right before it turns down to the low-water crossing, you can make your call from there."

"I guess you saw the generator quit."

"There was only a tiny bit of fuel left in the tank. I had to run down to Peterman's to get another tank, and ... sorry I was gone so long."

"I enjoyed being up here in the quiet. No problem."

While Andy was changing out the tanks, I set off down the road to find the cellphone spot.

It was a pleasant deep dive into the dark. Being the dirt road that started at the entry gate and led up to the house, my path was wide, without obstacles. Easy to navigate in the moonlight. The moon was a handbreadth higher into the eastern sky. The towering canopy of trees overhead felt protective, only occasionally giving way to astral vistas. Those million shimmering dots so much more dramatically clear and crisp than seen from the city.

Already, my body was adapting to the slower pace of rural life. Ambling, my strides were short and without urgency. My eyes wandered about, peering contentedly into the dark scenery. I'd periodically look down the road to maintain my orientation. I knew where I was now. There was no possibility of getting lost.

I arrived at Andy's suggested spot. A few steps off the road was a fallen tree, which made for a good temporary seat.

I tried to call Michael, but no answer. However, there was a short voicemail from Steve. "No news to report, but when you get a chance, I'd like to visit with you." I put that onto my mental to-do list for tomorrow. My conversation with Liz was brief. Neither one of us mentioned the earlier phone call when she hung on me. I had learned that for Liz, time had a great healing effect, and I certainly didn't want to poke the bear. She quizzed me about the drive in, how Andy was doing, and the state of the cabin. She mundanely reported that the boys were fine. I was a little annoyed she didn't ask one word about my work problems. On the other hand, there wasn't anything new to share with her. Regardless, the lack of sympathy made me feel utterly alone with my struggles. Rather than enjoying our talk, when I hung up with Liz, I felt relieved of the obligation, one more item checked off of my list. Resting on the log, from what had been a few moments ago a peaceful state of mind, I felt a turn. All of a sudden, I felt dislocated in a distant, alien time and universe. I felt sad. The forest's nighttime atmosphere was closing in on me. My chest was tight, and it was hard to breathe comfortably. I felt claustrophobic. The forest was impersonal and mindless of me and my problems.

Months before Dad's accident, I had come home early from work, around four p.m., removed my suit and put on my working-in-the-yard clothes. As I was walking through the kitchen, I saw Liz sitting at the counter, thumbing through some colorful catalog.

"I'll be out in my garden," I said.

Liz looked up, surprised and confused. Seeing myself in my tattered jeans and realizing the outfit was out of character for a Tuesday. I read her expression as a question.

"I don't know," I started. "Even though my desk is chock full of things to do. Nothing felt especially urgent, and I like the idea of getting a little sun."

"So this is how it's going to be?"

I withdrew my hand from the garage door and turned towards Liz. "And what exactly do you mean?" I asked. I felt like I had suddenly been accused of a crime with no idea what it was or when it had taken place. I walked back into the kitchen, closer to her.

"When we have a problem, you just disappear ... or maybe you just don't have a clue. I've given you a pass for the last several days — actually, it's been years." Liz sat up straight; her eyes narrowed and angry. "Off you go — into your shell, wherever it might be — outside, into your little garden — golf — I don't know where, but off you go. Leaving me alone. I'm tired of it. I don't feel like we're sharing a life any more. Just space — that's all we're sharing, just space." Her next words were emphatic. "Cole, I'm not sure this is working any more."

She continued to stare at me but was silent, waiting for my response.

"Liz, I'm sorry," I said. "Clearly I've offended you, but

honestly, I'm not sure what I've done."

"You aren't paying any attention, are you?"

There can't be a right answer to that question, and I had enough experience to know not to attempt one. So, I waited it out.

"I've been upset ... I guess you couldn't tell ... ever since we hosted the school fundraiser ... you really haven't noticed, have you?"

The fundraiser clue didn't help in the least, but my mind raced back to that evening. She was right; I hadn't noticed that anything was wrong. I had obviously missed all of the signals that she felt were so evident.

Liz took a deep sigh as though the telling would take some time. And it did. I sat on a stool on the opposite side of the counter, listening intently while Liz outlined a litany of disrespectful actions. The list began with me being late for an event that was at our own house. And the list continued, centered around the accusations that I was a narcissist, insular and neglectful. Plus, she had overheard me showing off our new house to a few of her friends, framing everything in the first person singular. "I found the lot." "I told the architect ..." "I decided ..." She said her contributions to the new house had been outright disregarded. "I matter," she said.

After a moment's pause, Liz added, "... and I don't like the way you fawn over my friends."

"You're jealous. That's the problem?"

"Well, I can't tell whether I should be or not. You had your arm wrapped around Grace's shoulders like you were on a date."

"I was just trying to be nice to your friends."

"I don't get credit, no credit at all. What do you think I do? You think I read magazines and get my nails done, but raising two young boys takes a lot of work, a lot of emotional work. You don't understand the strain. You're gone. And the house?

It doesn't take care of itself. And the thanks I get? Can you begin to appreciate what I'm doing? Of course, all this will fall on deaf ears. You bring home the money and pay the bills. Sure, but that's not enough, not enough in the right kind of way. The boys need you around. And I need you.

"You think you're doing fine, but I don't know how to say it more clearly. You're absent, body and mind. Of course, you won't admit ever to doing anything wrong. Never. There's something in that male ethic of yours that prevents defeat. You have to be tough all the time, never wrong, and continue to argue your side. Just onward. Off to war. You. Just like your Dad. Why is it that you men think you have to project a rock-hard exterior? Every problem is framed as a battle, only solved by getting tougher and stronger, winners and losers. It's worn me down. Cole, I hate preparing for war. I'm tired. And I pray, I so pray that my boys don't turn out like that. Like *you*."

That stung. Her anger was intense and broad. I had no clue how to respond. I truly couldn't distinguish the wheat from the chaff, what was the noise and what was the signal. Liz's list of complaints was long and disjointed, and global. What was true. What had been elevated. I knew that she wanted to be noticed. It was a constant need, like everyone. But I chose at this moment not to be defensive, to take her entire litany at face value and respond to each one, one at a time, or list all the ways that I attend to her and the boys. Topping that list would have been showing up at the frigging school function in the first place, an event I had not one iota of interest in. Second would be acting like I enjoy her friends. No, I couldn't argue the other side. It would have further escalated the problem. There was something fundamental gnawing at her, and I didn't know where it was, but there was some deeper wound.

Maybe if she had told me of her displeasures closer to the time of my infractions, I might have been better able to see my flaws and how to accordingly modify my behavior. I did want to please Liz, intensely so, but she sees me constantly failing at the job. My main challenge, one I had come to discover early on in our relationship, was how to anticipate what was going on in Liz's mind before she chose to share it with me. It was a game I was terrible at and was the first thing our marriage therapist had encouraged her to work on. "Liz, you should be more open in expressing your inner thoughts with Cole. If he hears from you what your concerns are, there is a better chance of them getting addressed. As much as you believe these things are obvious, they aren't to him." That suggestion had been lost somewhere.

I sincerely didn't believe I had done anything so terrible as to justify the intensity of her anger. And I certainly wasn't going to discuss some abstract state of mind, much less one about the generic male thought process – or lack thereof. I'd just been on my way to the garden, searching for a little quiet time. The worst part was, after everything she just spewed, if her goal was to seek greater intimacy, this unloading had the opposite effect. Liz was pushing me further away.

Liz continued, "When you're stressed, you always go ... retreat into that dark, dank depressing office or go play in your silly garden. Off on your own."

"I'm sorry, Liz, but that's just it. I just need a distraction from all the confrontations at work ... and, I guess, at home, too. Thankfully, I enjoy my so-called silly garden. For a few minutes I can relax and find a little peace."

"I'm sorry. You don't get it. Completely self-absorbed. The distance you're putting between us is growing further and further as time goes on. This isn't what I signed up for."

Not wanting to defend myself, I stayed quiet, hoping her anger would soon pass like it usually did.

Liz said nothing further, just continued to stare at me.

I then walked out of the house and made my way to my silly little garden.

I started back towards the cabin, self-consciously keeping my pace slow. The physical act of placing one foot in front of the other, one deep breath after another, combined to form a welcome meditation. The dark passage through the forest temporally erased the irritating noises from my head. Nature was again soothing my soul.

When I arrived at the porch steps, I heard the distinctive clanging of a metal spoon against the side of a large pot. Opening the door, I instantaneously felt a welcome wash of warm air. Andy had lit the potbellied stove, and it had done a quick job of heating the room. Standing proudly, artfully framed by the old fireplace hearth behind it, the squat black furnace was the focal point of the cabin's living area. It had not always been that way. A long time ago, the furnace had replaced the stone fireplace as the cabin's only source of heat. Dad permanently sealed off the fireplace not long after he bought the cabin. The primitive foundation couldn't resist the weight of the stone tower. The metaphorical heart of the house had become a potential fire hazard, and the only possible life-saving measure was a transplant.

And above, in the same place that had once been occupied by an elaborate chandelier formed from the intertwining of deer antlers, now hanging from a twisted extension cord, was a single bright bare bulb. The transformations from my last visit were jarring and not altogether positive.

Andy glanced up from his pot. "I don't suppose you've had any dinner yet."

"No, not yet."

"I've started a sauce. How about you boil some water for pasta? I need to go back outside and check the propane tank. I don't think the valve is all the way open." The sureness of

Andy's request surprised me. He'd never delivered orders to me so casually before. "I have some lettuce and tomatoes in the fridge that we can make a salad out of." I was now under his dominion.

The kitchen, in contrast to the rest of the cabin, was clean and well ordered. On an open shelf neatly arranged in rows were four of everything, likely the result of an all-in-one package that he found on sale at Walmart. Four plates. Four glasses. Four forks. Four spoons.

Andy grabbed a bag of trash and walked past me and back outside.

The long heavy wooden table still dominated the room. At one time, it had twelve or fourteen chairs lining its sides, but that evening there was just one wooden chair set next to the table, with two tall stools in front of the kitchen counter.

It wasn't difficult to imagine the table with the usual cast of characters: the waving bear mailbox neighbors and their kids, Pete's grandfather, and the occasional friend of Dad's from work. Holding court, Dad would sit at the end of the table, spinning stories about the best bends in the streams for fishing while broadly gesturing with his arms. On a good night, he also found time to sneak in one of his "how great is America" philosophies as well.

Still in their same places but a lot worse for wear, the dark red plaid sofa and the matching pair of armchairs surrounded the black furnace. They were one day short of disgusting. At that moment, I made up my mind I wouldn't be sitting on any of that furniture anytime soon. Liz would no doubt have insisted on a quick exit and a trip back to the interstate to find a modern hotel.

Where the light barely reached, in the far corner, several stacks of cardboard boxes were piled chest high. Those on the bottom were being crushed by the weight of the boxes above them, with papers erupting out of the open corners.

Andy yelled from outside the kitchen window. Unable to hear him clearly, I opened the small kitchen window above the sink, which to my surprise, glided open smoothly.

Andy repeated his question. "Can you check the gas pressure on the stove?"

I turned one of the black knobs and heard a steady hiss, "It seems to be working fine."

"I have to check a couple more things. Be back in a minute."

I opened the refrigerator door to see what foodstuffs Andy had brought in. It was the same Kenmore model I used to pull open for Popsicles. Contrary to the scratches and patches of corrosion on the front, I discovered the inside of the machine to be spotless and odor-free. Checking around the rest of the kitchen, I opened one drawer after another and then the cabinets one by one. Mostly they were empty, but what was there had been carefully thought about. The cooking utensils had been packed into plastic bags; all the spices were stored in similar-sized plastic containers, with one very large plastic container under the stove holding a variety of pots and pans.

As I started on my assignment and began the salad, Andy walked back in and went right back to work on his sauce. Opening each container and taking a deep sniff, he examined the spices individually before dipping his finger in and deciding which ones best suited his taste.

I removed a beer from the fridge and found a seat on the stool on the other side of the counter.

Glancing up from his work, Andy said, "I'm really looking forward to this weekend."

"There's so much here that I had totally forgotten about. Those plaid sofas, the stove, the long table. How many meals did we have there? Must have been hundreds. There were a lot of stories told around that table ... spread thick. It's been a long time since I sat there."

Maintaining concentration on his marinara sauce, Andy hesitated a brief moment.

"Do you need any more help?"

Andy's pace was relaxed. He covered his pot and let it simmer. "That's all right, I've got it. Why don't you go ahead and bring your things in? We have a few minutes before dinner is ready."

I grabbed my bag from the car and brought it into the cabin.

Behind the old stone fireplace, the back half of the cabin consisted of two neglected back bedrooms, and between them, a small bathroom with a rust-stained sink. To call it acceptable would be generous, but the linens were clean and folded in a neat stack on the bed, waiting for me to lay them down. On the nightstand was a round-faced, battery-operated drugstore alarm clock, surprisingly set to the correct time, the thread-thin second hand sliding steadily across the numbers. I flushed the toilet once to make sure it worked. One of the many lapses in luxury that I had forgotten about was the fact there was no shower in the house. As a child, this was rarely an issue. Dad didn't require a high level of personal hygiene while we were out in the wilderness. And us kids never found that to be a problem either. For desperate circumstances, when the caked-on mud was finally too thick, there was an outside shower. Like the water in the house, it came from a shallow well. It was amazingly cold, clear, and clean enough to drink.

As a young boy, this freedom from the details of our daily rituals was something I looked forward to, like a kid set loose at Disneyland. Upon arrival, Andy and I would sprint out of the car, drop our bags in the cabin, then head straight for the stream. At the cabin, we were untethered from civilization and loved the sheer wildness of it all, to a degree at least.

Out of the quiet, I heard my name being called. Andy and I were down by the pond setting up targets.

"Thomas!"

That familiar snapping voice. I'd done something wrong. Dad emerged from the side of the cabin, carrying a large ax off to his side.

"Thomas, listen up. I've got a job for you two. Take this," he said, shoving the ax in my direction. "I want you and Andy to go down by our road near the gate."

"Yes, sir."

"Let me finish. There's a dead tree there, not too big, that needs to be cut down. We can't let nature handle it on her own. Next big wind comes along, and it'll fall on our fence or worse, across the road."

"I'm thinking that if Andy and I were to...."

"I don't give a shit what you think." He glared at me with his dark eyes, then paused. "You boys can handle it. And when you get it down and out of the way, later on, we'll cut up the wood for the fire pile."

I leaned over to Andy and whispered, "'We' — like he's going to do anything to help us."

Hearing me, Dad grabbed my shoulder. "Listen, son – I don't need any of your damn attitude. You have a job to do. Let's get after it."

"But Dad, we've been here two days already, and all we've done is work. Can't we just do nothing for a bit?"

"Now! Get going. Rest is for the weak."

I glared back at my father. The order had been given. There was no arguing. I grabbed Andy's sleeve and started us off down the hill. "Come on. Can't win with him... never, ever."

Dad was still there, enforcing his immutable laws. No matter back at home or out at the cabin, respect for his authority was number one. Rule Two was, as the old joke goes, to refer back to Rule One. After that, I can't remember any specific rules. It depended on the day but with the general effect that a certain daily ration of work was expected.

Although there was a good side, once our chores were done, we were unsupervised with free reign to explore wherever we wanted. There were plenty of positive memories, and by coming back here, I was hoping to rediscover a few.

At a later age, my attitudes about the cabin and all its responsibilities shifted entirely to the negative. I began to wonder why someone would desire a vacation home that required so much upkeep and, despite the work, was perpetually substandard.

When I came out of the bedroom, I saw the table set, with Andy tasting from the steaming pot of sauce.

He had brought out a second chair from the desk in his bedroom. It matched the one at the table. Both ladder-back chairs, worn and splintered along the edges, colored a hue that can only be called old brown. Apparently, these were the last two survivors of the original set. I remembered them having matching striped cushions, but those were apparently gone leaving just the hard naked worn wood.

We sat across the table from one another, eating quietly in alternating rhythms of salad, pasta and beer. I was tired from the drive and anxious for a decent night's sleep. Back in the day, the cabin had held dozens of family events with wives and kids, full of energy and life. Other times, it was just Dad, Andy and me, but just the two of us, eating alone? I don't believe that had ever happened.

The dinner was a nice salve, but I wasn't sure how to start a conversation with Andy. I hardly wanted to start with the probate update. Marcus had taken that worry off our hands, and the process seemed to be going smoothly. Enjoying Andy's pasta, I simultaneously tried to think what common ground we might have left. Andy concentrated on his meal, and I wondered what was going on in his mind.

I pulled back the last slug of my beer and watched as Andy finished his dinner.

Andy broke the silence, "I'm sure you know, but I'm pissed about the for-sale sign up near the gate."

"Hey, I'm really sorry about that. If it makes you feel any better, I'm pissed as well. I had asked a realtor to look into what we might get for the property. I never expected him to do that on his own. I'll get it taken down ASAP."

"Okay, I see. But you must know it made me feel like crap. Like my opinion doesn't matter. You do know you need my consent. And just to make myself ultra-clear again, I don't have any interest in selling. Period."

"Like I said, it'll come down. It was a mistake. It's gone. Sorry. But, in any case, it's not like anybody is going to drive by the sign in the next day or two."

If my intention was to eventually convince Andy to sell, this was the worse tactic ever. His forceful opinion didn't bother me. I knew time would be my ally. It did bother me, however, that the sign was now a wedge when Andy and I were struggling to find common ground. I felt bad for Andy. I did. I wanted to find a normal brotherly relationship between us, but I had no notion what that should look like nor how to get there.

Andy, perhaps on the same page, offered a way forward. "There's a couple of things I'd like to do together while we're out here. You know, there are a lot of Dad's things stacked in the corners. Like those crushed boxes and even back in his closet. I'm not sure what's here. Most probably it's just his work records. But there's a lot of it here, and we need to go through it. If it's trash I'll haul it out. Maybe, I don't know; there's something worth saving besides his old shirts. Of course, it's too late tonight to worry about any of that, but we could try to sort through things tomorrow ... Or, in the alternative, if you want, we could leave that work until later and instead do a little deer hunting tomorrow."

"Hunting?" I laughed. The idea was absurd. "Sorry ... I didn't mean to laugh. That's rude. But I don't think so. I haven't touched a gun in years. Besides, just the thought of shooting a living thing. I feel like I've evolved past that." I instantly realized that might be taken as a judgment. "Don't get me wrong, though. It's perfectly fine for you to hunt. I don't care. But for me it just doesn't feel natural any more."

"You don't have to decide this second. But, here's how I see tomorrow starting out —"

Andy's enthusiasm became clear, and his plans were well thought out. First, my brother shared the chores he intended to accomplish in the morning; I listened carefully, and at the same time, with the small clues gleaned from Andy's brief itinerary, I was reconstructing my mental map of the property, its many landmarks. But while listening, I was also questioning. I did not understand the necessity of half the chores Andy laid out. It was like Dad all over again. What on earth could be gained by fixing the fence line on the northside of the property? That fence served no purpose; it was keeping nothing out or in. It sounded like so much meaningless work, especially in the aftermath of Dad's death and the uncertainty about the property's eventual disposition. But in no way did I want to argue. It was just one day of being with Andy. And after my short visit was over, I wouldn't care about any of these details.

He interrupted his summary with a question, "... and you know that stream coming down from the south line?"

My partially reconstructed mental map was unclear on that detail. "Yeah, I think so."

"I want go by there to make sure it's clear, that no trees have fallen into it. I wouldn't want it to dam up."

"You mean the stream coming out of the government's property? Does it still have fish in it?"

"When the water is high enough. Sometimes. Haven't been up that way in a while. Why?"

"Isn't that where we built the weir?" I asked.

"Didn't catch any fish that day."

"Exactly! Not a one. But wasn't that such a blast? We were jumping in and out of that freezing knee-deep water, trying to scoop those little guys out with our hands. I can still see all those baby trout scurrying around inside our trap. I think every last one of them found their way out, and those couple that were slower than the rest were way too slippery ... they were impossible to catch. But we tried."

"Was fun. A net would have been handy."

"True, but counter to the point — not how the Indians did it. You remember? Dad explained to us how to build it, how they would read the stream and discover where the water was calmer, how deep the water should be, and how to stack and layer the rocks. We understood the concept, but, hell, we were what ... eleven and eight?"

I had Andy smiling. And it was nice to see.

"I bet we can find that same spot again," he said. "It's on the way to where I'd like to take you hunting."

Andy glanced over at the pot-bellied stove, grabbed a couple of logs and threw them in, "We need to see if we can keep this thing going all night. It might get a little cool back in your room."

19

I finished the dishes, opened the refrigerator, and pulled out a couple more beers.

"There is something of Dad's I'd like to show you," Andy said with some unusual enthusiasm. He'd obviously been thinking about whatever he was about to reveal to me.

He disappeared into the other room, returning with an old, small suitcase. From its size and design, it looked like an artifact from an old black and white film of a hatted, trimly tailored businessman stepping into a sleeper cabin of a train. The leather was smooth and a rusty, dark brown. There were a few minor scratches along its edges, but overall, it was in good shape for an antique.

"Dad's closet had a few things in it," Andy started explaining. "Boots, a large assortment of flannel shirts. Clothes mostly. But on the top shelf, I found this. It's locked, and there's definitely something rattling around inside. A bit of mystery. I thought it would be fun if we opened it up together, maybe like a time capsule."

On either side of the leather handle were two keyed locks, although conveniently tied to the handle was a red string and two identical keys. The two locks snapped open with ease. Inside we discovered a loose cluster of a dozen or so photos, along with a large legal-size manila envelope. We briefly studied the jumble in front of us before we each pulled out a picture, examined it, laid it out on the table, then pulled out another. We spread the pictures across the table, looking for any connections between the people in the pictures. Scrutinizing each one closely.

"See anything familiar?" Andy asked.

"No. Not me. Dad never showed us a single old picture, except those couple from his wedding. That was it."

Silently, we continued shuffling the images as if we were trying to solve a jigsaw puzzle. A couple of faces repeated, but still, it was difficult to decipher the code. Although, one picture intrigued me. I pulled it close and examined it in detail. The setting was either someone's large dining room or, more probably, a restaurant, being that the background was a wallpaper painted with a hazy, pastoral scene. Dominating the composition was a long table with a tablecloth loosely draped down to the floor. It must have been taken just after dinner. Although there was no food on the table, there were many half-filled glasses and, off to one side, a pair of candlesticks with no candles. I assumed they had been fully burned. The photo was organized as a multi-generational portrait, centrally seated in two matching chairs was an elderly couple. Their refined clothes were in sharp contrast with their weathered faces. Behind the table were younger couples, men in suits and women with feathered hats. And on the floor in front of the table were three young children. I squinted intently at their faces and, in particular, the oldest of the three, who was dressed in a coarse tweed jacket and a short tie.

"I couldn't say for certain, but could that be Dad as a little boy?" There was something in the face that seemed to connect to the older man.

"Mean anything to you?" I asked.

I handed Andy the picture.

"I don't see it," he shrugged his shoulders. "But I have a hard time remembering someone's face from one week to the next. The style of the clothes and the setting makes me think it might be from the generation before Dad. Maybe if you're seeing a resemblance, it's our grandfather."

Andy double-checked the interior pockets of the suitcase but found nothing else.

I looked inside the legal-size envelope and discovered ten or twelve smaller yellowed envelopes. The script on each was confident florid, yet precisely crafted, and they all appeared to be written in the same hand. They, just like the pictures, were from some ancient past. All had been sent to the same address in Ohio, with the same name on the address, but it was not a name too familiar to either Andy or me. I carefully opened a couple of the fragile envelopes and unfolded the letters inside.

I speculated they were written in German — a language which neither Andy nor I could read. As I examined the text looking for anything familiar, I asked, "What does one do with old stuff like this? Do you suppose we keep it or think we just toss it?"

"No," Andy said, offended by the suggestion. "You don't know yet if they're important somehow. Absolutely, we keep 'em. Who knows, one day, we might find that there's some connection to us."

"Even if these people are related to us, who really cares?"

"Maybe your boys." Andy looked at me with an, *of course you idiot,* look. "One day, they might have an interest in their family history, even if it's simply something about the aura of their ancestors' lives. That alone could have meaning to them — no? Dad kept all this for a reason. And what's the downside? It takes up almost zero space."

"I hear you. But in truth, they aren't anybody's memories any more."

"It just makes me sad to throw them out. It'll be as if these people never even existed. There'll be no evidence left. Their faces will no longer live in anyone's memory. Their faces vanished, never to be seen again."

"Yeah, I get it. It seems a shame, but if we can't make sense of them, nobody can."

I reached for a third letter. Through the top corner, a straight pin attached a small newspaper clipping to its back. Wary of the pin and the brittle newsprint, I pulled it out slowly. It was a short one by two-inch column article with the headline reading: "Accident Kills Two."

I read the article once, and then after not fully comprehending what I'd just read, I read through it slowly again. The victims' names were Mr. and Mrs. Cole. I couldn't believe what was so clearly factual. My heart was suddenly racing. This was bizarre news.

"Accident Kills Two." I repeated the headline, adding, "It goes on here to say that their teenage son was the driver. But Dad's name isn't mentioned." I turned my attention from the clipping, looking up at Andy. "Clearly though, Dad was driving."

"This ... this is ... I don't understand." Andy's face contorted into some combination of shock and confusion. "He told us about the crash, but ..." Andy tried to frame this new information. "... Does it say anything about rain or ice?"

"Nothing about the weather. Just says, 'one car accident' and on a 'Highway 40'... nothing about an investigation or any other details. It's a short piece ... what, three sentences."

There was a handwritten date on the top of the clipping. It was the year Dad turned seventeen, and Andy and I agreed, also the same year that Dad said he had entered the Marines. I carefully handed Andy the fragile newsprint and let him read it for himself.

"I don't get it. Why did he hide this from us?" Andy asked.

"Maybe it was embarrassment? ... Guilt? ... Shame?" Maybe he was avoiding the pain of the loss. Trying to forget. I speculated wildly. I had no evidence as to his emotions. "You know, he had always told us that the long jagged scar across his forearm was from falling into a plate-glass window. And if he lied about one thing, why not another? Maybe he got the scar from the car accident and made up the other story about chasing a dog — that story never sounded true to me."

"Would you call not telling us about the accident a lie?"

"The most believable lies are ones that contain some element of truth. Maybe in his telling of the story, he was thinking about the car window. So maybe over time, it became true to him. Weirdly, all of a sudden, I feel disappointment in the man. A single lie puts into doubt everything he ever said."

Andy looked at me blankly. He sunk into silence, and I couldn't sense where his thoughts had retreated.

"Are you okay?" I asked.

He gently nodded, but said nothing.

I surveyed all the meaningless photos and letters spread out on the table between us.

"And what's the deal with all these pictures. Why'd he keep 'em? If he wanted to hide his past, wouldn't he just throw all this out?"

"Well, that's in character," Andy said, back to his normal disposition. "He never threw anything out. It might be this suitcase is all that he had left from his parents' lives."

"But what kind of history is this when you don't have any understanding of what's left to you? Like these pictures prove, our family history is limited to just one generation, and there's not much there. We can't connect with anything beyond that. We have no roots to speak of."

The evening was getting old, and with no place to go and with this new information about the accident, we took a new interest in the photos and examined them again. But after several minutes of quiet shuffling, neither of us had discovered any new insights. I wasn't sure what to do with this news.

We repacked the suitcase and left it sitting at one end of the table.

I went outside and leaned against the porch rail. Night had settled in around the cabin. The moon was still high in the sky. A light wind rustled over the pond, pushing rows of silvery ripples across reflections of the dark mountains.

With both of our jackets in hand, Andy came out to join me. Sitting in a chair, he set down a couple of beers on the floor next to him.

"So Tommy," Andy said as he shared my gaze of the pond. "How are you feeling? Like being back in the wilderness?"

As I walked across the porch to sit next to him, one annoying board after another creaked underfoot. I settled down into the chair next to Andy and grabbed a beer. "Not sure. Feeling a bit unsettled right now. I don't know if I belong here." We sat there quietly together, awkwardly. I took in the view, breathing in the cool air.

20

Late in the night, restless, uncomfortable and no longer able to resist the cold, I yanked the thin mattress off its sagging frame. I dragged it out of my bedroom and set it down in the corner of the living room floor, close to the warmth of the potbellied stove. The stove was doing its job, but for the front room only. The uninsulated cabin walls offered only a meager defense against the cold. From my youth, I remembered many nights like this. Staying warm seemed to take less effort back then. I often had, without complaint, slept in my clothes, tightly cocooned in a single thick blanket. But unlike in youth, a time when falling and staying asleep was never a problem; sleep had of late become troublingly elusive. I spent a good part of that first night simply staring at the ceiling, not so much trying to untangle the birds nest of emotions but instead hoping to visualize, visualize the origins and extent of each strand and thread. There were many. It wasn't so much a worry. My mind was busy, very busy, reviewing minor annoying details, the borders between this version of this new world and the one from my memories: Dad and his absence; Andy as a child and the adult in the kitchen cooking pasta; the confusion with the photos; the ragged cabin and its past tidiness. The constants, too: the rippling pond and the smell of the trees.

The newfound warmth of the front room relaxed me. I looked out the un-curtained windows, studying the different qualities of black wrapping the back of the house. The trees were several shades darker than the night sky that rose high. In the gaps between the trees' high angles, a small array of stars, some bright, some more muted. The room's warmth and the relaxing view worked their magic and soothed me into a deep sleep. My next recollection was looking back out of those same windows, seeing in the deepest gaps between the trees the eastern sky starting to brighten into a light blue haze. Checking my watch, I felt that there was little chance of falling back to sleep. Sunrise would be soon.

While quietly picking up my things, returning them to my room and back into their proper order, I glanced over to Andy's room. I noticed his door was cracked open, his bed already empty and made. I couldn't recall hearing Andy move about or leave. He must have snuck out during one of my moments of sleep.

Making my way over to the kitchen, I tried to turn on the lights but quickly remembered that the generator was still off. In the dim light, and adding to my confusion, I found on the counter a large French press filled with brewed coffee, a still-warm kettle of water on the stove, and all the ingredients to make pancakes miraculously arranged on the counter.

I slid open the kitchen window. The wash of cool air was refreshing. Awake, I leaned my head out to look for my brother. Down toward the woodpile, I spotted his silhouette near the shed, silently framed inside a flashlight's beam. By the looks of it, he was pulling out and rearranging tools. It was strange not only to witness such work going on at this early hour in the dimmest of light but also to see the way Andy moved. His actions appeared like that of an old man. He was somehow smaller and less vigorous in his movements than I had remembered him being just the evening before. And then the realization hit me: Andy was now about the same age as Dad had been when we were teenagers. The busy little man working at the shed could easily have been Dad.

Seeing Andy consumed with his work, I was attracted by the opportunity for a bit of solitude. I poured a coffee, grabbed my jacket, and went to sit on the porch. I studied the sky as it slowly faded to light.

After the sky achieved a silvery blue, I set off walking down the road back towards the front gate. The same path as last night, leaving Andy in the opposite direction, alone with his busy work. After a couple of hundred yards, the cabin was out of sight. The air was noticeably cooler under the trees. I turned off the road and strolled deeper into the forest. The soil underfoot was damp and layered with recently fallen leaves. It was almost silent except for an occasional crack of a dried twig or a bird fluttering above the bushes. A light wind weaved through the upper branches, rustling the leaves. I had walked less than a few dozen yards and already felt completely isolated from any sense of civilization. Pausing, I stood, observing the space surrounding me. I reached out and slid my fingers across the trunk of a pine tree, feeling its harsh texture like it was a new experience. I caressed the soft reaching ferns. I knelt down and placed my hands on the cool, damp earth. I closed my eyes, absorbing the sensations, breathing in the subtle scents emanating from the trees. I hadn't been within this restorative peace in ages.

It was the exact same forest I had been in years and years ago — the same trees, the same trail, the same smells. When Andy and I ran these trails as boys, we never paused to touch a tree or stroke a fern. We were on a mission - to the outcrop where we could practice a bit of rock climbing, up to the next vista, over to the next peak. We didn't stop or have the inclination to pause along the way to notice. Intellectually, I grasped that in that long gap of time since I was a boy, everything had changed: that particular tree was not the same tree as thirty years ago, nor that fern, nor that birdsong. But on another plane, it remained as it was, exactly the same. Time felt deeper. The present and past interconnected, more than unchanging, unchangeable. The forest's constant renewal erased time — at least any human conception of it.

At dinner last night, Andy had said, "The last time we were together at the table, just the three of us, I was twelve, and you were fifteen." I was caught off guard by the clarity of Andy's memory. At the time, his interjection had merely been a non-sequitur in our broader conversation. But his memory was accurate. It was like a flip of a switch. That day, while not always at the top of my mind, never drifted far below the surface. I'd never realized before that Andy held the exact same memory as well. He was so young at the time. I had never revisited that moment with anybody, including Andy.

That moment occurred during my freshman year in high school. At a point in my life when baseball practices, games and tournaments were consuming my weekends. And there were girlfriends and parties. As a socially active athlete, I had plenty of things I wanted to do, people to see. The last place I wanted to be was alone with my father and younger brother out in the woods, isolated from society. As a teenager, those weekends felt like a prison sentence. I was way past playacting the cowboys and Indians that Andy and I had mimed when we were younger. The adventurous explorer was not a role I wanted to play any more. At fifteen, it all seemed like kid's play, a thing of the past. I was ready for a new life.

The tension between Dad and me peaked that weekend. It became crystal clear. Dad stopped asking me to come up to the cabin; didn't even make the pretense of an invitation. But at least afterward, on those weekends he'd come up to the cabin with Andy, he trusted me to be on my own. We both knew our mountain time together was over. I moved on, never looking back until now. With Andy dragging me back, I never gave a thought as to whether he was aware of the break between Dad and me or whether or not it meant anything to him. Andy seemed to be such a little kid back then.

The taste for coffee had come back to me, but when I sipped the last bit, I found it cold and bitter. I walked back out of the forest, onto the road, continuing on towards the phone spot. I wanted to catch up with Michael. Our conversation was very brief. There'd been was no progress, and we were still in the same untenable position. He did tell me he had set up an emergency morning meeting with our partners, which was a sign that things were not yet under control. I was more than a little perturbed that he hadn't clued me in earlier. But I withheld my protest, as my isolation from the phone was a valid excuse. Plus, it was a fait accompli, and it indicated some evidence of forward motion. I told him plainly that I wanted to be included on the call. But, the problem was that it was set to begin in just forty-five minutes. Nine my time, eleven back at the office — and I was in the mountains with bad reception. There were additional messages from Steve and some of the other employees that I had to ignore for the moment. My acute desire to solve this nagging problem gripped me. I felt desperately disconnected from the office and intensely wanted to end this deal's up-in-the-air status. There was an instant tidal change in my disposition.

In a small panic, I called Peterman and was pleased to learn that his office had a robust wi-fi connection. He offered me his front room as a temporary office. Elated, I rushed back to the cabin.

As soon as the cabin came into sight, I heard the generator running and saw the bluish fluorescent lights glowing from the kitchen window.

When I opened the screen door, I was out of breath. Andy was busy in the kitchen.

"Sit down. I've got breakfast ready."

Unbothered by my presence, Andy continued his work in the kitchen. In the center of the table was a large stack of pancakes, with a nearby stick of butter and a large container of syrup. This was a sight that I hadn't seen in a long time — not something Liz would allow in the house. Andy took out a half-dozen pieces of bacon from the skillet, brought a plate over to the table and sat down.

Then, noticing me still standing, he asked, "You okay?"

"I've got to go down to Peterman's. He's letting me use his place for a conference call."

"No breakfast?"

"I can't. I'm really sorry, but I really can't."

With all my rushing, I was able to quickly set up at Peterman's and was ready to go three minutes before nine. The technology worked better than expected. Waiting for the call to begin, I peered through the screen, seeing the conference table and a couple of partners in their usual seats, typing on their computers. I saw Steve, head down and focused on his machine just like the others. A few stragglers entered the room. It was the same pattern for each; they each offered a cursory "Morning guys," but not a person responded. In the background the digital clock ticked relentlessly well past our start time, and I was ready.

When Michael joined in from Houston, the clock read 11:08:04, and the conference call began in earnest. Around the table, they debated the accuracy of the cash flow projections. But I wasn't in the mood for a line-by-line analysis. A rectal exam would be quicker and more revealing. My mind was not in the proper frame to focus on these minute details. I was more interested in the big picture, if we had convinced the London folks to stay in the deal or if we'd found a better Plan B. I kept my mike on mute and listened in.

After fifteen minutes, Michael chimed in. He let the financial people leave the room and told the rest of us to wait while he brought in our attorney. The clock marched on, and I could barely make out the gentle white noise of clicking keyboards.

My table in Peterman's store was the same table where my dad had once sat and visited with his friends. Crossing my arms, I leaned back in the chair, trying not to get anxious. The large plate-glass window framed a clear view of the freeway, the intersection and the front parking lot. It was a good place to monitor who was coming and going. I watched the traffic sail down the freeway. So many people in a hurry to go someplace else, along with the occasional pickup making the turn onto the county road. Looking past the visual noise at ground level, ignoring all the concrete, my attention shifted to the irregularly shaped mountains in the near distance. The slow pace of the cloud's shadows as they subtly transformed shapes crossing the ridges and valleys took my attention away from the computer screen. It was a sharp contrast to the busy little motions of people running down the freeway. I could appreciate Dad's attraction to this spot and its view.

My screen all of a sudden timed out and faded to black. I touched a key to bring it back to life, but nothing new was happening on the other end. Michael's screen within a screen was still blank. Another ten minutes passed, and I finally took my mike off mute. I asked anyone listening where Michael had gone. No one had an answer. Nor did they look bothered. They all continued with their typing.

My frustration with the meeting was acute. Nothing productive was being achieved, and from my place of detachment, I felt powerless. The contrasting dissonance between the sterile fluorescent office setting inside my computer and the green mountains outside Peterman's window made me nauseous. Observing my office in this context made it feel like a very unfriendly place, one that I wasn't anxious to return to. I put the mike back on mute and continued my watching of the clouds.

Eventually frustrated, I called Michael, but he didn't answer. I lost my patience and closed my computer. Unsure of what the next steps should be, I returned to my view out the window. My fascination felt primal, part of some inborn consciousness — or were my childhood experiences with Dad and Andy what actually cultivated this allure? Within the mere minutes of my gazing at the mountains, the patterns evolved moment by moment in their shading and colors. It was easy to recall how, depending on the season, the mountains would be awash in green, brightly lit by a summer sun; or alternately, in late fall, wrapped in shades of grayish brown, the colors blending, absent a clear edge, with the cold, clouded sky, appearing soft, but perhaps more stoic; and in the winter, the crystal white snow sharp against the deepest possible blue sky.

This uncanny intimacy with the mountains felt familiar and calming, like the resurrection of a long-forgotten friend. I started to think that somehow in my effort to bury my bad memories, the good memories had disappeared with them. But apparently, locked in storage, not entirely erased.

Michael's number flashed on my phone. When I picked up, he quickly asked, "Hey man, did we lose you?"

I had outlined a long list of questions in my head: "*What was the deal with the attorney?*" "*Is there some problem going on behind the scenes I don't know about?*" "*Are there any possible new partners?*" and on and on. What I said instead was simply, "I'm worried about this deal."

"I know what your priorities are — you don't want to lose any of your money," Michael responded. "I've got good people working on all the possible options. You should just relax and focus on your brother."

"I know. I know — Andy is my job for the moment. That's why I'm here. But ..."

I let my sentence hang unfinished. I withheld from Michael my internal doubts, the anxiety I felt eating at me. Michael might have known me better than I had let anyone else know me, maybe even Liz. I had met him five years before her. But, our relationship was purely set in the context of business, whether explicitly or in its related activities, be it golf outings or steakhouse dinners. He had witnessed me perform under all kinds of stress, but it was only rarely that I shared my personal thoughts with him, even the most generic ones: about Liz, the boys, Andy, or my father. He knew something of my struggles with Andy; how I had periodically buffered his financial difficulties and shepherded him through his lawsuit. But while Michael knew the broad details and certainly had some empathy, we never unveiled our personal pains to one another. For someone I had to work with every day, it was certainly the correct posture. Michael couldn't understand the deep distance and mutual disregard between Dad and me. Nor could he sympathize with those feelings, being that I never shared them with him in the first place. We were business partners, nothing more.

"That's why you're there. Don't worry about any of these details for the moment. I'll untie this mess. Can't you trust me?" Michael asked.

"Of course," I answered. For some unexplained reason, Michael's reassurances relaxed me. Maybe because I had no choice but to rely on him. I needed to trust him. I continued our conversation with some perfunctory updates, sharing some of the issues regarding my dad's estate, issues I knew he could relate to.

"You can't believe the tall piles of papers stacked everywhere. And file cabinets with a million years of receipts. He never threw out anything. It has an order, but an idiosyncratic one and one that's taking us some time to figure out. Lots of handwritten leases, and worse — we're discovering he made a lot of handshake deals with the tenants."

"Sounds quaint and old-fashioned."

"Lucky is what it is. Lucky nobody ever sued. He trusted people to do what they said they'd do. He was so naive, but you know, for all those years, he got away with it."

"Those might have been better days. Today, you can work for months and months, creating an eighty-page document, and regardless, if the other guy wants to sue, they're going to sue, no matter how thick the document is. You never even see the other guy's face, much less shake his hands."

"Thankfully, we have a patient attorney who is doing a great job sorting things out."

My phone vibrated. Andy was calling, but I rejected it and stayed with Michael.

"So, where's the problem?" Michael asked.

"My brother and I are not quite on the same page — about whether or not to sell the mountain property. You'd think he could use the cash. He's only got a part-time job."

"So there's money out there?"

"Over the years, my Dad ended up assembling a nice size tract of land. I think it's worth a lot of money. It's nestled in a long valley backing up to a government wilderness area. You can walk for days without seeing anyone. It's beautiful — and who wouldn't love to buy a little retreat in the mountains? Since I've been out here and looking around, I'm surprised from what I'm hearing and seeing ... lots of new developments cropping up."

This news piqued Michael's curiosity. He quizzed me about the acres, the roads and double-checked my math on the economics. Talking numbers, not feelings, disguised my tension with Andy as one of business and not anything personal; the sort of shading I had no interest in sharing with Michael.

"So, what's the deal?" Michael asked. "Sounds like a good time to sell."

"And the cash would help us reconfigure our Atlantic City deal."

"I don't think so. Your timing is way off for this deal. You can't pull off a real estate deal of that size quick enough. We have to concentrate on more immediate options."

My phone vibrated again. "Hey Michael, that's Andy's calling. But, before I go, did anything good come of the meeting?"

"Didn't we just agree? I'll find us the best resolution. Go. I've got Bob working on a new option."

"You sure he's the right guy?"

"Quit worrying." Michael hung up.

I picked up Andy's call. He told me to stay at Peterman's. He wanted to run some errands together and, on his way, would pick me up. I went back to my view and waited.

Ten minutes later, Andy stopped his pickup in front of Peterman's front door. I got into the passenger's seat. Leaving the transmission in park, Andy turned to me.

"How did your call go?"

"Not sure... at least not yet. By the way, where are we going?"

"Down the road a bit, to the Walmart. I want to buy some more ammo."

"Ammo? For what?"

"You know, we talked about going deer hunting. You still down with that?"

"Well, that was your idea."

"Oh, come on. You don't want to go? I don't want to force you into anything you're uncomfortable with. But really, it'd be fun."

"You mean with rifles and all," I said in the sarcastic voice that only one brother can use with another.

"You're an idiot," Andy replied, his voice equally filled with sarcasm. "Of course, ... or would you rather go bowling?"

"Man, I haven't shot a gun since..."

"I'm guessing, since the last time you were here... when you and Dad had that fight."

I was fifteen, sitting on the cabin's porch, rifle across my lap, wiping the barrel with a lightly oiled cloth. Of all the rules we had to follow regarding keeping our stuff in order, the one I somewhat enjoyed was cleaning my rifle. There was something about the blue steel barrel and the slick feel of the oil that made me appreciate the art of tooling metal, manipulating the pieces into a precision work of art.

The screen door suddenly snapped shut. Quickly followed by two thunderous steps on the hollow porch. Then as if hit by a cannon shot, me, the chair, and the rifle went flying off the steps. Strewn in the dirt, laid out like a rag, I looked back up to the source of this unexpected violence. He had planted his boot squarely on the back of the chair and kicked. Hard. My idle daydreams immediately extinguished. Dad came down off the porch, towering over me with his scarred right arm, flexed, ready to strike.

"Damn it! If I've told you once, I've told you a million times." He grabbed me by the arm and yanked me up. "When you're done with your tools. You clean them up. And then you put them back in the shed — back where they belong. Now get after it."

"But dad, I was ..."

"Don't talk back. Now go!"

"Andy needed help with ..."

"You take care of your chores, and he'll take care of his."

"But, Dad, Andy doesn't know how to..."

He swiftly swung a blow across my jaw." Don't smartass me! I said no talking back, and I mean it."

Frozen by fear, I resisted the impulse to examine my face. Instead, I kept a watchful eye on the monster. Not sure what I was supposed to do next, I cautiously wiped a bit of dust from my pants.

He started in again, "I don't know what it is with you." He paused, looked like he was thinking hard. And then, suddenly, to my instant relief, he turned and walked back inside the cabin, muttering, "You can't ever finish anything properly."

I took in a deep breath, but I was still trembling. I lifted the chair onto the porch, putting it back in its place. Then bent over to pick up the rifle. The screen door snapped shut again. Dad reappeared this time with his plaid jacket on. He was heading out on some sort of mission. He came back to me. "Thomas, what the hell are you doing? Quit dawdling and get after it."

He grabbed me by the sleeves and got in my face again. "You know what? When we get back, you're going to stop wasting your valuable time throwing that stupid fucking baseball around. Where do you think that's going to get you? You need to spend more time with your books — that's why you're in school, not to play games."

He loosened his grip; his face was still two inches from mine, "How do you expect to get anywhere in life? I really don't understand you. Maybe try taking a clue from your brother. He knows what's expected of him."

"What did I do so wrong?"

At that, he turned from me and took one step towards the shed. Stopped yet again. Almost as if he had forgotten something. He turned. Stared at me, his eyes irate and fiery, "You know. You're a worthless piece of shit. Never going to amount to a hill of beans."

As he walked away, I saw him from behind, shaking his head. I pulled a single round out of my pocket, placed it in the chamber, raised the rifle, and put the bead squarely on my father's back. With my finger lightly on the trigger, I put the crosshairs on the plaid jacket and followed it down the hill.

Five steps. Ten steps. A dozen. As Dad turned the corner and out of sight, a shot burst out. I wasn't surprised. A small puff of grayish smoke erupted off the pine tree next to the shed. I stayed steady, with my eye to the sight.

The shot's echo recoiled back sharply but quickly dissipated.

Silence.

I continued looking downrange. A minute passed, an hour? I couldn't tell.

I heard the wind blowing through the trees.

I lowered the gun.

Time lost measure.

No response. I waited. There never was one. Not that day. Not thirty years later. My father and I never talked of this moment.

My heart wanted to erupt like a volcano out of my chest.

I sucked in a deep breath, then another. I checked the rifle to make sure the chamber was empty and then went to put the tools back in their proper place.

I walked up the hill to do my chores for the last time.

"Fuck you. Fuck you, old man." I said quietly to myself.

Was Andy's use of the word "fight" some sort of euphemism? But for what? What did he know? Andy wasn't there. He didn't witness the moment. I certainly didn't ever talk to him about it. I wondered now if, at some point, he had talked to Dad about it? If so, what might Dad have said to Andy? Clearly, Andy knew about the break in our relationship — that was plainly evident. My relationship with Dad from that point onward was, to put it mildly, cold. But the shot — did Andy know about that? Or did he just sense my anger? This moment, some thirty years later, sitting in Andy's truck in front of Peterman's, I had no appetite for reopening those emotions.

I chose not to probe for those answers.

"Andy, I don't know if I can stay out here any longer. This deal at work is blowing up. And I really should get back to the office ASAP. It's not your fault, you know, but out here, I'm feeling out of touch, so far from everything."

"That's kind of the point."

"I should head back home in the morning," I said to Andy, trying to sound assertive but feeling tentative.

"You aren't serious? We made plans."

Although Andy's sympathy skills weren't great, if he had been sensitive, at the beginning of this reunion, of my malevolent feelings towards Dad, and if he had any modicum of compassion, he would have been aware that this so-called fight was a subject to be avoided. But on the other hand, his mentioning of the fight was probably innocent, and he had no intention whatsoever of opening up a discussion about my past wounds. Probably, I overreacted to an instantaneous feeling. It erupted inside of me unfiltered. Andy didn't need to know.

"You've told Liz you're spending another night here." Andy continued. "In fact, I have the strong impression that she's happy you're taking this break. You need it. I can see your stress; it's all over you. And your work? You told me, as well, and just last night, that it's beyond your control."

Listening to Andy's voice, I wanted to give my brother what he needed. But I felt a growing internal discomfort, a compression around my heart. I could plainly see the highway in front of me. My instinctual yearning was to get back on it and head home. I had no interest in putting a rifle in my hands again.

"Yeah, but that's not a good feeling. It's like I've been demoted, cut out of the process." I said.

When I had agreed to join Andy, defying my nagging id, I'd hoped that I could see this remote and beautiful garden as the refuge it truly was. I had hoped for a brief separation from the daily burdens of my life. I had thought the bruises of history had faded and healed. How naive I'd been, they all were finding a way to follow me out to the middle of nowhere.

"Well, there you go, Tommy. You've got no reason to leave. You should feel lucky that you've got somebody you trust to run things."

"When I'm not in control, bad things happen."

"Believe me, I've learned, control is an illusion. The world is chaotic and essentially indecipherable."

"You're not helping."

"You know hunting is ninety-nine percent just a walk in the woods. Relax, unburden yourself. Let yourself enjoy this beautiful spot. If you went back, you'd just be sitting there wringing your hands. Wouldn't it be better to stay here, breathing in all this cleansing fresh air? At least here, there's a chance you'll find a bit of peace. Can't you just take a load off for one brief weekend? You'll be back in civilization by Monday morning. What can you possibly accomplish before then anyway?"

I had no rational response. Andy was being entirely reasonable, but I wanted to continue fighting his logic. I was feeling manipulated, entrapped inside Andy's scheme. Although, that's not how Andy operated. He was being authentic. He enjoyed hunting and wanted the camaraderie of his brother. What could be wrong with that?

But just the thought of staying at the cabin surrounded by all those toxic memories invoked disquiet. The last thing I wanted to do was unbury ancient arguments and artifacts, accidentally or purposefully. I didn't want to stumble onto a heart-to-heart conversation about some childish feelings. I had long ago moved beyond them; sealed them in a box, and locked the closet door. At least I had thought so. Now, they were flowing through me unabated like fish through our weir.

I was a weak person posturing as a strong one. I wanted a physical separation from my bad feelings.

But leaving felt like a mistake.

Sitting inside Andy's truck, I was feeling claustrophobic. It was hard to breathe. Even in one of the world's most isolating places, I still didn't feel far enough away. I had nowhere else to go. There was no place further away. I had to be there with myself. Just Andy and myself.

I'd have to make the best of it and stay upbeat. My brother wanted to move forward; I realized that much and I liked that. I heard the excitement in his voice about us spending time together. I felt that saying "Yes" was thus pleasing him in the right way. I didn't want to create any unnecessary tension in our relationship.

"That's why I thought I'd make it easy," Andy said. "We can practice shooting a little, set up some targets... just like the old days. You always enjoyed that. It's like riding a bike, something you never forget once you learn. Once you start back, you'll remember how much you loved it. You were an ace — for sure, the best shot between us."

"You're right. I've been overly tense about work. Sorry for being such a yo-yo."

"Well, finally. Glad you're agreeing with me for once." Without hearing me dissent, Andy assumed I was agreeing. Internally though, I wasn't agreeing as much as giving in.

"Thanks," Andy said. "I really appreciate this."

"But I don't have a license," I said, my last attempt at a lame objection.

"Technically, you're right. But you know as well as I do, we've never ever seen a warden out here. We'll be fine. Trust me."

I had no intention of shooting a deer, but Andy was insistent. For him the trip to Walmart was a part of the family ritual, and I no longer wanted to interrupt the flow. This expedition was all a part of his sincere desire to create new memories. I couldn't disappoint him, and I was worn out from arguing — not with Andy but with myself. My anxieties felt misplaced and immature. I needed to be a man and do what was required. Stand strong, step up. But ironically, doing so made me feel deferential. I didn't like that feeling, never had, don't think anybody does. I just couldn't bring myself to say, "No. No, I don't want to go hunting, shoot anything, not now, not ever."

"I made you a promise and I want to keep it. There is no other place I need to be than with my brother. Wherever you want to take me, count me in. That's why we're here — together."

"Tomorrow morning, I'll set up the targets. And then in the afternoon, we'll go looking for some deer." Andy's voice was bright with excitement. I loved hearing his tone. "At a minimum, you'll enjoy the walk. I promise you that, brother to brother."

21

"Andy, that chicken was delicious."

"Isn't it strange that an Asian restaurant out in the middle of nowhere is cooking the best fried chicken in the state? Just the right spiciness, not too hot. One day, while waiting for my order, she told me her secret — she fries it in one hundred percent peanut oil. The next time we try to fry some chicken, we should try that — but on second thought, maybe picking up to-go is less dangerous."

While I cleared the table, Andy moved over to one of the big, red plaid chairs, one of the ones I swore I'd never sit in. He rested in it and watched as I did the work in the kitchen. Engrossed in my cleaning, I had moved on to drying the plates before I remembered what Andy was talking about.

"Wow, can't believe I forgot that one," I said. "We had that one old beat-up cookbook ... what was it, Helen Corbitt? We were working our way through the whole book, page by page. And then fried chicken. It sounded so easy, egg, flour — and a frying pan full of boiling oil. What could go wrong?"

"I'll never forget that image of you running out the door with a flaming skillet," Andy said from the comfort of his seat.

"Real lucky we didn't burn the house down."

"But that is how it was, right? Dad worked late, and we

were left to fend for ourselves, like a couple of feral cats."

I liked that we had found a fun story to share. With the sun down, but still a couple of more hours before bed, I thought we could capitalize on the good vibes. I offered a plan. "Speaking of fires, for old time's sake, what do you think about making a campfire and ending the evening out by the pond?"

"Good idea. I tell you what — you finish in the kitchen, and I'll go work on the fire."

I continued my work and, through the kitchen window, watched Andy's shadow retrieve the wheelbarrow, head out towards the woodpile, then over to the pit. Soon, I saw a spark and then a small flame.

After putting the last dish in the rack, I put a couple of six-packs in the cooler and followed the fire's beacon, finding Andy sitting at the picnic table, idly admiring the night sky.

I handed Andy a beer and sat next to him. I looked up into the blackness, sharing Andy's view.

"I feel somewhat responsible for sparking your interest in the night sky."

"Maybe at the beginning, sure. I'll give you credit for that. You're my big brother. You led the way on a lot of things. But then I turned the tables. Tried to teach you the constellations — but I think that was deeper than you wanted to go."

"True, none of that stuck with me."

"See that?" Andy pointed towards the east. "We've got the moon in Aquarius now, and Aries is rising."

I strained to put the stars in the right order to make out Aries. Couldn't do it.

"You remember Mr. Simpson, our high school physics teacher?" Andy asked and continued, not expecting an answer. "Kind of a short guy, always wore black pants, white shirt, glasses? Classic nerd."

"Mr. Simpson or you?" Hoping for a laugh.

"You took his class a couple of years before me." Andy

ignored my joke. "It was in my sophomore year when you were already gone to college. He was the one that seriously encouraged me to study astronomy. He set the hook perfectly. Knowing Dad and I were headed out here one weekend, he suggested I stay up late and take a look at the Leonid meteor shower. I don't know if it was some great coincidence, or if you prefer, providence — but the peak viewing time happened to be that Saturday night. It was a chilly, clear night, with no moon, perfect conditions. Dad had lit a fire here in this pit, but as always, he didn't last ten minutes. He left me and went to bed, leaving me alone. He had no interest. The anticipation energized me, though. My eyes were as wide as I could make them. I stared deeply at the constellation Leo waiting for the stars to fall. I tended the fire, keeping the coals going but careful not to induce any flames. I needed warmth but not the glare. And I waited."

Andy's droll tone was quiet and hypnotizing. Although he had an audience, the telling was like a story to himself.

"Finally, it must have been well after midnight. I was entertaining myself by watching an occasional ember from the fire float lazily up into the sky until it quietly extinguished. I followed one ember after another. Then, one spark rose to a record height, where it seemed to amble for a while among the treetops, and then suddenly, it was met by a brilliant downward streak — like a collision right above my head. It was less than a tenth of a second, but it was a magical moment. A perfect symmetry, sparks rising and sparks falling — a glorious spectacle. As I watched, the sparks from the sky kept coming. I jumped onto those ephemeral embers like they were steps on a ladder leading deep into the cosmos. Moving faster and faster, I was soaring through the universe, the stars ceaselessly streaking past. Each bright dot was more luminous than the last. It was so beautiful — but also so fleeting."

Andy paused and I let his words hang with me. But after a

moment he continued, still as if he were talking to himself.

"I felt connected to something much bigger than myself, the sky, the stars. I lost a clear definition of myself. No substance. No form. Aware of nothing and everything at once, as if I was floating in an infinite ocean. No good. No evil. No judgment. Safe and vulnerable at the same time."

"Were you high?"

"No." Andy's retort was quick and certain. "It was way before I knew anything about that stuff. It was awe ... in its purest form. It was much bigger than any of that nonsense. Drugs didn't do anything but blunt the brain. Believe me on that theory. No, this felt authentic — perfection. I wanted more. I watched for what seemed like hours. I was captivated."

"But you had surely seen a falling star before, as many times as we'd been out here."

"Odds are, you're right. Maybe I hadn't been in the right frame of mind before that moment. Maybe I hadn't been quite ready. Inspiration needs fertile ground. Maybe Mr. Simpson plowed the furrow to just the right depth. Whatever it was, nothing beforehand made an impact like that night did. Having had that experience once, I decided then that it was something I desperately needed to repeat. That night is what motivated me to know more."

"I really like that story," I said. "It sounds so you."

"Of course, when I got to college, they managed to suck all the magic out of it."

That sudden huge dose of negativity dropped me back to earth with a thud. But such a flip-flop was so typical of my brother. I got up and walked over to the cooler and grabbed a couple of more beers. I would have enjoyed lingering in Andy's state of marvel a bit longer. It was the best part of him. When his energy bubbled up from his intellectual curiosity, you couldn't help but be endeared to him, reveling in his passions, oblivious to everything else — those were the moments when

Andy was most authentically Andy.

Back on earth, Andy was in his damaged form. His face had lost its openness, and he looked worried. I offered him a beer, placing it on the picnic table in easy reach. We were sitting on the same side of the table now, gazing across the black pond. The fall out of his delicately detailed dream was saddening.

"They drowned us in long equations and pages of data." Andy continued to talk about college, occasionally glancing up at the night sky. "The more precise the mathematical description, the farther away I traveled from this picnic table — on that night. I was lost all over again. It took until the end of graduate school before I realized that my love of the sky was not about the precision found in the numbers. In fact, the obsession with complete knowledge is itself a black hole. The searching is a fundamental urge and needs to be attended to, but diving into the infinite is a seduction that must be resisted. At first, you feel your mind open and expand, then you get sucked in further and further... until finally, you no longer have any connection with day-to-day reality. If you're not careful, you'll go insane. Diving into the obscure minutiae distracts you from life. It wasn't until I gave up on that struggle that a calm reappeared in me.

"I discovered that it was the complete opposite of certainty that appealed to me. I wasn't really interested in a better grasp of the mathematics behind neutrinos or pulsars. Do we really need to know what the stars are made of? Actually knowing the details, the mechanics, or the formulas, none of that made the sky more meaningful. Greater knowledge wasn't helpful. I preferred the notion that the sky is resistant to understanding. I enjoyed basking in its mystery. I didn't care if it was Aristotle, Ptolemy, Copernicus, or Hubble. The specific theory didn't really matter any more. The idea that there was some sort of cognitive progression became meaningless. I learned to appreciate them all. They were each right for their time. All I really cared about was their internal motivations. I tried to put myself in the mind of each of those guys at that inspirational moment, like the one I had sitting right here that night so many years ago. When they, I, looked up towards the stars in wonder — real genuine wonder — I felt something inexpressible. I wanted to embrace it, as ephemeral and difficult to grasp as it might be. But they, those thinkers, like me at first, tried to untie the mystery with their intellect. That yearning is hard to dismiss. But now I wonder — why are we so hungry to understand. What's the endpoint? Maybe the unfulfilled yearning is a good enough place. Why can't we just leave fascination as fascination? As much time as I've spent trying to decipher the mysteries of the sky, the further intractable the problems become, the less connected I feel to my original emotions. Maybe it might have been more pure in some way to have left it as undefinable, to remain in a permanent state of wonder. Some things are unknowable and best left at that.

"Not everything has to be, or should be, explained. Maybe it's better to luxuriate in the mystery. Knowing why the sun rises and sets provides no benefit except for the vanity of knowledge. It confers some sort of control over the natural order. But it's the other way around that's more important; nature is in control, and we have to adapt to its order. We do. That's no different than the interior mystery of free will. For all the tests and endless discussions, there's no definitive solution, never will be. It's a question for which there is no answer. And that's okay. It's a topic for philosophy or religion, but not science. As I've grown older, I've found comfort in the uncertainty. In framing it that way, we aren't any smarter than the ancients, and that's a connection I like to know exists."

His narrative sounded for all the world to me like his excuse to abandon ambition, revealing my brother's tendency to acquiesce. It was simply not in his constitution to fight.

Fighting Dad was never a viable option. His fierce disposition made that path unrewarding. Disagreement, which in Dad's eyes equaled dissent, was not tolerated. I chose the path of confrontation, never backing down from an argument. But in the end, it never got me what I wanted, at least not from my father. I never won. Never.

Andy had chosen the alternative path, the path of least stress, avoiding confrontation at all costs. But, in shying away from the fight and giving in to the bullying, he had sacrificed his identity. He had given up on striving for anything. Moreover, his rationale sounded purposefully naive.

Andy started up again, "You know, still that night, that moment of clear self-awareness, that epiphany, as much as I've tried, I've never been able to repeat the awe of it. I guess you can only go through that door once."

"But you have your teaching. Isn't that where the fascination leads to? You share it with the kids and it reignites within you. No?"

"True. Nothing beats seeing their young eyes light up with amazement. You can feel their joy — and certainly, that reinvigorates you. Especially if you can find them in that brief moment between achieving the sufficient intellectual capacity to conceive of the infinite when new ideas can still inspire, and before society has beaten them into new cogs for their old machine. After that, the practical demands of life hit the reality of having to pay rent and make a buck; there's no time for contemplation. But you're right, teaching has been somewhat of a redemption. I, never for a moment, had any second thoughts about that decision."

Andy sat up, opened the cooler and grabbed two more beers, handing me one. He stuck a stick into the fire, brightening the coals and provoking a few flames. He sat back down on the other side of the table.

"It was, in fact, the only good decision I ever made. But you

216

know... the only people that take me seriously now... are a bunch of children not even half my age. At my age and with all the people I've met ... I can't find anybody to share these conversations with. I feel alone with these thoughts."

"Man, that does sound sad."

"I don't need your pity." Andy's retort was instant and sharp.

Instantly, I regretted how I said what I said. My sarcasm wasn't intended. I was just echoing what he had said a moment earlier. I thought I was being empathetic, but my words came across as callous, even mean-spirited.

"That's not what I meant," I said, trying to correct myself.

"You should only say what you mean."

"C'mon, Andy. Give me a little latitude here. You know me better than that."

"Oh, I know you. But often I can't tell the difference between your teasing and your judging. You do both quite frequently. ... At least Dad approved of my work."

"What makes you think I don't approve? You have my absolute total respect. For all your struggles, you've kept an enviable enthusiasm for your work. Just because I tend to focus on more pragmatic pursuits doesn't mean I'm judging you for being different."

His face, lit by the fire's meager light, tightened like he were about to cry. But he didn't.

"But you have to admit it," I said. "Don't you think it's kind of strange that we came from the same father?"

Andy added, "... amongst other things."

Without warning, Andy had disappeared into a funk. He pulled a long sip of his beer. His gaze was unfocused. I was confused by his cryptic comment, "amongst other things." I didn't anticipate the turn. Maybe Andy was suggesting that beyond our shared childhood experiences, our spheres had little overlap. Andy's interests began and ended inside academia. Mine was business.

Although I had anticipated that this trip would be emotionally fraught, I had no clue how thin the ice actually was.

The other thing was that, when we were kids, Andy rarely ever ventured outside of his limited circle of friends. There weren't many like him in high school, but they were a tight-knit group of science nerds with strange habits. Like his friend, Ed, with whom Andy regularly played chess — over the phone — at two a.m. Completing his strange circle, he found companionship with a couple of teachers, Mr. Simpson, the physics teacher, and the chemistry teacher, whose name I forgot. On Saturday afternoons, these two teachers, who were good friends, would invite Andy and a couple of his classmates over to play bridge. Membership in this crowd was based on an inborn quirk for intellectual oddities. But these two teachers served as the most on-point role models Andy ever had, maybe, as he suggested, the primary reason Andy had gone on to be a teacher.

Out of the blue, Andy said, "Maybe I got more of our mother. Perhaps there was something good there."

We both might have needed it, but it wasn't the time or place to delve into a psychotherapy session. I wasn't prepared to be the supportive older brother. I was tired. Too much was stewing inside my head. I, too, had lost my father. I didn't have a firm grip on my own emotions. And I didn't feel Andy was respecting my emotional stress. Add in my worries from work, the several beers, and voila, guaranteed impaired judgment. I chose not to pursue his meaning.

We sat in silence for a while before I offered another new line of conversation. "Do you remember how Dad would go to the bookstore and pick up a stack of math workbooks?"

"Sure. ... always two of each." Andy responded quickly.

"He loved competitions." I heard in Andy's voice a willingness to re-engage. I enthusiastically pushed forward. "We'd sit at the kitchen table and he'd stand over us, pull out a stopwatch to see how fast we could finish a page. You loved the challenge. You were doing my level workbooks, three grades ahead of where you were at school, and you were still faster than me."

"It was his bizarre way of motivating us," Andy said.

"It worked for you. But it was more than just that; it was his way of compensating, of fixing his inadequacies through us. Never finishing high school bothered him deeply. It made him feel intellectually inferior. I think that's part of the reason he quit school early and jumped into the Marines. He was never going to be a good student. — If you think back on it, when was it that you ever saw Dad read a book?"

"Yeah, I noticed that, too. Never."

"If he were growing up today, I'd bet he would've been diagnosed with some version of a reading disorder. The military was the best place for a man like him. A place where the world feels concrete. That's the world where he could thrive, the world of physicality, things, not abstract ideas."

"But why pit the two of us against each other?" Andy questioned. "It was always some competition. And you remember, that whole deal about the push-ups. That was so unfair. Of course you were going to do more. I get the being all Marine-like, strong young men. But so unfair. An eight-year-old can't keep up with an eleven-year-old. And worse, you were a great athlete."

"Not exactly."

"Oh, c'mon. Didn't you dream of playing professional baseball?"

"Dreaming is one thing. That's such a kid thing. But when you measure yourself against reality and see the impossibility of it all — that's another thing entirely."

"Aw, man, you were great. How many school records did you set?"

"It was only one. — A good one, though. Most RBIs in a season."

"Tommy, you didn't give yourself the chance. You could have gone further. You never put in your 10,000 hours. You cut your dreaming short because you claimed it was the quote-unquote not-practical choice."

"Why do you feel it's okay to critique my life? I've done quite well, thank you. No regrets. And by the way, I barely made the team in college."

"Sure, but you were only a freshman. Pretty impressive and a walk-on at that. You could have given it a little more time — but if you weren't the star, it wasn't good enough."

"Andy, you're getting a little too heavy here. Can't two brothers sit side-by-side and just enjoy being outside? Do we have to get all so psychoanalytical?"

I tossed my empty aside. Grabbing another couple of beers, I asked Andy if he wanted another.

He snatched it. Andy still had an agenda he wanted to tend to. "While you're living this good life, the one that you think Dad wanted you to live, you missed his point entirely."

"So now you can read my mind? But yes — Dad was all about success."

"Success doesn't only mean making lots of money and producing nothing."

"That's fucking rude. You clearly don't have any clue about what I do."

"You push money around. Admit it. That's all you do. You don't produce anything. Trade one building for another and make a profit on the trades, sucking a little juice out of somebody else's money. So what? You call it creating liquidity or streamlining or whatever ..."

"Tell me. What is it? You jealous? You talk of passion, but where did that get you, huh? Teaching at a junior college. Yeah, that's impressive."

In the dim light of the fire, I could see Andy sending me a glare.

"Sorry, that was mean. — But clearly, something has you tied up in knots. What's really on your mind?" I asked this last question, instantly uncomfortable, anticipating his answer.

"I don't know." Andy's shoulders slumped, and he looked down at the ground.

I waited.

He looked back at me, expecting a reaction. I didn't know how to respond. Not yet. I needed more from Andy. There was a long silence before Andy spoke again. "I'm lonely."

His turn from critical judgments against me to an apparent deep inner angst left me perplexed.

Andy looked back towards the ground, slowly adding, "As sad as our relationship is... and you have to admit, it's sad. You are the one person in the entire world I am close to... and at that, we're not even that close. Now that's truly sad... isn't it?"

I had no answer for him. Yes, what he said was sad. He even looked dejected. I felt bad for Andy. It was true; close wasn't how I would have described our relationship. Certainly not now. Although it once was. Maybe Andy was drawing that comparison. But on the other hand, I wouldn't have described our current relationship as distant either. It was also true that I felt guilty, guilty that I hadn't worked harder on our relationship. Andy had poked a sensitive spot within me. Perhaps I had unintentionally abandoned Andy for more urgent needs.

Perhaps Andy was measuring our closeness in the aftermath of our father's death and his fondness for Dad. Making a comparison I could never match. While I had sought distance from Dad, Andy's attachment to Dad had always remained tight. Perhaps, in my mind and not fair to Andy, I had unintentionally linked him to the taint for which I held my father. All of my built-up crappy feelings about Dad had been collaterally deposited onto Andy merely because of his closeness. Not fair, but a theory for sure. I didn't know how to explain to Andy these half-baked speculations. I was afraid of how they might be heard. So, I didn't. We remained in silence.

Andy laid flat on the picnic table, looking up into the dark sky.

I found a few sticks close by and added them to the fire, then laid back down in the grass.

After a few minutes, I offered, "I know Dad was a big part of your life, and now you're left with this huge hole."

Andy said nothing. I shared Andy's view of the night sky and tried to find comfort in the darkness.

I awoke, finding myself still laying in the grass next to the picnic table. The fire had burnt down to a fistful of glowing embers. I looked at my watch, "Shit. It's almost midnight."

I looked over at Andy. "You asleep?"

"No. Just thinking."

I was too worn down, out of energy, and wary of how I'd respond to ask what he was thinking about.

We poured out what little beer was left in our half-drunken bottles to snuff out the embers. I picked up the cooler and we started back towards the cabin.

Andy started off in a different direction, but he abruptly paused.

"Do you need to use any water?" Andy asked.

"Hadn't thought about it. Why?"

"It's just that the generator needs to be on to power the pump, and I only brought up ten gallons of fuel. I'd like to conserve it for as long as possible."

"I guess we'll lose the lights then, too?"

"You're not still scared of the dark, are you?"

I sat on the edge of the porch and watched Andy walk around the corner to cut the machine off. The house went dark. He reappeared a moment later, a flashlight leading his way. He sat down silently next to me, looked over at me, then, in a soft, tentative voice, said, "You know, over the years, I spent a whole lot of time out here with Dad. And even though it was just the two of us all those weekends, with nobody else to talk to, I can't say we ever were the best of friends."

Andy turned off his flashlight.

As we sat in the dull blue light of the moon, I thought for a moment about what Andy had just said. Not only was the comment a revelation to me about his relationship with Dad, but I was also surprised about his sudden openness. And why now, after an already long and stressful day? It didn't feel like the right time to talk about his feelings towards Dad. I tried to understand not only what he was saying but, more bothersome, why he said it.

"I hear the not-friends part — one hundred percent. He certainly didn't make that effort with me. — So tell me, why the hell did you keep coming?"

"To boil it down to a word, I'd say loyalty. I don't know how else to describe it. I felt like I owed him that much."

"There must have been something in it for you. No?"

"It was like an obligation, I guess. Don't know how else to describe it." Andy struggled for the first time to describe to me his relationship with Dad. "For some reason, I have a hard time calling it love — but can you have devotion without love?"

"For me at least, I never felt that sense — of what did you call it? Obligation. He demanded something like that, for sure. More precisely, I'd say it was obedience he demanded. End of story. He wanted to call it respect. But it wasn't anything like that. He never earned the respect he wanted. My theory is, you have to give it first before you earn it. The best he did for me felt like some perfunctory protocol. Dad would occasionally ask cursory questions about my life, my work: 'How's that deal going? or whatever, but even when I tried to answer, in the end, all he wanted to hear was 'great.' He'd never follow up with deeper more probing questions, like — 'How are you going to handle this or that?' or 'How does that make you feel?' or 'What do you think about whatever?' It was always about what was on his mind, on his agenda, what he wanted. No respect for me or my wishes. He didn't respect me enough to encourage me to be myself. He demonstrated the exact opposite. — You know, he actually wanted me to skip college altogether and work with him building homes."

"Couldn't see that working out. Not the two of you." Andy finally had a smile on his face. It was nice to see. "He never asked that of me, but that does sound like Dad."

"He cared not a whit about my likes, my dislikes, what sort of career would be best suited to my competencies or passions. He was in no way the mentor that I needed. I had to figure out my path all on my own."

"But look at yourself, where you are in your life. You're a success. Just like he wanted for you."

"Feel like a success? You're kidding me. Aren't you?" I couldn't tell if Andy was purposely or accidentally goading me. "He did nothing except make me feel like an absolute complete failure — repeatedly and repeatedly reinforcing it. Whatever effort I put forth was never enough. I always fell short. How else was I to view myself? As failure, not a success. He never hesitated to point out how I could improve. A discussion about an A-minus grade was not about how difficult the material might have been, or the two hours a night of homework per night, or the four hundred question exam. No, it was about the one question I missed and how I needed to ensure that I didn't make that same mistake again. There was a huge gap between where I was and his expectation of me."

"Sure, he encouraged hard work and had high expectations. And isn't that the heart of what he taught us? Don't you think that's the part that rubbed off on you? To work through to the finish. You're so caught up in the illusion of your own autonomy that you alone, all by yourself, are solely responsible for your own success. No recognition for what anybody else has done for you."

"I didn't owe him a thing."

"You've created this strange distorted imagery all on your own. If you were just a bit less narcissistic, then maybe you could see beyond the end of your nose."

"You're defending him?" I was tired, and my filters were no longer working. Why this midnight provocation? "Didn't you just tell me how disconnected you felt from him?" I returned the challenge to Andy.

"But c'mon, you're painting him like some sort of tyrant. Was he perfect? No."

"I wasn't motivated to succeed as much as I was terrified of failing. How many times did he bring out the belt? For what? For being disrespectful. Not saying, 'Sir.' For talking back. Tell me you weren't scared of getting hit? Scared of our own father?"

"You're exaggerating. It wasn't so bad. Sure, he was occasionally strict, but he was teaching us the difference between right and wrong. Isn't that a worthy goal?"

"No... he was a plain mean man. He'd sooner hit me than look at me. And he did that plenty. If he had used his head a little, think, he would have realized that we were good kids. We knew what was expected of us — and we did those things. But he leaned on us way too hard."

"He grew up in a different time, a different culture."

"That's a crap excuse and you know it."

"You need to give the guy a little more slack. He started with nothing, no education, no money, no family. He parented out of desperation, with no wife, and still he made a good life for us."

"He reminded us all the time about how hard life was. Like there was a debt we owed him for his suffering."

"But we never went hungry. And had luxuries he never got

to enjoy. He denied himself for us. Now that he's dead, maybe you could put all this anger behind you and show a smidgen of gratitude?"

"The more I think about it, the more upset I get. I was always disappointing him, never good enough." My blood pressure was up. I fumbled open the cooler and discovered there were no more beers.

"Where the fuck are you getting all this? He was proud of you."

"You don't know that. He loved you. He was easy on you. I had to fight back in order to have any sense of my own self. Why couldn't I be recognized for being me? Just good enough me, without having to constantly prove myself worthy of his love — and failing? I couldn't get away from him fast enough. I fought for everything and for nothing, never winning, not one lousy fucking time. He was a mean son-of-a-bitch, taking out his pile of insecurities and then dumping them on me. He was the one that made everything a competition. I battled and took the bruises for you, so you didn't have to. And you? What did you learn from all his wise counsel? You gave in. Surrendered. You decided it was easier to just go along. You didn't have the courage to fight. What's your struggle? Nothing motivates you. No sense of urgency about anything. How is it you spend your time? You're lazy, bored and … wasting your time on this earth, just checking the days off one at a time."

Andy stood up, looking down at me,

"You know. — You're a narcissistic ass."

I stood up. We were nose to nose. I smelled his beer-laden breath.

Andy continued, "The world flows in one direction, only through you. This entire mythology, nothing would exist today if not for your heroic efforts. And you don't give one ounce of credit to the man who sacrificed everything to build the foundation on which you are now standing."

"An ass? If I didn't stand up for myself ..."

"You! That's right! You're an ass."

Andy threw both his hands solidly against my chest, shoving me off the porch.

"Whoa!"

The short fall splayed me out onto the dirt. Unharmed but surprised, I looked up at Andy looming over me. He was yelling, irate like I'd never seen him before. "You have no fucking respect for anybody. This so-called winning wasn't Dad's thing. Not my thing, either. It's you. You're the one who decided everything is about the score — whatever that's supposed to do for you? What is it with you? What game are you playing? Whatever it is, I want no part of it — never have."

His physicality shocked me. Never once had either one of us pushed the other in anger. Through all the years, I had always thought we were on the same side.

Andy watched as I picked myself up. I didn't bother brushing off the dirt that was now pasted to my shirt and pants. I sat back down on the edge of the porch.

"I don't need your help or anybody else's. I'm just fine, thank you," Andy said. "Go fuck yourself."

Andy disappeared into the house, letting the screen door slam behind him.

22

Andy's tug on my shoulder caught me in the middle of a semi-comatose sleep. My disorientation was severe. With some effort, it took me a minute to realize I was in the cabin's front room.

"C'mon, let's get up," he said. "We have a lot to do today."

Again, I was with my mattress next to the pot-belly stove, although this time, I had decided to start the night that way. My fitful sleep had done little to rejuvenate me. Widening my eyes, I assembled the fragments of consciousness. Opening my eyes, I saw Andy disappear into the kitchen and, even from my low vantage point, a table already set with plates and glasses. Andy had been at it for some time and had been superbly quiet. The kitchen looked a lot like yesterday. Several bowls of ingredients were staggered across the kitchen counter. Even though this was only my second day here, waking up and seeing the French press next to the makings for breakfast felt routine and extraordinarily welcome.

My head was still swollen from the beer. I slipped on my jeans while looking out the window to see an overcast sky and made my way to the bathroom. I found a few aspirins and swallowed them, cupping a little water from the sink, before crawling back into my still-warm spot under the blanket.

While I recovered, I observed Andy's efficiency as he assembled an omelet and toasted a couple of English muffins. He even put the store-bought jam into a small serving bowl.

When the plates landed on the table, I made the four-foot walk over to the table, sitting down on the opposite side of the table from my brother. I carefully sipped my coffee as I watched Andy artfully arrange his plate and start to enjoy his breakfast.

"Tommy," Andy said. "I'm really sorry for last night."

"It's not your fault. We've both been through a lot ... and I don't know if you noticed, but we went through a whole lot of beer."

"I noticed, all right. I already dragged out a couple of bags of trash."

"But, seriously," I said. "I don't want to use alcohol as an easy excuse."

"I behaved poorly and used some unkind words."

"They were all true," I said. "I really don't blame you for anything. Not at all. Your reaction was completely understandable. You know, it might be hard to accept, but those harsh words I released last night were not intended for you, if you know what I mean. You just happened to be in the way. And that's not right. I'm sorry."

"I know that — at least that's how I'm feeling this morning. When I dragged you out here, I wasn't quite sure what we'd get into. I suspected that there were some lingering emotions that still need to be unknotted."

"This trip has surprised me probably more than you. My anger hasn't been as permanently buried as I had thought it was. It's been lurking, hidden for all these years, waiting for a fissure like this to erupt. ... Dad's death has made me unexpectedly raw. Right now, I'm having a hard time separating the place here from the man. I'm sorry for unleashing on you all my bad shit. I should be in better control of my emotions."

My gut remained the same, to turn my back on the cabin and never return just like I had intended to do thirty years ago. But here I was — again. I had thought I had appropriately processed all these bad feelings. I had thought all of these variable moods were so far behind me that this trip would be different. I had thought I was more stable and stronger than my toxic past. I was wrong.

"What's the matter? You all right?" Andy asked. "You look worried."

"I'm fine. Just fine. ... but maybe ... I've been doing the math. ... You know, selling this property could put a lot of money in both our pockets."

"You've got to be kidding me. Not this bullshit again. ... Seriously, Tommy?" Andy, bewildered, rose with his plate in his hand and stared at me more intently than I had ever seen. "You are all over the fucking place. Just eat your breakfast, and hopefully you'll feel better in a few minutes." He landed the plate on the counter with a solid thud and went outside, leaving me alone in the cabin.

I started with the eggs and ate in slow motion. Andy was right. I was stupid to bring up the subject of selling. Especially now. Andy and I were both fully formed in our opinions, and neither one of us was likely to change. Whatever value that was tied up in this place was going to stay locked up here for a long time, and I didn't have the key. I honestly didn't care if Andy kept the property. He could have it. And, I didn't want to make an issue of leveling the score by demanding something else of value. I hated the idea of keeping a tally with my brother.

I started washing the dishes, enjoying the mindless manual labor. No thoughts, just sudsy water, stacking dishes, and a dry dish towel. But before I could finish, Andy came back in, put his hand on my shoulder and gently nudged me out of the kitchen, in a not so subtle way, taking command of the sink.

He said, "Go get yourself some of this good fresh air. You look like you could use a little downtime. Relax, and I'll get us ready for the day."

His directive was welcomed. I walked out onto the porch. The morning air still held acrid remnants from last night's fire. I sat in one of the two chairs. Its arm felt unsteady, although I attributed the feeling to my hangover. When Andy eventually came through the screen door, he let it go, the spring snapping it back sharply against its frame. The loud slap struck a nerve. My heart began to race.

Andy continued past me and out towards the lake. I watched him go, thinking for a second to follow him, but I needed a few more moments to calm my jitters. The scene was the same as thirty years ago — and I felt the same shame as I had thirty years ago. I hadn't made any progress in all that time. I was mishandling everything in my life, my wife, my business, and right now, my brother.

I stepped off the porch, turned left and headed down the road, trying to empty my brain of its turbulence. A walk seemed like it would be therapeutic. I relied on my primal brain and simply took in the forest's smells and visuals. I almost instantly felt much better, more relaxed. The sun was breaking up the clouds, and it was looking to be a warm day.

When I returned, Andy was by the pond holding a rifle and pointing it downrange. He had another four rifles laid out in a neat row across the top of the picnic table. About thirty yards away, he had positioned a long log with about a dozen tin cans lined up on top — just like when we were kids.

As I approached the weapons, I was struck by the sight of my old lever-action Winchester.

"Where did you find this?"

"You abandoned it. It sat in Dad's gun closet along with the others for years and years. The locks quit working, and after a while, I got nervous about leaving multiple guns here.

So, one day, I took them home. It was not one of Dad's best habits — he started to let things go."

"He gave me this on my twelfth birthday. This thing is as old as the hills but looks almost brand new. You've done a nice job of keeping it clean and pretty."

Looking at the weapon on the table, I was still afraid to touch it.

"You been shooting often?" I asked.

"Not too much. I'll come out here and fire off a few rounds before looking for deer. As you know, hunting is mostly walking and waiting. Not much shooting. It's more about the walk than the hunt. I haven't shot anything in a long time."

"You sure about this?"

"How hard can it be? You point it. You squeeze the trigger. If you keep it pointed that way you can't hurt anything or anybody. It's just a few cans and a lot of trees out there."

I lightly slid a finger along the Winchester's smoothly worn stock.

Reacting to my hesitation, Andy grabbed my rifle off the table and laid it firmly in my hands.

I instinctively pointed the barrel downward, racked the lever forward with a solid pull, then checked the chamber to make sure no rounds were loaded.

My hands quickly became reacquainted with the gun's weight. It felt familiar and somehow relaxing. I slowly brought the gun up to my eye, feeling the stock lightly touch my chin. I caressed the trigger and applied just enough pressure to feel its release point. But went no further. The memory was still deeply embedded inside of me.

"Do you want to give it a try?" Andy asked.

"All right," I said.

"Thomas, we are going to start this by lying on the ground. They call this the prone position. As you get better, you will learn to do this standing up. Okay, check your rifle again. You can't do this too much. Always, and I mean always, son, treat every gun under any circumstances as if it is loaded. Got that?"

"Yes, sir."

"And what's the most important rule?"

"Never point a gun at anything you aren't willing to kill."

"Good. Exactly. This is a very dangerous tool, but if used carefully, it can be the source of a lot of pleasure. Maybe even one day save your life or someone else's. ... Is the gun pointed downrange?"

"Yes, sir."

"Now check your background real carefully. If you miss, which you'll probably do a bunch at first, I don't want you accidentally hitting anybody or anything. Understand?"

"Yes, sir."

"Now, for the moment, let's keep your right hand away from the trigger. Grip the stock behind the trigger with all your fingers closed, but not too tight. We're just going to practice aiming. Now get comfortable. Put your left hand about halfway towards the end of the forestock, the wooden part, not the metal. Press your face close to the stock."

"Okay."

"You see the two parts of the sight? You want the top of the rear sight — the 'U' shaped piece closest to you — to line up with the top of the front sight. And, of course, centered in the 'U'. Move around slowly until you have the two sights lined up with one of the cans on the log. Got it?"

"Got it."

"Okay, now carefully take your index finger and lightly touch the trigger. I don't want you pulling it yet. I want you to learn the feel of it."

Without warning, the gun fired. As if the weapon had become a red hot poker, I instantly dropped the Winchester to the ground

"Damn it, son. What the hell is wrong with you?"

"But Dad, I barely even touched the trigger — and it went off."

"Okay, don't touch the gun. Stand up and take a step back."

Dad took hold of the rifle and examined it. Consciously modeling the proper inspection technique, he pulled the lever sharply forward and loaded another round in the chamber. He assumed a wide stance and fired a shot, hitting the log just below one of the cans. He put another round in, fired again, this time hitting one of the cans square. With hardly a pause, same thing, he aimed at the next can, fired, and knocked it off the log. And again, another can killed.

"I should have looked at this gun a little more carefully first before giving it to you. This gun has a very light touch to it. We can adjust this later, or you will just have to learn to be extra careful. Let's try again. But son, no more dropping the gun in the dirt. Keep your head in position and stay mentally in the shot until the bullet hits its target. You were surprised this one time, but now you know what to expect. Don't let it happen again."

Back on the ground, we ran through the checklist again. There was only one can left on the log.

"Okay, Thomas — let's be extra gentle with the trigger this time. Take a deep breath and try to relax. Keep your finger off the trigger for just a little bit. I noticed this gun shoots a hair low, so raise your aiming point a little bit above your target. I mean, like just barely an inch or so. And pay careful attention to your breathing. Relax. Now, breathe in slowly. And hold it for a second. Breathe out. The hardest part of being a good target shooter is controlling your breathing. Take a couple of more long breaths and relax. You good?"

"Yes, sir."

"The shot might surprise you again, but you're ready this time, right?"

"Yes, sir."

"Finger back on the trigger. Watch the sight as it gets in position... and gently squeeze."

The shot rang out, and the can bounced off the log.

"Excellent! That's amazing — hit the target with your first shot. Good work, son."

"Actually, it was my second."

"We don't need to count that other one. Okay. Ready to try again?"

We reset the cans and the lesson continued for another half-hour. The next several shots were not quite as precise, but the feel was there, and by the time we had finished, enough cans had been hit to induce a sense of self-pride.

After several rounds, Andy asked, "How is it feeling?"

"Not bad, not bad at all. I'm kind of surprised and proud of myself for hitting seven out of ten. And you, what's your score? How many did you hit?"

"Man, not everything needs to be a competition."

"Oh, don't be so sensitive."

Not unexpectedly, Andy had all the preparations for our hike readily accessible. It took him all of ten minutes to assemble a pair of backpacks before slapping them down, ready to go on the table.

"What you got in there? They look awfully big for a day hike."

"The typical stuff: a Ziploc with some trail mix, a couple of bottles of water, binoculars, and a first aid kit. Not much. We'll be gone just a couple of hours. And they're not too large if we're going to bring back any deer meat."

"Whatever." I remained skeptical of Andy's agenda.

"Anyways, after you warm up, there's plenty of room for

you to put your jacket in."

"Seeing all this laid out reminds me of how Dad used to make us carry our tin drinking cups on the outside of our packs so that their rattling noise would keep the bears away. Seems silly now ... and that racket was annoying as hell."

"But you might say it worked. We never saw any bears."

"Except for that once. You remember?" I looked for Andy's reaction and he clearly didn't remember. "A mama bear and her cub were about a quarter-mile down the valley on the opposite side of the creek." Now I could see the memory surfacing onto Andy's face, but he was squinting at me, almost angry. "I took out my binoculars to get a better look and you slapped my arm down. Remember that?" The memory put me in a better mood, and I felt myself on the verge of laughing. "I can't believe how you jumped into that bear's mind and thought what the bear thought — that I was pointing a gun at her. You didn't want me to scare her." I guffawed with pleasure.

"I was just a kid back then."

We lifted our packs, grabbed the rifles, and set off together towards the forest. The sky was now nearly cloudless, and the deep blue was dominating. As if pulled by a string, I felt absent of any volition, passively letting Andy lead the way. We walked west, down the dirt drive to where it ended at what was left of the firewood pile. The same spot where we would back up the pickup, push the wood off the tailgate and then assemble the cut wood into Dad's particular pattern, converting the chaos of the dump into an organized stack. Having sat undisturbed in its current condition for several years, it was now disintegrating into mulch.

We walked side by side towards the forest. The first hundred yards were on the eroded remains of a little-used road.

Andy had explained his plans for the hike to me earlier in the day, while we were target shooting. Our destination was a large meadow. We would walk about three miles in and arrive by mid-afternoon. This was a place Andy often saw deer, but typically late in the day. But since we wanted to be back before sunset, he wasn't certain our luck would be so good today. As Andy emphasized again and again, and although our goal was more about the walk, we headed in that direction anyway. "Who knows. We might get lucky." Andy said. As was my brother's way, he was managing expectations towards the worst possible scenario. Although our potential bad luck was welcome news to me since I still had no interest in shooting anything. As we turned into the trees, the path narrowed, and I was still struggling with how to balance the backpack and my rifle. Andy walked ahead. The weight was no burden, but the pack and the gun were a cumbersome combination, and they didn't hang well together.

The path, a narrow earthen scar, was clear and easy to navigate — remarkable to me for how infrequently it was used. The unfolding scene resonated as familiar, accessing old hidden recesses in the back of my mind. This trail had existed long before Dad bought the property. And as we walked I wondered how long ago the first person had blazed it and who he, or she, was. How long into the future would this path continue to exist?

Andy's stride was strong and confident. He effortlessly moved faster than me and was quickly further ahead of me. I felt my heart beating harder, my breathing more labored as we gained elevation. I had to focus on the trail as it was revealing itself. My walking became deliberate and self-conscious. I was now concentrating solely on the location of my next step and not where we were heading.

At its best, hiking is a Zen exercise that focuses the mind, clearing away extraneous thoughts and allowing the senses an unburdened notice of one's specific place in the world. The air was thick with the scents of plants and earth, scents that are entirely missing from the urban world. The uncorrupted experience was gradually soothing my agitated mind. With little effort, I yielded to its impact, falling into the steady rhythm of one foot after the next. I watched for the next rock or root and listened to my breathing as it coordinated with my steps. The walk was having a positive effect. It felt freeing, as if I were shedding the detritus of the city life one step at a time.

Lost in my inner Zen, I found myself moving slowly, and Andy was somewhere ahead of me, out of sight.

This was a path I had taken many times as a young boy. While I could not have described any part of it prior to returning here, it was becoming familiar once again. The first landmark would be when we arrive at a low ridge, absent of trees with a long view to the south. Then a quarter mile after, we'd cross the fence line separating Dad's property from the government's wilderness area.

When I arrived at the fence, I was surprised that I could barely make it out. The fence posts had fallen, and strands of wire weaved in and out of the ground; all had been fully absorbed by new growth. I never understood why, but Dad had made maintenance of the fence an important mission, one assigned mostly to Andy and me. Since his absence, clearly no one had taken on the responsibility.

The next section of the trail was a steep decline down to an abandoned logging road, one the government still maintained as a Forest Service trail. It was wide and made for easy walking. It paralleled a stream that, depending on the time of year, could vary between a bare trickle to a rushing brook. However, it was never any wider than a young boy's best jump.

At the stream, the water was low, making for an easy crossing. The trail remained parallel to the stream on the other side for a few hundred yards, and then it headed up out the valley.

Andy's goal, the meadow, supposedly with deer, was at a higher elevation, and from here it was all an ascent. Every once in a while, looking over his shoulder to check on me, Andy led the way. As we crossed the ridge, the forest then became noticeably denser; the southern exposure, water, and quality of the soil were apparently advantageous to the flora. Nearly choking the trail at the ground, soft new-green tendrils reached into the ribbon of blackish soil. In their attempt to impede my progress, the branches were, with each stride rubbing against my pants. Although seemingly benign to the traveler, each step was destructive, one that discouraged the delicate sprigs of new growth from reaching any further. I suppose there's a metaphor for life buried in that observation. As we do what we need to do to move forward, we unintentionally leave little bits of unnoticed destruction. It's inevitable. It's not possible to travel without leaving behind a footstep, and no matter how light the footstep disturbs the ground.

Blanketed with fallen leaves, the trail felt moist underfoot. It was soft like a thin cushion, allowing my footsteps to be nearly silent. The soil revealed each imprint left behind by Andy's boots. We proceeded up the hill, now heading east. Just past its peak, the sun was beginning its descent. The foliage thickened, and within a few turns, Andy was again out of sight.

"You still with me?" I called out.

"I'm here," I heard him shout from a short distance away.

As I made the next turn, I saw Andy up the trail waiting on me. Once he saw me, he continued on as if there wasn't any time to waste.

Fixated on the narrow path curling forward, I concentrated on each step, constantly adjusting them to the ever-changing terrain. The induced semi-meditative state was a feeling I had long forgotten and was happy to rediscover. We stayed in this pattern for a good twenty minutes, with Andy occasionally stopping to check my position.

The hill gradually gave way to a straight, level section. Andy was still in sight, but the separation between us had grown and he had quit checking on my progress.

The walking became easier, more automatic. My thoughts wandered, and I unfortunately kept returning to the night before. I quickened my pace until I was a few steps behind Andy.

"Andy. About last night ... do we need to talk?"

Andy maintained his steady pace.

"There's nothing to revisit," he said. "You've made your feelings crystal clear."

"I made some mistakes ...and I'd like to apologize."

"No worries."

"But I'd like to make it better."

"You shouldn't worry about me. I'm fine."

"But it's about us."

"If only."

"Not true," I said. "We can work on this."

Andy laughed. He pulled away from me, shaking his head. I froze in my tracks.

Andy's objective for this hike — to kill a deer — was never my goal. I'd only conceded to this plan so that I could be with my brother. His brevity was justified. I had screwed up; I had disrespected him. Andy pressed forward, or maybe it was away. He was obviously angry with me. This trip, this brotherly get-together, was all about appeasing his wishes. And, after my less than adequate efforts, he had rejected me. So now, what was it I was doing out here if not being with Andy? This hike didn't have the feeling of togetherness. No longer did I try to match his pace. My walking slowed. With Andy no longer in sight, I again focused on my footsteps, trying to find the meditative state that I had enjoyed earlier.

We began a steep climb, with the turns becoming more frequent. My legs ached and my chest heaved. But, along with being more aware of my body, I was also becoming more aware of the forest's sweet smells. Within a couple of minutes of ascending uphill, I heard Andy's gear rattling against the branches, but I didn't see him. My pace must have quickened, or his slowed. The sound of Andy once again disappeared. The trail crested, followed by a short downhill incline that led a short distance ahead to a threshold between the woods and a clearing. There was something about the view that looked vaguely familiar; or perhaps, my memory was playing tricks on me.

I paused at the threshold to the clearing and enjoyed a view of the tall yellowing grasses scattering sunlight like a pointillist painting. A thousand tiny gnats swarmed above their tips. The clearing was large, like a small baseball field, an ideal place for the deer to gather, but Andy's goal was still farther up the valley.

Through the opening in the trees and across the field, I spotted Andy beyond the grasses walking towards the woods at the clearing's opposite end. The trail through the tall grasses was difficult to discern, but using Andy as my reference I soon saw the path. The gentle curve of the trail coming out of the trees took me through a sea of blackberries spreading left and right. As a younger explorer, this would have been a delightful discovery. Berries were everywhere, all around me.

Having climbed and conquered, my legs felt strong again, and my physical confidence had also returned. I pulled one ripe berry off the shrub and put it to my nose. The sweetness reminded me of t-shirt stains and stomachaches.

Snap. Snap.

The sound of breaking branches came from nearby, close

to Andy. I spun towards the noise and saw a dark mass darting out of the woods. A bear.

She was instantly at Andy's back. Shadows and glare confused my eye. Her sounds were loud and clear. This was her territory. I strained to see. They were twenty or thirty yards away.

The bear was easily a foot taller than Andy. She snarled and I saw Andy move into the trees. In a few strides, the bear was on top of Andy as I watched in horror. Andy disappeared under a raging mass of brown fur. The bear's growling over-whelmed any scream Andy was capable of issuing.

I dropped my backpack, pulled the rifle around, flipped off the safety, raised the scope to my eye, and aimed across the green field. The crosshairs shook while I tried to identify a target. The bear's midsection moved through the frame. She disappeared. Then appeared. Then disappeared again. I needed a perfect shot, otherwise I'd only further anger a bear that size. There wouldn't be time for a second shot. My finger lightly touched the trigger. I hesitated. She moved left. The crosshairs followed. A green plaid shirt was now facing the gun. I waited. The scene flipped again. I saw fur and pulled the trigger.

The concussive crack resonated into the woods and back again. The sound waves dissipated through the trees, echoing back to me like a soft breath. And then silence. Absolute silence.

I quickly maneuvered another round into the chamber. Click. Focused. I kept my head down.

The rhythmic bursts of my breathing suddenly became apparent. My arms were steady. My eye stayed glued to the sight.

Where had my bullet gone?

Both the animal and my brother had dropped out of sight. I saw nothing but grass and trees. I kept my cheek pressed to the stock, ready to take aim again.

Nothing moved.

The background noises of the forest began to rise. The breeze through the high branches rustled the leaves overhead. No bear. No Andy. Nothing but the wind. Squinting into the forest, I expected the danger to re-emerge. My gaze was still tautly locked downrange. As the adrenalin drained, I let the barrel fall slowly. Whatever lay hidden beyond the berry patch wasn't something I wanted to see. Had my shot gone astray? Had I missed the bear and hit my own brother?

"Andy! Andy, are you there?" I yelled.

No response.

As if a cold wind had grabbed me, I shivered.

"Andy?"

I reset the safety on the rifle and slung it over my shoulder, then ran the trail towards my brother. The bear was nowhere to be seen. I found Andy sprawled haphazardly across the trail. His face was turned down. Soaked in blood, his shredded shirt exposed multiple, deep, ragged scratches across his back. I knelt down next to him and placed my hands under his shoulder. I gently pulled on his now limp body. More scratches were visible across his arms and neck. His eyes were shut. In spite of all evidence to the contrary, his face was calm.

I touched his cheeks, feeling for any movement, a twitch, a breath. I put my face next to his, desperate for any hint of life.

"C'mon, Andy. Breathe! ... Please!"

Only knowing crudely where to look, I grabbed his wrist and then touched his neck, desperately searching for a pulse. Not knowing the first thing about CPR, I nevertheless put my mouth over his, trying to force the life back inside him. I tried and tried a dozen times. Out of breath, my brain told me this work was senseless, but my heart insisted. I tried again and again.

No response.

Finally exasperated, I fell back onto my knees.

Survival was not possible. It was over.

Rivulets of blood rolled off Andy's body, pooling around both of us and seeping into the porous soil. Small air bubbles percolated up from the ground. I pulled at his blood-stained shirt, looking underneath to see if I could find the bullet hole. I had to know. The bear was gone, having disappeared into the woods. I assumed that the bear was a mother protecting its young, but how could I have known that. I didn't see or hear any cubs. What the bear had previously viewed as a threat went instantly inert. And the loud concussive noise of the gun was enough to drive her away. Whatever, she and her babies must be safe now. I had obviously missed my intended target. The bullet certainly must have hit my brother. Although my target had appeared so large through the scope. In that brief instant, when I pulled the trigger, I had been sure of myself. I rolled Andy over and checked all sides. But the haphazard gross violence inflicted by the bear must have hidden the tiny bullet hole. My blood-covered hands slipped across Andy's back, frantically searching for a bullet wound. But all I found were the raw, still oozing wounds left by the bear.

Andy was gone.

23

Andy lay dead at my side. Looking at his mangled body, I was in shock. Grief was yet to come. I was alone and unsure what had to be done next.

"My god ... what have I done?" I said to no one in particular, a broad forest, whose only response was a persistent wind rattling the leaves above.

My trembling hands cradled Andy's head. I sobbed and stared at my brother. Whatever was my brother's essential essence had vanished, leaving behind a hollow shell. My heart disintegrated into sharp painful bits. My body was limp, as well, like I was melting and merging with the blood-soaked soil.

A curse had been set upon me, both my father and my brother dying in the same week. I gently placed Andy's head back onto the damp earth. Of all places, deep in the woods, why did my brother have to die here? Far from anyone, from any help. Isolated. I felt empty, lost, confused, and most of all, guilty.

The decision was impossible. I had no other choice but to shoot. But I failed; my choice was the wrong one. There was no other way to judge it. I had reacted too slowly. None of what I saw made sense. I had pulled the trigger only a moment ago, but I was already uncertain of my recall. The results didn't reconcile with what I plainly saw. I had the target in my sights, but the turmoil must have confused me. How could my aim have been so poor? The crosshairs were on the bear's chest. In the instant between recognition, reaction, the trigger, and the distance, could the bullet's destination have been Andy?

The bear had wreaked havoc on my brother's body.

If he suffered, it wasn't for long. It was only seconds between the awful rancor of the bear raising up and the end of Andy's life. The blood continued to drip off my brother's matted clothes. Slower now, the ground absorbing it all.

A milli-second quicker might have made a difference. If I had been more attentive to the details or if my decision had been more acute, could I have saved Andy?

My shaking subsided. I cautiously wiped my tears with the back of my hands, then gazed at my bloody palms. I grabbed a handful of dirt and vigorously rubbed it over my hands, trying to remove the stain. After the futile effort, I let the impure soil cupped in my hands sift through my fingers, falling onto the blood-soaked ground like the performance of some shamanistic primitive ritual.

I stared again at my muddy and bloody palms. Resolved. Self-pity and doubt — useless and suffocating emotions, at least for now, had to be set aside. I had no means to summon help, nobody to call, no 911. But I had to act.

"All right, Andy, it's time to figure this out. Don't worry ... at least, not yet."

My guess was that we were two and a half to three miles out from the cabin. The sun would soon be falling into sunset. There wasn't sufficient time to hike back to the cabin and come back with help. Abandoning Andy and exposing him to the wild predators and scavengers would be a desecration, a gruesomeness I closed my mind against.

Andy and I had to return together.

My pack held only a sweatshirt, some trail mix, and a bottle of water. Also, I had that awful rifle, which still reeked from its recent discharge.

Andy's backpack had fallen to the side of the trail. It never crossed my mind to question what he might have packed and for what reason. I had deferred to Andy the schedule, the gear, every part of the agenda. This was his domain, and I had complete confidence that he had prepared for any eventuality — almost any. This scenario was one that he could never have anticipated.

Stuffed in at the top of his pack was his fleece which I spread out like a small blanket on a barren patch of the trail. Painstakingly I reached into the pack, removing the contents one by one and assessing their utility; I placed them orderly on the fleece. There were two small Ziploc bags, one contained more trail mix, and another had two Snickers bars — a childhood favorite for both of us; apparently a surprise Andy intended to lay on me later. A large red first aid kit with a white cross on its face. Matches. A lighter. A pair of leather gloves. At the bottom of the main compartment was a large nylon bag containing the tools needed to dress a deer. A necessary component I would have never thought about beforehand — having not seriously considered that we would actually kill a deer — but Andy had thought of that. Inside the nylon bag were two pairs of latex gloves, some folded up paper towels, several large plastic bags, zip-ties, a small whetstone, a short length of climbing rope, ostensibly for dragging the deer, and of immediate benefit a bottle of hand sanitizer — which across my hands not only felt cleansing but calming as well.

Also, inside one of the pack's side pockets, I found the gem of the trove, a brand new package of paracord — 100 feet worth. This was the key I needed.

Dad found a flat area in a clearing for us. He then sent us

out on a search, telling us to gather several sticks of a specified length and diameter. He insisted that we use already fallen or dead limbs, not to cut anything off a living tree. When we returned, Dad sat off to the side while he instructed us on the proper pattern. As he watched us work, he told us how the Native Americans used a travois, dragged by a horse or sometimes, even a dog, to move their supplies and the occasional slain animal from one camp to the next. The work that Andy and I were doing was for the singular purpose of pulling firewood from the further reaches of the property back to the cabin.

On Andy's belt was the next tool I needed, a large folding knife. Unfolding it revealed two blades, a dangerous-looking gut hook, another preparation for dressing a deer, and a long smooth blade. I removed my belt and added the knife's holster to it.

My next step felt like a violation of Andy's little bit of remaining privacy. I wanted to see what else Andy had brought with him. Kneeling next to him, I said, "Excuse me, brother, for just a moment." I took a deep breath, suppressing my urge to cry, and dug around in his pockets. I had no time for emotions. There was nothing in Andy's pockets, empty.

Andy's knife was sharp but cutting down two long saplings with a smooth blade proved to be hard work. I didn't have the luxury of time to search for dried wood.

I trimmed the wood to size and laid the two long pieces into a narrow 'V', next placing several shorter pieces across the broad end and another short piece across the narrow end. I parsed out the paracord into the many short lengths I needed to lash the sticks together and began tying my knots.

"Andy, we're doing great. I'll have you back down the mountain soon."

Although I was speaking to Andy, I was the one who needed encouragement. That morning I had expected nothing more than a walk to spend time with my brother. The intention was a half-day hike, a few miles out and back to the cabin. Something a freshman boy scout would have no problem with. But what I was faced with now was the most difficult of tasks imaginable.

Andy's agenda had been more ambitious and thoughtful. He had described in detail the hike and his intended destination, a large clearing in the government's wilderness area. The choreography had been carefully planned in his mind, and he had diligently reviewed the agenda with me as we started out. By this hour, Andy had fully expected to be settled into a relaxing spot and watching for deer.

The real trick was how to load and balance the travois. The sticks provided a minimal platform. It was easy enough to stack and haul back two or three pieces of firewood. That was literally child's play. Hauling in a dozen or so pieces was more of a challenge. Back when we were young, failure was funny. By the end of the summer, we learned how to stack the wood, properly securing the load.

Loading the travois this time was a task I took on with significantly more gravity. This wasn't a pile of wood; it was many times more difficult, not only because of the physics. I focused on the task in front of me, blocking the emotions.

By the time I was done, even with our gear stacked between his legs, Andy looked reasonably comfortable strapped in the contraption. I looked at Andy, murmuring, "This will be a bit uncomfortable. I know. The ride's going to be a bit bumpy, but we're heading down now."

With the focus of building the travois out of the way and my energy now drained, I was suddenly exhausted. And I still had so much work ahead of me. I had to move forward quickly. Slipping on Andy's leather gloves, I stepped inside the travois and grabbed its handles. I instantly gave in to the burden and collapsed into a weeping heap. The travois coming to the ground with me.

"Sorry, Andy. Not a good start."

This beautiful, verdant patch of earth, this Garden of Eden, had within a few moments been transformed into a threatening chaotic void. I was in the middle of nowhere. Evicted, dislodged, uncertain, with few resources — with my dead brother in tow. I checked my watch. It was already after four o'clock. If there was any chance to make it back before sunset, I needed to start heading downhill immediately. I braced myself for the challenge and again picked up the travois.

The weight was not quite as enormous as I had expected, but still it was substantial. Setting the crossbar against my hips, I tentatively tested my contraption, feeling its resistance as I took the first step. Instantly clear, this was going to be a monumental job. I took several more steps forward. The travois' tail dragged heavily against the ground. A few steps were okay, but I wondered how the weight would feel later, an hour later, two hours. I pressed onward.

In the shade of a tree, I set Andy down and double-checked all my lashings and straps. I took Andy's fleece out of the packing and wrapped it around the crossbar to reduce the harshness of the rough branch against my hips.

I started the trip in earnest. I leaned into the wood. The new cushion worked brilliantly. The load followed compliantly with the noise of the back end scrapping along, offering a steady grinding background noise that overwhelmed the sound of my boots.

I headed back on the trail in the direction from which we had arrived. It was easy to follow. It traced the edge of the clearing, and we soon came upon where I had been standing just a few minutes earlier. The overhang of the trees to my right and the tall grasses to my left. The sun to my left dropping towards the horizon. Without pause, I moved past the spot from where the fatal shot had been fired.

With my destination in mind and Andy firmly in tow, I refused to look back at the site of the crime. Pushing the travois, I kept my eyes focused forward. The first few yards were remarkably smooth, with my mind finally unburdened from the logistics of getting started. From here, it was a question of following one step after the other.

Within a few more paces, I had turned into the woods, the trail narrowing. My focus returned to the design of the newly built contraption. I stopped for a second and set Andy down. I let my arms relax a little and looked at Andy to make sure he was still secure, and to catch my breath. The travois was designed to be narrow enough to slide along the trail without getting wedged between trees or rocks. So far, so good, but I expected the path would become more challenging as we went along.

I wished for a meditative state, one with a singular focus on physical exertion, nothing else, but my memories from an hour earlier were still fresh, vivid, and raw. In an incessant and tireless loop, the videos started playing back in my mind. Another iteration. This time the tape began with my glancing across the grass-filled clearing, then sequel into an impossibly long exposure of the bear leaning over and clawing fiercely at Andy. Then my frantic fumbling for the rifle. The checklist. A jump to the indelible image of my peering through the scope, seeing Andy with the crosshairs on his chest. I pushed the travois on. I already doubted my own memories. The previously resisted emotions emerged full-scale. The physical struggle offered resistance to the emotional one. But they fought against the other, unleashing their violence into my swollen chest. My breathing labored from the effort. My face constricted, trying to suppress the pain.

I remembered the perfect silence that followed the shot.

Had I hesitated before pulling the trigger? Could my aim have been better? I pushed harder, one step at a time. I concentrated on the travois' resistance and the physiology of my muscles, trying to find the best rhythm for dragging the load across the field. My legs felt the sled's heavy resistance, my arms felt the weight of the front end. I stepped deliberately one foot after the next down the trail, trying desperately to banish my thoughts.

But, suddenly, my eye was back on the scope. The cross-hairs on the bear's chest. I felt the trigger's light resistance on my finger. And I peered now across the yellow field, with the gnats circling low everywhere. But my brother did not appear anywhere.

The beads of sweat started rolling down my forehead, over my eyes, and off my chin. I needed a rest, but I had gone barely but a hundred yards. The burden was becoming heavier and I was tiring. I recalled Dad's admonition that rest was for the lazy; there'd be plenty of time to rest when you're dead. Time was pressing. I'd not a clue how Andy's condition would change over the next few hours. And I respected him too much to do anything but hurry home.

The trail turned uphill and the strain increased by an order of magnitude. Each step became more difficult. The length of the trail home appeared now more daunting. I tried to calculate my pace and how long the whole journey might take, but I found it difficult to not only determine my pace — which was now crawl-like — but also I was completely uncertain of my progress, unable to locate any familiar landmarks.

The pressure on the trigger was light, but the image of the bullet passing over the tall grasses was illogically time-warped and graphic. My memories had swiftly transformed into feverish hallucinations.

Turning level again, the trail became a little more forgiving. Sensing progress, I was back to following the stream where Andy and I had once built the weir so many years ago.

Those many years ago, while poised next to my watchful father, his ever-discerning eyes on me, my first rifle shot had surprised me. But with my second shot and every subsequent shot since, I was prepared, prepared for that sudden sharp concussive explosion. Ever since I'd always kept my eye on the sight and my focus downrange. Before my shot, I was certain the crosshairs were on the bear's chest, but in one quick beat, the scene had changed. Maybe I blinked. Maybe there was a glare from the sun. Suddenly, maybe it was Andy that had become the creature in my crosshairs. And then, in the next instant, both had disappeared below the grasses. Could it possibly be that I had shot my own brother? But I saw no bullet wound on Andy, but within that bloody mess, how could I have known? The bear could have killed Andy. That was certainly possible. But if so, what happened to my bullet? Where did it land? I know, just know, that I couldn't have missed everything. I needed to know what the truth was — or did I?

I trudged on, taking deep breaths and, for the moment, trying to forget.

A couple of weeks before Dad's fall, it had been a good day. Kevin and Alex were running loops in the front yard while I worked in the garden, organizing my flowers. I felt good about my time with the boys, a little catch and a run to the store. At lunch, Liz and I took a long walk. And by late afternoon, in my study, I was catching up on my reading. That evening, I took my family out for dinner — a family dinner. The world wasn't perfect, but it felt pretty close. Everything felt orderly. Everything had its place. A house, a garden, a wife, and good children. I was proud of all of it.

I had no sense of the distance I had traveled. The work was catching up with me, and my stamina was being tested. Out of breath, I set my load down for a moment. Tightly tucked on the travois, Andy looked secure. When wrapping him with the improvised ties made from the sleeves of his shirt, I had taken extra care with the presentation. I knew it was only me that was going to see him this way, but I wanted him comfortable and, in a weird way, attractive. This wasn't an inert pile of firewood or sack of potatoes I was carrying. He was still my brother. The only concession I was forced to make was that I had to awkwardly spread his legs a bit so that I could nestle our gear in the gap. Still, he looked peaceful. I wanted to believe that.

I wished I could have spoken with him for just a moment or two, but I had no idea what I'd say.

"Hey Andy, how's the ride?"

By this point, I had walked for almost an hour. The sun had just fallen below the peaks and I knew darkness would not be far off. I was straining from the burden, and the harder effort weakened my resistance, allowing me to cry. The tears flowed unabated and uncontrollable while I continued with the contraption down the path. Surprisingly, this emotional relief worked to lessen the physical pain.

Reaching a flat open area, I set Andy down. My arms were now quickly tiring between rests. I removed Andy's belt, then mine, connecting them into a single, long strap. I had plenty of paracord left to fashion for myself a crude replacement belt. I stepped back into the travois, then looped the belts over my shoulder, tying the ends to my handle. This effectively transferred some of the travois' weight to my shoulders.

The air felt cooler here but my body temperature was still high. With its impending arrival, I started to worry about the evening. My perception of distance was severely damaged. Intuitively, I felt as if we might be nearing the halfway point, but I really had no clue. If I were truly at the halfway point, that meant the time I'd already spent walking would have to be repeated. And that consequently meant that it would be impossible to return to the cabin before dark. Walking the trail at night, even without this load behind me, would be a foolish choice.

"I spoke to Andy this morning."

Liz had called me at the office before I flew out west.

"He says you're not answering his calls. I hope you're not doing to him what you do to me, ignoring him until you're ready to talk and ... treating him like some ignorant fool. I hope that's not the case, Cole. And, he did share with me a great idea. He said he wanted to invite you to your father's cabin for the weekend. I think that's brilliant. This is something you need to do with your brother. You could even take the boys. I could send them later if you want."

"But you've been telling me about feeling abandoned and neglected. — Liz, I'm confused."

"This isn't about me... it's about the boys ... our boys matter more than me. Don't think of it as giving in to your brother. Do it to spend some quality time with your sons. Go. Just Go. Maybe some brother-with-brother time together would be good for you, as well as Andy. You grew up with him; you know him and trust him. Right or not?"

"Yeah, sure ... but ..."

"Maybe if you can open up with Andy and get some things off your chest. Talk about your father and your relationship with him — and with Andy. He told me about how peaceful and beautiful it is out there. Never mind that I've never had the chance to see it for myself, that I was never asked to go out there. But that's a different story for another day."

"We've never talked like that."

"You and Andy need each other. Your family is small, but don't minimize its importance. The way you've been lately, you're not any good to the boys. You treat them like the little minions at your office. They are not cogs in some machine, Cole, waiting for their next set of orders. They are people, young ones, full of potential, like seedlings that need sun and water. They need a connected father to nourish them, to show them how to become good men. Are you listening to me, Cole?"

The improvised strap around my neck had helped save my arms, but my shoulders were paying the price. They were desperately asking for a reprieve. Surrendering, I stepped out of the contraption and looked back at Andy.

"Sorry, Andy. I know it's been a bumpy ride."

He appeared calm and unperturbed. I took several deep cleansing breaths, stretched my neck and rolled my shoulders to loosen the tension. A fallen tree served as a temporary seat while I ate the trail mix from Andy's pack.

I pulled down a generous slug of water. The short rest was of little help, but I was not yet ready to give in. Using Andy's knife, I cut off a piece of my fleece for padding and re-situated how the strap crossed over my shoulders. I picked Andy up, and we started off once again.

As before, each step was a focused, deliberate, concerted effort. I leaned into the contraption with my hips. Although having learned how to support weight partly with my shoulders, the real burden was still on my arms. It all hurt. Although I was not in bad shape for a middle-aged man, this was by far the most taxing ordeal I had ever experienced, and I was ill-prepared for the effort. The drag of the travois against the ground vibrated through my arms and shoulders and my entire soul. The exertion was consuming the limits of my physical energy, and the anguish about what had happened was taxing my mental capacity. I was overwhelmed by the task, but I had no choice but to continue.

24

I made the final turn towards home ... and could only laugh. On both sides approaching the house, the street was packed with cars. A uniformed valet met me at the front gate, then gestured me around a yellow cone up my own driveway. Rather than explain who I was, I let him take my car.

This was our third house since being married, and hopefully, this one would be permanent. It was everything we wanted, a great neighborhood, lots of trees, plenty of room for a pool. Liz liked showing off our backyard and had decided that Kevin's birthday was as good an event as any to do it.

The front door was framed by an archway of red and blue balloons. Two steps into the entry hall, I was confronted by a jungle of streamers, and to make my way to the back yard, I had to pass by three large pasteboards on which Liz had attached three dozen photos of Kevin tracing his life since birth. This most assuredly embarrassed him to no end, but Liz was a proud mother, no arguing about that. Dangling from strings surrounding the boards were brightly colored Sharpies; these allowed his friends to write their inane if affectionate comments.

Liz had the backyard fitted out as if for a wedding, with rented tables scattered across the lawn, and a pair of open tents were set up off to the side. In one tent, servers were preparing hot dogs for the kids. In the other, a chef, complete with a toque blanche, was preparing made-to-order fresh salads for the moms. Nothing about this seemed appropriate for a twelve-year-old boy's birthday party.

With the boys huddled on one side of the pool and the girls on another, they used the water as a place to mingle. Boy/girl pairings were in no short supply; a portend of what must be ahead for Kevin. I hadn't imagined he'd arrived at this stage just yet, but I could plainly see his arrival happening before my eyes.

Kevin sat at a plastic-littered table surrounded by several of his friends — all boys. I recognized a few from his basketball team. He acknowledged my presence with a cautious wave; under the circumstances, that was all the attention I expected, but sufficient. I maintained a distant vantage point, only engaging with his friends as they wandered by. I didn't want to interfere with the party's natural choreography.

Not much of a surprise, I was the only father here and, as a result, wasn't sure what to do with myself. I said hello to a few of Liz's friends, but they were far more interested in sharing with each other the interpersonal dynamics of the children. I kissed a few cheeks, then followed the smell of grilled meat. I hadn't indulged in a hotdog craving in a while, so I ordered one with a light touch of chili and onions. I took a bite. While it had been viscerally appealing on the grill, it ended up being less than satisfying in its eating. Although I was glad to have indulged in my spontaneous urge, after a couple of bites, I considered myself done with hot dogs for a while.

Liz came up from behind and touched my shoulder, followed by a peck on the cheek. "I'm so happy you're here," she said. "I know it's hard for you to take off in the middle of the day."

"I didn't want to disappoint you."

"It's Kevin who you don't want to disappoint."

"He's fine with his friends, I think. From the looks of it, he hardly cares that his dad is here or not."

"More than you realize."

Liz paused and studied me for a second before saying, "By the way, it was super nice that your dad called earlier before the party."

"That was his once-a-year call, I guess."

"He deserves a little more credit from you. He talked for a while with Kevin and said he was sending him a present in the mail. But, you know, listening to Kevin's tone, I think there is some real desire to connect more with his grandfather. I think he'd like to know more about that side of the family."

"There's not much there."

"I know that's how you feel, but let the boys form their own opinions. Let's see about inviting your dad here for a few days. Or maybe, we go out and see him. He's always talking about the mountains."

Liz meant well but envisioning that scenario induced a sense of palpable discomfort. Pondering the thought took me to a place I preferred not to go. In order to preserve the light-heartedness of the day and not disappoint Liz, I lied, knowing I could pull back later. "That would be a great idea, sure. Let's talk about it later after I get this deal at work settled."

I received the smile and twinkling eyes that told me I had said the right thing.

"It's a beautiful party. I hope you're having fun," I said.

"Fabulous. It brings me such joy seeing all the boys together."

"So, how much is this costing me?" I was hoping to sound sarcastic.

"Stop it. Why do you do this to me? Quit counting the dollars. This is for your son, you know. Really, it's no big deal.

You just need to relax sometimes. It's all fine. Enjoy."

Liz gave me a quick kiss, then walked off to attend to a newcomer, leaving me holding the remnants of my now cold hotdog. I wadded it up inside a napkin and threw it away. I grabbed a drink to go and headed back out the door.

I gave the valet guy a few bucks and drove towards the office.

I was almost there when Liz rang my cell phone.

"Where the hell are you? You're always hurrying off someplace. Couldn't you stick around another ten minutes?"

"Seriously? What do you expect of me? Hang out there like some idiot? Jump in the pool with the boys? Flirt with your girlfriends? Shit, give me a break for once."

I regretted it later, but at that point, I hung up on Liz and went straight into my next meeting.

I ended up on calls all evening. By the time I got back home, it was nearly midnight and Liz was asleep. I turned my phone to silent, making sure nobody would wake me up in the next couple of hours, then I set the alarm for five. I left the house the next morning before Liz or the boys were up.

25

In a concession to my aching muscles, I set Andy down often. I'd take in a quick sip of water, trying to achieve some brief modicum of recovery, before moving on again. The crossbar against my hips became more resistant with each step. In consequence, my hips were feeling bruised and tender. I related my fate to that of Phillippides' agony, although without the good news of victory; my mission was undoubtedly urgent, but I wasn't sure my body could complete the journey. Brother or no brother, I wasn't sure how much longer I could drag this contraption.

My sense of the distance I had traveled continued to be very poor. After a couple of hours of trekking, I intellectually knew I was making some progress, but I was unsure how to measure it. I hadn't seen any familiar landmarks, and my pace was awkwardly slow. The rapidly fading light now started to dishearten me. I realized that I'd be spending the night in the woods and had to start thinking about where to stop. I wouldn't need much space. It only had to be somewhat level and big enough for the two of us. The trail before me was narrow and either side thick with understory. I needed to continue on, plus there was still some light left.

Luckily, the next stretch was downhill, with the trail

widening out a bit. The weight compliantly followed along and my walking grew a little easier, with gravity helping out. The sun had disappeared behind the mountains and wouldn't be long before it was set.

Why had Andy and I been walking so far apart earlier? He was mad with me — and I suppose justifiably so. That much was clear. I had tried to apologize for last night, but he didn't want to hear any of it. Was the failure all mine ... or, perhaps, partly his, for not engaging with me? ... or, perhaps, there wasn't any failure whatsoever — it was what it was?

I gave a glance back at my brother.

"Andy, tell me. What was on your mind?"

I knew that we would never be friends again like when we were younger. We had become too different over time, and that ancient history couldn't be recreated, nor would anybody want that. But, when I first heard Andy's pleading with me to join him on this mountain adventure, I believed that a middle place was possible for the two of us. A better place than where we had been for the last thirty years. A place where there was a possible foundation upon which to build.

But my decision to visit this property — Dad's property, I still thought of it like that — assumed a major self-deception. I had wanted to prove to myself that I was man enough to walk here again and pretend that my pain was gone, that it had been processed and dealt with. But it turns out that I was wrong about myself. The pain wasn't gone, and, in fact, it was not even much less potent. That's just the way it'll be; I'll be forever plagued by my father. I had regrettably transferred my anger for Dad onto Andy. I knew that wasn't fair, but he had enmeshed his being with Dad's; they were interlinked and inseparable. I couldn't see Andy without also glimpsing Dad's shadow hovering nearby.

I continued to scan ahead for a spot to pass the night.

The trail turned down towards the stream I'd been walking parallel to, steeply declining below me, with a series of tree roots forming a set of irregularly spaced steps. I stepped down and across each one, then braced myself for the travois' jolt as the back end dropped off roots behind me. Although I was going downhill, my pace slowed considerably due to the tedious footwork. As treacherous were the switchbacks that were accumulating more frequently as we descended. I crept forward, planning our path carefully around each root and each bend, dragging the travois in the widest possible arc. At the tightest turns, I had to stop and set Andy down before going back and picking up the rear of the travois, realigning it to a new orientation. And then starting back down again. My pace was slowing, the work exhausting.

The roots eventually receded from the path only to give way to a thick understory. The unruly shrubs crowded my path, scratching against my legs and pulling at the sides of the travois. At one sharp switchback, a branch snagged the travois' back end, seizing our momentum and jarring me, pulling my shoulders backwards. My left foot slid out from under me. My right leg strained to hold the shifting weight, but the travois twisted out of control. My balance gave way, jerking me together with Andy and the entire contraption into a fateful fall downhill, the shoulder straps dragging me into the thicket. Restrained by the straps, my arms couldn't guard my fall. My face slammed into a bush, with my forehead leading the way.

Luckily, we hadn't fallen far. My immediate assessment found no severe pain. Nothing broken. That was the good news. But now I was twisted like a pretzel, uncomfortably crammed underneath the travois, with a bunch of leaves pushing into my face. Andy's weight was pressing against my back, aggravating my predicament. I knew I wasn't sliding any further. We were static, at least for the moment.

"Damn it. Just what I needed."

I freed my left hand, instinctively slapping the bushes

away only to have them instantly return the favor — a further insult, but with the benefit of stilling my anger. With a few contortions I disentangled myself. I touched my forehead and cheeks, feeling drops of fresh blood. The damage didn't feel serious, just a few sensitive scratches.

I worked my way out of the A-frame and checked Andy's condition. He still appeared to be comfortably snug. Now leaning onto a narrow tree, the travois was surprisingly undamaged. I was proud of my construction skills, and I think Dad would've been proud, as well. The travois had withstood the accident. It had remained solid, intact. The lashings had held Andy in place, and he looked unperturbed by the whole incident.

Having resettled myself, I rolled Andy and the travois back to their proper traveling position. Between the shock of the fall, exhaustion and the rising bump on my head, I felt a new urgency to find a place to rest for the night. With the travois righted and centered on the trail, I moved forward again, fast as I could move, into the diminishing light.

My forehead throbbed. I had no mirror, but my fingertips kept trying to describe the damage. Blood, mixed with my sweat, found its way onto my lips. I was annoyed and ripped the tail off my shirt to use as a handkerchief. I dabbed at the wound, but despite the extra care, blood continued to drip over my eyebrows and down the side of my face. As I needed both hands for the travois, it was an aggravation that I had to get used to.

The forest was darkening, and the sky's blue was beginning to deepen. The sun was certainly now below the horizon. The dim light would soon prevent me from moving forward.

The trail dipped down next to the stream. On the opposite side, I spotted a narrow sandy beach, framed on the low side by the water bending through a long gentle turn and on the upper side a tall protective bank. From where I stood, the sandy area appeared to be temporarily dry. This was not my planned crossing; that was still further ahead, where the trail exited the government property and onto Dad's property. This was a good enough place to lay down for the evening. I blazed a short new trail for several yards through the undergrowth and forded the low stream, knowing that I would have to reverse this same crossing the next morning.

The place felt safe, enclosed and protected. The beach's U-shaped area, semi-cave-like, with tall trees growing above the steep embankment, was easily adaptable to our needs. I placed Andy parallel to the stream and situated my own resting spot a couple of steps upstream.

With the physical strain and urgency now set aside, I felt a welcome ease. I savored each drop of water, the unique flavor of each nut and raisin. For the final part of my mini-meal, I ate one of the two Snickers bars, heartsick that Andy wasn't able to share this minor pleasure with me.

The beach was level and soft. I balled up Andy's fleece and used it as a pillow. Being horizontal allowed my muscles, in particular, my back, to relax. Despite the horrors of the day, my mind was used up and numb. Lying silently, looking through the trees at the quickly darkening sky, every part of me gave in to a nothingness. My mind quieted, and I found myself in a meditative state. I was acutely aware of my surroundings, the vanishing light, the almost inaudible wind in the upper branches, the gurgles from the stream, and the earthy smell of the forest's decomposing residue. Once I cooled down from my exertions, I became sensitive to the evening's cool air. I dug around, finding the few bits of clothing that might serve as blankets and laid them over me. I closed my eyes.

I awoke underneath a pitch-black sky. I checked my watch and saw that I had only been asleep an hour. The only light was the faint glow of the stars coming through the branches. I reached out through the darkness and touched Andy. I could tell he was fine, just like I had left him.

Staring at his silhouette through the darkness, I could not believe he was gone — and that my brother had died only a couple of hours ago.

The memories of the day started to plague me again. It was a choppy, disconnected sequence, everything playing out of order: standing next to the grassy field, the huge bear rising, breakfast in the cabin, running up the path, the expanding pool of blood, the view through the rifle's sight. It was a disjunctive mash-up, void of any sensible pattern. That singular image, what I saw through the gun's sight, repeatedly reappeared and magnified as if that were the single critical moment upon which the world hinged, when a slightly more cautious decision could have resulted in a dramatically different result — an innocuous moment that wouldn't haunt me like this one was promising to do.

What if I had pulled the trigger a microsecond faster? Was my aim off by an inch? If we had started our walk an hour earlier, the bear would have been elsewhere, not there, not when we crossed the berry patch. Would two minutes have made a difference? Would two seconds have made a difference?

Moreover, and this is more of something that was in my control, what if my conversation with Andy had been more sympathetic? What if we had walked side by side? A few poorly chosen words shouldn't have that much significance — but are a few words what made the difference between life and death? I tried to apologize — but he rejected me — just as my father had done. He pushed me away.

My head throbbed, my mind spiraling with confusing questions. I was fully awake. I dug through Andy's backpack and found his medical box, grabbed the vial of Ibuprofen and took four pills, chasing them with a slug of water.

I remade my pallet and tried to find comfort again. Before finding a halfway tolerable position, I reshaped the improvised pillow a half-dozen times. I laid with my back on the ground, my eyes staring aimlessly up through the trees at nothingness.

For one exciting moment, I thought I had spotted a meteor, but it was, in fact, the blinking red light of a jet flying high above, noiseless through the maze of other lights. I let myself imagine where those people were headed, their lives and jobs. That led me back into the reality of my own work. All that felt so distant from where I lay but posed just off-stage waiting for its cue. I knew there would be no escaping its re-entrance, but I had no interest in playing that game at that moment. In fact, the sharp contrast between the glare of the office world and my current spot in the dark woods induced a nauseous disorienting dissonance.

I knew that my work would soon enough find its way back in. I forcefully set those thoughts aside and turned my thoughts to Liz. Realizing that she was not at the top of my mind surprised me. I had let other issues dominate. The boys, too — they had dropped down on my list. How sick? How could I have placed thoughts of work before family? I chastised myself. I sat up. My mind raced. None of these thoughts were useful, at least not in this situation. With this much mental activity, sleep felt impossible. I needed a distraction.

I turned on the flashlight and assembled our remaining food, including the second Snickers bar. Taking the smallest bites possible, I lengthened my enjoyment. I slowly ate all that remained. Those small remnants were satisfying and enough to squelch the hunger pains. Although, after that brief indulgence, there was nothing left to eat. And I was still awake.

I laid my head down again and covered myself. I saw the glimmering moon rising in the eastern sky, and although extraordinarily beautiful, that sight provided me with no help.

With my eyes closed, Liz appeared as an apparition, laying beside me, talking in long involved sentences. I struggled to understand, but couldn't make out what she was saying. She was propped up on one elbow, talking urgently and looking right into my eyes. Her eyes glistened in the darkness, catching many points of light, like a mirror to the night sky. I returned her direct gaze, straining to understand her words. Her presence pushed in close to me and then closer, to the point I was completely enveloped by her atmosphere.

I awoke. And I wept.

I refilled the water bottles in the stream. I let my hands linger in the freezing water as a way to distract my mind's machinations. I went back to my resting position on my back, but sleep was elusive. Peering up through the trees, I tried to think like Andy would have. He would have been basking in the stars' infinite wonder. It would have helped ease his pain.

The ocean was vast. I was floating alone. The waves caught the moonbeams, scattering them in a thousand directions across the surface. There was no panic. I was alone.

I was alone in a field of tall, wavy grasses. Across the clearing, I saw Andy walking towards the looming bear. I was desperately yelling at him to go in the other direction.

Andy and I were on the street running through the neighborhood with the other kids, playing a game of kick the can. Down at the far end of the block, in the middle of the street, Dad stood outside our house, appearing about a thumb's width high. He whistled like no other person I have ever met. It was a crystal clear signal we were to stop whatever we were doing and return home immediately.

The air had become cold. I curled up into a tight ball the best I could and reset my blankets again. I shivered.

The three of us sat down to dinner. Andy rattled off stories about all the tiny creatures he had discovered in the woodpile. Dad politely engaged him. Other than that brief exchange, there was a long uncomfortable silence extending through the post-dinner clean-up. Rather than our usual routine of leaving in the morning, Dad had us pack up all of our things that evening. We began our drive home well after dark. Andy fell asleep in the car. If Andy knew of our fight, he kept his knowledge concealed.

I thought I had shielded Andy from my secrets. I wasn't ever quite sure — and even less so now. But if my brother knew then, might Liz also have known? And if Liz knew, might the boys know? Know or sense, did it even matter? And if they didn't know now, might they soon come to know? And what about the rest of the world — how well could they read my feelings, my innermost thoughts? And if all those people knew so much about me, why didn't they ever say anything? Did my projected demeanor fend off inquires? Or was this part and parcel of normal societal respect? A world my family knew nothing of — we didn't speak — about how we felt. We didn't bring up bad memories. We moved forward, on to something productive. I must have had put so much energy into suppressing those bad feelings — and to whose benefit? To whose cost? Did I even know I was doing it? It certainly didn't make me any closer to anyone. Alone, next to Andy, I realized that I had spent most of my life constructing walls — like my Dad? But protecting what? Protecting whom? The inside from the outside or the outside from the inside? Who amongst all the people really knew me in a way anywhere close to the way Andy did? In the entire universe, it had to be Andy who had the best perspective on who I really was. And then again, maybe it was only Andy who could see through the façade? Perhaps our shared genes had more power in that way? Perhaps it was because we shared the same antagonist?

The moon was high in the sky, broken by the high branches. My head continued to throb, and I touched my forehead, careful not to disturb the newly formed scabs.

I rolled over and reset my makeshift blankets.

I could see in Dad's mannerisms the occasional reflection of myself. Our hands were the same shape; I remember comparing them as a kid — and we actually resembled each other in our appearances, quite closely: the same slant of the eyebrows, the same nose. But it was like observing that horses and their offspring each had four legs; it was a scientific fact devoid of emotional content.

The rifle sight was pressed uncomfortably against my eyebrow. I felt like it was bruising my eyeball. The crosshairs were circling in tight, very tight, random arcs.

I awoke. In the west, the moon had settled behind the mountains. Down the valley, to the east, the sky was shifting through the subtle gradient of colors that precede sunrise. Anxious to make progress again, I repacked my few belongings onto Andy's sled. I took out the flashlight and carefully reinspected all of my lashings. I was still proud of how well my improvised assemblage had performed. I splashed some of the stream's cool water on my face and drank a fair share as well.

I was ready to go once again. But I sat by Andy for a while, waiting for a bit more light.

"Why," I asked Andy, "are we so fascinated with the sunrise and sunset and not so much with the sun in the middle of the day? Once the sun rises above the horizon and the color transitions to a brilliant white, the fascination disappears. Have you ever thought about any of that?"

I let Andy mull on the question for a while.

Andy would have had an answer much better and more philosophical than simply, "It's pretty." He could never be so trite. He surely would have something profound to say about the ethereal nature of time and how it flows differently depending on the observer. He might have quoted Einstein on the relative difference between kissing a lover versus sitting on a hot stove. Or maybe he would have waxed on about our humanity's time-based anxieties. Namely, how packed our agendas are and how the brief distraction of a sunset can help re-center us, by simply focusing on that slowly descending celestial body, we can match our slowness to that of the earth's internal rhythm. Andy might have said that we are but tiny specks within the cosmos and, at the same time, are connected to its deepest vast outer reaches. Or maybe he would have digressed about how the ancients managed time and their mechanics of timekeeping, how the sky was integral to our daily lives. Or whether we were regretting the day that had just disappeared? Or were excited with anticipation about the day in store? For Andy, a sunrise would never be just a sunrise. Even though it happened daily, it was a moment of joy.

I was worried about what this particular sunrise was going to bring forth. How was I going to explain my dead brother? To whom? In a few hours, I had phone calls to make. What was the world going to think of me? I had killed my brother — either directly or indirectly — I still didn't know. I had failed him.

As the sky lightened into a pale blue, I faced my new harsh reality and set out again with Andy in tow.

I pulled him across the stream. As I made my way up the small rise back to reunite with the trail, my bodily aches, which I had briefly forgotten, arose again, reminding me of the previous day's work and impressing upon me how much strain still lay ahead.

I straightened the travois into the center of the trail. I took a swig of water, checked on Andy, and made sure all the packing was still stable. He looked comfortable. I lifted the handles, threw the strap over my shoulders and leaned into the crossbar — again.

It wasn't long before the sun was glaring into my eyes. Rolling down my forehead, the sweat irritated my scratches, and the pounding of my heart, coupled with my rising blood pressure, produced a monumental headache and further reminded me of yesterday's injury.

With the trail narrower than yesterday's and with no interest in repeating yesterday's fall, I stayed sharply focused on the travois' track. Although the width of the travois was generally wider than the trail, along the edges, the only impediments were the easily pliable ferns and delicate understory plants. Except for catching on the occasional stone, the travois thankfully pulled smoothly.

"But you were the one," I prodded Andy, "who sped away from me. Why were you so upset? You know, you could've made an effort. It wasn't entirely my fault that we were separated. Why am I assuming all the blame here? And you know, you can be a bit too sensitive at times. Admit it. It takes two to make peace. Sure, my choice of words was poor, but you need to take ownership of your mistakes."

Andy was quiet.

As I walked, I thought of the many curiosities Andy and I had discovered as young boys playing on this mountain. I imagined Andy in fifteen different versions, from young and naive to older and still naive. But the good memories, however hard I forced them to the forefront of my mind, quickly ground to an abrupt halt. What separated Andy and me of late was not any interpersonal conflict but our fundamentally different attitudes towards our father. I wondered how a simple difference in point of view could be so divisive.

In the mountains, Dad and I argued all the time. At least that is how I remembered it. Always arguing. How it started and when I can't remember. I do remember my emotions that controlling me, that heat rising up, that need to take him down a notch, that intense desire to be heard, and that infuriating frustration that came with not being heard — and I remember all the versions of how it finished: "I don't understand you." "Why can't you be more like your brother?" "What's the matter with what I've given you? You lack for nothing." "After all that I have sacrificed for your benefit, you still care only about you. You show no fucking gratitude."

Stunned and incapable of retorting, Dad would leave me alone, stewing, and head back to the cabin. I would stand silently glaring at the old man. The conversation was over before it began.

My legs burned with each step. I felt we were making progress — but slowly.

I set Andy down for a water break, wishing I had another Snickers bar. Hunger gnawed inside my stomach.

My body ached ... all of it. The strap was heavy on my shoulders, the weight insufferable.

26

Around the next turn, the expected stream crossing quickly came into view. It was less than a hundred yards out, closer than I'd thought.

Arriving at the stream, I set Andy down. We had been walking for only a half-hour, and I already needed a short rest. I had fooled my stomach earlier by downing a fair quantity of water, but with my stomach empty, my energy was now gone. My thoughts were of that last Snickers bar; that would have been perfect now.

From the crossing I could easily visualize the rest of my journey. The end was in sight. Emboldened by the nearness of my goal, I picked Andy up again and pushed forward. The landmarks were familiar and predictable. The physical hangover had caught up with me. I was beyond tired, but that didn't matter as much. Concentrating on the next step and the next and the next, I broke the trip into a series of short journeys, with an extended rest at each juncture. The weather was good, and the urgency of nightfall was no longer a factor. I had time. I kept my focus on the next easily achievable goal.

Soon we were back up on the old logging road, and even though the path was slightly uphill, it was wide, and my anxieties about snagging the travois disappeared.

We paralleled the stream for a while until we arrived at the last fork. We rested there for a moment. Narrower and rarely used, the trail that would take us back home was shrouded with low-hanging trees, as if we were sneaking in by the back entrance — which we were.

Although this newest segment of path again made for challenging navigation, it was the last leg, and knowing that we were so very close, my energy remained bolstered by the anticipation. We crossed the fence line and were now back on our property. In the bright sunshine, the terrain felt like home, and my breathing felt more relaxed. The trail turned twice, and I saw the woodpile. The weight felt momentarily lighter and my pace quickened.

The end of our trip had been much closer than I had anticipated the previous night. Nevertheless, I didn't doubt my decision to stop. It would've been foolish to attempt those last steps at night. I walked past the spot where the trail spilled out beside the woodpile, but I couldn't stop, not yet. Our front porch was mere yards away. My arms ached, and the final few steps felt like my last. Even though relief coursed through my body, my exhaustion was complete.

"Andy, we're home."

I pulled Andy to the edge of the porch. Through a couple of lifts alternating between the front and the back of the travois, I soon had him comfortably situated on the porch's edge with his head turned so that he could look out towards the pond. Andy's face was placid. I think he liked being back home.

I sat on the porch beside my brother, and we shared the same view. Sucking in the vast quantities of desperately need-ed oxygen, my chest heaved. My body convulsed in rhythm with the pounding of my heart.

As my pulse slowed and my body relaxed, I paid attention to nothing but the steady in and out of my breathing. With each expansion and expulsion, the effort slightly lessened.

I looked at Andy, putting a hand on his cold cheek. "So, that wasn't so bad ... was it?"

He looked disinterested.

I hadn't thought through what came next. Sitting in the calm and taking note of my place in the world after such an ordeal, I half-expected that with the complete evaporation of all my strength, I'd succumb to the emotional toll and collapse into a hysterical messy blob. But I didn't. I think I was too tired for even that.

After a couple of minutes of sitting, my plan became obvious. First, I needed to call the authorities, then Liz.

I found my phone just where I had left it, on the nightstand next to my bed. When I came back out of the cabin, the screen door slammed. The loud snap startled me, momentarily freezing me.

"Sorry, Andy, but I need to leave you alone for a few minutes. I have a couple of calls I need to make. I'll be right back."

I tried running down the hill, but my legs only allowed for an urgent walk. Even at that, I felt the fatigue in every muscle.

I reached the special telephone spot, sat on the log, and dialed 911.

"911. What's your emergency?"

The question was expected, but I hadn't planned exactly what to say. The operator's voice was pleasant, bland, and helpful. My body, however, descended into a total meltdown. Saying out loud what I had been experiencing in my head took me to a new level of reality and vulnerability. Slightly concerned now, the operator asked, "Hello, how can I help you?" In response to this simple question, all I could do, though, was shiver and weep. It was an effort to keep the phone next to my ear. How does one say, "I just killed my brother?"

The operator repeated the question yet again. This time all

I could brokenly utter was, "Please hold."

I put the phone down next to me on the log and brought both hands onto my face in an attempt to arrest my emotions.

The shivering softened, but the tears flowed unabated. I took a couple of deep breaths and picked up the phone again. "There's been an accident."

My composure returned enough to cite the necessary facts and location. I needed to be clear and concise, and I was.

The operator responded, "I'm contacting the County Sheriff and the State Game Warden. They should arrive shortly. Do you need me to stay on the phone with you?"

"No. Not now, thank you. I need to get back to my brother."

The morning air was cold. Inside the cabin, on a hook by the front door, I found one of Andy's heavier jackets, one colored a dark red plaid. Why always plaid? I sat next to him on the porch while I waited for everything to start happening — the shit to hit the fan.

Burning out of the clear blue sky, the sun radiated a satisfying warmth. Even though the kitchen was only a few steps away, I let my hunger sit as a mild form of punishment.

I had resisted calling Liz. I wasn't yet sure how to break down for her the events of the last twenty-four hours. For the time being, it was only Andy and me who knew what had happened, and that felt right. The news, soon enough, was going to ripple out to the world, and that prospect terrified me.

While trudging through the forest, the physical suffering had overwhelmed my ability to think clearly, but, back at the cabin, with the struggle over, the journey in some sense finished, doubt surfaced as dominant — mixed with guilt. I worried about how I would be judged. How will my decisions while out in the forest be seen by others? What will the police think of me? Liz? The people at work? My boys? In that one decisive moment, did I pull the trigger a tenth of a second late ... or a tenth of a second too early? The what-ifs were not knowable — never — but I continued to torture myself, thinking of them over and over again. I strangely wished if I could ask Andy. Would he judge me harshly? Would he understand?

"I missed our conversations," I said to Andy. "Like the one we had the other night. It was mostly good, but I'm terribly sorry, it didn't end well. That was my fault."

It'd been a long time since we shared our inner thoughts and feelings honestly with each other. We had once been best friends. We knew everything about each other. Why had I let all that change?

Dad was strict, and getting out of line was a scary place to be, but at the end of the day, as long as our work was done, we had all kinds of freedom. We could roam the neighborhood, eat when we wanted and what we wanted. Dinners, Andy and me, alone together at the tiny kitchen table. Baseball in the front yard. And out here, in the woods, co-conspirators, exploring nature's vastness for hours on end.

"You really enjoyed this place, didn't you? ... And there was a time when I did as well. But I changed. It wasn't a choice; I had to protect my dignity. I admit I have some of Dad's characteristics. I know that. Not all good. I'm a bit hard-headed, perhaps. Two stubborn people aren't a good mix. You were different — but still stubborn in your own way. You held tight to your independent thinking. In fact, I think how to think is what you enjoyed most about your teaching. You wanted your students to be skeptical and enjoy the act of discovery. But, you never felt the need to confront Dad. What was it? Why were you so different from me in that way?"

At a slower speed this time, the tape played the events from the day before once again. The walk into the woods. The lengthening distance between Andy and me. The interstices of a second between seeing Andy enwrapped by the bear, the concussion from my shot all clicked by frame by frame, with every nuance becoming more vivid and less reliable with each replay.

The feel of the stock against my cheek.

I lifted my face towards the sun, hoping the radiation would obliterate my thought. It didn't.

My index finger lightly pressing the trigger.

I stood and walked towards the pond. My legs ached.

Looking back, I saw Andy nestled in his wrappings, laying comfortably on the porch, watching me.

If Andy were capable, what would he be thinking? How would HE judge me?

In the clear light of day, he looked pale and relaxed. Worry-free. I went over and sat next to him. We were once close, then distant, but I didn't know what we were now. Those many years ago, when I walked away from Dad, I never thought I was also leaving Andy. But I had. He reached out to me in his desperate, awkward ways, and I wrongly turned a deaf ear to his pleas.

I heard a vehicle coming up the drive. And now it starts.

The game warden and his partner showed up first. The warden made a cursory examination of the body, offering his polite sympathies. Knowing that the county sheriff was on his way, he expressed deference to him about the human aspects but was acutely interested in the bear.

"Can you tell me anything specific about the bear?"

"Don't know. What do you mean?"

"How big was he compared to your brother?"

"I assumed it was a she."

"Why's that?"

"I just figured she was trying to protect her young."

"Did you see any cubs?"

"Well, no."

"This sort of predatory behavior is more likely male. Could you make out any distinguishing marks?"

"Just a large brown bear."

"Can you tell me what direction the bear was headed?"

"When she — or he — dropped to all fours, I couldn't see the bear any longer."

"We'll have to track the bear down. Once a bear has killed a human, it's likely that they'll do so again."

"She didn't kill Andy; I did," I instinctively insisted.

"How do you mean?" The warden asked.

He gave me a long quizzical look. "Never mind. I'll stay out of that for the moment and let the sheriff get into all of that. Right now, I need to find a bear."

Although the sheriff was equally business-like, he was much more interested than the warden in my confusion about the ending point of my bullet. My words weren't heard or effective, at least there was nothing in his voice or demeanor that reflected the unambiguous horror that I had so recently experienced. He remained calm. We sat at the picnic table while he wrote long notes onto a yellow pad. I told him step by step what had happened over the last two days. His questions focused on the certainties to what I could truthfully testify as if I were already under oath. He expressed no surprise, no emotion. He nodded a lot, encouraging me to add as much detail as I could remember. The only physical evidence that was verifiable to him at this particular moment was that my brother was dead, laying near us on the porch, and my rifle. The rest was useless speculation. The interrogation was brief and rote. Nothing but the facts, times and distances.

At the end of his questioning, he closed his pad and only said, "You can go home. We'll be in touch."

"That's it?"

Another SUV had pulled up while we were talking and parked next to the other vehicles. The sheriff motioned to its occupants, who had been waiting for his command. As they started in our direction, he stated matter of factly that an autopsy would have to be performed. In all the turmoil, I hadn't thought about that detail. A sense of unease enveloped me, and my body tightened as if it were the one that was being threatened by the medical examiner's knife. At the thought of additional violence coming to Andy, the cutting and exposing of Andy's insides, I grabbed my gut and folded over in pain.

"Are you okay?" the sheriff asked.

"I'm sorry. Nauseous, I guess." I tried, failed to straighten myself up.

"Sit down here." He pointed to the edge of the porch where Andy had been moments ago.

"I'm exhausted and haven't eaten. I'll be fine." I refused to sit and forced myself to stand erect.

I couldn't rid myself of the image of Andy being incised and systemically manhandled like some farmhouse slaughtering. It was just a further desecration. I again felt as if I were about to faint. The sheriff and one of his associates grabbed me by the shoulders, placed me on the porch, and opened a bottle of water for me.

I took a long drink, and my dizziness slowly subsided.

They left me on the porch while the sheriff and the various authorities moved about, talking amongst themselves in muffled voices. I watched as they unceremoniously placed my baby brother into a thick black plastic bag, then loaded him into the back of an SUV modified for such purposes. The practiced routine of death removed what little bit of soul remained in Andy.

After several minutes the sheriff came back to me.

"I'll need your rifle and the remaining ammo."

"Of course," I pointed to the far end of the porch where all our gear was piled up.

"By the way, you need to have a doctor look at that forehead. That cut might need some stitches."

I soon found myself alone on the front porch.

Parked off to the side of the cabin was my dusty black rented Escalade, a symbol of the materialistic urban reality that I was about to reenter. A few yards away, next to the generator shed, was Andy's beater pickup. It appeared to be in the process of rusting and returning its minerals back to the soil. The contrast between the two vehicles could not have been more glaring, It must have been apparent to Andy as soon as I arrived, but he had the good sense and tact to avoid comment.

Sitting there on the porch, the cabin was familiar and newly alien. For the first time, I felt responsible for it. Since the beginning, Dad had been in charge, directing all the work. I knew well what came next, the closing process, preparing the house for abandonment and locking it up. I had performed all those steps before, but always as the subordinate, told and directed by those in charge. I had taken on a passive-aggressive approach. I would do the work but without any sense of ownership. I'd dawdle and resist as a form of protest. This had not been mine; the cabin belonged to someone else. I was now the undisputed owner, a fact that only became evident at that precise moment.

Not quite ready for the work of closing the cabin, not ready to face the long drive back to the city, I picked up a chair off the porch and brought it down to the flat spot by the pond. I needed some space before moving on. Just the night before last, Andy and I had watched the stars from this spot move ever so slowly in their circumnavigation around the earth. I set the chair contrary to what would have been my normal orientation and faced the cabin. I studied my view. My hand could remember it all, even at this distance. It could trace the outlines and feel the roughness of the wood railing, worn by the many years of exposure. Smoothed by a thousand grips, I could feel the screen door's worn handle. My feet could remember. The give and the individual squeak of each board on the porch. Without a noise present, my ears could recall the snap of the screen door. And without a flame in the fireplace, my nose still smelled the ashen haze of an old blaze tiring out. It was all there — and still was.

The screen door slammed shut, and Dad stood on the porch surveying the horizon. He whistled. Arriving from behind the woodpile, Andy and I ran towards the house.

Jubilant, Andy strode, no, jumped off the porch with a mission in mind.

Dad called from inside that dinner was ready.

I was on the porch looking at Andy. Oiling his guns, he was sitting where I was now sitting, so many years later.

I looked to the right, and I saw Andy and me side by side, walking towards the forest.

I felt the gun's sight against my brow, the crosshairs on Andy's back.

I saw the ground absorbing Andy's blood.

I felt the weight of Andy's head in my hands.

I tried to breathe.

27

I finally called Liz. I was sitting on the log at the telephone spot. It had taken me a long time to walk here. While I spoke, my emotions were absent — I think used up. Liz struggled to understand me through her own tears. I had to repeat myself and clarify many of the details.

"It's like being in a horrible nightmare and not able to wake up."

"Cole, I wish I were there with you. You need to come home as quickly as possible."

"I'm still numb ... and barely conscious."

"Get yourself some coffee. You still have plenty of daylight for your drive. You can do it. After all that's happened, you shouldn't stay there another minute."

"Basically, I'll just need to lock the door. That's it. And then I can leave."

"Hurry up, darling. We need you here."

There were a thousand unanswered emails on my phone, but I had no patience or desire to tackle any of them. I ignored the whole mess, but I still felt the need to touch base with that world. It'd only been seventy-two hours, but it felt like a lifetime.

I called Michael.

"Where the hell are you? Are you alright? You never miss the Monday meeting."

"I'm not all right. ... No. ... Well, I am ... but ... Andy is dead."

His shock quickly moved to compassion, but without giving him the opportunity to question me further, I said, "But for right now, I have so much on my mind, all I can say is I'm fine and that I'll call you later on with the details. In a word, it's horrible. I need to go now. I'm sorry."

"I completely understand. But before you go, I want to take one thing off your mind; you shouldn't worry any more about the London deal. I've got it taken care of."

"Michael, maybe later. I'm sure everything's under control."

I didn't know if he was lying for my benefit or if it was true. For the moment, I didn't care one way or the other.

I propped the screen door open, so my comings and goings out of the house would be uninterrupted.

The back of the Escalade was full of the things Andy would have carried had he been able: the extra food from the kitchen, his guns, the newly discovered suitcase. And all the miscellaneous weekend crap: the trash, empty propane tanks, dirty clothes, in short, everything that we would normally haul out after a short stay.

I had saved entering Andy's room for last. As expected, everything was well-ordered. The bed was made. Three shirts and a couple of pairs of jeans were hanging in the closet. Next to the bed, a small nightstand, a lamp and a mystery novel about a red wolf. There were no pictures on the wall, and the curtains were fully open, revealing an interior view of the woods. A monk would have been happy there.

I opened the nightstand's single drawer. Inside there were

several pens and a journal, exactly similar to the one I picked up at the diner a few days ago, except this one was brand new. I refrained from opening it. Certainly not now, maybe not ever. I instead took it out to the car and loaded it alongside the rest of Andy's belongings.

In all of my trips back and forth across the porch, I couldn't help but glance over occasionally at Andy's truck. I couldn't take it with me, nor was I sure what to do with it, but it did look quite at home next to the cabin. The rust around the wheel wells seemed to be the earth's way of reaching up, asserting dominance while reclaiming the raw materials. Maybe it would be best to leave it here and allow nature to unleash its mechanisms on it, swallowing it back.

The cabin was still full of a million other things that would need to be dealt with later. Dishes, pots, furniture, pictures, and whatever else lay hidden in closets, under beds, or in drawers. Dealing with that long list of chores required a trip back at some later date. That wasn't a job I had any interest in doing — or even needed to do. It was a job that I could perhaps hire out. Peterman, I'm sure, would know who to call. For the moment, I left everything in its place. Thinking about these minor problems hurt my head. For now, I just needed to leave and be done with the place.

I put my to-do list aside, focusing instead on how to get back home to Liz and the boys as quickly as possible. After double and triple checking the cabin, the valves and switches and locks, I surveyed the scene and wondered if there were any chance I'd ever return to this place — I didn't know how to describe it in my own mind, as Dad's place or as mine. I lingered on that thought while turning in circles, taking in the view one last time before I climbed into the truck.

I drove at a pace that I could have easily walked. I was leaving. Relieved, but I was caught like a fly trying to extricate itself from a sticky web. Attentive to every bump and pebble, swerve and turn, I inched forward. I came to the low-water crossing and stopped, watching the small stream flow down the valley towards the larger stream where I had spent the night with Andy. I turned off the car and felt the quiet. After a moment, I waded into the water and submerged my hands in the cold liquid. I pulled out a small smooth stone, worn by years and years of the water's incessant flow. I put it back in the water, rinsing it free of grit. Taking it out again, I rubbed it in my hands to dry it. This little ritual provided a satisfying connection. I picked up a couple of more stones and washed them, then dropped them into my pocket.

At the gate to the property, I went through the routine of getting out of the car, swinging the gate open, getting back in the car, driving through, getting back out of the car, swinging the gate back shut and then finally securing the lock. I yanked on the lock, making sure it was firmly secure.

Once outside the gate and on the road, I felt as if I'd just traveled through a misplaced time wormhole, somehow violating its rules. I couldn't tell if I was going forwards or backwards. I was returning to the real world from which I had come, but a world that vaguely resembled the one I had left a few days ago.

As I approached Peterman's place, it dawned on me that I hadn't eaten a decent meal in a couple of days. I walked under a sign reading *Tacos y Bebidas* and ordered two carne asada tacos. I took the loaded paper bag next door and made myself at home at my spot in the front of the window. Peterman, who had been sitting at his desk when I came in, walked over to join me. He sat by my side and then, seeing I had nothing to drink, without asking, got up and brought over a Dr. Pepper.

It was the slowest I'd ever eaten a meal in my life. With the window so clean and transparent, I wasn't quite sure there was glass in the panes. I remained quiet, staring out at the mountains and the interstate, enjoying their firm constancy. I took the occasional bite, savoring the tingle in my mouth from the combination of picante sauce and spiced beef. Peterman sat silently next to me. He was right about their food.

"I'm so sorry about your brother," Peterman said during the gap between tacos. "I'll miss his visits, just like I'll miss your dad's. Both were great guys ... have you figured out what your plans are yet?"

"Not sure. But I'm taking the property off the market for now. I know that much."

"I'm relieved to hear it. Your dad put a lot of work into assembling that property. It's a special place. I'm glad to have met you, Cole. And I'd like us to continue getting to know you better."

I folded the foil wrappers into increasingly tiny triangles and swallowed the last sip of Dr. Pepper.

"I've left quite a few things up in the cabin for now ... we'll have to deal with them sooner or later."

"Well, let me know if there's anything I can do for you. I'm close by, and it's no problem taking care of any issue that might arise. You have my number."

I waited until I was on the interstate at cruising speed before calling Liz. There wasn't any news to add, only the details about the authorities. We talked for a long while. The conversation was like when we were first dating. After we had run out of things to say, neither one of us wanted to hang up. But finally, the gaps of silence were too long, and my mind shifted to work and the long list of unanswered calls. I called Steve.

"Sorry about the delay in getting back to you."

"Michael sent around an email about your brother. I can't imagine how heartbroken you must be."

"It's been a really tough few days. Thanks. But for the moment, I'd like to get back up to date with things at the office, and mostly I'd like to hear that the Atlantic City deal is done;

that'll relax me."

"The good news is Michael cut a deal with the guys in Houston."

"Is there bad news?"

"If you like, I'm willing to stick with you. If you want me, that is."

"I'm not understanding."

"Didn't Michael explain the deal to you?"

"Steve, I'm missing something here. I've had a couple of really bad days. Can you just cut to the chase for me?"

"When I left you that message a couple of days ago, I didn't know what to think. But then, Michael told me you guys had talked. So, I assumed you needed the details. He said you'd be happy to be rid of the risk."

"That much might be true."

"The other half of the story is that Michael is gutting the firm, which is what's upsetting to me. He's taking five guys and moving to Houston to start a new company."

"Say again."

"Apparently, there's still a lot of that wildcatter money flowing around that city. He asked me to go with him. It at first seemed like a great opportunity to make some good money, but I couldn't stomach the way he handled this ... after all those years, the two of you together, and none of that held any meaning for him. A total lack of loyalty. It's not right."

Steve was eager in his transparency, and I calmly collected the facts as Steve knew them.

As soon as I hung up with Steve, I immediately called Michael to verify everything. As I listened to his recitation of the story, I didn't get mad; I was resolved to stay neutral while I learned as much as I could. I didn't agree or disagree with his plan or anything; I wanted him to sell me on his agenda, and I wanted to take the proper time to plan my reaction. While I listened carefully to the details of his many conversations, I heard no regrets or apologies. Michael's explanation was simple.

"I know the timing for you is terrible, but I had to grab this opportunity and make a decision quickly. I'm sorry. It's just business. Don't take it personally."

After hanging up with Michael, I drove in silence while in the back of my mind, I formulated all of my possible responses. I could blow up his plan by refusing to dissolve our existing partnership, or at least resist it. That'd be the obvious first step. At least it'd buy me some time. Or I could find a new partner to outbid Michael's group and reassemble the partners and pitch them the benefits of staying together. However, all of the options I could come up with meant going to war. No question about that. And the thought of a drawn-out confrontation made my stomach knot up. My body and mind were spent. I felt pushed into a corner and saw no easy way out. I needed to relax. In an effort to drown out the turmoil induced by my plotting, for the balance of the drive back to Denver, I listened to the 90s radio station, tapping my hand on the steering wheel as the mountains faded deep into the background.

I drove to Andy's house, took the contents from the back of the Escalade, dumped them right inside the front door and placed the trash in bins out by the curb.

At the airport, waiting for my flight, I left a voicemail message for Marcus. I told him where I hid the key to Andy's front door and that I would need more of his help going forward. Between sorting out Dad's legal affairs and all the property problems, he now had the added burden of Andy's death. I ended up on the redeye back home, with a seat in the very last row. Between my long list of anxieties and the all-night logjam around the bathroom, I couldn't find a minute's sleep.

28

The cab dropped me off at the house before sunrise, well before the boys were to get up. I was worried about waking Liz, so I came in through the garage. I pressed the garage door button, stopped and listened to the door ramble through its motions. Although intimately familiar, a noise I had encountered every day for years, and as familiar as it was, it creaked louder than normal, as if it were on the verge of jamming. The slow whirr of the gears, the rattle of the chains, the rollers squeaking across their tracks all combined to irritate me, as if it suddenly became some strange metaphor for my life. I waited at the step into the house until the noisy machine finally jerked to a stop.

As soon as I walked through the kitchen door, I saw Liz already sitting at the counter flipping through a magazine. Bizarrely, the garage door's noise had not been audible inside. My opening of the door surprised her. My worry about the noise had been senseless. Liz, knowing my flight plans, had been up waiting for me to come home. She jumped off her stool and threw her arms around me, using the entire force of her body.

"Oh, Cole, I am so so sorry."

"I'm beyond exhausted."

"I can only imagine."

"Don't be mad, please, but I don't think I can talk about any of it right now."

"I understand."

Liz poured me a cup of coffee, but I declined. Normally, I'd be on my way to work, but all I wanted right then was to crash in my own bed. To sleep for as long as possible, not hours, but perhaps days, weeks even.

"I wish I could have been with you."

"The worse part ..."

Scenes of the mountain tragedy instantly reappeared in my mind's eye, intensely vivid. Liz hugged me again.

"The worse part was when ..." I braced myself against my emotions, "... when they put Andy into that thick black plastic bag."

Emotion won. It grabbed hold of me. Tight. I couldn't resist its power. My body convulsed, and I cried uncontrollably.

I looked around for a place to sit.

"Oh, Cole." Liz guided me to the counter stools.

Aggravatingly, my words weren't wholly accurate. There were several layers of worse beyond what I was willing to share. I would never be able to describe to her Andy's mutilated body. I was not yet to express my feelings of guilt, my doubt about how Andy died, how it might have been my bullet that killed him, how I failed my brother.

Liz sat next to me, and thankfully, silence reigned until I felt back in control. I used a napkin to dry my eyes.

Liz stared at my forehead.

"What happened to your head?"

"It's just a scratch."

"It's worse than a scratch. You ought to see the doctor."

"Don't worry about that. Of all things, that's the least of it."

Silence reemerged. Liz, I'm sure, was struggling to find the right words to comfort me.

"In the back of my car, I've got some of Andy's stuff, and Dad's, but there is so much more I left behind."

"Have you thought yet about when you'll go back?"

"I don't have a clue yet. I don't know what it is I want."

"There's no rush. No need to make any decisions now. Why don't you go, clean up and lay down for a while? I sent the boys to spend the night with my mother. So it would be quiet for you, and I didn't want them waiting up, worried. She'll bring them back this evening after school."

"I'm a little disappointed."

"I'm sorry, but it's better this way. You need your rest first and to get cleaned up. Later you'll decide about how you're going to speak to them about all this."

"It feels good to be home with you."

I shed my clothes and within minutes was asleep in my own bed.

29

I awoke mid-afternoon. Nobody was in the house. I made a sandwich and ate it alone. With a blessedly empty mind, after about half an hour, I went back to bed.

At some point, I was briefly aware of Liz climbing into bed and nestling next to me, but time had lost measure, wavy and borderless.

It seemed like an instant, but my next memory was of my bedroom filled with light. Liz was gone.

The house was quiet as I made my way to the kitchen. Anticipating that the boys would soon be in, looking for breakfast, I started making eggs and bacon.

I heard the boys bickering as they made their way across the house. They were dressed for school, their backpacks dragging behind them. Liz behind them like a shepherd. When they stepped through the door, whatever was their controversy ended. Looking confused, they froze for a long second. It was probably seeing me with a spatula in my hands. After the hesitation, they ran to me. Kevin came in first with a hug. Following his brother's lead, Alex then ran in for an extended three-person hug. I pulled their heads close to my chest.

As the hug loosened, nobody spoke. Unsure about what to do next, the boys looked expectantly at me. I asked them to sit down at the table. They had never had to deal with death in such a personal way before. Their grandfather's recent death had been merely a conceptual concern; their emotional connection to him could not have been much different from their father's conspicuous prejudice. And although they knew their uncle Andy well, it was clear they were waiting to see my reaction to all this loss, as if my emotional state would be conveyed upon them, and only then would they own it. Liz went about finishing their breakfast, but I knew she'd be listening to every word.

"Boys, you first need to understand that a terrible accident occurred back at Grandpa's cabin in the mountains."

They were riveted by the story. I told them the basics as simply as possible, in much the same way as when I talked to the Sheriff, only the certifiable facts, no speculations. When I came to the shooting, all I could say was, "I took aim at the bear, and I fired. I'm afraid to say I missed."

I admitted none of the culpability that I'd been feeling since that initial moment after my shot, guilt still burning hot in both my gut and my head.

"So the bear killed Uncle Andy?" Kevin wondered.

"I couldn't stop the bear."

Kevin was hungry for more details, like the time of day and the clothes we were wearing. He was creating the picture in his mind's eye.

"Did Uncle Andy cry?" Alex asked.

"No. It all happened too quickly, in a matter of seconds. I don't think he felt any pain."

"Where did the bear go?"

"Son, I'm not sure. She ran off, scared by the gunshot."

"She?" Kevin asked.

"Well, my guess is that it was a mother bear protecting her cubs."

"Was Uncle Andy hurting her cubs?" Alex asked.

"No, but they must have been nearby. I'm sure they're fine now, Alex."

"Then it must be a bad bear."

"No, son, bears are neither good or bad. It's just a bear doing what a bear does."

Liz set their plates on the table and said, "Boys, eat something, quick."

Alex didn't move. He looked closely into my eyes.

"Dad, do you feel sad that your brother died?"

30

The next couple of mornings, I fell into a pattern. I'd awake around four in the morning, stare at the four walls, and with no returning to sleep, I'd briefly consider getting dressed and driving into the office. There would be no traffic at that hour. But my energy level wasn't ready for the office yet. An apathy had settled in. I had no motivation to get back into the fight.

Instead, I'd pace the empty house, landing in different places. But I had no interest in TV, reading, or eating. No place in the house felt right. As the sky lightened, I'd move outside, pacing up and down the neighborhood. A nervousness had taken over my body like I'd taken too much of the wrong drug. My garden called to me, but that didn't feel right either. My mind was unsettled, unable to concentrate on one thing for more than a few moments.

I didn't resist the memories — as if I could. The tape played and played and played. I granted myself the gift of time and tried not to judge myself. But the images carelessly distilled became more focused, more intense with each rehearsal, with less variation in each iteration. My mind was editing the events down to their essential elements.

Co-mingled with all those thoughts of the recent past, thoughts about the near future emerged. I conjured strategies for defeating Michael's mutiny, but I wasn't sure what my end goal should be. I couldn't be partners with Michael any more, that I knew. That bridge had been burned and I wasn't interested in repairing the rift — and he probably didn't even see whatever it was as a rift — "just business, nothing personal." Nor was I interested in elevating it to an existential crisis. That would be overly and unnecessarily dramatic. Although new to the company, Steve seemed loyal. Intuitively, I liked him. But who else in the firm could I actually trust? Half of them had agreed to leave with Michael. The other half, I wasn't sure about.

Once being a time and place for a bit of calm, even dinners with the family felt confining, I would eat two bites, then excuse myself, saying I was walking to the store. I'd walk miles and return with nothing bought. Liz remained patient, while the boys had no connection to my pain.

While I paced the streets and strained my memory, I asked, was my life with my father really so bad? Hadn't he, in essence, been a well-intentioned person? A good provider. A man working under difficult circumstances? How could I become so angry over words — just words — a few poorly chosen words? ... and stay so angry? ... for so long?

By avoiding the office, I was, by default, ceding control to Michael. With each passing day, the knot was being pulled tighter and tighter. My desire to untie it, however, was slowly dying.

Dad certainly heard the shot, but he never said a word — nor did the shooter. I'd arrived at a place of regret. I'd never know what passed through Dad's mind that day. Never. I now lusted for that difficult conversation. I wanted to have it out with him. Rip the scabs off. Let the emotions fly. Silence and rumination were my worst enemies. My desire to know his thoughts would remain with me forever now, but only in the abstract — certainty was out of reach, not possible, now unknowable.

I heard nothing from the Warden or the Sheriff. Nothing about the hunt for the bear, nothing about the autopsy. I felt like the accused while the jury was out, anxiously awaiting the verdict. *"Am I guilty?"* Of what? It irritated me that, even though I was present at the scene, right there, in the middle, involved and immersed, I had to rely on an outside authority — one who wasn't even there as a witness — to tell me the truth. While my memory was fixed, the veracity of what I had done or hadn't done remained in doubt and evasive. An epistemological conundrum I couldn't escape from.

On Friday, I awoke early, still in that pattern of little sleep and constant agitation. I quietly dressed so as not to wake Liz, made a quick breakfast, then drove to the office. The stair-stepped skyline, silhouetted in the predawn light, vaguely resembled the mountains I had left just a few days ago, but the manmade peaks and valleys were dotted with the flares of mercantile hubris waiting to be fanned.

I unlocked the office, the first to arrive, and sat down at my desk. My typical rhythm was, at first meditative. Reading proposals, reviewing financials, and approving spending requests were all easy tasks that didn't require a lot of thought, but just enough. For a couple of hours, I felt okay. I was alone. A couple of hours later, as the office began to awaken in earnest, I heard doors open and saw bright fluorescent lights turn on. Voices echoed down the hall. Everyone paused at my door, offering a pleasant acknowledgment, but they also had the good sense to divert their questions to the other partners. I'm not sure what signals I was sending out or whether they were the manifestations of palace intrigue. In either case, I was granted a very wide berth.

Mid-morning, I found myself daydreaming, staring out the window at nothing in particular. I easily imagined myself sitting in Peterman's front room, looking out from a similar window but at an entirely different view. It didn't particularly matter where my mind started; it always ended out there, beyond the horizon, in that clearing, high in the mountains. I was still out there. On some level, I'd always be out there.

Puttering in the office, I was faking my routine. Beyond the most simple tasks, work was impossible to sustain. After several nonproductive hours, I left. Not in any particular hurry, I drove back on the slower streets, through neighborhoods I hadn't seen in years. I stopped at a Korean BBQ, distracting myself while indulging in a few spicy wings.

I eventually made it to my house, changed clothes, and set out for my garden. There wasn't much for me to do. I was pretty well caught up. All that needed to be done was a little weeding. Bizarrely, I thought, Dad had never planted flowers, nor had he ever done any form of gardening.

My phone rang. It was Steve.

"I heard you had been in the office this morning but left early. Not feeling well? Or is something else going on?"

"I feel terrible that I haven't been of much help to anyone lately."

"You shouldn't worry. But when you're in the mood, I'd like to talk with you, one-on-one."

"Some problem?"

"No, not exactly. I've been thinking a lot about my future. I don't agree with Michael's direction and want to see what you're thinking about."

"Starting over?"

"There are a couple of us that would like to continue working with you. We have some new ideas we'd like to talk about, perhaps a new paradigm."

As Steve outlined who the players were and the kind of deals he wanted to chase, I watched Liz pull into the driveway. She stopped short of the garage, giving a little wave through the windshield.

Kevin and Alex jumped out of the car.

I interrupted Steve.

"Steve — hold on — can we talk about this later? My boys just came home."

Both of them came running my way.

"Dad, do you want to play some catch?" Kevin asked.

Everything in my gut told me that Liz had given him that hint, but I didn't care.

31

On one of my now regular drifting directionless drives, an incoming call displayed the same area code as Dad's property had. I pulled off the road into a small shopping center parking lot, suspecting the call would require my undivided attention. Taking a deep breath, I pressed 'accept.'

The sheriff came on the line. "Mr. Cole, I apologize for how long our process has taken. But it is our job to be deliberate and exercise caution. Just to formally confirm what you already know, you've been cleared of any responsibility in your brother's death."

"Thank you. That's such a relief. You have no idea." At the same time as I said those words, I doubted the conclusion, wondering how it could be possible. I know what I had seen through the scope. I asked, "And how is it that you're so certain?"

"The medical examiner's report left no doubt."

"But, my shot, where did it go?"

"I'm sorry, but didn't you hear from the Warden? I thought I was following up on his call to you."

"No, sir. Haven't heard a word."

"That's surprising ... the report was completed ... let me see ... three days ago. He must be an awfully busy man. His report is crystal clear. Your shot went right where you intended it to go. The bear was struck a few inches below his heart. The warden found him about thirty yards from where you shot him."

I couldn't process what the sheriff was saying. He contradicted what I knew to be true. I was shaking my head. When I arrived at where Andy lay, the bear was gone. I didn't see her — him anywhere around.

"Are you sure it was a male?"

The sheriff continued, "It's clear here, in black and white. If you'd like, I'll send you the entire suite of reports. Just let me know. Regardless, the proximate cause of your brother's death was a deep wound just below the base of his neck, causing a major tear to the carotid artery. Your brother lost consciousness within a second or two. At that point, there was nothing you, or for that matter, anybody on earth could have done to help him. Again, I'm sorry for your loss."

I didn't know what to say; I couldn't respond; I couldn't continue. Sitting in my car in an anonymous parking lot, I fell into an emotional wreck, a million pieces, tears flowing uncontrollably. My hand covered the phone, so the sheriff couldn't hear any of it. But he must have been aware of the lingering silence.

"Not that it matters much," he continued. "But we've decided to overlook you not having the appropriate hunting license. And by the way, let me ask, how's that forehead of yours? That was some ugly cut."

It took no more than a moment or two before I composed myself to answer, "That's kind of you to remember. I'm fine now. Got a few stitches, but I'll be living with the scar."

I didn't even say "thank you" or anything further. I just hung up the phone.

32

Once home, I found the house empty. I went straight to my study and closed the doors behind me, creating the solitude and silence I desperately required. I was confused. I was relieved. I sensed I had crossed some ill-defined finish line, not winning, but at the same time, not at all sure what it was that I had finished. And even more aggravating, I had no idea what lay beyond this threshold. How was my future going to reconcile with this recent past?

From the liquor cabinet, I grabbed my oldest single malt, sat at my desk, and poured out two fingers. Behind the desk was a tall leaded window with multiple diamond-shaped panes, intricate joinery, facets and antique glass. A window that dominated the room's east elevation, framing and distorting the view of my garden into a pleasing impressionistic tableau. The returning fractured late afternoon light entered the room, filling it with a pleasant soft green glow.

I loved that connection to the garden from my study. The architect's sharp intuition permitted me to rediscover my connection with the earth and living things. It has evolved into an enjoyable distraction. Nothing I did at work was directly connected to anything living. Papers, computers, and the transactions were only theoretically and, at best, distantly related to life. Whatever contrived connection was easily dismissed as a distraction from the adding of sums. Numbers and percentages were what I believed in. Those abstractions, though — were they metrics of something that truly existed or were they manmade inventions? Had I bettered mankind? As Andy appropriately asked of me. Is providing liquidity to a bloated market and capitalizing on the occasional hidden inefficiency a betterment? I could rationalize the linkages, that I was participating in the creation of jobs and providing fuel for the capitalist system to churn out an ever-rising GDP. But now that all felt so remote. In the real everyday-at-work sense, I pushed symbols from one computer to another, hopeful that at the end of the day, the accounting worked out in my favor. The symbols had taken on a far greater importance than the things they actually signified.

The walls surrounding me carried a diary of my past, a conspicuous display of mementos and commemorations. In the north bookcase, next to the never-read volumes on world history, were scattered plaques commemorating business and charitable achievements. On the opposite wall, above two leather club chairs, were more indications of my connections to power, photos of prominent dignitaries, a mirror image of my office downtown.

Outside the closed doors of my study, I heard the boys and their friends running down the hallway to their den. Liz followed shortly. She cracked the door and asked if I was okay. I nodded yes. She reported that some of the other mothers were over for an afternoon glass of wine, adding that dinner would be ready in about an hour.

After these many years of working, all the manifestations of my success boiled down to a bunch of colored pieces of paper entombed inside clear plastic forms, eight by ten photos in expensive frames, a string of bytes in a distant bank computer representing my net worth, and proudest of all; I owned a big house on a big lot.

Those adornments never impressed my father. At least, he never expressed any pride to me about any of it. There were moments when I heard his pride secondhand, sure, in the context of a socially correct brag. Instead, unheard but clearly felt, was his sense of disappointment. Somehow, I had failed to achieve what he wanted of me. And I could never figure out where it was that I let him down. That wish for approval would have to remain unanswered.

A quote I'd read a long time ago had resonated with me. The exact phrasing had escaped me, but, in effect, it stated that a man is not truly a man until his father dies. For all this time, I had understood this adage as a poetic metaphor, not a literal death. It was about the freeing of oneself from the constraints and opinions of one's parents. A burying of the past and assuming responsibility for one's own future. In that regard, at least, I felt as I had long ago crossed that threshold. My respect for my father had so diminished that I easily arrived at the point of ignoring any of his advice. I didn't trust any of it. It was no longer meaningful to me. I heard criticism from my father, but what I wanted was support. I had become my own man, capable of standing on my own. I wanted to be recognized for that.

Dad's death and Andy's death compounded to crack open my perfected shell. My formerly trusted self-conception was all of a sudden in doubt. A wounded child, still residing in my adult body, was crying for attention.

I worried that my father's spirit would continue to hound me after his death. Buried events, ones I had thought were long dead, would resurrect, seep out, run in and around my mind, control my thoughts, reappear like dancing ghosts. No amount of blinking would dislodge them. There wouldn't be any refuge by running. I had to fight the battle from where I stood. I couldn't expect events as potent as what I had experienced to wash through me like water through a sieve; I needed to hold them, at least for a while, to process them, to absorb their impact. I had something to figure out. Was there meaning hidden in all this chaos?

Out the large window, the darkening shades of green and gray of my garden indicated the sun's recent absence.

Andy's two journals, the one I found in the cabin and the one I stole from the diner, sat closed on my desk. They held a mystery. Maybe on a closer reading, Andy had something to tell me. I poured another glass of scotch and decided it was time. I prayed for some insight.

While the older journal was almost completely full, with only about a dozen blank pages remaining, the newer journal had but two pages of notes. There's an odd conceit to a journal. Are the words meant only for the writer? Is the meaning embedded within the act of writing? If it's only about the writing, you write, read and toss. Why keep it? Who reads a journal after it's written? And when? But anything that is cached will one day be found — and the writer knows this.

With the texts in my hand, the crime of violation that I had scoffed at last week now felt like a more serious transgression. I could burn the whole lot and avoid the temptation to read them. I could shrink-wrap the journals, leaving their contents to some future generation to decipher. Wouldn't Andy have suspected that his pages would one day be found and revealed? Did he have an expectation about who the reader might be? Did he perhaps intend for me to be the reader? Or was I the last person on earth he would have wanted to peer into his inner recesses? But who now could possibly be hurt by reading them? Who would that be — who was connected to these words? Me and only me. This self-serving logic crafted for me a permission. Eliciting a sense of relief. Wouldn't the highest honor be to read the journals and, by doing so, come to know Andy better?

That it took his death to bring me to this desire was an irony not lost on me. But it cemented my resolve to carefully study his words. The journals projected a new power that I couldn't ignore.

In the hotel, after the diner theft, after I had scanned the first few pages, the part where Andy had described losing his job at the high school, that event being the impetus for his writing, I found myself in sympathy with my brother, feeling the pain of that unjust injury. Those events would be a challenge for any rational mind to reckon with.

I was absent in his rendering of that story. Although I had helped him financially, directed him to lawyers and paid some of his bills, I was not mentioned at all. I realized that I wasn't there as part of the generative action, at least not according to his telling. Yes, it was he who had lost his job and his wife. And as much as I thought I was a participant, in his eyes, amid one of his deepest tragedies, I was not even a fellow traveler. I was so far in the background as to not be seen. I'm sure Andy felt that my money was a weak substitute for compassion.

I had let him fight alone throughout. But that was how we were raised, every man for himself. Independent. Self-reliant. I had rejected Dad, but I suppose not his methods. And as a consequence, I had abandoned Andy. And worse, even after recognizing my sin, I had made no effort to come back into his life, repair the harm, apologize, or simply reach out. I had failed at the essential element of being a big brother. When he needed a mentor, he had none, neither Dad nor me. In terms of being a brother. I had lost my bearings

Liz knocked on the door, asking if I wanted dinner. I declined, waving her off. The light outside my window was dimming. I pivoted into my desk, turned on the lamp and continued reading.

I flipped the pages of the older journal and came across a passage about Dad.

...I don't think Dad had the tools or the experience. His upbringing didn't provide him any guidance ... he grew up even more feral than Tommy and me. ... We came and went as we pleased. When it came to his two sons, he kept a tight restraint on us in only some regards, ... but when he wasn't dominating, he was the opposite ... either completely clueless, trusting, or just plainly didn't care. The problem was, you never knew which one was walking in the door that evening.

On this topic, my thoughts mirrored Andy's exactly. The pattern was clear. Dad taught us self-sufficiency. Dad taught by example; rugged individualism was the one true path. But what were the consequences of going it alone? From his own life, he learned that you couldn't depend on anybody but yourself. He had no choice. He lost his parents and was out on his own when he was not much more than a boy. And how did the accident affect his mindset? He never shared that with us. Did he feel guilty? Was he at fault, or were their deaths the result of some random act over which he had no control? He had nobody to rely on, no place to turn for help, no one to guide him through tough times.

I picked up the second journal, the more recent one. The ink and the script were exactly like the first journal, precise and even. I read the first page:

Why did Tommy lie to me? He put me in an impossible position. I couldn't challenge him or wouldn't. I didn't want to be confrontational. If I had asked him again if he possessed my journal, would he have changed his story? Not likely. It's not in his character to admit fault. It's sad that it's taken me this long to learn that I can't trust my own brother about the simplest issue ...

That stung. It was about the most disappointing thing I could have read about myself. I felt the urge to weep — but the tears didn't come.

... I understand his curiosity, it's natural, but certainly, he should have known that I'd share anything with him. I have nothing to hide from my brother. Maybe, this episode points to the core of our problem; we aren't in the habit of sharing our secrets ...

I wished I could have explained to Andy why I kept his journal, but of course, there wasn't an acceptable answer. What was there to explain? Maybe I could have formulated a reason, but I didn't have an excuse.

I was desperately desirous of forgiveness, something that now could never be granted.

I flipped to the end of the second journal and studied his final entry:

... the battles with Dad have scarred Tommy more than I had realized. Coming out to the mountain property has unveiled a deep tension ... his bodily posture instantly morphed from one of a confident businessman back into a pissed-off teenager ... You can see when a person is carrying anger, like they're constantly preparing for a fight. ... I never understood Tommy's sudden shift. It was like a dam had broken. ... One moment, I had a best friend, the next, he was alien to me. ... I'm not sure how to relate all this. ... his instinctively combative nature, ... Dad was certainly

stubborn and provided an obvious adversary ... I'm baffled that the two of them could never find some common ground ... their postures came from different places ... Dad was single-minded and not interested in alternative points of view, his proven recipe. ... Tommy was born defensive as if attacked ... what was he protecting? ... Tommy scores himself with dollars. More money means more winning. Winning equals approval. And that's the heart of it. He was fighting for Dad's approval. ... but Tommy couldn't see or hear what was plainly there. Dad gave it. It might not have been effusive enough for him ... Dad could only give as much as he was capable of giving. ... Learning about Dad's car accident, I can see how that singular event might have shaped him, ... losing his only family ... when the only people who love you are suddenly taken from you, ... maybe by your own fault, ... maybe you abandon the capacity to love, give it up, it's so painful you can't go there again ... it's stunted ... for Tommy, Dad couldn't do enough, no matter how much he did. ... Tommy's always having to win fouls his personality with the stink of arrogance. I'm tired of it. Perhaps this trip was a big miscalculation on my part; I had hoped with Dad gone, Tommy and I could find a new relationship. But I can't bet on that any more. ... Playing hard is one thing, but was winning so important to him that lying was permissible? ... Was he even being authentic with himself? ... Was he counterfeit as well to the rest of the world? ... He proves his worth to the world according to some ever-shifting set of external standards, not his internal standards, at least none that I know. What fiction of himself has he constructed?

I put the journal down. Never had I been so harshly judged by my brother. Or perhaps I had but had never properly heard him. He had earned a new special power with his new status, one that demanded that I listen more intently to my brother's words. I wondered if Andy's opinion was unique to him. Could it also be this is how the rest of the world sees me?

My glass was empty. I generously refilled it with more scotch.

What if? What if Andy were right? That all these symbols of success that I've surrounded myself with and have been so proud of were merely a thinly erected facade reflecting my pitiful narcissistic attempt to bolster my worth in the eyes of my incapable father. I knew in my gut that no matter how many trophies I lined up along the wall, there could never be enough. Yes, I was truly proud of my accomplishments, but I wish I had heard that pride expressed by my dad, and not to others but directly and intimately to me. Why couldn't he give me that one simple pleasure?

Liz opened my door, inquiring as to my status. "Fine," I said. "I still need some time alone." I suspected she heard some irritation in my voice.

The window behind me had turned a deep black. The desk's small reading lamp was now the room's only illumination.

I could easily rationalize the chase for money as having all kinds of consequential benefits: liquidity to the markets, jobs for others, taxes, and the ability to give to others. But none of that was my honest motivation. Those other things allay the guilt that one should feel. Like almost everyone I know, money equals status. Money satisfies the passion to accumulate beyond need. Greed. Money, yes. When is it enough? And to what good other than greed? What good to others was I providing? The thought of chasing another business deal evoked dread, making me gag. I felt piggish, like some cartoon caricature of a robber baron, fat, slovenly, stepping on the unsuspecting. I wanted to throw up. My legacy was opportunism. Is that what my boys were going to be proud of me for? Andy was right. My life was constructed by discovering tiny inefficiencies in the system, the occasional accidental gap between the ask and the bid.

Even if his expectations for us were manufactured according to his own idiosyncratic understanding of the world, to my core, I believed that Dad had wanted what he thought was best for Andy and me. He was hard on us. His methods were often revolting. He knew only one path, the path that worked for him. He was also hard on himself. The end result, he taught me to be hard on myself.

Although Andy, unlike me, projected to the world a reserved caution, with most people characterizing him as *easygoing*, I thought of my younger brother as submissive. At some point, he had experienced the death of ambition. He had surrendered. When did that happen? I couldn't say exactly. Did he choose it? Was it his reaction to a demanding father? Or his reaction to a highly competitive brother? It's also possible he wasn't born with ambition in the same way I was. But maybe that was all to the good. Spending time on things that interested him, he found a way to be authentic to his own needs. What I pejoratively judged as goalless was perhaps something else. Maybe he had goals that, for reasons I didn't understand, goals that he felt no need to advertise to me or anybody else, quieter goals. If not to impress, what point is there in announcing a goal to others? For some sort of public accountability? Perhaps he had found a life absent of the need to prove anything to anybody.

I thought about Andy's journal as a tool. I wondered if the writing had provided him any cathartic help. My mental tape from the previous week still played over and over in my head, and there was no structure to it, much less understanding.

Ruminating in circles felt potentially perilous.

Desperate for some sense of clarity, I honored Andy's lead. I spontaneously reached into the side drawer, pulled out a pad of paper, and began writing. The words came easily. In no particular order, I wrote down the events as they came to mind. They were only governed by the strange links the mind makes in seeking coherence. The events appeared scrambled. There arose an urgency to disgorge all the noise, to build a solidified order to what I was remembering. I poured myself another glass. While the lines unspooled across the pages, I was unsure of what problem I was seeking to solve. I didn't judge. I knew there was a disturbance within me that needed to be excised, and only by going deep was I going to find its source. Sitting at my desk in the dimly lit room, I wrote page after page after page.

Maybe minutes, maybe hours later — it could have been days for all I knew — I awoke. I found myself with my back on the floor, lying next to my desk. I didn't actually remember making that decision. Pulling myself back up, I saw dozens of pages of barely legible scrawl. And a dry scotch glass.

I walked over to the large dark leaded-glass window. Putting my face close to the glass, I peered out into the obscurity of the night. I could barely make out the contours of my garden.

I put my palms to my face in a vain effort to rub the glaze off my eyes.

Looking down at my watch, I saw that it was after three in the morning. Although it seemed unwise, I poured yet another glass of scotch. As I sipped, I slowly deciphered the words I had just written, the scratchings of a lunatic. Their logic was barely coherent. I quietly laughed at myself. I had transcribed a long timeline of facts. Missing were any words of feeling, no sympathy for my brother. Only some selfish angst over my pitiful plight, a litany of all the terrible, unfair, unforeseen circumstances that had fallen upon me. This cathartic writing exercise was a bust. It was just grievances. But against who? There was no use in any of it. I balled up each page and threw them one by one in the direction of the trash basket.

My mind never drifted far away from Andy. And all I saw were my failures towards him. I was not with him in his last critical moment of need, nor in any of his moments of need — none of them. We had parted paths long ago, the unconscious collateral damage that arose from my rift with Dad. And that physical and emotional separation had become a permanent condition. In retrospect, it all seemed so callous of me, and childish. When we walked that morning into the woods, it was not as brothers should. Although we were mere yards apart, it was as if we were as far apart as our habitual two time zones. Maybe if we had somehow figured out how to walk in together, the bear wouldn't have attacked. Together we would have been more imposing against the threat. I had failed my brother for years, and it all culminated in one final failure.

The life that I had chosen suddenly felt fraudulent and misdirected. I had chased power, winning as the primary metric. But power for what purpose, to what end? I was self-aware enough to realize that I was especially seeking power over my father. I had known that for a long time. But why was I looking for power over my dad? Was it defensive? Retaliation? Was he resisting my desire to individuate? Power destroys intimacy. Both dynamics can't coexist between two people. Or was his harsh parenting his way of pushing me to individuate, challenging me, forcing me to stand up for myself, even if it compelled me into a confrontation?

And what about my boys? What was I doing for them — or to them? Had I already begun pushing them towards aliena-tion? They lacked for nothing. I had performed all my parental obligations to them, like my dad had done for me. With all the money I'd made, they would never have to worry. But was removing that challenge a disservice to them? Isn't the strain of striving, its risks and rewards, at the essential heart of each person's journey?

Stacked in front of the sofa were the four cardboard boxes of items I had removed from the cabin. On the sofa's seat was a large blanket, one that I had laid over the several guns.

I stepped across the room, pulling off the blanket to reveal the small arsenal. On top, I saw the Henry 22 caliber from my youth and picked it up. With the Henry in my hands, I checked the chamber yet again, more out of habit than any conscious desire to be safe. From the shine, it looked like it had been recently oiled; something Andy probably did in preparation for the trip. I slid my hand down along the stock, feeling its smooth polished finish.

I lifted the weapon, set its butt into my shoulder, and eyed along its sight. With this one, I had aimed at my father.

Oddly, this silly bit of playacting made my heart race. The fear was still there. I carefully set the gun back down onto the sofa and took a deep breath. The evil had lingered within me for all those years. I felt my soul harden, angry again with my father. My malicious intent had reappeared front of mind. Relief was found the moment after, by some accident of fate, some divine intervention, I was overtaken by an instinct that knew better; my better angels took control — placing the aim on a tree and not on my father's back. It was a terrible deep sin, one for which I had been unable to forgive myself. With my raw insides seething, that unattended guilt reemerged, gnawing at me anew. It was wrong back then, dreadfully wrong. But I had tried to simply forget about it, to move on and not look back. How naive could I have been? Never did I attempt to heal with my father. Never brought it up. Some brave guy I was.

Lying next to the Henry was Andy's Marlin, the one he had carried with him on his last day. I picked it up, my hands touching where his hands had been only a few days ago. I felt Andy's essence, his memory being forever attached to this gun. I put it back on the sofa, next to my childhood favorite, the Winchester 92. It was with this one — in one moment, I was aiming at the bear, and in the next, I was pointing it at my brother — that I pulled the trigger, unsure of my aim. I left it untouched on the sofa along with the two others. My instincts were good, thinking wasn't involved, and by an act of grace, Andy didn't die from my bullet. But he might as well have. It was my spiritual distance from him that killed my brother. If I had been with my brother the way I should have been, there would have been no bear, no need for me to raise my rifle. I failed my brother. I had pushed him away. Despite the verdict, despite the objective, verified by others, truth, that my shot did not kill Andy, I still felt culpable for my brother's death.

I sank into the leather chair. I resisted opening another bottle of scotch, mostly because it would have required me to walk across the room. I wanted to give in to my intense fatigue.

I set a blanket across my chest. But the stack of guns within arm's reach radiated evil. They were insanely powerful instruments of death. Inanimate objects, they were not inherently evil, of course, but they were easily capable of magnifying the malicious intent of their user. My resident evil reflected back at me through those guns. If I weren't possessed by evil, why would I ever consider pointing a gun at my father — with intent to kill? What punishment is just for such a thought?

I escaped the blanket, letting it fall to the floor. I grabbed the Marlin with its large scope and, on the way back to my desk, grabbed that second bottle of scotch I had been lusting after. I laid the weapon on top of my desk, focusing on it. Andy's gun.

I returned to my now blank pad of paper and tried writing

again. I wrote again about our walk into the woods. But more about the walk out, with Andy dead. Dragging him on that strange contraption through the mud and rocks. I cried for Andy. I told him how sorry I was, how I should have done more. Tried harder to connect. My mind again flooded with a tsunami of images. Views through the scope. Down long barrels, at targets ... at people ... at my father ... at my brother. I was angry. I ardently wished I could have erased those thoughts ... but I could no longer repress them. I'd write, and they'd quickly reignite. I was no longer sure of their relevance or why one idea was followed by another. I held Andy's gun. I looked through its scope. I felt the tension of the trigger. Gently pressing until that final bit of resistance gave way. The click of the hammer. I pressed again and again. I saw the forest from all its myriad angles, inside, above, long trails, clearings, from thirty years ago, from forty years ago, from a few weeks ago. I was scared. The images were bright and airy; they were dark and obscure. A pool of blood seeping into the earth. The tape had gone wild and spooled wildly out of control, spinning off its sprockets. I didn't like the scenarios my brain was drawing up, nor could I stop them. I felt shame. Intense shame. In an attempt to quiet my mind, I closed my eyes.

I needed to better know what it felt like to be at the wrong end of a gun. It was my turn to look at the large lens on the front end of the scope. That would be fair. I turned Andy's gun so that it pointed in my direction. It was all completely unfair. I propped the gun up with a rigging of books and a side chair. I returned to my seat, looking numbly into the barrel, that barrel pointing into my face. The front end of the rifle was narrow and cold. The dark hole from which the bullet emerged was darker than any night sky. There was no definition inside. I felt myself as the target. I could almost see the bullet emerging. I was the problem, and the best solution was to take aim at myself. Wouldn't that be a fitting punishment?

I jumped, uncertain. I vividly dreamt of calmly drifting in a vast sea, gently swinging my arms back and forth against the water, trying to stay buoyant. A young boy standing on the back of the boat was looking in my direction without any discernible emotion. No shoreline in sight. The water was warm and soothing. Emptiness. Endless blue-green waves. A tiny dot in a vast ocean. I was alone and afraid.

I opened my eyes. I took a quick look around to restore my bearings. It was just a dream. I was drenched with sweat but pleased to find myself sitting in my big brown leather chair.

Andy's gun was ever-present. I felt cold. I set the rifle back down next to the others. I pulled the blanket up past my shoulders. This time the writing experience had a curative effect. I felt some satisfaction with my progress. I would later decide to let those scrappy notes be the foundation upon which I could build my story. The alcohol had done its job; I was sleepy.

33

Refracted by the waves of the leaded glass window, the sun projected a radiant pattern of points across the study's floor. Still lit, I turned off my desk lamp. Outside the window, I watched the play of light scattering through the leaves. The scene provided a pleasant remedy to my very groggy mind, easing my transition into wakefulness.

I slid open the doors from my study and walked down the hall into the kitchen. I turned the TV on low and filled the coffee kettle. Before the water had a chance to boil, Liz walked in, dressed in her workout clothes and her bright white running shoes. If she was startled to see me or pleased, she didn't show either emotion. She didn't acknowledge me, not even saying "Hi." My heart suspected a chasm between us, and I was confused. I couldn't understand why she might be angry with me.

While watching Liz begin her morning routine, I sat numbly but attentively at the counter, looking for clues into her emotional state. She was into the refrigerator, pulling out the milk and a carton of eggs. And next into the cabinets for the dishes.

I asked, "Liz, have I been a good father?"

Staying focused on pouring two glasses of milk, she said,

"Fine." Her answer was brusque and barely audible. She sighed and shook her head.

She walked across the kitchen to another cabinet, then asked, "By the way, where have you been?"

I chose not to answer. She knew precisely where I was.

Liz opened a drawer, grabbed a handful of silverware, and dropped it noisily on the counter. "It's not me you need to ask; it's your boys."

"Seriously. I need to know what you think." I strongly emphasized the "you."

"I am serious." Her emphasis on "serious" was equally assertive. "On this subject, their opinions are the only ones that matter." I couldn't piece together why she was being so strident. She was hardly concealing her anger. I watched her face as she removed the kettle from the stove and poured the hot water over the coffee grounds, still looking for a clue.

"Please, answer me. I need to know what you think." I insisted, again making the "you" emphatic.

Liz emptied her hands and crossed her arms across her chest. She faced me from the other side of the room, "Cole, I know this isn't the right time — as if there's ever a right time. I haven't given you time to grieve. I know. And I also know this process of yours is not anywhere close to over. I get all that.

"But, Cole, I'm worn down, completely worn down. My patience has run out. I didn't sleep at all, and my opinion right now might not be fair to you — especially now. But I gotta tell you this — you can't possibly solve your problems by isolating yourself, locking yourself away in that room, ignoring your family, and ... and ..."

Her frustration boiling over, she turned away and began laying the placements on the table. Sounding even more exasperated, she let out a long sigh. Then, in a surprisingly quiet voice, almost pretending to talk to herself, she said, "This is the weirdest fucking time to be having this conversation." Finished with setting the table, she said, "We need to get going. Why don't you go find the boys? It's time for them to eat."

Still confused about her emotional location, I kept my eyes on her, watching her as she moved about the kitchen. She cracked four eggs and stirred, striking the bowl sharply with her fork as she did so.

Suddenly, she stopped her breakfast-making motions and looked at me with an intensity in her eyes that almost frightened me, "Okay. ... Okay, Cole, I'll be frank. Here it is."

Not gently or gingerly, but with a thud, she put the bowl down. She grabbed a dishtowel, rubbing her hands vigorously. Then with her eyes again directed at me, "You have been here ... mostly. Although a lot of in and out ... your physical presence has been a constant within this house, and that's not something every wife can claim. Growing up, I understand that you had to fend for yourself, and that made you one hundred percent self-reliant. There's value in that, but your version is not what I want for my boys. You felt like you were alone and had to do it all by yourself. I get that. But understand your pain is not just your pain; it's our pain. My pain. And I'm sure the boys are feeling it too. It's here today, which isn't much different from most other days around this house — it's ... it's not like we're living inside some fanciful old Western movie, where it's every cowboy for himself. We're a family — a family that looks out for each other, that works together as a whole. Sure, you're at every third or fourth soccer game — great. Is that enough? To have checked that box ... of how a father is supposed to behave? Do you have any clue who their friends are? Do you know their music, the latest fad, which tennis shoe? Do you know Kevin is fascinated by, of all things, World War 2? Bizarre? Sure, but that's him. And Alex — I think, inside that big heart of his, he's an artist. He sees the world in his own unique way.

"These boys of yours are not like your expendable employees, who you love to throw into the river and watch to see if they can sink or swim. I get the tough love thing. That's how you were raised. But my children, they are precious seedlings. They need constant, consistent nurturing. And we are just now witnessing them bloom."

I had asked for her opinion. But to hear Liz say these words laden with her motherly ferocity made my heart even heavier than it already was.

"I'm sorry," I said.

"For what?"

"I've let you down ... the boys, too."

She looked at me with a new directness. Her emotions were shifting, but I couldn't yet describe them. Her forehead furrowed, and her bright eyes still burned. Trying to protect myself from further judgment, I turned from her piercing gaze, focusing on whatever was outside the window. The long night in my study had drained me of all energy, my ability to resist. I knew Liz was my fiercest ally, but I felt under attack. She was scratching a primordial wound, a deep cavity that I always knew was there but had protected it behind a false courage, a courage that I could no longer prop up.

"Cole," Liz called to me. "Cole ... listen to me." Her second intonation of my name was much quieter.

With a gentle touch of her fingertips, Liz pulled my face back towards her. I gave in. A softness had washed over her face. "Cole, we're good. I promise you that. You're a good man. You've provided for all our needs ... beyond all my dreams ..."

"Needs ... I know that. But I'm not sure about ..." My face was suddenly flush, my eyes swelling with the sense I was about to cry. Feeling an intense shame over my fragility, I dropped my head into my hands; I couldn't finish my thought. I didn't know how to speak to Liz. Sitting in my own kitchen,

I didn't feel safe. She was sitting there right next to me, yet I was unmoored. I had no concept of what anchor to reach for. I was terrified of being abandoned, forever alone. I looked up at Liz anew as if she were my only possible salvation.

Liz walked around the counter and stood next to me. Reaching for me, she grabbed my hands and said, "Don't try to say any more. Just relax." She urged me off of the stool and hugged me. "Cole, I'm so sorry you hurt so bad. I feel it." She said softly into my ear, "I love you."

A dam around my heart cracked wide open, and pain flooded through me. My chest hollowed out. I closed my eyes. I trembled without control. I sobbed, but sobbed without tears. I sobbed because I was weak.

Liz tightened her embrace. I felt her warmth, her familiar smell. She slowed my fall. Inside of her arms, I felt small ... defenseless. I had no will. My arms remained powerless at my sides. But I fell away, like the water draining from a cracked bowl. Dark shards scattering into dust. I couldn't reciprocate her embrace. I wanted to melt into the floor and just disappear. I thought briefly of retreating back to the comfort of my study, but I couldn't muster the energy to separate from Liz. I yielded to her support. I felt her near, but I was distant. My mind faded into a vague childhood memory from my deep past. I saw myself as a young boy in pale blue pajamas, forgotten on the floor of our living room. A small toy rocket was just out of reach. The room was empty of people, empty of furnishings. I sat alone in the midst of a vast sea of gray-green softness with no horizon in sight.

"Are you okay?" Liz asked.

I couldn't answer.

"Cole, you're still in shock. Stay with me. ... I'm here."

She squeezed tighter. Her energy seeped into me and calmed my trembling. After a moment, my composure slowly approached something close to normal. I lifted my arms and returned her hug.

I rested my head on her shoulder.

My weeping was over.

Unexpectedly, another set of arms grabbed my waist.

I looked down. Alex had joined us for a three-way hug.

"Dad, we'll make you feel better."

I released Liz and stared at my boy. I wiped my face with my sleeve and focused on my son. We were locked eye to eye. Alex remained still with a beatific expression, looking for me to provide the next clue.

"Thanks, son."

With both hands, Liz grabbed my head. She kissed me firmly and returned to the stove. "You two visit for a moment. I have to finish breakfast."

Wiping my face again, I took Alex's hand, leading him to the table. "Come on; it's time to get ready for school. ... And by the way, where's your brother?"

Stuck, still waiting on his father for clues, Alex kept his blank expression. "Don't know," he said.

"Okay, we're in a hurry now," I said. "We need to leave in a minute. How about some eggs?"

Alex shifted gears and began to focus on his food.

Ignoring the sizable pit in my stomach, I left the kitchen to look for Kevin.

34

Not finding him in his bedroom, I called out from the hallway, "Kevin." Hearing no response, I continued through the house, checking each room.

At my study door, I froze. Kevin was standing next to the sofa. He was holding the Winchester up to his eye, pointing it out the window. I suppressed my instinct to yell, knowing Kevin was totally naive about guns except for what he had seen inside of a video game.

"Kevin," I said calmly.

He glanced in my direction and the barrel turned with him.

Grateful for my father's lessons, I knew the rifle's chamber had been checked multiple times and was empty and that the ammunition was stored away in a closet, out of reach and locked.

I went to my son. I put one hand on the barrel of the gun and the other on his shoulder.

"I need to explain something to you."

He readily let go of the rifle, and I returned it to its previous resting place on the sofa.

Even without its bullets, the gun's lethality still felt razor-sharp.

"This is way cool! Where did all these guns come from?"

"The clock is ticking. I need more urgency." Liz's voice echoed down the hall from the kitchen.

"Kevin, a rifle is a very powerful tool." I then added the second part of Dad's instructions, "But like any tool, it can be used for good, or it can be used to destroy. It could even one day save your life or someone else's ... Those are the words my dad used when he gave me this gun."

"How old were you then?"

"I was about your age."

Hearing myself blithely state that simple fact out loud shocked me.

"So, does that mean I'm old enough to have my own gun?"

Kevin said out loud what I was thinking internally. His voice was full of enthusiasm, while I possessed trepidation. Readily recognizing the symmetry in ages, I didn't consider our maturities equal. It was hard for me to fathom that my boy was ready for something as serious as a gun.

"Well ... perhaps." Maybe this was a risk that I needed to take. "But you'll have to learn the proper way to handle it. And we'll have to do it my way. Understood?"

"Yes, sir."

35

After we landed, I rented a car and drove Liz, the boys, and myself to Marcus' office. The timing was arranged so that we could efficiently meet and sign a few papers in the morning before the afternoon funeral. I sat at the conference table while Marcus's assistant pushed back and forth across the table a long series of documents. Marcus himself cared less about the legal work, entertaining the boys and offering them strips of beef jerky, a product from his ranch. Despite being much longer than necessary, he held their attention tight with a story from his youth about when he first tried to ride a horse — including the embarrassing ending, whereby he slid off the side of the saddle and broke his collar bone.

When I finally set the pen down, Marcus turned his focus to me, sending Liz and the boys to wait out on the leather sofa.

"I received a serious inquiry about the property. Do you still have that broker involved?"

"No. That guy? I fired him."

"This time it's not a developer. The buyer is interested in keeping the entire property intact, just as it is, a weekend house for him and his family, and likes the idea of exposing them to the wilderness. He'll accept your price, but he wants you to take care of the deferred maintenance on the cabin. It will be quite a bit of work on your part. Some big items, like the roof, repairing the fence and leveling out the road. And, ..." Marcus paused and then reminded me, "You'll need to remove all the personal items you still have at the cabin."

"I know someone who can help get all that done."

"So, we have a deal?"

For Andy's funeral service, we had no church, no rows of unknown guests, no organ. Like Dad, Andy had never expressed any religious inclination, but I nevertheless felt the need for solemnity, and to me, that could only be provided by some sort of religion. So, to oversee our tiny gathering, I again contacted Preacher Dan, who had assisted us with Dad's service.

We assembled back in the same graveyard next to the still fresh grave of my father. Standing around the open grave, in addition to Liz and the boys, were a scattering of Andy's friends, mostly colleagues from the junior college, plus Peterman, who had driven in with his wife, and also Marcus was there with his wife. Preacher Dan didn't summon the same enthusiasm for the service as he had done at Dad's. His rhythm was expert but without personality. He hadn't known Andy and it showed. Despite the service's perfunctory nature, the formality felt authentic. Preacher Dan's practiced words hummed as if he were coaxing me into meditation. I fell into a strange mix of emotions. On the one side, I was clouded in an incoherent daze, like a boxer who had been punched a few times too many in the head. At the same time, I possessed a quiet satisfaction about my momentary place. I was fully present, feeling the world about me but with no need to react to it, listening with no need to answer, a psychic space absent of thought, devoid of self-consciousness.

Preacher Dan intoned a simple rote phrase. It jumped

apart from the background. "He will be missed." Words, routine and ordinary, words which outside of this specific moment I would find benign or trite. But today, they resonated true, a small arrow hitting its target. Exactly pinpointed, although common as they were, those words connected me with Andy. Hearing Preacher Dan's quiet voice, I swelled with emotion, an emotion that I don't think was visible on the outside.

In that narrow moment, I couldn't analyze. I couldn't step back and examine the swing and depth of the emotional journey I'd recently been subject to. I only knew that I hurt. Although surrounded by family and a few of Andy's friends, I felt as if I were alone by myself, absent from those other people, passively watching the shiny, gray-steel cables lower the polished wood casket out of sight into its dark hole. I was witnessing the concrete finality of our relationship happening in an anonymous distant life-denying cemetery, a place that I probably would never visit again.

And a few inches away, confronted by their graves, there was more loss, the recent loss of my father and the long distant loss of my mother. The enlarging permanence, the feeling of abandonment, all that loss gnarled inside my gut. There was an isolation I needed to solve.

The heavy sense of loss was already beginning to edge away my anger. The unevenness of all those problematic relationships was diminishing in importance. I was resolved to focus on the positives. It was as if the argumentative part of me was being buried along with my brother. I wanted union, not separation, for us to be whole like when we were kids. But there lingered an aching incompleteness that I was afraid I would never be able to cross, no matter all my promises or intentions. *"I'm sorry, Andy. I'm sorry for not being the brother you needed when you most needed me, and sorry for all the times, less urgent, when I wasn't there."* My apologies felt hollow, and they drifted away with the breeze. *"But Andy, I'll try to keep you close in my heart."* I worried, though, that there would be parts of our relationship, parts of me, I'd never again have access to.

Although I was surrounded by my wife and my boys, I felt no succor from their presence. They lived in different universes. Despite Liz's proclamations, she didn't know my pain. And I wasn't sure if I truly wanted to take her down into that hole. It was a complicated and damaged past, to which there was no longer any opportunity for repair. Maybe that was it and all it ever would be. Redemption no longer seemed possible. I would have to learn acceptance.

I found my stoic face and shook hands with Andy's friends. I shared a few words with each of them and had a brief visit with Peterman, but I can't remember a word from any of those conversations. It was as if I were briefly another person.

Afterwards, I took Liz and the boys to an early dinner at Andy's favorite diner. Paul, the waiter I had met on our last visit, was off that day.

36

With a coffee in hand and a newspaper, I began the morning sitting in the hotel bar, watching pontificating political pundits wallow in hypocrisies from above the whiskey bottles — a delightful synergy.

Liz arrived soon and sat on the stool next to me.

"Not sure where I'd find you," she said.

"Just thought I'd catch up on what's going on out in the world. I was up early and didn't know what else to do with myself."

"Have you thought about how you'd like to spend our last few hours before the plane?"

"I forgot the time of our flight?

"It's right after lunch. That's not like you."

"Maybe we could squeeze in a short drive. Take the boys around town and show them some of my old life. That sort of thing."

"I'd enjoy that, but do you think you can hold their attention?"

"It's probably not a good bet, but I should try."

A little later, I watched the boys devour a mammoth breakfast. They at least feigned excitement about a drive. But I knew better. I would have liked to find an activity that was fun, but the heavy solemnity that still hung around my shoulders prevented me from thinking about anything fun. As we headed out of the hotel lobby towards the car, I asked Liz, "Why don't you drive?"

She gave me an appropriately curious look. It was outside of my character to give up that control.

"I'd like to absorb the view." I offered as an explanation.

Without dissent, she took the driver's seat, and the boys sat in the back without comment. I had occasionally shared stories with the boys about my life growing up: friends, street names, favorite restaurants. I had planned for a quick biographical tour of the main landmarks. We first drove by my old high school, which looked exactly like it did three decades ago. Well maintained, the building had aged gracefully, and the ballfields in the back looked just the same as they did when I played on them. The trees along the edges were a little taller. The weather was good, and although baseball season was over, we saw a small group playing in a pickup game. The scene brought a moment of warm memories back to my heart. But when I directed the boys' attention to the ballfields, they only briefly looked in that direction, seeming not to care much. I'm not sure what I expected from them, but the details of their dad's early life didn't produce any enthusiasm.

On the way to Dad's old house, we passed my elementary school. My narration was apparently boring the boys. Their polite attention had waned, and both of them were absorbed in their phones. Neither one was listening. I stopped trying to share with them and remained quiet. I decided not to bother them further. They were my memories, and, I suppose, only meaningful to me. But I wondered as they aged whether my history might eventually become of interest to them.

Liz continued driving with no particular destination in mind. Having forfeited my original agenda, I thought about Liz and what she might like to see. I simply watched the scenery unfold until I could guide her to some place worthwhile. Soon, I directed her to the scenic road along the river. We passed the park where I used to meet friends after school. Liz slowed the car while we enjoyed the river views and took notice of the fading fall colors. I remarked once again on my passing memories, even old girlfriends and movie dates. Liz asked prompting questions, at least pretending interest in my anecdotes, but the conversation was only between the two of us. Alex had fallen asleep, and Kevin continued tapping away at his phone.

After about ten minutes of meandering along the river, everyone was quiet. I gave up on trying to maintain anyone's attention.

"At the light just ahead, can you turn right?" I asked Liz.

She followed my instruction and the several others that followed after it. Within a few minutes, we had arrived back at where we had been just the day before. The parking lot in front of the reception pavilion was a modern addition to the 150-year-old cemetery. Standing prominently to the left of the pavilion were the original limestone pillars that framed a gracious entrance to the grounds.

Stubbornly attached to the pillars were two large rusty iron gates. Having failed to properly function for many years, they were frozen in a wide-open, welcoming position. Fascinated with the rusting metal and the pillars' spalling stone, the boys dragged their hands over the stone blocks and started the motions like they were about to scale the wall.

"Boys, you can't do that! Show some respect," Liz protested.

I knew she was right, but I was just glad to see them animated again. "Let them be boys for a bit. They can't hurt anything."

A series of heavy bollards protected the old entrance and prevented all but walking traffic. Inside the gate, a crushed rock plaza gave way to a broad path leading deep into the property, with a large fountain in the distance creating a focal point. As if entering a lost ancient world, we walked inside the walls. It was instantly a realm with an integrally slower pace; nothing new existed here except for the occasional extra bright white headstone.

Although I had been there twice in the past couple of weeks, I was disoriented. The property spread for acres in each direction. The two earlier times I arrived, I had been sheltered inside a darkly tinted limousine and had entered the grounds from the opposite side of the property.

Along the path in front of us, we approached a caretaker, an older man dressed in a dull gray uniform, pushing a wheelbarrow loaded with several gardening implements.

"Excuse me, sir. I was wondering if you could help me. We buried my brother here yesterday ..." I started my question, but the caretaker answered before I could finish.

"That would make you Mr. Cole, correct?"

"Yes, sir. That's right."

"My condolences. Losing your brother must be hard enough, and so soon after your father. Hard times."

"Thank you," I said.

Pointing down the path, the caretaker continued, "You'll need to walk down to the large round fountain at the center. Go past it a short way, and at the very next path, take a left. You'll see your place right away. Just look for the freshly turned soil."

I looked at Kevin and Alex. They had been here before, but it was under different, more serious and constrained circumstances. I knew I had already tried their patience, so I told them, "Boys, if you want, you can go explore for a bit. But please be respectful. I need some time alone. I'll be right back."

"Cole, do what you need. I'll look after the boys," Liz said.

I walked for a while, and it seemed far from where we

entered, but as the caretaker suggested, the new graves were easy to spot. The two mounds of fresh earth were the only recent disruptions within the tightly packed rows of stones. The fall air was brisk and cool. The trees towering overhead had shed many of their leaves, and the morning sun drew dark, sharp lines across the gray monuments.

To my left was my mother's headstone, discolored by age and difficult to read, pitched ever so slightly forward as if she were reaching towards me, wanting to touch me. To alleviate her frustration, I stepped over to her stone and laid my hand upon it, closed my eyes and prayed for some connection. My father was in the center of the group. And now, joining my parents, Andy lay to the right. Neither of the men had their stone yet. But two small bronze stakes with paper inserts indicated their names.

After a few moments of studying the arrangement of graves, I drifted off into a fantasy, a silly, irrational and pitiful dream, but I wondered what it would be like if the four of us were to sit around the kitchen table and what we would talk about. What stories would we tell each other? Could we express our regrets? Make the much-needed apologies? Would it be a softer conversation? Might my anger be gone? Might we feel connected as a family? But I knew that would have never, could have never happened in any reality. My history had been written in ink. Nothing in it could be erased or undone. The needed conversations were impossible, always were impossible. My already aching incompleteness was destined to become even more profound and even more difficult to define.

I looked over at Andy. Of all my talking with him on our walk out of the woods, I never found the right words. There was no salve that would be or could ever be sufficient. But I sincerely believed that I was becoming aware of my shortcomings, albeit slowly. I owed him much more than I gave. I wondered if my sins towards my brother could ever in any universe be forgiven. My instinct said no. It would be a burden I'd have to carry for the rest of my life. Some way or another, my future life had to be dedicated to his memory.

Standing above my father's grave, although distant and now very much muted but not entirely absent, I easily recalled the true terror I often felt in his presence. Wary of his judgment. Wary of his power. Love never feeling as if it were a part of our transaction. If only to avoid his wrath, I did what he wanted of me, possessing a clear conception of what was expected, how to perform. Like a dog, who had been trained to avoid punishment and seek reward, I provided him that impression of obedience; a stimulus-response behavior learned to satisfy the desires of the owner, knowing in my heart of hearts that I was ultimately headed in a different direction.

I consciously chose to define myself as the opposition to my father, designing myself as a reaction to, not a reflection of the man. However he did it, it was wrong. I knew better. I was smarter. I firmly believed that I understood the modern world better than him, that the world was radically different than it had been a mere generation ago. Although, after my many years immersed in the practicalities of life, I've learned that the ways of the world have barely changed at all. The colors, the textures, the stage set, the actors, are all different in detail, but their essences, the interpersonal interactions, the necessary grit, the loyalty, all the aspects that make for a meaningful life have remained constant across all time. The frustrating part, recalling my father's teachings or should I say instructions, was that these eternal truths were presented to me as his epiphanies, the truths he discovered on his own — and as far as I was concerned, if they were his alone, they were wrong. I was that angry. The intoxication of my anger impaired any possible objective perspective. I resisted the view that the rest of the world had presented to me of my father.

Where they saw him as confident and fearless, I saw reckless. Where they saw him as caring and loving, I saw excessive control.

What lessons does the father choose to teach his sons? Are they the exact same lessons that were the hardest for the father to learn? Or perhaps they're the tools that worked the best for the father? But no matter what the lesson, even a good teacher needs a willing student. I acknowledge I was too impatient, too often in a hurry to properly listen. I always wanted to be someplace else other than where I was.

Perhaps he understood me more than I realized. We both had defined our lives similarly by rejecting the place we'd come from. We possessed radically different frames of the world and how best to navigate it. We both craved our own particular form of independence and thrived within that definition. I suppose a strong sense of individuality is necessarily born out of revolt. Conflict not being something to be scared of but a potent component of independence.

He didn't know me, what I wanted, nor how to lead me. Perhaps he learned the limitations of control, the limitations of conflict, and as a result, he let me run loose without a leash. Perhaps he thought that was what I needed, the best way to raise a proto-man — let him do it by himself, the way he raised himself.

I tried desperately hard for years and years to find some common vocabulary where we could forge a rapport and bridge the chasm. I really did try. I truly believe with all my heart that it was not a question of trying hard enough. And carefully looking back at our long history, I'm certain that there was never a moment when the connection I longed for was possible; our energies didn't match, like mismatched cogs inside a machine, making lots of noise and producing nothing of use.

Eventually, I did learn to respect the man. He certainly

worked hard. Never deceitful. Day in and day out, he tried his damndest to do his version of the right thing. And he did it all with one hundred percent sincerity. He constructed his life in service of what Andy and I needed, and we lacked for nothing. And he did it by himself, with no help from a wife or a large family. His life was difficult, and I took for granted the grace with which he approached his struggles. It was all too complicated for a young boy to understand. And then, as an adult, I chose the safety of my arrogance in order to avoid the deference required to ask about his life.

Nowhere is it written that a father and a son are supposed to be friends. That would misdescribe the relationship. But I admitted to myself that, for my part, there were many times when my behavior was inexcusable. We start life tied to others, and as we leave, hopefully, we will leave a part of us for those who follow next. I know now, much of what I ignored before needs to be heard. I promised my father that I'd honor all that he gave me as good and carry it forward to my sons. Hope is not yet gone.

"Dad?" Kevin's voice came from behind me.

I reached out a hand to bring him closer.

"You shouldn't sneak up on a guy like that. You scared me."

"I've been here waiting."

37

Alex and I were a few steps behind Dad as he walked through the cemetery's grand gate with our mother by his side. I saw a distinct aberration in the way he was walking, a gait slowed by the weight of his inner angst. He hadn't talked about how he was feeling, but the unease was evident. It didn't affect his still erect posture. His head was still held high, and his gaze remained direct and focused straight ahead. No, it was a slight shortening and slowing of his stride. Almost like his thoughts were consuming so much of his energy that there was barely enough momentum left to propel him into the next step, like a resistance holding him back. He didn't hesitate in his pace. His walk was steady and purposeful as if making his way through a deep river. His facial expression was short of being worried but not quite a frown. His normally shiny confident aura had phased into a grayish cloud.

On the one hand, there was an obvious understandable reason why we had returned to the cemetery. We were leaving town soon, and there was a distinct possibility that we might never return to this spot. Our home was elsewhere, on the other side of the country, and there wasn't any reason for us to return to Denver, and it made sense that Dad wanted to underline his memory, make it more solid. But I felt there was something more to our coming back than just that. There was always little access to what was going on inside my father's mind. He wasn't one for sharing his thought processes. Before words came out of his mouth, they were certain, unambiguous and direct, never containing doubt.

Alex tried to interrupt my thoughts and began quietly muttering into my ear about being bored, about how this whole trip was boring. I was sympathetic. Dad's car ride storytelling was lame. His stories about his growing up here and there were plainly boring, like listening to someone read the index in the back of a textbook, a recitation of facts and figures. As if we cared about his baseball team's won-loss record. While sitting in the back seat of the rental car, I wanted to explain to him that history is much more than a chronology of facts. The interesting aspect is the *why*. We weren't getting any of the *why*. Then Alex followed with the as yet unanswered *why* question, the same one that was on my mind, "Why are we here again?" Dad's decision was seemingly spontaneous, and so far, he was keeping his reasons to himself. I had no answer for Alex.

We were barely a dozen yards inside the gate before Dad stopped. He scanned around like he was lost, unsure which of the several directions to take. It wasn't like him to be confused directionally. Nearby and a little further ahead on the main path, he walked ahead of us up to an old man in a uniform. The man was pushing a wheelbarrow which in turn held an assortment of gardening tools. Dad talked to the man, and as Alex and I approached, I could hear the old man's reply to Dad's question, "Well, that would make you Mr. Cole, correct?" I thought how clever of him to figure that out so quickly.

"Yes, sir. That's right," my dad replied. And for the first time that day, Dad's face brightened with a smile, also enjoying the man's cleverness.

"My condolences," the man said. "Losing your brother is

hard enough, and so soon after your father." He shook his head softly. "Hard times for you and your family."

I soon noticed that Alex had wandered off, examining some of the old headstones, attempting to read the fading dates. Mom, noticing the same thing, told me to retrieve my brother before he got too far away. I tracked him down and pulled him back by the arm, telling him we couldn't do that right now and that we needed to stay with our dad.

The old man continued telling Dad something about the fountain while at the same time pointing further down the main path.

Dad turned around, looked down at Alex and me and said, "Boys, if you want, you can go explore for a bit. But please be respectful. I'll be right back."

Mom, Alex and I turned and started back towards the way we came in. But in an instant, Alex left us again, running down one of the paths. Mom passively watched him go, this time apparently unconcerned. Understanding that we were now free, I told her I wanted to explore on my own. She gave an approving nod. "Go do what you want," adding that she'd meet us at the front gate.

I watched my mother walk away from me in the direction that Alex had run. Alone in the cemetery, I pivoted around and thought about what I wanted to do with myself. The place was beautiful and begged for exploration. The light streaming across the hundreds of stones was brilliantly clear, creating sharp patterns of black and white. Scattered around were a few larger monuments. The occasional leaf floated down from the towering trees as they prepared for winter. I wondered who decided that certain individuals needed a more special recognition. Was it the person's family who felt the extra love and appreciation necessary to honor the person's impact, or was it the individual's own ego that required the planned recognition in his afterlife?

My uncertainty was short. I was drawn to follow my father. My curiosity about the man was peaking. I don't remember ever before understanding my father as a real flesh and blood person, instead of the master-of-the-house, the person-who-makes-all-things-possible, the way that a father impresses on a young child. For the first time, I saw a man with his own particular set of problems. His history was becoming of interest to me. How did the events in his life bring him to this moment? What drives did he possess? What pains had he overcome? These recent tragedies revealed a fragility I had never seen before. A man damaged in his own unique way. Except for the now smaller bandage on his forehead, covering the stitches from his fall, there was nothing visible, but the way he moved reflected a still simmering internal turmoil.

Dad's demeanor towards Mom, Alex and me had shifted in the short time since his father died, in a way I was struggling to understand. Ironically his pathetic stories during our short car ride at least revealed a new desire to connect. I appreciated that, but he had no idea as to which channel to tune into. And I wasn't sure either how to set the stage for him.

While Dad returned to the graves of his father and brother, I followed, staying a distance behind, thinking it was more respectful to walk instead of run. Dad passed the fountain and turned left on the next path.

He was a man, like any other man, a man with a history, one that I hadn't paid attention to. I was intrigued and, at least for the moment, too intimidated to ask. As the gardener had acutely observed, my dad had experienced a double shock to his system. Either one would be enough to unseat a stable person. It was obvious he needed time to process. Losing an elderly father to an accident I can understand as tragic, but the emotional drama of being so closely intertwined with your brother's death coupled with the suspicion of culpability had to weigh heavy on his heart. Imagining myself in his position, I'd be devastated about Alex's death, especially if I were in any way remotely connected to the incident.

When I arrived at the fountain, I sat on its edge, deciding to let Dad have the space and time he needed. From my vantage point, I saw him arrive at the Cole plot, a section of land capable of handling several more graves and surrounded by a stone curb with the family name carved at its center. From my time at the funeral, I could easily recall the arrangement of the graves: my grandmother on the left, her headstone blackened and difficult to read; my grandfather in the center; and Andy laid to the right.

I studied my father and waited. Dad stood stiffly in front of the three graves staring at them. He looked fragile standing alone amongst the white stones, his shoulders bent and his head lowered. Maybe it was the cast of the cemetery's effect, with its open and raw exploitation of death, our fragile mortality so evidently designed into this context.

As terribly tragic as these recent deaths were, their impact on my father seemed strangely and disproportionately intense, a sharp contrast compared to the sparse involvement those two people had had in our lives. There were perhaps only a half-dozen times I can remember that either Grandpa or Uncle Andy had come to visit us — and never did we travel to see them. When you grow up within a settled pattern, there isn't the perspective to question those habits. It is simply the way it is.

Until now, I had lived without much reflection on this web of fundamental relationships. Grandpa and Uncle Andy had lived far away in another city, and to me, it seemed that the physical distance was reason enough for an equal emotional distance. Our lives in New York were complicated and full. It didn't enter my mind to think about any missing family connection. Alex and I were immeshed in our schools. Dad was so incredibly busy with his own work. And with Mom's family close by, we spent every holiday and birthday with them, filling those celebratory spaces entirely. I hadn't recognized any gap in attention from Dad's side of the family. Although, during those infrequent visits from Grandpa or Andy, or sometimes both, we'd spend every meal together. They'd attend our basketball games, or baseball, or soccer, or whatever was happening at that moment. On those few occasions, our time together was fun — but brief. I never thought to ask for more. I never contemplated how quickly that could all end.

I recalled the preacher's words from my grandfather's funeral. The very words he used to describe Grandpa could easily have been used to describe my father. He characterized my grandfather as sociable and driven. My father was the same. The intense desire for achievement was common to both. My father postured himself as sure, confident, unerring, firmly in command, like a mirror image of his father, but also like a mirror; the reflected image, deep on the other side of the glass, was disconnected, and the two could never possibly connect.

My uncle Andy, somehow, was cut from an entirely different cloth than my father, a softer man, less impressed by success. He embraced doubt. What he didn't know was more intriguing than what he already knew. He was less concerned with goals, per se, and attracted to the simple pleasures derived from exploring new realms. His highest delight was discovering something interesting and then sharing it. I had always enjoyed our conversations and felt he listened carefully to me. The contrast in the brothers' personalities was distinct, and I could see now that there was little overlap in their interests.

My formerly firm impression of my father was being challenged by my emerging perspective on the complex formations that built his character. How much of his character resulted from his clearly sour relationship with his father, one that I now yearned to know more about. I wondered about my father's early life and what it must have been like to grow up without a mother, no female influences, and no broader family. The isolation of three men in one house. How was it that the hard-driving father made one son in his own image, and he ends up pugnacious, while the other son is completely unlike the father but intensely devoted?

After several minutes of watching, I noticed that my father appeared to be talking to the graves. I couldn't hear his words, but his body language was suddenly looser, and his hands were animated as if moving in some coordination with his words.

I wanted to be near my father. I rose from my seat and walked to him.

As I approached, I could hear the tenor of his voice. It was soft, not angry. But the only words that I heard him say were, "Hope is not yet gone. Please help me find a way to forgive."

"Dad, you okay?"

Surprised by my voice, he turned suddenly towards me with a confused face.

I reached my hand to his.

"You shouldn't sneak up on a guy like that. You scared me," he said.

He squeezed my hand tightly.

"I've been waiting on you. You seemed like you were someplace far away," I said.

His eyes were swollen, but there weren't any tears. He held them back. No tears flowed that day. I knew enough about my father that he wasn't going to openly and freely share his feelings. I had the urge to probe — and probe deeply. But it was not yet the time for that. Those questions would have to wait.

"I'm here now," he said.

Dad took his hand back and rubbed his eyes. Glancing back towards the cemetery's entrance, he said, "We can go."

We walked together in silence past the fountain and onto the path towards the gates. As we started out, Dad reached into his pocket and pulled from it several small round stones. He began rolling them around in his palm.

"What do you have there?" I asked.

"They're remnants from the mountain."

Over and over again, he twisted them between his fingers. Working them tightly as if he was working to make them even more smooth.

A few yards past the fountain, he stopped.

"Wait here a minute," Dad said.

But I went with him anyway, and he didn't object. We walked the short distance back to the graves. He knelt down on the fresh earth of his father's grave, and with his bare hand, he smoothed a spot in the soil and set a stone on top. He did the same for Andy's grave and again for his mother's. He stood up and took a brief glance at his work. He kept one stone in his hand, looked at it, rolled it around, and then returned it to his pocket.

Back past the fountain, in the distance, we could see Mom and Alex sitting on a stone bench next to the pillars, waiting for us. As we got closer to them, we passed the caretaker, who at that moment was lifting a load of dried leaves into his wheelbarrow. He paused in his work, and we stopped.

Dad said, "Thank you for pointing me in the right direction."

The old man seemed to inspect us anew. He looked at me for a second and then back at Dad. He studied my dad's face; perhaps it was the bandage on his forehead that attracted his attention. After what seemed like an awkwardly long time, he said to my father, "I see that you have been blessed. May peace remain forever with you and your family."

"Amen," my father said.

about atmosphere press

Atmosphere Press is an independent, full-service publisher for excellent books in all genres and for all audiences. Learn more about what we do at atmospherepress.com.

We encourage you to check out some of Atmosphere's latest releases, which are available at Amazon.com and via order from your local bookstore:

A Cóndor Dies, a novel translated by Jonathan Tittler

Facehash, a novel by Reuben Percival

The You I See, a novel by Danny Freeman

Neanderthal Gita, a novel by Michael Baldwin

Tsunami, a novel by Paul Flentge

Donkey Show, a novel by Stephen Baker

The things we left sleeping, a novel by Kathryn Lund

Take a Bow: An American in Tokyo, a novel by T. Stonefield

Original Mind Disconnect, a novel by Michael R. Bailey

Paper Targets, a novel by Patricia Watts

Don't Poke the Bear, a novel by Robin D'Amato

Tubes, a novel by Penny Skillman

Skylark Dancing, a novel by Olivia Godat

ALT, a novel by Aleksandar Nedeljkovic

The Bonds Between Us, a novel by Emily Ruhl

Dancing with David, a novel by Siegfried Johnson

The Friendship Quilts, a novel by June Calender

My Significant Nobody, a novel by Stevie D. Parker

Nine Days, a novel by Judy Lannon

Shining New Testament: The Cloning of Jay Christ, a novel by Cliff Williamson

CPSIA information can be obtained
at www.ICGtesting.com
Printed in the USA
LVHW101913290822
726885LV00003B/73

9 781639 884902